"A multilayered Regency-era mystery with unexpected twists, appealing characters, sweetly satisfying romance, and an ending worth waiting for!"

—Julie Klassen, author of *Shadows of Swanford Abbey*

"Steeped in charming historical detail, *Children of the Shadows* will tug you deep into an Agatha-Christie-meets-Jane-Austen story world. Snuggle up, grab a cup of tea, and enjoy this intriguing Regency mystery."

—Hannah Linder, award-winning author of *Beneath His Silence* and *When Tomorrow Came*

"In this captivating conclusion to the adventures of Thorndike & Swann, Juliette and Daniel face their greatest tests yet—both in solving the case and in their unfolding romance. A deftly plotted mystery and a dash of romance combine in a page-turning tale sure to satisfy readers of Regency-set fiction and mystery fans alike. Twists abound and rich historical details vividly bring Regency London to life. A reading experience destined to delight!"

—Amanda Barratt, Christy Award–winning author of *The White Rose Resists* and *Within These Walls of Sorrow*

"An intriguing and compelling conclusion to the glittering Thorndike & Swann Series, and another great installment in the Haverly Universe! *Children of the Shadows* is Regency sleuthing at its finest. Full of romance, mystery, and the drama of the English aristocracy, this story will appeal to history lovers and those who enjoy PBS's *Miss Scarlet and The Duke*."

—Gabrielle Meyer, author of *When the Day Comes* and *In This Moment*

"With a cast of likable characters and Vetsch's perfect pacing, *Children of the Shadows* is a thoroughly enjoyable read sure to delight fans of Regency romance and mystery. Every word from start to finish weaves an engrossing story that is hard to put down and satisfying to finish. Readers will not be disappointed with this third book in the popular Thorndike & Swann series."

—Kimberly Duffy, author of *The Weight of Air*

Children
of the Shadows

THORNDIKE & SWANN

REGENCY MYSTERIES

Children
of the Shadows

ERICA VETSCH

KREGEL
PUBLICATIONS

Published by Kregel Publications, a division of Kregel Inc., 2450 Oak Industrial Dr. NE, Grand Rapids, MI 49505. www.kregel.com.

Published in association with the Books & Such Literary Management, www .booksandsuch.com.

The persons and events portrayed in this work are the creations of the author, and any resemblance to persons living or dead is purely coincidental.

Scripture quotations are from the King James Version.

Cataloging-in-Publication Data is available from the Library of Congress.

ISBN 978-0-8254-4715-0, print
ISBN 978-0-8254-7762-1, epub
ISBN 978-0-8254-6915-2, Kindle

Printed in the United States of America
23 24 25 26 27 28 29 30 31 / 5 4 3 2 1

To Heather and Benjamin—I wish you as much happiness and joy in your marriage as your dad and I have found in ours.

And as always, to Peter, with all my love.

Chapter 1

April 1816
London, England

"How CAN YOU BE LATE for what might be the most important meeting of your life?" Daniel Swann muttered under his breath, weaving his way through the pedestrians clogging the sidewalk on Drury Lane just around the corner from the Bow Street Magistrate's Court. Sir Michael had kept him for ages, wanting a firsthand accounting of the investigation he had sent Daniel and his partner, Ed Beck, on to a county in the north. Daniel's frustration had grown as he reiterated the information contained in the written report in Sir Michael's hand.

The superintendent of the Bow Street investigators took perverse delight in ruling his domain, particularly when it came to showing his disdain for Daniel. He had questioned their every action, parried any explanation, and generally faffed about until Daniel feared he would be seriously tardy for his evening appointment.

Half a block up, Daniel spotted a familiar carriage. Cadogan's hackney sat at the curb. The driver, a friend to whom Daniel owed his life, always seemed to be around when Daniel needed a ride. Cadogan's knife flashed through an apple, cutting off wedges and splitting them between the carriage horses, Sprite and Lola. A mismatched pair—

chestnut and dark bay, one lean, one well-fleshed—they weren't the most elegant team, but according to Cadogan you wouldn't find a better brace in all of London. The driver affectionately rubbed each horse's nose, then returned the knife to a sheath at his waist.

"Evening, guv." He touched his hat brim. "Need a ride?"

"I do." Daniel reached for the carriage door.

"I been meaning to have a word. Have you heard anything about some street children going missing lately?" Cadogan's brow furrowed. "I've heard some rumbles, a few children not showing up on their street corners. Not hereabouts exactly, but over in Spitalfields maybe? I dropped a fare there earlier today and caught a whiff of a rumor that a chimney sweep's boy had gone missing."

Daniel shook his head. "No, I've not heard anything, but I don't know that we would unless they found a body or someone made a formal report."

Cadogan grimaced and glanced down at his lapel, straightening the white flower slotted through his buttonhole.

"You look smart." Daniel indicated the blossom. He'd never seen the jarvey so tidy. Polished boots, brushed coat, clean breeches. The coach appeared freshly washed, the brightwork gleaming. And a new brass plate fixed to the side—Mr. H. Cadogan. "Putting on airs, are we?" He smiled to indicate he was teasing.

Cadogan's teeth flashed. "Thought I'd groom more than just the horses. See if I can get a higher-tone client. I came into a bit of money recently and thought I'd polish up the old girl." He swung open the door and held it for Daniel. "Thought the flowers might be a nice touch. I know a little flower seller who needs to empty her tray before she returns home each day, and I helped her out."

In a bud vase between the windows on the opposite side of the carriage, a trio of the same white flowers as in the driver's lapel brightened the space. The benches and squabs had been brushed, and the floor swept clean.

"Looks nice. Sorry I'm not quite the caliber client you're looking for, but at least my destination is. I need to get to Westminster."

"Are you in a hurry?" A frown touched Cadogan's eyes.

"A bit, yes. Sir Michael kept me longer than I intended. Is there somewhere you need to stop first?" Cadogan had never asked Daniel for such a concession before.

"No, it's not that. It's Sprite. She's showing her age, and I don't like to push her. She's let me know today that she's not up to trotting on the cobbles for miles. A bit stiff in the joints, she is. I suppose I'll have to look for another horse soon, though it pains me. She was my first carriage horse, and she wasn't young when I got her." He dug a rag from his pocket and swiped a smudge of grease off the side of the carriage. "My worry is, I can't afford to keep her if she's not earning. I rent space in a livery near my house, and what with feeding and shoeing and the like, a horse is a powerful expense. Still, I can't see parting with the old girl. No telling what would happen to her. 'Tis a quandary, for sure." He shook himself. "But that's no bother of yours, is it? We'll get there if we go steady."

"You can let me off at the abbey." Daniel climbed aboard, sat on the bench, and leaned back as Cadogan shut the door. The potential change in Daniel's circumstances and his true parentage were hardly common knowledge, and the Duke of Haverly's message calling him to the home of a barrister had been quite cryptic. Daniel felt it wise not to draw attention to his destination, hence why he asked Cadogan to drop him off a few blocks away.

Daniel touched the flowers in the carriage's vase, and a pair of white petals fluttered to the floor. Chagrined, he picked them up and dropped them out the open window, not wanting to leave a mess in the pristine vehicle.

With a lurch, they were off, joining the evening traffic heading across the river. Daniel had never met with a barrister before. At least not on his own behalf. He'd been called to the Old Bailey to testify when one of his cases was tried, but this was vastly different.

Was he, with the help of this unknown barrister, about to change his entire future?

Half an hour later, and dangerously near the time of his meeting,

Daniel wrapped his cloak tighter against the wind and alighted from the carriage. This prosperous area of London near Westminster boasted gaslights, and the lamplighters were out now with their long brass rods, hooking open the glass doors and turning the keys to start the gas flowing.

Daniel kept to the shadows, head down but walking purposefully, as if he had a right to be there.

Cadogan hadn't been exaggerating when he'd said the ride from Vauxhall would take longer than normal. The sun had set, bringing chill dampness to the air. A fresh breeze whipped his lapels, and he anchored his hat atop his head. This had been the latest spring Daniel could remember. The latest anyone could remember, if the old tars who chewed their clay pipe stems and commented on the weather while toasting themselves around the pub fireplaces of London were to be believed.

Turning onto Cowley Street, Daniel quickened his pace along the pathway in front of identical brick townhouses. At the end of Cowley, where it turned right and became Barton Street, a five-story, many-windowed residence marked his destination. No carriage waited at the curb. Had the duke not yet arrived?

Squaring his shoulders and wiping his palms on his breeches, Daniel inhaled the cold evening air to fortify himself. He clacked the brass knocker against the strike plate twice, and before he dropped his hand, the glossy black door opened.

He offered his card to the rotund butler, who held out a small, silver tray to accept the bit of pasteboard. "Daniel Swann to see Sir James."

"This way." The portly servant turned, carrying the tray before him as if it held the Crown Jewels, and Daniel followed. A footman in full livery closed the front door behind them.

Parquet floors, curving balustrade, heavily framed portraits . . . all the accoutrements of London prosperity. The place reeked of money and respectability.

Though dressed impeccably, Daniel felt out of place. A simple Bow Street investigator had no right calling on a respected barrister, and a knighted barrister at that. Yet Daniel's potential membership in the peerage was the subject of this very meeting.

The butler mounted the stairs, his footsteps heavy and his breath coming in puffs. Daniel followed and, at the top of the tall flight, waited while the servant opened the double doors.

As Daniel entered, a surge of pleasure went through his chest. What a library. Books from floor to ceiling on three walls, tall windows that would let in light during the day, rich dark wood everywhere, and a carpet so plush, it felt as if his boots were sinking.

Carriage or not out front, the Duke of Haverly had arrived first. He rose as Daniel approached, as did the man seated behind a Brobding-nagian desk.

"Good evening, Your Grace." Daniel bowed slightly.

"Sir James, may I introduce your client, Mr. Daniel Swann. Daniel, Sir James Durridge."

"Sir James." Daniel made a quick assessment. The barrister appeared to be about fifty, with impressive side whiskers and a full head of gray-ing hair. Impeccably tailored, though a bit ostentatious for Daniel's taste with a green waistcoat and bright-blue coat. His eyes were pierc-ing and his face longish. It was a learned countenance, with intelli-gence emanating from his heavily browed eyes.

"Sit." He indicated a chair. "You're behind your time. I hope tardi-ness isn't a habit with you."

Daniel glanced at the case clock. Two minutes past eight. Hardly late, as he'd knocked on the door at precisely eight o'clock, but he wouldn't quibble.

The door behind the barrister opened as they all sat, and a slight man of perhaps thirty-five with dark hair and eyes slipped into the library. Smartly dressed, but much less flamboyantly than his em-ployer, the man's gaze moved from one to another quickly, as if assess-ing the occupants for their suitability.

"Ah, Henry. Thank you." Sir James took the meerschaum pipe and leather pouch the man handed over. "I shall need you to take notes, of course. Your Grace, my clerk, Henry Childers."

Mr. Childers removed a portable writing desk from the bookshelf and set it upon a small side table. He adjusted the wick in the wall lamp above him and tilted the reflector to direct the light downward. But rather than take his place, he went to the fireplace, removed a taper from a box on the mantel, and lit it from the flames.

Sir James had busied himself with stuffing tobacco into the meerschaum, which had griffins carved into the bowl. The clerk brought the taper and held it to the bowl as the barrister puffed on the pipe. The pair must have worked in tandem for some time to be so well rehearsed.

When the tobacco glowed sufficiently and smoke billowed from Sir James's nostrils, the clerk stepped back, inserted the taper into a holder, and placed it beside the writing desk.

"Now, Your Grace," Sir James said, "I have been retained by the solicitors Coles, Franks & Moody to represent a claim of inheritance. I have read the relevant documents Mr. Coles supplied." He clamped his teeth on the pipe stem and leaned back, his brows lowering. Before him on the broad expanse of leather blotter, he had spread several pages into orderly rows. "An interesting and challenging case. Don't you agree?"

Daniel wondered why he had bothered to attend the meeting. The barrister had addressed his comments only to the duke. Shouldn't Daniel be the one to whom the inquiry was made? Was there some protocol he didn't know at play here?

"And what is your opinion of our chances of proving the claim?" Haverly asked. The duke appeared casual, as if the answer wouldn't change every facet of Daniel's life.

I'd be casual too if I was only a bystander in this affair. If I had my title sewn up tight with no need to fight for it.

"The precedence for such a case is narrow, thankfully. Though previously unknown offspring will occasionally pop up, it is rare that they have a strong case for being named heir. I will tell you now, cases like this are difficult to win, which is not a bad thing. Otherwise, the aristocracy would be chaos." For the first time since they'd sat down, Sir James looked at Daniel. A look of mistrust and doubt. "Even the thought of admitting hitherto unknown heirs to the peerage, of having them stroll out of the woods, as it were, terrifies the establishment."

Wasn't this man supposed to represent him to the attorney general and possibly to the regent himself? To put forth his case for the title of Earl of Rotherhide? If Sir James was so pessimistic at the outset, would he be wholehearted in his work on Daniel's behalf?

"Traditionally the House of Lords, should the petition get that far, tends to side with the heir presumptive, making our job an uphill battle. However . . ." Sir James leaned forward and scrutinized a page. "You do have strong evidence, not least of which is the declaration of the late earl himself. Often the petitioner is fighting against the wishes of the previous holder of the title, but in this instance, the old earl declared you his legal heir in a witnessed document before his death."

"So our chances are better than average?" Haverly asked.

"I do not like to give percentages. If there is anything I have learned in my long career, it is that anything can happen when it comes to the law. Juries are unpredictable, and lords even more so. The gentlemen who will be deciding this case come from well-established families, holding titles that date back centuries. They will not be eager to discard Viscount Coatsworth's claim to the title, no matter how strong the evidence. To do so would open the door to other such claims, and no one wants the proceedings of the House to be clogged with by-blow children screaming for their rights."

Heat trickled under Daniel's skin. Though he had recently learned that he was not the illegitimate child of a domestic servant as he had always thought, he had worn that label a long time. It would not come off easily, though he now knew his mother had been rightfully married to the Earl of Rotherhide's son and Daniel's birth had been within the bounds of a legal union.

What a tangle. What should have been his by birth was now something for which he would have to fight in a public battle that pitted him against his half brother, Alonzo Darby. If he won, it would be

Alonzo wearing the brand of illegitimate and who would have no title and standing.

If he did not prevail, it would be himself who was ostracized. Would he even be able to stay in London? And what would that mean to his budding relationship with Lady Juliette?

Daniel did not look forward to Alonzo's return to London. Alonzo had fled to the West Indies upon learning from his grandfather the truth of his birth—but Alonzo's mother, the current Viscountess of Coatsworth, had sent a fast ship after him and was determined to contest Daniel's claims on her son's title.

Brother against brother, where one would win everything and the other be left with nothing.

"What evidence do you still need to build your case?" Haverly asked. "The solicitors have tasked me with heading the investigative portion of the petition, and I feel strongly that this wrong must be righted, no matter how the lords might detest or fear it. If the claim is true and Daniel Swann is the heir to the earldom, it must be put right."

A different heat lit Daniel's chest. For most of his life, he had been alone, with no one to fight for him. Taken from his home by a mysterious patron, evicted by his mother—who had been only too glad to be rid of him—he had been on his own at school and at university, not fitting in with or accepted by the wealthy boys in his classes. It wasn't until he'd joined the Bow Street Magistrate's Court as an investigator that he'd found a family of sorts, a brotherhood in the investigators' room.

He'd had a powerful patron working in the background, paying school fees, paying for his tutelage at Oxford, procuring him the job of his choice. A shadowy figure who dictated the parameters and perimeters of Daniel's life. And all that time Daniel had never known it was his own grandfather, the Earl of Rotherhide, acting from a guilty conscience rather than benevolence.

But now Daniel had the Duke of Haverly working on his behalf, standing by him in this totally foreign arena.

Sir James inhaled deeply from his pipe. "I will need sworn statements from anyone still alive to make them. You will need to take a local magistrate with you to hear and witness the statements. Because you are clearly biased toward the petitioner, you must take along someone to corroborate the gathering of the information." He spoke as if choosing his words carefully, not wanting to give offense.

"I understand. Do you have a list of those with whom I should speak?"

At a nod from Sir James, Mr. Childers dipped the tip of his pen into the inkwell, ready to write the dictated list.

"First will be the plaintiff's mother, a Mrs. Dunstan?"

"Excuse me." Daniel held up his hand. He could keep quiet no longer.

Sir James looked up, his brows rising.

"Did it perhaps slip your notice that I am, in fact, sitting here before you? I have a name. I have a brain, a tongue, and the ability to use both. I would appreciate it if you would cease calling me 'the petitioner' and address me as the individual human person I am. Mr. Daniel. Swann." He emphasized each word.

The barrister looked from Daniel to Haverly and back again before harrumphing and shuffling papers. "Very well. *Mr. Daniel. Swann.* Here is something important for you to remember as we make our way through this case. You are to say nothing. You are to draw no attention to yourself. In the eyes of the law and the peerage, unless or until you prevail with this petition, you have no standing. You are nothing more than a nuisance making an extraordinary claim against an accepted member of the aristocracy. This is an academic issue, not one of personalities or entities. This case must be decided upon its own merits and nothing else. You will not address the lords, you will not talk to the press, and you will do nothing to put yourself forward between now and the hearing of your petition. You will not accompany His Grace to interview or otherwise influence or intimidate the witnesses who will be giving statements. You, Mr. Daniel Swann, will be a silent bystander. The lords will be looking for any reason to dismiss your claim, so it will be best if you are seen and heard from as little as possible. We're already straining our credibility with the earl's codicil, expecting them to believe (a) your mother married the earl's son, and (b) that he never had that marriage annulled."

Haverly nodded. "We must have evidence that will hold up at this hearing, legally and credibly, for every aspect of this story. You must first convince the attorney general, who must then convince the Prince Regent. If he deems the petition to have merit, he may then put it before a select committee in the House of Lords. Every step of the proceedings will be scrutinized with the hope of being able to dismiss the case before it goes to the next step in the chain. To avoid any appearance of influence or interference, you must remain away from the collection of that evidence.

"We're asking those who will decide the merits of the case to be impartial, and we cannot be seen as having any interest in anything other than bringing them the truth of the matter. I'm sure an Oxford-educated man such as yourself is intelligent enough to see that and not get himself into a state because of the way he has been addressed in his barrister's office?"

Daniel felt properly chastened. He tried to ignore the chagrin squirming in his chest. "Am I to have no part in the proceedings at all? Will I not be called upon to address the attorney general? Should I bother to attend when the case is heard or just wait for you to inform me?" He hadn't quite managed to eradicate all sarcasm from his words.

"I will inform you when and if your presence is required." Sir James harrumphed—a favorite mannerism, apparently. "I would not have had your attendance this evening if His Grace hadn't insisted."

Daniel glanced at Haverly and nodded, subsiding into his chair. Sir James went on to list several more people Haverly should interview. Daniel's late grandfather's physician and valet, other servants at the Rotherhide estate, and the local vicar, as well as searching for the forger who created the false annulment documents, the investigator who had located Daniel as a child, and the man who had performed the marriage ceremony in Scotland, if possible. If the man no longer lived, then a records check would be the next best thing. Haverly was to speak to Daniel's tutor at Oxford and the headmaster at the boys' school where Daniel had been sent, in order to attest to his character while a student.

"Speak to the man who agreed to employ Mrs. Dunstan at his estate when she was exiled from Rotherhide, and barring that, anyone else who might have been there when she arrived. Find the midwife who assisted her in giving birth, so we can confirm the dates. If there are others who come to mind, get their statements. As I put together the case, there may be other individuals who crop up to whom you should speak, but for now, this list should keep you occupied. These people will not be easy to track down, some may be reluctant to speak to you, and others will have died. We're talking about an event that took place a quarter century ago."

The clerk's pen scratched and scraped as he wrote his list. When he'd finished, he showed the paper to his employer, who nodded, and then handed it to Haverly. "Will this do?"

"Yes, thank you. I'll commence my investigation at once. When I know more, I'll contact you."

"And I shall begin work on the presentation documents. As to when we will meet with the attorney general, that will depend upon the speed with which you can verify the claims we are making." Sir James peered into his pipe, but the tobacco no longer glowed, and only a faint wisp of smoke drifted up. "If there is nothing else?" He looked to the duke.

"Not on my end. Swann?"

"No, Your Grace. If there is any way I may be of service, I trust you will inform me?" Though he had been relegated to the role of watcher for the time being, it didn't mean there wouldn't be something in the future that he may be able to contribute.

When the duke rose, the others did too. "Sir James, Mr. Childers, I bid you good evening. Daniel, walk me out."

The stocky butler waited in the entry with their wraps. It always mystified Daniel how butlers seemed to know exactly when a meeting or gathering had ended. They never needed to be called to fetch coats or open the door.

Once outside, Haverly headed north on Barton Street toward the abbey. Daniel matched his stride.

"My carriage is up this way. I didn't feel it wise to advertise my presence at Sir James's. Not that I believe anyone would be watching, since no one knows about your claim just yet. Habit, most likely. Did you arrive by hackney?"

"Yes, Your Grace."

"I shall save you the difficulty of procuring another. Ride with me. I'm attending a dinner party tonight, but once I've been delivered, I'll have my driver take you home."

"Thank you, Your Grace."

Once seated in the luxurious carriage, Daniel grimaced. "Something about Sir James rubs me raw. He acted as if I was invisible, and when I did speak, he gave me a setdown, didn't he? One would think I was a street urchin coming hat in hand, begging for something to which I wasn't entitled."

"He was abrupt, but in essence he isn't wrong. It's best if you let us go about our work on your behalf and be patient. At this point he's approaching the case as if he were one of the committee members who may be called upon to decide your fate. Extreme skepticism and prejudice against your claim until it's proven to him plain enough that he can be confident in what he's presenting. If we convince him, he will be much more persuasive before the committee."

"When will you interview my mother?"

"Soon. Tomorrow evening, most likely. Why? Have you spoken with her yet?"

"No." And he wasn't certain he wished to. Every time he thought of her, his heart burned with abandonment and shame. "We've been estranged more than a dozen years. What is there to say?"

Haverly stirred in the darkness of the carriage, flashes of light crossing his face as they passed beneath the streetlamps. "What is there to say? More than a dozen years' worth of your lives? Explanations, comparing of experiences, and what the plan will be going forward? Those might be good places to begin, I should think."

Daniel said nothing. He would have to deal with his relationship with his mother at some point, but he was in no hurry. Until last month, he'd been forbidden by his patron, his grandfather, from having any contact with her. And she had done nothing since his grandfather died to seek him out to explain herself. For all he knew, she was as reluctant as he to dig up the past.

That she lived in Juliette's house would complicate his efforts to avoid her. What odds that his estranged mother would be employed as housekeeper for the woman he loved?

As always, the thought of Juliette made his heart soar. He'd sent a note asking permission to call tomorrow morning. It was time to share first with her parents and then the rest of the world their intentions. Though, as he traveled across town with this man who was his advocate and his superior in rank and employment, it occurred to Daniel that he should tell the duke as well before word got out.

"Your Grace, there has been a development regarding another relationship. You should be apprised before it travels outside a small circle, since both parties are in your employ." Daniel rubbed his palms on his thighs as heat built along his collarbones. "I have made my heart known to Lady Juliette, and she reciprocates my feelings. Tomorrow we intend to inform her parents and ask their blessing on our association. It is my objective to ask for her hand in marriage."

The duke was quiet for so long, Daniel wanted to squirm. Had Haverly not heard, or was he outraged that someone like Daniel would reach so high up the social ladder as to fall in love with an earl's daughter?

At last Haverly let out a sigh. "You have excellent taste. Lady Juliette is both kind and beautiful, and I can see how you might come to have feelings for her."

Hope sprang into Daniel's heart.

"However, I must caution you. You are embarking on delicate maneuvers as your case is presented to the attorney general. Any whiff of scandal attached to your name will give the committee reason to toss your case aside without giving you a proper hearing. Courting Lady

Juliette at this sensitive time could be seen not as a harmless romance but as you currying favor or trying to manipulate the outcome of the case by making yourself more acceptable to the aristocracy."

"What are you saying? That I shouldn't . . ." He couldn't possibly stop loving Lady Juliette. "I've already declared my feelings for her. That particular bell cannot be unrung."

"I'm not asking you not to propose to the lady eventually. I'm asking you to wait. Wait until the hearing is over, the inheritance decided, your position in society made plain. If the committee rules in your favor, you will be an earl. You will be of the same social standing as Lady Juliette, and no one can cavil at your offering for her. But if you move now, before the hearing, it will not reflect well on your cause. And if you are unsuccessful in the petition, you will put Lady Juliette into a position of having to renege."

Though there was wisdom in what Haverly said, Daniel scowled. Renege? He assumed Juliette would not marry him unless he was an earl? But she loved him, or so she claimed, and she wasn't even aware that an earldom might be in the offing.

But the duke wasn't finished.

"Daniel, I must also caution you. You and Lady Juliette are from vastly different social strata. The possibility of your inheritance may have emboldened you to declare your feelings for Juliette, but if things do not turn in your favor, are you prepared to still offer for her? Are you prepared for her parents to deny permission? Most would under those circumstances."

A pang hit his heart. He probably should have waited to tell Juliette of his love for her. In truth, he hadn't expected her to return his love when he'd blurted out his feelings. He had simply been unable to stop himself.

"Have you told Lady Juliette about your new circumstances?" Haverly asked. "About the petition for the earldom?"

"No. I plan to tell her tomorrow. Both her and her parents."

"If I could keep the petition quiet until it was decided, I would, but word is going to come out. The moment we make our case, London will be abuzz with speculation. I suppose it is better to inform the Thorndikes beforehand so they can prepare. However, tomorrow you will only have Juliette and Bertie to brave. The earl and countess are leaving before dawn on a diplomatic mission for the Crown. I'm having dinner at their home tonight along with my countess and sister-in-law by way of a send-off."

"Another mission for the Thorndikes? They've only just returned from France." Poor Juliette. She must be so disappointed. "They're leaving her again."

"It cannot be helped. This time it is not I who am sending them, but the regent himself." The carriage stopped in front of the Thorndike townhouse. "Keep your head down, do not draw attention to yourself, and await developments. Let Juliette and Bertie know what's happening, and then trust me and Sir James to see this through. I will keep my own counsel regarding the petition and the situation with yourself and Lady Juliette."

"Thank you, Your Grace." Disappointment warred with frustration in Daniel's gut. The duke was good at keeping secrets. Too bad Daniel wasn't good at waiting.

Chapter 2

"MOTHER, MIGHT I HAVE A word before our guests arrive?" Lady Juliette Thorndike hurried into the drawing room, her white organza overskirts whispering against the silk linings of her evening gown. She'd spent the last few moments in the foyer, giving herself a stern talking to, gathering her courage to tell her parents her secret. She had stared at herself in the hall mirror, berating her cowardice and calling on her fortitude while pretending to fuss with her hair. With her parents finally home and getting settled into the routine of the Season, it was time to inform them of what had occurred and ask their blessing.

Because Daniel's note said he would call on her tomorrow morning. She must speak with her parents first.

Would they approve? Would they be happy for her? The last thing she wanted was to disappoint them in any way.

Her heart gave an odd bump, and she gripped her gloved hands together, feeling the ridge of her garnet and gold ring bite into her skin. Her parents were not ogres. They would be calm and sensible and, she hoped, joyful that she had found someone to love, even if the rest of the world would think it an ill match.

The Countess of Thorndike turned in her chair, looking up from the papers on the table before her, her dark eyes glittering in the lamplight. She was stunning, as always. Her emerald necklace replicated the colors of her dress, and the matching drop earrings emphasized the length of her slender neck.

Juliette swallowed, in awe, as she often was, that this woman was her mother. So graceful, beautiful, intelligent, and wise. A sought-after guest at society functions, an excellent judge of character, with impeccable taste. She could carry on an engaging conversation with a courtier or a chimney sweep with equal panache and had a lively sense of humor that never bit or dripped of sarcasm. That she was also one of the most talented and skilled spies in all of the kingdom only enhanced Juliette's admiration.

"Ah, darling, you look lovely." Mother shook the last drops of ink from her quill into the reservoir and lifted one of the pages to blow gently across the wet ink. "Are you looking forward to this evening?"

"Yes, of course. I always enjoy spending time with the Haverlys."

The door on the far side of the drawing room opened, and her father strode in. He caught sight of them and beamed. "Whatever did I do to deserve such a blessing as to have you two lovelies in my life?" He shot his cuffs as he crossed to his wife, bending to kiss her upraised cheek and clasp her fingers. "Devastating as always, darling. You'll show up your guests, appearing as you do, so young and fresh."

He turned to Juliette. "And you, young lady." He opened his arms, and she went into them. His hug, though emphatic, also took care not to crush her dress or dislodge her carefully coiffed hair. He cupped her shoulders, holding her away from him and studying her from crown to hem. "You do realize I shall soon have to hire another footman for the sole purpose of receiving all the notes, nosegays, and invitations that flood our front entryway the morning after every event."

She smiled at his exaggeration. "You're looking well yourself. Is tonight purely social?" The guest list was comprised of several members of the agency for which her parents—and she—worked clandestinely. "Will you need the War Room?" Juliette spoke of the hidden room at the top of the townhouse, used for secret meetings, briefings, and storing the accoutrements of their trade, as well as for the training sessions Juliette underwent almost daily with her Uncle Bertie.

Her father ran his hand down his golden waistcoat, his fingertips tripping over the long row of buttons. His fitted jacket hugged his shoulders and fell in tails almost to the backs of his knees, and his shoes gleamed with fresh black polish. He looked exactly as he should, an elegant member of the peerage. No one would guess how he could disguise himself as a beggar or highwayman in his work as an agent for the Crown.

"Tonight *is* purely social. I want you to enjoy yourself and act as a young debutante should." He touched the tip of her nose. "No intrigues, unless it's catching the attentions of a young man, right?"

"Speaking of intrigue, perhaps now is the proper time to discuss things with her." Mother consulted the clock on the mantel. "Before our guests arrive."

She focused her attention on her father, a thrill going through her. A new mission in the offing, perhaps?

"Of course, my dear. Juliette, won't you sit? Bertie will come down soon, and we wanted to have a word with you in private."

Uncle Bertie, her father's brother, lived with them when they were in London, and Juliette adored him. What would her parents want to speak to her about that Bertie shouldn't hear? She perched on the edge of a chair, pairing her feet close together, her back straight as she had been taught.

"Jules." Her father went to stand behind her mother, resting his hands on her shoulders. "You know that our lives are given to the service of our king and country and that we have spent our entire adulthoods working secretly for the Home Office. When it came my turn to enter this service, I was given several years to decide if I would follow in my forebears' footsteps. My father informed me of his true occupation and that of our family going back to the Norman Conquest before I went to university. He wanted me to study, to consider, and to weigh up all that being an agent would mean in my life. He wanted me to choose my path well before I considered taking a bride—what the consequences of my choice would mean not only to myself but to my wife and family."

He bent and kissed the top of Mother's head. Warmth seeped through Juliette at their obvious affection, but why was he saying this?

"When I met your mother, I knew beyond a shadow of a doubt we were destined to be together. I had finished at Oxford, taken up the family business, and even been on a mission or two. I was committed. Your grandfather approved my choice of a wife, but he advised me to go carefully. He wanted me never to reveal to her my life as a spy, but I knew that would not work for me. And I believed Melisande Wyn-Jones would not only make the perfect wife, but she would make an excellent agent if she so chose. But the decision needed to be hers, and I wanted to give her plenty of time to consider before committing."

Puzzled, Juliette nodded. Where was this going? Could they possibly already know of her feelings for Daniel Swann?

"We each had time to contemplate whether we would enter into a life of espionage," Mother said. "You, on the other hand, were hurled into it with no time to ask yourself if it was even what you wanted. We had intended to inform you rationally and calmly, give you this season and summer to think and evaluate, and then you could decide."

Her father leaned against the table, picking up the quill, running it through his fingers. "You've done remarkably well up till now, but you have not been afforded time to truly consider the path you're on. It was more chosen *for* you than chosen *by* you."

"What we're trying to say is, we want you to take your time. A period away from any missions or activities related to spy craft to consider the true ramifications of this life." Mother stood and removed the quill from Father's hand, replacing it on the blotter.

Juliette didn't know if she was relieved or disappointed that they did not appear to know about her feelings for Daniel, but were they cautioning her because they doubted her suitability as an agent? She had no such doubts. Not about her calling, at any rate.

"I know it's been a whirlwind, but I truly have given thought to the matter." Juliette spread her hands. "I feel as if it is what I was destined to do. As you—or was it Uncle Bertie?—said, God didn't make a mistake when He put me in this family. He knew what He was about, and I have no regrets. I love the work. Has the Duke of Haverly expressed any doubts?" The duke, as their superior officer in the agency, had the final say as to who was given missions and who wasn't.

"Marcus seems more than pleased with your progress, but we have discussed with him the need for you to take your time making a final decision. You've only known of our calling for a few months, and those months have been full of missions and investigations and training. Not to mention, we've hardly been home to guide you through these early stages," Mother said. She looked into Father's eyes, grave and a touch troubled.

The door opened, and Uncle Bertie, resplendent in evening dress, entered. He looked from one to the other, then back at his brother. "Have you told her then? I've been waiting tactfully outside. I am not known for my tact, so I hope you appreciate the difficulty I've had. Guests will arrive momentarily, and you must be on hand to greet them." He gently flexed his arm, now free of the sling but still recovering from the bullet wound he'd suffered on their last escapade.

"No, we haven't told her yet," Father said. "We had that other little matter to discuss first." He turned to Juliette. "You cannot know how sorry we are, but we've been ordered to go on another mission. This time to the Low Countries."

"Again? So soon?" Her heart fell. "You've only just returned from France."

"We are sorry, but there's nothing we can do. This time the mission is on behalf of the foreign secretary, and I suspect the regent himself." Father shook his head. "Lord Castlereagh has requested . . . actually, he was more insistent than that. Regardless, he's sending us to the Netherlands. There have been some rumors that the Belgian people are considering breaking away from Amsterdam to form their own country. Castlereagh believes a bit of diplomacy is in order, as well as information gathering. He was pleased with our efforts recently in France and feels we could be adept at investigating while not appearing to do so."

Juliette stared at her hands for a long moment. "Am I to go with you?" She asked the question, though she wasn't certain what she wanted to hear. To go would mean being with them, something she longed for fiercely. But to go also meant leaving Daniel behind, and how could she bear to be separated from him? Even now, after only a fortnight of being apart, he was never far from her thoughts.

He'd been away on a case up north, and in his absence, she had begun to doubt. Not her feelings for him, which seemed to grow stronger by the day, but his feelings for her. Was he certain? What if, in their time apart, he had reconsidered? What if he regretted all he had said to her that night? Their attachment was so new—was it tenuous as a result? And what would happen when they made the attachment known? Would her parents be amenable, or would they refuse to entertain the notion? And what would the rest of society make of this? Would she and Daniel be ostracized? Or would it be a nine days' wonder? Was that truly the reason she had yet to speak of their love, because she was afraid of what others would say?

Father released his hold on Mother and stood. He crossed to Juliette and took her hand, rubbing his thumb over the bump her ring made beneath her glove. "You are to remain here in London. It will give you time to consider your future and to make a rational decision. Bertie is under instruction not to involve you in cases while we're gone. You can work at your training if you wish, or better yet take a complete break from it." Father bent a knowing gaze on her. "I told you to stay out of the Montgomery affair last month, and what did you do? You helped capture the killer. However, while we're on the Continent, you are to behave yourself and do as we say. The Duke of Haverly concurs. He is, in fact, providing his mother as your chaperone once more in our absence. Rest and think. Agreed?"

"Yes, Father." She tried to keep the disappointment from her voice, but when he stroked her cheek, she knew she hadn't fooled him.

Bertie shrugged and shook his head. "I don't see why you're taking this tack. She's a natural. She won't change her mind, not now that she has a taste for it."

"We're well aware, Sir Bertrand, of your feelings on the matter." Mother lowered her chin and looked at her brother-in-law through the tops of her eyes. "That's why we wished to speak with her in private without you butting in."

Bertie took this mild setdown with grace, bowing and grinning, as unabashed as ever.

The knocker sounded on the front door, as did the echo of Mr. Pultney's shoes on the foyer floor.

"Our guests are here. Let us go greet them. Juliette"—Mother arranged her skirts and checked her hair in the mirror—"did I tell you I invited Earl Winslow and his son? Henry Winslow is such a nice young man. Have you been introduced? At Almack's, perhaps?"

Juliette shook her head. "I do not believe so." Sad that her mother would not know to whom she had been introduced. If she would stay in London longer than a fortnight at a stretch, perhaps she would be more *au courant* with Juliette's social encounters.

"Ah, Diana, Evan, welcome. Always a pleasure to have the Earl and Countess of Whitelock in attendance." Father held out his hand to the couple Mr. Pultney showed in. "How are those delightful young sons of yours?"

"Growing like well-watered weeds." The countess's voice was filled with pride. Mother had told Juliette how Whitelock had been rewarded with an earldom for bravery on the battlefield, had been mentored by Marcus Haverly, and married the daughter of a duke.

Mrs. Dunstan opened the door at the back of the hall, poking her capped head out, making eye contact with the butler. He nodded and whispered to Mother. Discreet. No doubt the signal that dinner service could commence at their pleasure.

Mr. Pultney opened the door once more and admitted the Duchess of Haverly, the dowager duchess, and—a ripple went through Juliette—Miss Pippa Cashel.

Miss Cashel was Charlotte Haverly's half sister and had, until not long ago, been a courtesan. Juliette had heard she was once the most sought-after Cyprian in the city, but Miss Cashel had left that life behind her and was now on a mission to rescue other unfortunates and rehabilitate them.

Juliette stole a glance at the dowager to assess her displeasure. Oddly, the dowager looked as serene as Juliette had ever seen her, which was to say, she didn't appear totally disgruntled and displeased with life.

"Marcus had business to conclude and is arriving separately," Charlotte began, but stopped as her husband nipped through the door before Pultney could close it.

"Business done," Marcus said, bending to kiss Charlotte's temple. He winked at her, and she laughed at his cheekiness.

It was sweet how the duke showed attention to his wife, keeping her arm tucked through his. Charlotte's condition was evident now, her shawl covering the gentle roundness of her unborn child.

Another pair followed the Haverlys inside, an older gentleman and a younger. These must be the Earl of Winslow and his son, the viscount. Straightening her posture, Juliette considered the viscount. No doubt her mother had invited the young man as a potential suitor for Juliette, and though there could be no satisfaction there for Mother, Juliette determined to be polite and use the manners she had spent so much time acquiring.

"With everyone arrived at once, I believe we will expedite going in to dinner." Father offered his arm to the Duchess of Haverly as the senior ranking female. The duke bowed and took Mother's arm. It was a ritual for which Juliette's etiquette lessons had prepared her, this pairing off by rank to go in to dinner. The Earl of Whitelock took a subtle hint from his wife that he should escort the dowager. As a man still fairly new to the peerage, the earl must rely often on his wife to show him the way.

Juliette vowed to do the same for Daniel should they be allowed to wed and should they be invited to any societal events.

She partnered the viscount, who bowed crisply and looked her in the eyes as she took his arm. "Good evening, Lady Juliette. I suppose, though we have not been formally introduced, we can dispense with the ceremonies and greet each other?"

"Good evening to you, sir." She inclined her head. He had nice gray eyes, and chestnut hair, but the most striking thing about Viscount

Coverdale was his confident bearing. Not bragging or snobbish, but sure of himself.

Juliette had to smother a smile as Uncle Bertie partnered Miss Cashel. What an unlikely pairing. She a former lady of the evening, and him a supposed sot and dilettante.

Miss Cashel was stunning, with glossy brown hair, a regal carriage, and intelligent brown eyes. Her golden gown flattered her coloring. She moved with grace and an air of aloofness, as if holding herself separate though surrounded by people. This gave her an air of mystery that piqued the interest. She looked nothing like Charlotte, who had curling blonde hair and eyes the color of the jade dragon Juliette had acquired on her first case as a spy.

Once seated at the dining table, again by rank, Juliette found herself across from Earl Winslow and between Whitelock and Uncle Bertie. Miss Cashel sat opposite Uncle Bertie.

With a mixed group, Juliette had expected there would be no mention of her parents' departure, but from the end of the table, the dowager spoke up. "Off on another trip, Lady Melisande? I must say, you've spent more time packing and unpacking this Season than attending events. Marcus tells me I will be called upon to chaperone Lady Juliette once more?"

"We are appreciative, Honora. Hopefully, it will be a quick voyage. Tristan has business interests in Amsterdam and Brussels that are urgent. Did you know he's branching out into the import trade? I am using the trip to stock up on chocolates and lace and to have a look at the latest fashions while I am there. Is there anything I may bring you as a thank-you for looking after Juliette so well?"

If by "well" Mother meant all but locking her into a tower. Juliette poked at the fish course. She detested fish.

The Earl of Whitelock looked at Juliette's plate and leaned close, lowering his voice. "I hate it too. Fish, oysters, eels, anything that lives in water." He had rearranged the items on his plate, but he'd eaten none of the filet. "I wouldn't dream of sending it back untouched. I hear cooks are a testy lot and must be studied lest they decamp in a huff."

They shared a conspiratorial grin. "I hear our cook has a tender heart and takes any uneaten fish into the mews to feed the cats that gather there," Juliette whispered back. "I like to think I'm doing my part to sustain the mousers in the neighborhood."

"Ah, reprieved. I shall join you in our support of the local felines." Whitelock laid his fork on his plate. "Though when I was at war, we got so hungry at times, we would have fought the cats for the scraps."

Juliette had heard his story, how he had saved one of the Prince Regent's godsons during a battle in Spain, and as a reward, the prince had made him an earl. She liked the man and had a feeling Daniel would as well.

Father set down his glass. "George," he said to Earl Winslow. "I am pleased you accepted our dinner invitation. And you as well, Henry. Whitelock here can appreciate the difficulty you may have acclimating to civilian life now that you've mustered out of the army. How are you finding your first few weeks back in London?"

The viscount dabbed his lips with his serviette. "It has been an adjustment, as you say, but most have been very kind."

"He's not met many new people yet, as his wish was to spend time at my estate when he first returned to England." Winslow leaned across Miss Cashel to nod to his son.

Almost as if Miss Cashel wasn't there. It dawned upon Juliette that thus far, no one had addressed Charlotte's sister directly. Seated as she was between two men who were strangers to her, she must feel isolated.

Juliette nudged Uncle Bertie with her foot. He raised one eyebrow in silent inquiry. With a slight inclination of her head, she motioned toward the lady opposite.

He exhaled a small huff and put on a pleasant expression. "Miss Cashel, I understand you're looking to expand your charitable efforts here in London."

Her brown eyes widened a fraction, and her chin lifted. "That is correct. The greatest need is here in the capital."

Perfect diction. The voice of a well-educated woman.

"And are you being met with resistance or welcome?" Bertie asked.

She studied him before answering, as if judging the sincerity of his inquiry. "Both, though more of the former, I am sad to report."

"What charity would that be?" the viscount asked. "And why would someone resist charitable efforts?"

The dowager's fork froze halfway to her mouth. Though she might have assisted in the retraining and reformation of streetwalkers, it appeared she wasn't prepared to discuss it in polite society.

Miss Cashel had no such qualms. "I seek to help unfortunate women leave their way of life and learn skills that will see them able to support themselves without selling their bodies to men in order to survive."

"Pippa." The dowager's tone held a warning.

"I've asked you to call me Philippa, my given name. Pippa is a pet name used for a child, and I am hardly that, Your Grace." A firmness in her tone drew Juliette's admiration. The only other person she knew who could speak like that to the dowager was her son.

Philippa turned to the viscount on her right. "I have been involved in this work for a year and more now, and we've been able to help several women, but I can hardly continue to impose upon my sister and brother-in-law. Most of our work has taken place at their Oxfordshire estate. I'm raising funds to open my own mission here in London. I hope to have medical care, skills training, and a safe refuge for women in need. If you are willing to contribute, I can guarantee the money will do much good. In addition to skills and schooling, we also instruct the women in the Scriptures and seek to save their souls along with their bodies."

The viscount blinked, and the dowager gasped, rolling her eyes. "Really, *Philippa*. This is neither the time nor the place."

"I beg to differ, Your Grace. Everyone at this table has been blessed by God with great privilege accompanied by great wealth. With that privilege comes responsibility to help those who are in need, and I challenge you to find someone more in need than a penniless woman forced to sell herself to buy a morsel of food." Miss Cashel kept her tone civil, but Juliette could sense the passion behind her words. She truly cared about her cause and the women she could help.

"Here, here." Bertie raised his glass to her. "I shall be happy to subscribe to your charity, Miss Cashel."

She eyed him, her face revealing nothing. "You have my appreciation."

"I believe we all shall be pleased to donate." Father looked with raised brows to his guests. "It is our obligation, after all, as Miss Cashel says, having been blessed by God with position and wealth."

Juliette looked from face to face, and she stopped on Earl Winslow's. He stared at his plate. The muscles of his jaw stood out, his neck rigid.

Philippa Cashel watched the earl as well; her eyes were knowing, but with that icy aloofness that Juliette had sensed in her from the start.

A new thought struck Juliette, and she barely stifled her gasp. Was it possible that the earl was a former client of Miss Cashel's?

How terribly awkward. Poor Philippa must dread these encounters, and yet she handled it far better than the earl, who wore a pinched expression, as if he'd just encountered a foul odor.

Or perhaps she did Winslow an injustice. Perhaps he, like the dowager, would merely prefer not to discuss such matters over dinner.

Chapter 3

"THE HANDS ON THAT TIMEPIECE will not move faster because you stare at them." Bertie chucked Juliette under the chin as he passed. He flopped onto the sofa in the drawing room, managing to appear elegant even as he sprawled, though he favored his mending arm.

Juliette scowled at the offending clock. "How is it that time goes so quickly in one instance and so slowly in another?"

The moment their guests had departed last night, a flurry of packing and preparations had begun, with the staff carrying cases and boxes and trunks into the front hall. Early morning had flown by even more swiftly, and before she knew it, she stood alone in an empty foyer.

But now, when she anticipated Daniel's arrival, the clock plodded and inched and scraped forward one agonizingly slow moment at a time.

"Why didn't you tell them about your changed relationship with Daniel before they left?" Bertie asked. "Not that it is any of my affair, but I am curious. Young ladies aren't known for keeping such things to themselves, after all. I know they were in a bit of a rush, but if you had wanted to, you could have wedged it into the conversation somewhere."

She turned and surveyed his lean, well-dressed form. His dark eyes studied her in turn, and she shrugged, though she did not feel nonchalant. "There might have been time enough to blurt it out, but not time for a reasoned discussion, for them to consider and advise, for them to give their blessing in a measured, thoughtful way. It would have been madness to broach the subject when their minds were clearly on their next assignment. Imagine if I had tossed it casually into the conversation? 'Oh, by the way, I have fallen in love with a Bow Street runner who is the furthest thing removed from the aristocracy, and as a matter of fact has no idea who his father is. I know you have to leave, but don't worry. It's not anything too momentous in my life to have found myself in love with such a man. Have a nice voyage.' Yes, I can just imagine how that would have gone."

"That's a fairly dramatic rendition, I must say." Bertie gave her a droll look. "I had rather looked forward to their reaction. Do you anticipate resistance?"

She spread her hands. "I don't know how they will react. I think if we can have a rational conversation, if I can tell them of my feelings and we can work through any concerns, that they will warm to the idea. From what I can tell in the fleeting amounts of time we have together, they aren't bound by the closed-minded strictures of class and social barriers, but it will most likely take them by surprise. Only recently I had drawn the attention of a foreign duke. The rest of society will feel I've fallen in my aspirations, don't you think?"

Bertie propped his boots on the tea table. "I believe you should take things with Daniel slowly in your parents' absence. Be circumspect and discreet, as I know you will be, and bide your time until they return. It will only be a few weeks at most. They're to complete their business in Brussels and give a report with all haste. The Prince Regent expects them to make an appearance in Brighton while he is in residence. He will spend a few weeks lolling about at his seaside residence once he dispenses with his tedious duties as titular head of the Church of England this Sunday by attending Easter services. There will be time for you and your investigator to declare yourselves and seek their blessing when you join them in Brighton. If you still have the same feelings in a few weeks, that is."

Juliette rounded the sofa and gripped the back of it, leaning over him. "You think my affections so fickle that I will have changed my mind before they return?"

Bertie closed his eyes, leaning into the cushions and lacing his fingers across his trim middle. "I think you are young, and young people are more likely to be in love with the idea of being in love than anything else. I think you've been caught up in more than a few intense situations over the past few months, many of them involving Mr. Swann, and that perhaps if you step back and take some time to consider, you might find that you've romanticized him to a degree. He did rescue you from kidnappers, after all. Love addles people's brains, preventing them from making rational decisions. That's why I've steered far away from the shoals of romance. I prefer my judgment unclouded."

Juliette laughed, though his assessment stung. "I think, when you meet the right woman, you will be so bowled out, you won't be able to help yourself. You'll fall head over hessians and will do the most irrational things and will offer your heart freely and without thought to the consequences. I hope I live to see that day and that when it arrives, I'll be lady enough not to laugh in your face at all your 'rational' objections to romance." She straightened and crossed her arms, scowling at him.

Bertie opened one eye and gave an exaggerated shudder. "That's hardly likely. I am heart-whole and carefree, and I intend to remain that way. I foresee you, on the other hand, having great difficulty in concealing your budding romance until your parents return. You light up like a firework at the mere mention of Swann's name. Prudence will be required, especially around the dowager. If she tumbles to it, there will be an almighty stramash, and she may well lock you in your room until you 'come to your senses, young lady.'" His voice rose to a higher pitch as he imitated—rather well—the disapproving tones of the Dowager Duchess of Haverly. "You would do well to inform Daniel that you can do nothing now, that you would prefer to wait to make anything public."

Disappointment warred with the good sense of her uncle's words, rankling Juliette. She didn't want to be wise and well reckoned. When she thought of loving Daniel, she wanted to fly around the room like a giddy butterfly, laugh at nothing, and hug all that joy to herself. Uncle

Bertie cautioned her to be rational, but what did love have to do with rational thought?

Bertie continued. "Though I voiced doubts last night, I now think your parents were wise to have you consider seriously whether you were called to this life of espionage. I suggest you add to those considerations a serious contemplation about the likely longevity of your attachment to Daniel Swann. You can practice your spy craft, your ability to keep a secret, by pretending not to be in love with Swann when you're with other people."

"I don't think Daniel will be best pleased at the delay." At least she hoped he was as eager as she to tell the world. "I believe he intended to make his intentions known to my father today."

"Since that is not possible, and waiting is your only option, you might as well wait gracefully. While you bide your time, you can weigh the consequences of your decisions moving forward and decide if you are willing to take on the responsibilities of becoming a spy and the possible social recriminations of marrying an illegitimate public servant."

She flinched at his description of Daniel. While true that he did not know who his father was, Daniel was so much more than his origins. He was brave, thoughtful, kind, diligent, intelligent. He was educated and athletic, a talented horseman, and a good investigator. Listing his attributes made her pulse thrum. Handsome, well-built, courteous, humorous . . . his fine qualities were too numerous to count.

Though she understood Bertie's concerns and could see the wisdom of his advice to take it slowly and consider her future and what God would have her do, it stung that both her parents and her uncle thought she needed time to know her own heart. Would her parents also think her love for Daniel a passing fancy? Did they consider her impetuous and feckless? Leaping first and regretting later? Her decision to become a spy hadn't been without consideration, and her feelings for Daniel . . . she couldn't help. Whatever she decided about her future as an agent for the Crown, she was certain she would not change her mind about Daniel.

The knocker on the front door sounded, and Uncle Bertie stood, adjusting his jacket and smoothing his waistcoat. "There's your young swain now, I imagine."

Juliette's heart bumped against her stays, and her skin fizzed. He was here. A fortnight apart had never seemed so long.

She moved around the settee and stood before the fireplace, careful to position herself well away from the screen guarding the low-banked coals. The last thing she wanted was for her skirts to catch fire and ruin their reunion. She could only imagine Uncle Bertie dousing her with the water from the vase on the side table, Daniel's aghast face, and her, sodden and singed and sorry for herself.

Mr. Pultney opened the drawing room door. "Mr. Daniel Swann, sir." He bowed to Uncle Bertie. "Shall I tell him you are receiving?"

"Send him in." Bertie flicked his hand.

When Daniel entered, Juliette bit her lower lip, her heart soaring as she examined him from head to toe. He was as handsome as ever, his brown hair curling slightly, his blue eyes rimmed with dark lashes, a bit of color riding his cheekbones, no doubt from the fresh breeze today.

But there was a tightness around his eyes, a set to his mouth. Concern flickered through her. Something troubled him.

"Swann." Bertie held out his hand. "Good to see you again. I hope you don't mind, but I have to retrieve something from upstairs. I'm certain Juliette will keep you company in my absence. I won't be gone long."

Juliette didn't know whether to hug him as he went by or roll her eyes at his obvious ploy to give her and Daniel a moment alone. Though it wasn't proper at all, she appreciated his thoughtfulness. He even closed the door as he went out.

Juliette wanted to run into Daniel's arms and have him kiss her as he had twice before, but that would be unseemly. Wouldn't it?

Daniel had no such qualms apparently. He crossed the room and enfolded her, crushing her tight against his chest. "Ah, love, it's been an age." He kissed her, his lips warm and fervent, commanding her attention. Her head spun delightfully, and if he hadn't been holding her so steady, she might have melted into a puddle on the floor.

He broke the kiss but not the embrace, burying his nose in the hair at her temple. His heart thudded against her palms, and she breathed in his scent of soap and sunshine. All her fears that perhaps he had changed his mind in their time apart fled in the security of his arms.

"I missed you," he whispered against her skin. "You smell like roses."

Leaning back, she studied his face. "I missed you as well. Did you end your case satisfactorily?"

He nodded. "Not as quickly as I would have wished, but the arrest was made and the perpetrator tried and sentenced by the local magistrate. Justice is swift in the north counties, I'll say that for them."

Again she sensed strain in his voice. The skin around his eyes was tight, and his jawline pronounced. "Are you on a new case now?"

He shook his head. "Not yet. Sir Michael gave me some meaningless work last evening, though we'd only returned to London yesterday afternoon. He had me in Vauxhall looking for pocket-dippers." He shook his head, his frustration evident. "Ed and I will be assigned the next case that comes in." Reluctantly he stepped back, but he raised his hand and caressed her cheek. "I have much to tell you. I understand from Haverly that your parents have been called away again?"

Juliette leaned into his warm palm for an instant, nodding. "They left this morning."

"Do you know how long they will be gone?" He took her hand and led her to the settee. "I'm sorry, Juliette. I had intended to speak to your father about us this very day."

She allowed him to lace her fingers with his as they sat close. "It cannot be helped. When the government calls, they must go."

"The government should call on someone else from time to time. This is unfair to you." He pressed his palm against hers. "What did your parents say when you told them about us? Were they shocked by the notion?"

"I had not yet told my parents about us . . ." Heat built in her cheeks. Saying it aloud to him made it all the more real. "I intended to. I wanted to, but I was waiting, at first because it was so new and amazing and . . . well, precious, that I didn't want to share it with anyone. Then I realized I should tell my parents before you called, but they announced their departure for Brussels, and I knew I should wait until they returned to discuss it with them." She lifted their clasped hands, thrilling to the contrast of his long, tapered fingers, broad palm, and rougher skin against her own smoother, paler, more delicate hand. "Uncle Bertie says it is just as well, that we should hold off telling anyone until we can inform my parents and get their reaction, and that the interval should be spent assessing what we really feel and what we want."

Daniel pressed his lips together, his eyes narrowing. "Does that mean he thinks you should change your mind? Or does he hope you will?"

"I don't know what he really thinks. He talks a lot of banter, but he has given us time together alone. He wants me to be sure both of my feelings for you and about my decision to become an agent. I'm to use the time until my parents return to pray and think things over."

Bertie returned before Daniel could say anything further. "Did I wait in the hall long enough?" He grinned broadly. "I seem to be waiting in the hall quite often these days."

Daniel released Juliette's hand and stood. "Sir."

Bertie waved him back to his place beside Juliette and seated himself once more on the sofa, flipping the tails of his jacket out. "I'm sorry you missed my brother and sister-in-law this morning. I suppose Juliette told you of their departure?"

"She did. I wish them safe travels."

"And has Juliette also informed you of the need to wait to apprise anyone of the . . . *tendresse* . . . that has arisen betwixt you?"

He eyed them, and Juliette was aware of how close she and Daniel were sitting. Her thigh brushed his, and she felt every inch of contact. His arm rested against hers, and warmth seeped through his sleeve.

"Yes, which relieves my mind somewhat. I didn't have the chance to tell Juliette yet, but I have been advised by the Duke of Haverly to keep our relationship private for the time being."

Juliette studied his profile. He was relieved not to reveal their love for one another? And the duke had advised him? Did Haverly, like Bertie, feel perhaps they had been precipitate in declaring their feelings after only knowing each other for a few intense months? Or did he disapprove of the differences in their stations? Was Daniel himself hesitant? His kiss hadn't felt unsure.

"There have been some developments of which I must apprise you, a rather delicate state of affairs in which I find myself. The Duke of Haverly has been tasked with managing the situation on my behalf. The information is known only to a few, but in the coming days, will become known to all." He shifted on the settee, as if ready to spring to his feet and pace the floor. "I have learned the identity of my father as well as the name of the man who has been my hidden patron all these years."

She reached for his hand, only to find it fisted on his thigh. The muscles of his forearm bunched, and a tremor went through him. What had he learned that was so terrible? Did he think it would make a difference to her? Is that why Haverly wanted them to wait? Because once she learned the truth, she would reverse her feelings?

Bertie leaned forward. "Have you now? And Haverly is involved?"

Daniel turned to Juliette, taking both her hands in his and looking into her eyes. "I was summoned to my solicitor's office just over a fortnight ago, where a codicil to the will of the Earl of Rotherhide was read. In this codicil, he testified that his son and heir, William Darby, eloped with one of the housemaids at his country estate, running away to Scotland and marrying her. However, when they returned to the Rotherhide estate, the old earl was furious and demanded the marriage be annulled as quickly as possible. He banished the maid to the estate of one of his friends in another county, forced his son into a marriage with a woman of his own class, thinking he'd solved the problem. However, a few years later, after the new wife had given him a son, William Darby, then Viscount Coatsworth, was severely injured in a riding accident. He confessed to his father on his deathbed that he had forged the annulment papers and that he was still legally married to the housemaid."

Bleakness entered his blue eyes. "That housemaid was my mother. At the time, she went by Catherine Swann, though you know her now as Mrs. Dunstan, your housekeeper, from whom I have been estranged for thirteen years."

Juliette squeezed his fingers. Mrs. Dunstan? Daniel's mother? He must have recognized her, the woman he claimed had leapt at the chance to be rid of him as a boy. That would explain the restraint and coolness she had sensed the few times she had seen them together. She studied Daniel but could see no resemblance between the two. Did he favor his father?

"You are saying that you are the true heir of Rotherhide and our housekeeper is your mother?" Bertie tumbled to the paramount issue, drawing Juliette's attention away from her thoughts.

A frisson went through her. Daniel was the eldest and legitimate grandson of the Earl of Rotherhide? She bit her bottom lip to stifle a laugh. If this was true, then Daniel was extremely eligible and would be more than acceptable both to her parents and to society at large. This was perfect.

Daniel nodded, looking at Bertie. "If the codicil and his dying confession are to be believed. However, proving it is far from a certainty. Haverly has instructed me to stay away from the proceedings so as not to appear to be influencing them in any way. He will question witnesses, track documents, and gather information. The duke and my barrister, Sir James Durridge, walked me through the procedures. Alonzo Darby's mother has indicated that they will petition the attorney general for the succession of the title. Sir William Garrow, as attorney general, will then present the case to the Prince Regent. Because the title is in dispute, the Prince Regent and the attorney general will then have to present it to the Select Committee for Privileges for review. Those sixteen men will examine the petition, make a recommendation, and send the whole thing back to the Prince Regent, who will make the final decision. I've been informed that there is less than an even chance that things will break my way. The committee has historically favored the presumed heir rather than an outside petitioner."

Juliette tensed as a new realization hit her. "Alonzo Darby is your half brother?" Daniel and Alonzo had been at metaphorical daggers drawn since their first meeting, and all this time they were brothers. Another thought struck her. What would this mean for her relationship with Agatha? Her best friend was engaged to marry Alonzo Darby . . . or as near as made no difference . . . but this petition would pit the men they loved against each other in a public arena.

"Ironic, isn't it?" Daniel's mouth twisted in a wry imitation of a smile. "Just before his death, the earl informed Alonzo of the truth and bequeathed him some property in the West Indies as a consolation prize. The earl banished him across the globe. Alonzo must have thought there was no way to fight this and claim his inheritance, and he fled. That's why he left Agatha without a word. He was shocked and humiliated, I imagine. However, his mother intends to contest the codicil and my claim both for her son and for her own title and the legitimacy of her marriage. She sent a fast ship after Alonzo, hoping to catch him in the Canary Islands before he is off to the West Indies. If he's found quickly, we anticipate he will be back in England soon, most likely before the petition is filed."

Bertie let out a low whistle. "How soon do Haverly and Durridge plan to approach the attorney general? And are you ready for the firestorm when the news gets out? The broadsheets will hound you, and you will be the subject of every rumor the *ton* can generate."

"Haverly has already begun his investigation, and Sir James is preparing his paperwork even now. They plan to present the case near the end of the month if Haverly can gather all the bits together." He turned back to Juliette, his eyes bleak and pleading. "Until the case is settled, Haverly has also instructed me to keep mum about you and me, Juliette. He feels any public display on my part could be seen as trying to curry favor and bias the lords' decision."

She nodded, but her heart sank. "I understand." The wait would seem interminable, but if it helped ensure Daniel was given the title that was rightfully his, she would be patient.

Bertie rose and paced. "You learned all this through a codicil to a will, read out by a solicitor? That must have been like getting a punch to the brain. You had no idea?"

Daniel released her hands, clenching his fists on his thighs again. "None whatsoever. My mother never spoke of it when I was young. Once I was sent away, we had no contact. That was part of the agreement. The mysterious patron who paid for my schooling and set me up at Bow Street was actually my grandfather, the Earl of Rotherhide. He learned of the false annulment, sent an investigator in search of my mother, and found out about me. He then, through his solicitors, made a bargain with my mother. She would give up custody and anything to do with me, I would be sent to school and university, and her problems would be solved. She didn't know, any more than I, that her marriage had never truly been annulled until it was read out by the solicitor. The earl thought by taking on guardianship, he could make amends and that would be enough, but in the end, his conscience got the better of him and he spilled the story to his valet, who wrote it out and witnessed it. Still, the earl took the coward's way out, waiting until after his death to reveal the truth. If he had claimed me before his death, we wouldn't have to fight for the inheritance now."

Twisting the gold and garnet ring on her finger, Juliette tried to order her thoughts. Daniel was drawn tight as a bowstring. She had understood, since he'd first told her of his childhood, that not knowing who his father was had left a sizable hole in his life, but to find out in this way . . .

Bertie stopped pacing. "I don't envy you, what you're going to face when the *ton* gets word of this. Most will feel you're grasping at something you don't deserve, trying to invade their sacred ranks."

"That will be nothing new." Another wry grimace from Daniel. "From the moment I was enrolled at school, to my entrance at Oxford, and my placement at Bow Street, I've been accused of being an interloper. Alonzo Darby has taken particular satisfaction in 'putting me in my place' since I met him."

"All that ends when you're awarded the title and property." Juliette smiled at him. "You'll be the Earl of Rotherhide." *And when we marry, I'll be your countess.*

Chapter 4

JULIETTE HAD TAKEN THE NEWS better than he had thought. Though clearly disappointed, she understood his reasons and had her own for delaying any announcement about their relationship. There would be time enough to tell the world. For now, they would keep it to themselves. As Juliette had said, it was new and private and precious.

A shame Sir Bertrand hadn't left them alone for Daniel to say his goodbyes. He would have liked to kiss Juliette again. Though it was unwise, when so much of their future depended upon the whims of the Prince Regent and a handful of peers Daniel had never met, he could not help himself, dreaming of having her as his wife.

Pultney stood in the foyer with Daniel's cloak and hat.

"I'd like to have a word with the housekeeper before I leave, if I may." Daniel looked toward the back of the house where the green baize door marked the separation of the servants' part of the house and that of the Thorndikes.

The butler, ever the professional, gave nothing away in his countenance. "I shall see if she will meet with you." He laid Daniel's hat on the table and with his customary stately manner, crossed the space and disappeared.

In less than three minutes by the tall case clock by the library door, Pultney returned. "This way, sir."

Daniel followed the man down a set of stairs, his guts knotting and hands sweating. This encounter had been long in the making, and now that the strictures were off the agreement with his patron, he had a few things to say.

"Mrs. Dunstan's sitting room." Pultney held the door open, and Daniel entered. High windows looking out on the back garden marched down one side, and several built-in sets of shelves held household items. A spice chest stood on narrow legs along the wall, and a piece of American furniture, a rocking chair, sat before the fire.

His mother stood behind the chair, gripping the tall back. Her dress was black, a small timepiece hung from her lapel, and a chatelaine dangled from her waist. Gray streaked her dark hair, and wariness clouded her eyes.

"Daniel."

It was the first time she had spoken his name to him in thirteen years. Thirteen long, lonely years.

"Mrs. Dunstan." He couldn't keep the coldness from his voice, nor did he wish to. And he would not address her as "Mother." What he had learned in the solicitor's office did not absolve her of the harm she had caused.

She winced. "Won't you sit?" She gestured toward a cushioned chair opposite the rocker.

"No, thank you. I won't be here long."

Folding her hands at her waist, she waited.

Words roiled in Daniel's head. All the things he had wanted to say to her for all these years. The small child he had been, begging her in his mind to take him back, that he would be a good boy. No trouble, he promised, if only she would come rescue him from that cold, stone school in a distant county. The angry words he'd wanted to hurl at her as an undergraduate at university, accusatory, castigating her for her callous rejection. The cold, indifferent setdown he had dreamed of delivering should he ever happen to cross her path when he was an adult.

The silence stretched between them.

Finally, her chin came up. "If you've nothing to say, I have work to do."

He flinched. "Nothing to say? I've got thirteen years of things to say. I would think you do as well. I was waiting for an explanation."

"Of what? You now know everything there is to know. You found out many things at the same time as I." Her brows lowered. "What is it you want me to say?"

"'I'm sorry' would do for a start," he spat out.

"I'm sorry? For what do you wish an apology? For believing William Darby loved me and would honor our wedding vows? For believing the earl when he said the marriage was annulled? For doing everything I could to keep body and soul together when I was banished to an estate far from anyone and anything I knew? For believing the earl when he threatened to send me to prison with trumped-up charges of theft if I ever came near his son or his estate again? Or for finding out too late that I was carrying William's child?"

The earl had threatened her? *No, do not weaken. You've waited too long for this.* "For getting rid of me at the first opportunity?"

A sarcastic smile came over her face, something he didn't remember ever seeing before. "If you think I had no opportunity to be rid of you before you were twelve, you're mistaken. One of the laundresses offered to help me end the pregnancy before you were even born. There were parish orphanages where I could have taken you. I could have sold your services into an indenture by the time you were five."

"So you thought about getting rid of me long before you did?" Fresh pain sliced his heart. How had she deceived him for so long, making him believe she once loved him?

"Never of killing you before you were born, but trying to find a better place for you than I could provide? Of course. I was alone, poor, in service. I had nothing to offer you, barely keeping you clothed and fed most of the time. I was always looking for a better situation for you. When the solicitor from London approached me with his offer, he promised you would be educated, clothed, fed, established in a career. Things I could never give you."

"Those were just things. Things that couldn't take the place of love and a family. Somewhere to belong. Do you have any idea how scared I was, how alone? Despised by classmates as a nobody, never fitting in anywhere? How much did they pay you?" It was a question that had burned in his brain for years.

"Pay me?"

"Yes, how much did the solicitor give you to get rid of me? How much was I worth? Enough to leave your position on the estate and move to London, at the very least. Or did that happen after you married Mr. Dunstan? Where is he, by the by?"

"There was no payment. I didn't *sell* you. I signed the agreement for your guardianship freely, praying it would mean a better life for you. As to Mr. Dunstan, there isn't any such person. When I left the estate and came to London, it was safer and more expedient to pose as a widow. I felt like a widow in any case. I worked for a banker's wife for a period of time as a lady's maid. I took the job of housekeeper to the Thorndikes because it was an advancement in pay and responsibility. They have been very good to me, and they've even brought me into their work from time to time. Nothing dangerous or difficult. But it gave me a purpose and helped fill the emptiness."

Fill the emptiness? She would get no sympathy from him. Her *supposed* heartache was caused by her own actions. He hadn't asked to be taken from her, nor had he asked for the so-called "advantages" thrust upon him by his tyrant of a grandfather. Emptiness. He knew a thing or two about that.

This was getting them nowhere. "The Duke of Haverly will arrive sometime in the next few days, and he will have questions for you. He's looking to establish my claim to the Rotherhide estate. We plan to petition the Crown. If we are successful, you will be a titled lady, with no need to continue to work as a domestic. I hope you will assist him with his inquiries. A verdict in our favor will legitimize your marriage and my birth and remove any stigma that remains. If you have copies of those papers you signed to send me away, they could prove helpful." His face felt stiff, his tongue wooden.

Tears formed on her lower lashes, and for a moment he regretted his harsh tone, but then he remembered all the tears he had sobbed into his pillow as a lonely child, and his heart hardened.

They were strangers, and they would always be strangers. She had chosen the path for both of them.

He left without another word.

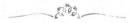

"I'll be candid, Swann. I had hoped to be done with your services when you reached your majority. I was told I only had to employ you until your twenty-fifth birthday, but now that the day has passed, what do I find? Whoever you have backing you is still moving in the shadows. Who is it?" Sir Michael Biddle smacked his palm on his desk. "Are you blackmailing someone into showing you favor?" His eyes burned like bright coals.

Daniel stood in Sir Michael's office at the Bow Street Magistrate's Court, his hands clasped behind his back, his face devoid of expression. Daniel didn't know which was worse, being called onto the carpet by his governor, or the brief conversation he'd had with his mother yesterday. Nevertheless Sir Michael wasn't to know that Daniel's original patron had died and that his new ally, the Duke of Haverly, was working on Daniel's behalf.

Sir Michael looked as if he'd swilled a tankard of vinegar. Why must he constantly abuse his power? Why couldn't he treat Daniel as he did the other investigators under his command? While not exactly cordial with any of the men, he seemed to save his most tyrannical behavior for Daniel alone.

"I've never blackmailed anyone in my life, sir." Daniel kept his tone bland.

"Who is this backer? Why does he care what happens to you? I demand to know whom you have under your thumb." Frustration leaked from every line of Sir Michael's face.

"I am manipulating no one. I only wish to do my job, sir."

"You only want to do your job, do you? That will include all the job, not just the glamorous parts that seem to land you in the good graces of your betters. You and Beck are up next in the rota. Until another case turns up, you'll stand watch in the court upstairs and move prisoners."

Court duty? That boring detail was reserved for a couple of old pensioners who escorted prisoners from the holding cells in the basement up to the court when it was their turn to stand before the magistrates. It was hardly a fitting duty for two trained investigators.

Sir Michael waited for Daniel to protest, but Daniel wouldn't give him the satisfaction. Any work was honorable, and a case would come soon, London being what it was, and he and Ed would be back out on the streets investigating.

And soon Daniel might be an earl, someone Sir Michael couldn't demean.

"That's all. Get out."

"Good day, sir." Daniel gave his boss a cheeky smile and bow before returning to the investigators' room.

Ed Beck sat at his desk, which was pushed up to Daniel's in the far corner of the room, perusing a newspaper.

"Enjoy yourself?" Ed flicked a glance up, his lips twitching. Everyone in the office knew Sir Michael had a bee in his bonnet about Daniel. "The boys are taking odds on how soon he can dismiss you."

Daniel shrugged. "If anyone chose today, they've lost their coins. However, you're being drawn into the conflict. He's relegated us to court duty until another case comes in." Daniel sat at his desk, leaning back and lacing his fingers over his flat stomach. "Punishment for being my partner, I daresay."

Ed lowered the broadsheet. "Indoor work. Hardly taxing. I suppose we shouldn't complain."

The door opened, and a young boy Daniel had not seen before came in, balancing a tea tray. Owen, part-time office boy and investigator in training, followed him.

"Put it on the corner of the desk." Owen pointed, and the boy obliged, only rattling the cups in the saucers a bit.

"Tea's up." Owen motioned for the boy to pour. "All we have is seed cakes today. The new boy forgot to pick up the order from the bakery this morning. This is Caleb. He'll be taking over most of my old duties, now that I'm helping more with field work. This is Mr. Beck, and that's Mr. Swann."

"Sir Michael has ordered us to prisoner duties up in the court until a new case comes in, so if you were hoping to accompany us on an investigation, you're out of luck." Daniel accepted a cup from Caleb, who poured and served deftly enough. He looked to be twelve or so, with a mop of curly hair, brown eyes, and a spattering of freckles across his nose. "What will you do while we're minding prisoners?"

Owen shrugged. "Wish the guv would settle on what my duties are. One minute he's training me to be an investigator, and the next I'm filing reports and making tea and teaching this pup."

Daniel hid a smile. It wasn't all that long ago that Owen had been a pup himself. "My fault, I suppose. Sir Michael was grooming you to take my place, planning on giving me my notice at the end of last month. But it seems he's changed his mind. I'll be here for a while yet."

"I thought he wanted to give your job to his nephew," Ed remarked. "At least that was the word going around."

"The nephew fell off a ladder and broke his leg something terrible. Had to have it taken off," Owen said. "Can't hardly walk, much less chase down cutpurses in Covent Gardens."

Daniel didn't question how Owen knew, nor the veracity of his story. He'd long ago given up trying to suss out Owen's sources. The tea steamed as Daniel blew across his cup. "Until a new case comes along, we're all stuck here on court duty."

Owen put his hands on his hips. "Caleb, go sweep the secretary's room, dust the shelves in the records room, and then run to the printers for that letterhead. You remember where it is?"

Caleb nodded.

"Good. And don't touch anything in the records room except the dust. I've got a system, and I don't want it upset."

Caleb nodded again, tugged his forelock with a slight bow toward the investigators, and hurried out of the room. When he was gone, Owen pulled up a chair from a nearby desk. "I might have a case for you. Something troublesome anyway. On my way to the office today, I crossed the Blackfriars Bridge and turned onto Fleet Street, my usual route. There's a little chap, Davy's his name, who sweeps the crossing there. He's been there every day for the past two years and hasn't missed once, but today he wasn't there. I asked the pie seller and the beer man who use that corner, and they hadn't seen him."

"Perhaps he got a different corner that was better or his folks up and moved?" Ed asked.

"He hasn't got any folks. We've chatted often, and sometimes, if I can spare it, I buy a pie and we split it for breakfast."

Daniel remembered the mean circumstances of Owen's home life. A widowed mother, several younger siblings, and miles to walk to get to Bow Street each day. Owen provided for his family the best he could, and he was proud of it. For him to care enough to share his own meager breakfast with a crossing sweeper . . .

"Street children are elusive. If he found a better corner or if he perhaps found a different position, he wouldn't hang around waiting to inform you," Daniel observed, taking a seed cake. Biting into it, he grimaced. Hard and stale. He set it on his saucer.

"It's odd, I tell you. He wouldn't miss unless something was wrong," Owen insisted. "Can you look into it?"

Daniel looked to Ed to give Owen the bad news, knowing it would come better from Ed.

"Unless we're certain a crime has been committed, we can't investigate. And you heard Daniel. We're on court duty until a case comes in."

"A missing person isn't a crime? Is it because he's a poor nobody that you won't investigate? Does he have to be rich for anyone to do anything?" Owen stood, his body rigid. "There's something wrong, I tell you. Davy wouldn't just disappear. Something's happened to him."

"Calm yourself. It's not that we don't care. You know us better than that. We don't show favoritism in the cases we take. But you've no proof of a crime." Daniel frowned. Cadogan had mentioned a missing child in Spitalfields, a chimney sweep's boy? Still, there were thousands of street children in London, and they traveled about the city with no one to track their movements. "A street child wasn't on the corner where you expected him, and no one in the area suspects foul play but you? Bring us evidence and we'll get to work." Daniel finished his tea. "Until then, we need to get upstairs to court."

At the rate Owen crashed the tea things about as he stacked the cups, he might be out of pocket for some crockery. Ed joined Daniel in the hallway.

"Poor blighter. He cares."

"I know he cares, and so do we, but we can't go chasing every rumor or suspicion, especially when it concerns someone as ephemeral as a street child. The ones I have encountered are next door to feral. The boy probably found a better crossing where he could make more money." Daniel eyed the staircase, dreading the boredom that awaited them in the court today.

"Blackfriars and Fleet would be difficult to beat for making coin. Lots of businessmen pass through there heading into the City."

The door to the street opened behind them, and a dark-skinned man came in, yanking his hat from his head. His eyes were round, the whites glaringly stark.

Daniel stepped forward. "Is there something I can help you with?"

"I come to report a murder." The man's voice was thick with a West Indian accent. "At the Olympian Club. On Red Lion Square."

A murder. That was more like it. "We'll come. Let us inform our superior. Flag us a ride."

"I've one waiting, sir."

His waiting carriage was owned by none other than Cadogan, who looked none too pleased about this particular fare. Did he have something against dark-skinned people riding in his cab? Cadogan had scowled and climbed to his seat, picking up the reins without offering his usual banter as they climbed aboard.

Daniel took out his notebook and pencil as they jounced toward the club. "Your name, sir?"

"Abel, sir."

"Abel what?"

"Just Abel, sir."

Daniel wrote down the name as the man rubbed his palm against his nape and then dragged his hands down his face. Was he normally this fidgety? He was certainly well dressed, with clean, fashionable clothes and shiny boots. "What can you tell us?"

"The boss, Mr. Jericho. He's dead. In his office, sir."

"You say he was murdered. How do you know?"

"The hole in his chest may have had something to do with it, sir."

Ed grunted, as if covering a laugh.

"This Mr. Jericho. Does he have a first name?"

"That is his first name, sir. Mr. Jericho Haskett."

"What is the Olympian Club?"

"It is a gambling hall, sir. There are rooms for club members if they wish to stay the night, and there is a bar and dining room."

Red Lion Square was bordered by row houses and businesses. A plaque on the black iron railing in front of their destination announced the Olympian Club.

Abel hopped out of the carriage first, holding the door as a footman would. Perhaps that was his occupation at the club.

They entered the club, and not a sound could be heard in the building. "Is there no one here?"

"Those who stay overnight are requested to be out of their rooms by eight o'clock, sir. To give the staff time to clean and prepare them for the coming day. Breakfast service concludes at nine, and the house is closed until noon."

"What about staff? Where are they?"

"When we found Mr. Jericho, the secretary, Mr. Alton, sent the servants to the hall downstairs to wait. Then he sent me to Bow Street, sir."

"Where is this Mr. Alton? We'll want to speak with him."

"I'll get him, sir."

"Wait. Show us the body first. Then fetch him."

Abel led them up the stairs and down the left-hand hallway to a room in the back corner of the first floor. "Mr. Jericho's office, sir."

He stood back, allowing Daniel and Ed to enter, then hurried away to find the secretary.

One shutter was open, letting in morning light, but the other three were closed.

"I imagine someone came in to ready the place, opened one shutter, and found him," Ed speculated.

A large walnut desk stood square and imposing in the center of the book-lined room, and behind it a portly man lay sprawled on his back. As Abel had said, a bloodstained hole just left of center in his chest had most likely contributed to his demise. Daniel squatted beside the body as Ed opened the other shutters.

With the end of his pencil, Daniel lifted the lapel on the man's waistcoat, peering underneath.

"Anything?" Ed asked.

"Something penetrated his chest, but it doesn't look like a gunshot. The wound is too narrow and long. Looks like a knife of some sort. We'd better send for Rosebreen. He'll be able to tell us more about what killed this fellow."

A man cleared his throat in the hall. "You wished to see me, gentlemen?"

"Mr. Alton?" Daniel asked.

"Yes." The man studiously avoided looking at his dead boss.

"You found the body?"

"Yes."

"Did you touch anything, move anything?"

"No." The man looked aghast. "I didn't see him until I'd opened the shutter. He isn't usually here at this hour."

"Is there anything missing, anything out of place?" Daniel asked.

Alton scanned the room, his gaze resting briefly on an interior wall, then he bent over the body. "His cravat pin is gone. A black enamel rose with a diamond center."

Daniel wrote it down. "Anything else?"

"Have you checked for his purse? He always carries quite a bit of coin in a leather pouch."

Ed dipped into the pockets, shaking his head. "Nothing there. Think this is a robbery that turned into something else?"

"A bit early for theories, but it's possible." Daniel noticed the ornaments on the desk, a silver inkwell, a brass letter opener. Those would be easy to fence at a receiver's shop. This murder scene had the feel of a single killer, not a group of thieves. Still, he must keep an open mind and gather information. He followed the clues rather than trying to find clues that fit a theory.

Owen Wilkinson edged around Mr. Alton. "Guv sent me to help. What can I do?"

Daniel smothered a smile, knowing Owen wouldn't like what he had to say. For once Daniel wasn't displeased to have the office boy, investigator-in-training appear at a crime scene. He waved his hand toward the desk and filing cabinets.

"You know where to start."

Owen scowled, but he said nothing as he stacked papers together.

Chapter 5

JULIETTE ENTERED AGATHA'S DRAWING ROOM, her stomach fluttering. *Do not mention the inheritance dispute. Do not mention Daniel. Behave as if everything is normal.*

"Jules." Agatha jumped to her feet and hurried toward Juliette. "You won't believe it." She engulfed Juliette in a tight hug, the black silk of her mourning gown rustling. "I am dumbstruck. It's the most awful thing."

"What is it?" Juliette took note of the other woman in the room, someone she didn't know.

Agatha released her. She put her hand to her chest, as if out of breath. "Oh, do forgive my manners. Juliette, this is Viscountess Coatsworth, Alonzo's mother. She's come with the most dreadful news."

Juliette's stomach sank. Did Agatha already know? She inclined her head to the guest. "Pleased to meet you, Lady Coatsworth."

The woman had a long, narrow face, pale hair, and pale eyes, and was so thin, Juliette feared her bones would poke through the fabric of her gown. She also had a pinched look of umbrage on her features. She gave a quick nod, acknowledging Juliette's greeting.

"Do continue, please," Agatha said. "Juliette, just listen. I never would have suspected it of him. He always seemed so nice."

Lady Coatsworth's nostrils flared as her mouth tightened. "There has been a claim against my son's estate. My father-in-law declared in his will that my marriage to his son was invalid, that our child is illegitimate, and some . . . some . . . money-grubbing by-blow of a kitchen maid is his true heir."

Juliette flinched. Daniel wasn't moneygrubbing. He was a victim of fraud and cowardice. Everything in her wanted to leap to his defense, but his words of caution filled her ears. *Say nothing. Don't indicate our relationship is anything beyond what it seems.*

"The claims are the false ramblings of a sick old man, and the moment Alonzo returns, we will quash these rumors. I am the legal widow of William Darby, and my son is his legitimate heir. This Mr. Swann will be exposed as a charlatan, my son will inherit the title, and we will put this farce behind us." Lady Coatsworth throttled her handkerchief.

"Mr. Swann?" Juliette feigned ignorance. "What has he to do with Alonzo's inheritance?"

"That man is claiming his mother was married to my husband and that the marriage was never legally dissolved. That he, being a year older than Alonzo, is the legal, legitimate heir to Rotherhide. He intends to present his claim to the Crown." The viscountess looked both enraged and appalled.

"Has he proof?" Juliette asked.

"Of course not. The earl was a sick old man, out of his head when he made those claims. It's all twaddle that should have been ignored from the outset. It's that Duke of Haverly who is pushing for an investigation. Him and his solicitors. I hear he's brought Sir James Durridge in to prepare the claim. Mr. Swann will rue the day he tried to steal what rightfully belongs to my son."

Agatha leaned forward. "I know he saved you from those kidnappers, Juliette, and I know he found the man who killed my father, but he's not a gentleman. You should stay away from him, though I can't imagine further situations where you will encounter each other. But if you do, cut him dead. It's what he deserves. Alonzo suspected him of something from the moment they met. You remember. Alonzo didn't like him, and now he has good reason."

"Does he? What if Mr. Swann's claim is the truth? He and Alonzo would be brothers, wouldn't they?" Juliette asked.

Lady Coatsworth gasped. "Bite your tongue, girl. You cannot think any of this is true? My son is in no way related to this grasping liar. He's the result of a loose woman's indiscretion. His father is probably a groom or gardener or gadabout, for all we know."

Juliette bit her lower lip. It was so hard not to defend Daniel's character, but she could see it would make no difference. The viscountess could not acknowledge even the possibility of Daniel's claim, because to do so would make her a bigamous wife with an illegitimate son.

Agatha sighed. "I am eager for Alonzo's return. It seems an age since I saw him, though it's not even a month yet. I understand now why he left. If his grandfather sent him to the West Indies, he would, of course, be obedient and go. It is only a shame the old earl passed away. If he lived still, we could get him to recant his statements."

The viscountess nodded once, hard. "Alonzo must miss you as well, my dear. The moment your mourning period is over, we will announce the engagement and see you properly wed. You will be the Countess of Rotherhide, and this nonsense will be over."

"When do you expect him?" Juliette asked.

"If the ship I sent after him can catch him up before they leave the Canary Islands, he should return within the fortnight. If not, it may take several weeks."

"It's too bad he won't be here for the Easter services tomorrow. Will you be attending church, Agatha?" Juliette hoped to get the topic changed. Agatha had not been seen in public often since her father's death, electing to remain in her house over the last month.

"Yes, I believe I will. Church is one of the few places it is acceptable for me to go while still in full mourning. I do wish Alonzo was here. How can he fight these false claims when he's not even in the country?"

So much for changing the subject.

"He has us, my dear. He has you and I, and he has our legal advisers." Lady Coatsworth nodded twice. "We will fight on his behalf until he can take up the matter himself."

"Wouldn't it be best to let the attorney general and the committee sort it out?" Juliette asked. "If there is no truth to the claims, then the lords and the Prince Regent will sort it out."

"Those incompetent buffoons don't know 'lie down' from 'fetch' half the time, especially the Prince Regent," the viscountess retorted.

Juliette smothered her smile.

The butler opened the drawing room door. "The Duchess of Haverly and the dowager duchess, ma'am."

Juliette bit her lip. How would Agatha and the viscountess react to having them here when the duke was clearly helping Daniel make his claims against the Rotherhide estate? This could put the cat amongst pigeons.

"Agatha, how are you, my dear?" Charlotte came to Agatha, who had risen, and cupped her shoulders, drawing her in for a kiss on the cheek.

"Your Grace, it's so nice of you to call." Agatha's eyes were wide. It was an honor to have someone of Charlotte's status call upon her, but the Haverlys were in the enemy camp at the moment.

Talk about avoiding caltrops in high grass.

Lady Coatsworth looked as if she'd just smelled bad fish. "How do you do?" she asked when addressed, but her tone could have frozen a brazier. What else could she do but show good manners? The duchess and the dowager held power of rank over her by several degrees. The viscountess couldn't cut them or behave with even veiled rudeness, or she would find herself on the wrong end of societal opinion.

Agatha invited the ladies to sit, and the dowager took the center chair, stacking her hands on her cane. "Agatha, you look well in spite of your trials. How dreadful of that man to shoot your father over money."

"Thank you." Agatha sounded cowed, and her shoulders sloped.

Juliette nudged her and straightened her back. Agatha caught her hint and sat up. "Yes, it was dreadful. I am glad Mr. Earnshaw was brought to justice. Your son recommended another man of accounts, whom I could trust. He has been helping me with my father's finances. It was most kind of His Grace."

Charlotte smiled, and her hand went to her middle, where a distinct bump was showing. "I'm glad. You can trust Marcus."

The viscountess snorted, then tried to cover it with a cough.

"Lucy, dear. I hope you're not coming down with something. It would be so flattening to be ill this close to the end of the Season. There are so many lovely parties coming up." The dowager turned to Juliette. "We must confer on our calendars. What invitations has your mother accepted on your behalf?"

"I am not certain. Thankfully, my parents will not be away long, as they have been invited by the regent to stay with him in Brighton next month." Juliette smiled politely at the dowager. "I do appreciate you stepping in for them once again."

"Juliette." Charlotte tilted her head as if an idea had occurred to her. "You know you are always welcome to stay with us."

"Thank you, but I wouldn't want to leave Uncle Bertie alone."

The dowager harrumphed. "I can believe that. That man is half-sotted every time I see him. I cannot imagine what he would be like left entirely to his own devices."

That hadn't been Juliette's meaning, but one corrected the dowager at one's peril. Poor Bertie. His drunken dilletante act was so successful, it was now a permanent part of his image.

The viscountess whispered into Agatha's ear, and Agatha nodded, looking at Juliette. She beckoned, and Juliette leaned close.

"Don't mention the inheritance, please. Lady Coatsworth thinks we shouldn't speak of it with the Haverlys here."

"Of course. Most wise." Though Juliette would dearly love to hear what Charlotte thought of it all. Juliette could predict the dowager's opinions, which were much more likely to align with Lady Coatsworth's than her own.

The dowager accepted a teacup from the parlor maid. "Young ladies these days need more oversight than ever. Did you hear what Lord and Lady Fresney's daughter did?" Without waiting for an answer, the dowager said, "She ran off with one of the footmen. How someone of her breeding and prospects could betray her parents by falling in love with a servant, I'll never know. It's disgraceful. Fresney spent an absolute fortune to launch her into society, her wardrobe, her dancing classes, her schooling, purchasing a voucher to Almack's, and how does she repay him? By eloping with the help. It's scandalous, that's what. I don't know what this world is coming to when young girls insist upon ruining not just themselves but their parents with impetuous acts. The family has fled London in disgrace. I cannot think who will invite them to any social engagement again. Believe me, I shall keep a much closer watch upon you than the Fresneys did upon Frederica, Lady Juliette."

Juliette blinked. Her parents had spent lavishly on her debutante's wardrobe, on the finest schooling, seeing her launched successfully into society. Would her love for Daniel scandalize them? Would it ruin their lives and reputations? Would marrying Daniel compromise their ability to do their work? Often vital information was gathered at parties and balls and social events amongst the aristocracy. If her parents were shunned because Juliette had "disgraced" them with a common husband, they wouldn't be in a position to gather that information.

Daniel simply had to win the petition for the title.

More ladies arrived, and Juliette checked the clock. Her half-hour visit was nearing its completion time. It was considered poor etiquette to stay longer than thirty minutes on an afternoon call, no matter how dear the friend one called upon.

"Did you hear?" one woman asked as she took her seat. "Jericho Haskett has been . . ." She lowered her head and her voice. "Murdered."

"Murdered?" The woman next to her had no such compunctions about being overheard. "By whom?"

"No one knows. He was killed in his office sometime last night. They found him this morning, and according to my footman, who knows one of the waiters there, Bow Street runners are swarming the club. I heard it just before I left the house. I doubt the papers even know yet."

Juliette's ears pricked at the mention of Bow Street. Daniel had said he and Mr. Beck would be the next investigators to be called out.

"Who is Jericho Haskett?" she asked.

The two women looked at each other, speaking volumes without saying a word. Finally, one said, "He was the owner of the Olympian Club."

She had never heard of the place. Was it like White's or Boodles?

At her puzzled expression, they shared another glance, then the first one leaned toward her and whispered, "It's a gaming club."

Light dawned.

"I know it isn't nice to speak ill of the dead, but can I say I'm a bit relieved?" The second woman gave an excusatory little shrug. "I owed a considerable amount to the Olympian Club, and now with Jericho's demise, I'm sure I'll have a bit more time to repay my debt. Not that I wished him dead, but a lady must take advantage of the opportunities given, mustn't she?"

Perhaps this woman wasn't the only patron of the club to think so? Had one of his debtors killed him to avoid paying? Surely Daniel would consider such a course of inquiry. Yet Juliette's interest was pricked. She would have no spy work assigned to her until her parents returned, and she wouldn't have her budding romance with Daniel to keep her occupied, as they had to keep their relationship quiet. Perhaps clandestine sleuthing would fill her time?

She could just see Uncle Bertie's disapproving shake of the head.

Juliette rose to say her goodbyes. Agatha came with her to the door. Once they were out of earshot of the guests, Agatha took her arm.

"You will stay away from that dreadful Daniel Swann, won't you? I know you consider him a friend, but with what he's trying to do to Alonzo, you will cut ties, I am sure."

Juliette didn't want to lie to Agatha, but she didn't want to hurt her, or worse, lose her friendship. "Why don't we both wait until we know whether his claims have merit before we make any decisions? If what he says is true, then justice will be served. If it cannot be proven, Alonzo has lost nothing."

"Juliette, you cannot think that any of it is true?" Her friend's eyes widened. "Daniel is jealous of Alonzo and has been since they first met. He's grasping at an opportunity given him by a sick old man. He went to visit the earl just before he died. How do we know he didn't exert undue influence on the man and get him to say he was his heir? Or perhaps the codicil to the will was forged."

Juliette stepped back. "Has Daniel Swann ever acted with less than integrity? Has he ever lied to you? You're casting aspersions on his character that are unwarranted. You don't know the entire story, and neither do I. But to claim he's a liar without hearing the evidence is very small-minded of you, Agatha, and you've never been small-minded before."

Agatha pressed her lips together for a moment, blinking hard. Juliette had never chastised her friend like this before.

"I suppose that is just, to wait for the proof, but when one's heart is involved, it is difficult not to take sides," Agatha said at last.

"Yes. Yes, it is." Juliette kissed her cheek, squeezed her hand, and left.

Daniel trotted down the narrow staircase to the basement of the gambling club, grateful to leave the removal of the body to Rosebreen and Ed.

The staff had gathered around a long table in the Spartan dining hall. Teapots sat on the table, along with plates of shortbread biscuits. When Daniel entered, conversation ceased.

"My name is Mr. Swann, and I am an investigator with the Bow Street Magistrate's Court. Mr. Alton, perhaps you can make introductions?" Daniel stood at one end of the table. Half a dozen faces looked back at him, three men and three women.

"This is Mrs. Woodlawn, the cook. And Naomi and Sue, her helpers." Mr. Alton indicated the older woman and then the two girls. "Then there's Abel here. He looks after the gentlemen who stay overnight."

The black man who had come to the station nodded.

"And Manuel. He mostly cleans and does maintenance."

"What about the waiters and the card dealers? Where are they?"

"The waiters will arrive soon. They are required to be in attendance at noon. We begin meal service at that time. Those who work in the gaming rooms will arrive later, around three. Because they work long into the night, they do not have to attend until midafternoon. Those who wish to play at the tables also keep late hours and often do not arrive before three." Mr. Alton spoke quietly and quickly with just a trace of an accent. Yorkshire, possibly?

"What can you tell me about Mr. Haskett's behavior last night? Did any of you notice anything odd or different?"

"The girls would not have seen him," Mr. Alton said. "Nor Mrs. Woodlawn. They stay belowstairs at all times. Abel? Did you see him last evening?"

"Yes, sir. I took him a meal at about nine, and he was counting money and writing in his ledger. He said to put the tray on his desk and that I should check that the rooms were ready, as there were several members staying over."

"Mr. Haskett counted money at least twice per night, recording it and placing it in the safe. Then he would return to the club to mingle with the patrons," Alton offered.

"The safe? Where is that?" Daniel looked up from his notebook.

"It is in his office. Behind a hidden panel. I checked it right away when I found him, and the safe is undisturbed."

"You looked inside?" That must have been the reason Alton's eyes had gone to the wall in Haskett's office when asked if anything had been stolen.

"Yes. I am the only one who has the key, other than Mr. Haskett, of course. When a table runs short of funds, I go to the office and procure more. That doesn't happen often. The Olympian takes in much more than it pays out." Alton spoke with a tinge of pride.

"Who has access to his office?"

Alton looked at Abel and then at Manuel. "The guests do not go into that wing unless Mr. Haskett invites them, and he only does so when someone is in considerable debt to the house. Beyond that, myself and Abel are permitted to enter when our duties require it. And Manuel here, who cleans at night."

Daniel considered the small Spaniard. "Did you clean last night?

"No, señor."

Alton frowned. "Why not? You were to remove the ashes from the fireplace and dust the furniture."

Manuel flinched and leaned away. "Please, señor, I tried, but the door was closed when I went upstairs to work. Mr. Haskett, he say I never go into his office if the door is closed. There was someone in the office with Señor Haskett, and they were . . . how you say it . . . *gritos* . . . shouting."

"Shouting? What were they shouting about?"

"I did not understand. The man, he said Señor Haskett was a black-guard? Is that the word? And he would make sure it never happened again, that the debt was paid. I think it is someone who owed Señor Haskett money, like all the rest. I know not to go into the office when he is getting his money."

"We all know not to go in there when Mr. Haskett is dealing with a club patron," Abel said. "I saw a man leaving late last night. After the gaming tables closed and the men staying overnight were in their rooms. I was surprised to hear someone at the side door, but perhaps it was the same man?"

"What did he look like?"

Abel shook his head. "It was very dark, and the man kept to the shadows. He went around the corner, and I heard carriage wheels and horse hooves. I assumed he got into a carriage or that his carriage was waiting there."

"What time was this?"

"Half three or thereabouts. We close the gaming tables at three."

"Mr. Alton, can you name anyone who might have owed Mr. Haskett enough money to be called into the office last night?"

The man shook his head, shrugging and spreading his hands. "I do not know. Mr. Haskett managed all of that. He never let staff see the accounts. He wanted us to treat every customer with the same courtesy, and he felt we could do that best by not knowing their financial affairs. One could guess, I suppose, if one watched the gaming tables closely enough who was winning and who was losing, but to be honest, most of our patrons lose more than they win."

Which narrowed down nothing.

Ed stepped into the servants' hall. "Rosebreen's gone, but he said there was something odd about the wound. He'll examine it further when he gets back to his office, and you can see him Monday for a report. And he said he would send the man's clothes over to Rhynwick Davies's place. Crocombe Abbey? Rosebreen said there was a strange substance on Haskett's wrist that he wanted the scientist to identify if possible."

Daniel gave a half smile. Rhynwick. The young genius who hopped about like a flea on a griddle, whose mind was never still, nor his body. He'd helped Daniel with the Montgomery case recently, and Daniel looked forward to working with him again. He hadn't known Rosebreen and Rhynwick were acquainted, but perhaps he shouldn't be surprised. The scientific community in London couldn't be that large.

Unlike the pool of gamblers, one of whom might be the mysterious man Haskett had quarreled with last night.

Chapter 6

How could one have both elation and dissatisfaction filling one's heart, and all centered on the same individual? Juliette had attended church with Bertie, and to her surprise, she had spotted Daniel in the balcony. Just seeing him brought her so much joy. And yet the dissatisfaction of the distance they must keep rankled. He had crossed town to attend her church on Easter Sunday, yet all she could do was catch his eye, nod the barest fraction to show how she appreciated his gallant gesture, and face the front, pretending he didn't exist.

And now Uncle Bertie, the moment they were home, had news.

"I am being sent on a mission, Jules. And if I don't miss my guess, it's a bit of a trial run in the agency. I'm being tested to see if I can handle taking on more responsibility."

"This is ridiculous. It's as if Marcus Haverly would prefer me to be abandoned to my own fate." Juliette laid aside her bonnet and prayer book. "Surely you don't have to leave immediately."

"It isn't personal, I assure you. If you wish to blame someone, blame the Prince Regent. He thinks of nothing but himself and his own appetites. He ordered Marcus to send someone, and Marcus has chosen me. I could think of lovelier destinations than Dartmoor Prison, I assure you. Someone must have put a bug in the regent's ear." Bertie rolled his eyes. "Prinny is now no longer satisfied with the investigation that was conducted following the massacre last year. The death of American sailors imprisoned while awaiting repatriation has not set well, especially considering the Treaty of Ghent had long been signed. I am to go to the prison and look into things myself, though what I am supposed to find after so much time has passed, I don't know." Uncle Bertie flexed his arm, wincing as he shrugged his shoulder. "I am leaving today, and I will be gone for a fortnight or so. However"—he held up his hands to stifle the protest on her lips—"I am not abandoning you to your own fate. You are to be a houseguest while I am gone."

"A houseguest? I cannot stay with Agatha. Not with things as they are. It would be torture. You don't know how much I want to fly to Daniel's defense every time she speaks of the inheritance dispute, and she speaks of nothing else these days. I'm surprised she didn't stand up in church today to air her grievance before God and the rector."

"You do like to leap to conclusions, don't you?" He rubbed his forehead. "You will not be staying with Miss Montgomery. You are to be a guest at Haverly House. Marcus and Charlotte have invited you to stay while I'm away."

A thrill tickled in Juliette's chest. Haverly House was magnificent, and Charlotte was a wonderful hostess. Perhaps it wouldn't be so bad after all . . . until she remembered that the dowager duchess lived there as well.

A mixed blessing, this invitation.

Still, it was better than sitting alone here mourning the fact that her family had all fled the city.

"You will stay for luncheon, won't you?" she asked. "Cook has prepared something special for Easter."

"I wouldn't dream of disappointing her, or you." Bertie touched her on the nose as he passed. "Haverly said he would send a carriage for you and your maid at three."

Promptly at three, Juliette entered the Haverly carriage wearing her Easter bonnet and carrying the two books she had borrowed from Charlotte the week before. Her maid, Miss Brown, sat opposite, surrounded by bags and boxes. Juliette's trunk had been sent ahead by Mr. Pultney. It still amazed Juliette how many things she needed as a debutante in London. She was required, on an average day, to change clothes at least four times, and each of those changes required appropriate accessories. After her life at boarding school in Switzerland, where she wore the same dress all day and only changed for dinner, it seemed excessive and tedious. And expensive, as the dowager had pointed out. The nagging unease that was never far from her thoughts pressed deeper into her mind. She rested her hand on the books on the bench beside her.

When they arrived at Haverly House on Berkeley Square, their carriage joined a queue out front. Footmen carried valises and trunks, and people emerged from the carriages in groups. What a melee.

When it was finally their turn, Juliette and her maid were welcomed inside the immense house by Charlotte herself, whose cheeks glowed and eyes sparkled. "Juliette, I'm delighted you accepted our invitation. We're going to have such fun. Oh, you brought back the Greek and Roman histories. We must find a quiet corner to discuss them." When Charlotte smiled, her entire face lit up.

Marcus joined his wife, slipping his arm around her waist and brushing a kiss on her temple. "My dear, don't you think you should sit down for a bit? You've been on your feet for hours. The staff will see that everyone has a place to sleep. Our guests are amassing in the drawing room for tea." Voices came from across the entry hall. Lots of voices.

Juliette's maid took her hat, gloves, and reticule and followed a footman up the stairs with Juliette's baggage.

"Come, Juliette, and join the fray. It will be a madhouse for the next week or so. Charlotte and my mother are throwing a party, and they've invited simply everyone." Marcus sounded aggrieved, but he winked at his wife.

The drawing room was so crowded, it appeared the festivities had started already. "I'll make the introductions." Charlotte threaded her arm through Juliette's. She pointed out several relations and then stopped in front of a woman with pale blonde hair, sky-blue eyes, and porcelain skin. An English rose, to be sure.

"This is Marcus's sister-in-law, Cilla. Cilla is married to Hamish

Sinclair, a talented artist. Perhaps you've seen some of his pieces at the Royal Academy?"

Cilla's husband, Hamish, had dark-red hair and a kind expression. He clearly doted upon his wife, for his eyes rarely left her, and he wore a besotted, almost bewildered expression, as if he couldn't quite believe she belonged to him.

"Pleased to meet you all."

"Later we'll take you up to the nursery to meet my niece, Honora Mary," Charlotte promised. "My son is quite taken with his cousin."

"Honora Mary thinks she runs the world, and no one has disabused her mind of the notion just yet." Hamish smiled. "She's a bonny lass, to be sure."

His Scots burr delighted Juliette, and the twinkle in his eye tickled her. She could see why Cilla Haverly had married him.

Cilla had been a lady, the widow of the heir to a dukedom, and she'd married an artist far beneath her social standing, but they seemed quite happy. Perhaps there was hope for Juliette and Daniel yet.

"Ah, Charlotte, who do you have here?" An older lady in a lace cap looked up over her eyeglasses. Her knitting needles never stopped.

"This is Lady Juliette Thorndike. She will be our guest for the next fortnight or so. Juliette, this is Mrs. Stokes. And of course you've met my sister, Pippa—I mean Philippa—Cashel. Mrs. Stokes helps with our work training young ladies for a better life."

Juliette nodded. "Good afternoon." Miss Cashel had mentioned their work to rescue and reform Cyprians at dinner the other night.

Juliette approached the dowager, who held court on the settee, her cane by her side.

"Ah, you've arrived at last. We're full to bursting here, but Charlotte insisted you come stay, and after I gave it some thought, I agree. It isn't suitable for you to remain alone at your townhouse with only the staff to look after you. We can't have you running afoul of demure behavior while unsupervised, can we?"

"A pleasure to see you again, Your Grace. Thank you for your most kind and generous invitation. I should very much not wish to run afoul of demurity. I am certain with your excellent guidance, I shall not even approach such a disastrous event." Juliette almost laughed as the dowager nodded, taking her remarks with all seriousness.

"If you do as I say, all will be well." The dowager patted the upholstery next to her.

The room buzzed with conversation and fellowship, and Juliette was both grateful and unsettled. What fun would it be to have a large, boisterous family? To have siblings and nieces and nephews, good friends and in-laws, all enjoying one another, being part of one another's lives?

This was how she had hoped her own small family would be, but alas, she couldn't keep them under the same roof long enough to become acquainted, much less to enjoy one another's company.

If she chose the spy life, would her family always be disjointed?

But if she didn't continue to be an agent for the Crown, would she have anything in common with her parents at all?

Crocombe Abbey was nothing like Daniel had envisioned. He approached the gothic monstrosity on Monday morning, eyeing the spires and ivy-covered facade. How had Rhynwick come to own such a place?

Cadogan had brought him out here, past Regent's Park and into the countryside north of London. The farther they got from the city, the more rutted the road became, and Cadogan slowed the horses to a walk. The gates leading to the abbey had been open with vines growing over them, and the gravel drive wasn't in any better condition than the road. Weeds grew everywhere, and if the hedges had ever been trimmed, it hadn't been in the last decade. The place was near to being a crumbling ruin.

Cadogan pulled up before a set of immense doors, and Daniel emerged from the carriage.

"Strewth! What kind of place is this?" the driver asked.

"It looks haunted. I knew Rhynwick was unique, but this is bizarre."

"If you aren't out in half an hour, I'll come looking for you."

"It might take me half an hour to find him."

The abbey was massive, with a central quadrangle surrounded by cloisters with groined ceilings, and in the middle of the grassy area, a garden enclosed in a high iron fence. Above the garden gate, which bore a padlock, a sign read, "Poison Garden. Keep out." A skull and crossbones emphasized the words.

Delightful.

To his right was what Daniel assumed must be the monastic cells, and to the left, the peaked roof of the church.

Before he could choose a direction, Rhynwick himself bounded from an unseen door. "Mr. Swann, welcome to Crocombe. Come in. I've something to show you."

The thin young man wore a canvas coat over his breeches and waistcoat. The garment hung to his knees, and he held a pair of spectacles with green lenses. Rhynwick strode across the quad with long, loping strides, coattails flapping behind him toward a door on the far side, and Daniel trotted after him.

Once inside Daniel stopped, his mouth dropping open.

The exterior of Crocombe Abbey may look derelict, but the interior was positively palatial. Rich carpets, tapestries on the walls, gleaming woodwork, candles and lamps everywhere.

Rhynwick disappeared around a corner, and Daniel hurried in his wake. "Hey, slow down."

"I can't. I have to check on my experiment. Come along."

They entered the transepts of the chapel and turned into the nave, and once again Daniel stopped. Large tables covered with glass containers, coils, and tools stood where the pews must have once resided.

"What is this place?"

"My laboratory. Stand back."

Rhynwick turned a crank on an apparatus on the nearest table, and a bolt of lightning shot out of a silver orb and crackled into a matching one two feet away. "Ah, most satisfactory."

Daniel realized he was clutching his heart, and he forced himself to relax. "Are you trying to scare me to death? Because you've nearly succeeded." His breath still hitched in his throat.

The young scientist blinked, as if he couldn't comprehend why anyone would be afraid of deadly lightning that could be summoned at will. "I'm building on the work of Allesandro Volta on storage capacity for electricity. Volta has begun the task, but I believe I can make it more efficient."

"Storage of electricity? Electricity is a fine parlor trick, but what possible practical use could there be for such an ephemeral element?" Daniel shrugged to loosen his tight muscles and reached into his inside pocket for his notebook and pencil.

"Electricity will open worlds of possibilities one day, I'm certain of it. We must find ways to harness that power. It will happen, and I intend to be on the front lines when it does." Rhynwick dropped his glasses on the table.

"I wish you well—only don't kill yourself in the process. I understand Dr. Rosebreen sent over some odd findings from my crime scene for you to analyze."

"Yes." Rhynwick snapped his fingers and rounded another table. He pulled a tasseled cord hanging along the wall, and somewhere deep in the building, a bell sounded. Within minutes a pair of tall young men, identical in every feature, appeared.

"Yes, sir?" They spoke in unison, and Daniel wanted to squirm. They were eerily alike, as if Rhynwick had created them in this very lab to be identical.

"Look after the combustion chamber, and don't let the water boil away on my hemlock concoction."

"Yes, sir." Again the disturbing duet.

"This way, Mr. Swann." The young Welshman was off again.

Rhynwick led Daniel down a long corridor with tall windows along one side letting in sunlight. Rows of armor and weaponry, shields and swords hung on the opposite wall. A plush red carpet ran down the middle of the flagstones. They passed several people busily going about their duties, women in aprons and mobcaps dusting and polishing, men in smart coats and shiny boots carrying parcels and buckets of coal or water. How many people worked here?

And how did Rhynwick afford them?

After climbing a flight of stairs and a few more twists and turns, Daniel found himself in one of the towers. A large desk, bookshelves, comfortable chairs, and papers everywhere. A black spaniel leapt off his pillow by the cold fireplace and wriggled his way toward Rhynwick.

"Ah, Faraday, did you have a nice nap?" Rhynwick dug in his pocket and produced a bit of dried meat for the dog. "Now, to Rosebreen's substances." He moved several papers on his desk and sat in the leather chair. "Here it is." He glanced up. "Do sit down."

"Faraday? What kind of name is that for a dog?" Daniel asked.

"He's named after a man I met at the Royal Society, Michael Faraday. I dithered between calling him Faraday or Humphry, after Humphry Davy, and Faraday seemed to fit best. I have a feeling Faraday will do great things for the scientific community one day. He has fascinating views on the unity of God and science that are running counter to most theorists these days, who seem to believe that God and science are separate and science is the greater."

Daniel didn't know what he expected next. Rhynwick had unplumbed depths that his busy-bee actions belied. "How did you come to live in a place like this?" He wanted to ask if Rhynwick was wealthy, but wouldn't commit such a breach of privacy and etiquette.

Rhynwick blinked and shrugged. "The abbey came down through my mother's family, a bequest from the king to my great-great-something or other in the fifteenth century. My English mother broke ranks and married a Welshman, but a man of considerable funds, from the Davies family who owned a fair chunk of land northeast of Swansea and all the coal mines his heart could desire. Mother's family didn't kick up too much fuss when he refurbished the abbey at his own expense."

"What about the outside of the place? It looks like a ruin."

"My grandfather's idea, actually. To say he was eccentric is putting it mildly. He thought if the place looked derelict, people would stay away. He hated parties and callers and intrusions into his solitude. My mother kept things the way he liked them, to placate him, and I've carried on the tradition, though my family are all gone now, of course."

If Rhynwick thought his grandfather eccentric, he must have been an odd stocking to be sure.

"Do you still own a fair chunk of land northeast of Swansea?" Daniel couldn't help himself.

The young man looked up again from his papers, blinking. "I suppose I do. I have managers for all of that. I'm only interested in science, not finance."

"What about my murder case? Did you find anything?"

"Yes." Rhynwick seemed pleased to be finished talking about money. He bounded up and paced. "There were several substances on the murder victim's clothing, some that one would expect to be there and some that were out of place. Rosebreen found what he believed to be ink under the man's fingernails, and when he examined the man's stomach contents, his findings concurred with my own about the yellow substance on the man's waistcoat below the wound site." Rhynwick stopped walking and met Daniel's eyes. "Custard tart."

"Ink and custard tart won't get us far in the investigation," Daniel observed.

"No, both of those substances could reasonably be explained, but I found other things. An odd mixture of axle grease, horsehair, and pollen taken from the body. It was on the cuff of his jacket and shirtsleeve, and Rosebreen said he found some also on the man's right wrist, as if someone with those substances on his hand grabbed our victim's wrist and the mixture transferred."

Axle grease, horsehair, pollen?

"Theories?" He wanted to hear what a mind as sharp as Rhynwick's might come up with, since he had known the test results longer than Daniel.

Rhynwick wandered the perimeter of the round room, his long fingers lighting on objects tucked on the shelves, skimming the spines of books. The dog, Faraday, had returned to his bed, but each time Rhynwick got near, his tail thumped softly and his dark eyes raised adoringly to his master.

"I cannot reliably draw any conclusions. How these substances got there or even when, I couldn't say. I did go to the murder scene and examine the room and the building, but nowhere did I find these three substances together. I am sorry that the grease made identifying the particular source of the pollen impossible. If I knew the plant, perhaps I could give you a location. I believe we can assume the mixture of substances was brought in by the killer and transferred at the time of the murder."

"Where in London would those three be likely to exist?" Daniel asked.

"Anyone who works with machinery would have contact with grease. Horsehair is everywhere, including furniture upholstery, carriage blankets, and on horses themselves, and it is springtime in England. Pollen of all kinds is prevalent."

Daniel closed his notebook and tapped his thigh. "It doesn't narrow things down much, does it?"

"I'm afraid not. However, Rosebreen allowed me to examine the wound on our victim, and if you find the murder weapon, it shouldn't be difficult to match. The man was stabbed with a rather unusual knife." Rhynwick went to his desk and drew a piece of blank foolscap toward himself. Dipping his quill into a porcelain inkwell and shaking off the extra drops, he began to draw. "The knife—at least I'm assuming it was a knife—was short, powerful, and shaped like a spear tip. Wide at the base, approximately three inches, and tapering like an equilateral triangle. The blade is serrated on one side, smooth on the other, and the quillons are wide, to protect the hand. It's a knife designed to penetrate rather than slice. Something like this, I imagine. Rosebreen concurs."

He held up the drawing, and Daniel shuddered.

A sinister weapon, to be sure. And unlike anything Daniel had seen before.

Chapter 7

JULIETTE, DIANA WHITELOCK, CILLA SINCLAIR, and the dowager alighted at the Water Gate leading into Vauxhall just as the sun was setting. Charlotte, in deference to her increasing pregnancy, had elected to stay behind and read a book, while Evan, Hamish, and Marcus had chosen an evening at White's discussing politics and policy rather than an orchestral performance at Vauxhall Pleasure Gardens.

The ladies were not left without protection, however, as Mr. Partridge, a large and capable man in Marcus's employ, followed them down the path.

The past two days had been a whirlwind with people coming and going from Haverly House, and party planning running like wildfire. The guest list had been the biggest bone of contention, with Charlotte's list differing from the dowager's in nearly every respect. Charlotte, like Juliette's parents, had a broader mind than the dowager, wanting to invite interesting people from all walks rather than the same members of the highest echelons of society.

Cilla quietly threw her support behind Charlotte, as did Diana, and eventually Marcus settled the entire thing by taking Charlotte's list to the printer's and having invitations and addressed envelopes produced and dispersed, over his mother's chagrined body. That lady had spouted dire predictions about the party's success from that moment on.

The dowager now leaned on her cane, and the group walked at her pace. Charlotte had confided in Juliette that the dowager had slowed considerably since breaking her ankle in a tumble down the stairs last autumn, though the older women defied anyone to mention it.

Gaslights illuminated their way, and the gardens were crowded. For the first time in what seemed ages, the temperature was mild, bringing people out to enjoy an alfresco concert.

Chairs had been placed in arced rows before the stage, and they found places near the front. In the row ahead, Lady Coatsworth sat as if a stair rod had been inserted where her spine should be. Her cheeks were reddened, and her eyes sparked fire.

What had happened?

It didn't take long to find out. The occupants of the seats behind them stirred and whispered, but not softly. "What do you think? It's all over London. The Earl of Rotherhide has left his title and fortune to a secret heir. That pompous jackanapes Alonzo Darby is a fraud."

"Maybe it's the secret heir who is the fraud. I heard he's a . . . policeman."

The scandalous tone rippled across Juliette's skin.

"It's the talk of London. Rotherhide was worth an absolute fortune, and of course, it's one of the oldest titles in the kingdom, dating back to William I. Alonzo Darby won't give it up easily. This challenger hasn't a hope, I shouldn't think."

Juliette's heart sank. Word was out, and now the case would be tried in the court of public opinion long before it made it to the Prince Regent. Who had leaked the particulars? Surely not Daniel or Marcus Haverly. And Lady Coatsworth was hardly likely to spill the news, at least not before Alonzo was home to refute the claims. Someone on the periphery? A servant, perhaps? Not in the Haverly household. Juliette would stake her life on that. Marcus would have examined every person he hired because of the sensitive work and meetings that took place in his home. It had to be someone in Lady Coatsworth's house, or even Agatha's.

"It will be in the newspapers tomorrow. The running patterers are already spreading it though the city. And Darby is nowhere to be found.

I would have thought he'd be here, strutting like a rooster and bleating that none of it is true." The gossiping went on.

Juliette adjusted her skirts and put her reticule in her lap. No wonder Lady Coatsworth was upset.

And what about Daniel and his mother? Mrs. Dunstan had refused to talk about the issue when Juliette had asked, saying, "God will work out the details. If He means it to happen, it will. If nothing else, I now know that my marriage wasn't dissolved, and that in his way William tried to make things right by telling his father the truth. I'm grateful to have His Grace and Sir James Durridge advocating on our behalf. In the meantime, I will continue with my work here as housekeeper and await events. Beyond that I would rather not discuss it."

Juliette had felt both chastened by and proud of this woman who had kept her dignity throughout years of being wronged, and she somehow seemed to bear no ill will or bitterness toward those who had treated her so badly.

And yet it seemed wrong to have a woman who might be the mother of an earl as housekeeper at the Thorndikes' London residence. A jolt went through Juliette as she realized that if she and Daniel did marry, Mrs. Dunstan would be her mother-in-law.

The women behind them weren't finished gossiping, however. "It isn't quite as delicious as a secret heir, but have you heard . . ." The lady on the left leaned over so the entire row could hear. "Miss Cashel, you know, the woman who used to ply her trade at a disorderly house on King's Place? I hear she's back in London and begging money at society parties to support a rescue home for Cyprians. And she's staying with the Haverlys. Attending social events as if she weren't a slattern."

"Shhh."

Juliette turned to see one of the speaker's friends nudge her and incline her head toward the dowager. Juliette wanted to scold them, both for engaging in gossip and for being so unkind to those in need, but she bit her tongue. It wouldn't do Daniel or Philippa Cashel any favors if she launched into a verbal brawl at a Vauxhall concert.

The orchestra began, and Juliette tried to focus on the music. She quite enjoyed Vivaldi, and the evening was beautiful, but she couldn't help the disquiet in her chest. As if something of moment was going to happen and she would be helpless to forestall it.

Stop being such a ninnyhammer. Enjoy the evening and try for some of the faith shown by Mrs. Dunstan. What God wills is going to happen, and your task it to respond well.

Easier said than done as the unease plagued her.

By the intermission, Juliette had earned several glares from the dowager for her fidgeting.

Diana smiled at her over her little cup of flavored ice served from one of several vendors along the walkway. "You seem to have spring fever. Are you as eager to get out of the city and back to your country home as I? Where is your family estate? I don't believe I've heard."

Juliette dabbed the corner of her mouth with her handkerchief. "A tiny village called Pensax in Worcestershire. My parents' estate is Heild House. *Heild* is Anglo-Saxon for 'loyalty.' It's a lovely home and a quaint village. The Church of St. James the Great is the focal point of the community."

"It sounds peaceful. I miss Whitehaven. It seems we've been gone ages. I want to get the boys home to the freedom of the estate. I feel the city hems them in too much." Diana laughed, and Juliette was reminded once again how beautiful she was. "Evan says it's really me who feels hemmed in by the city since the boys are really too small to know or care much. The changes to the house at Whitehaven weren't the only transformations since our marriage. I am a country girl through and through now."

One wouldn't know it by her stylish clothes and her perfect manners. She seemed to carry herself well in any situation.

Diana Whitelock reminded Juliette of her mother in that respect. The Countess of Thorndike was stylish and composed and beautiful too. Her mother was by this time now in Europe. Was she safe? Had she and Father gathered any pertinent information about the Belgians yet?

"What do you make of this rumor that there is another claimant to the Rotherhide title?" Diana asked. "It seems to be all of which any-one can speak. Does Miss Montgomery know? I was given to believe she and Lord Coatsworth were nearing an understanding before her father's death?"

"Agatha knows, and she's standing quite loyally by Alonzo." Juliette assumed there was no need to keep quiet about the topic now.

"Where is the viscount? I don't recall seeing him at any social functions recently."

"He's gone abroad, but he's expected back soon."

"Just as well, from the sound of things. He will need to muster a defense against such a claim, and he can't do it if he isn't here." Diana shrugged. "Still, it can take years for such disputes to be settled. It will likely die down until a decision is reached."

Years. How bleak for Daniel and for Alonzo . . . and herself. Surely Marcus didn't intend for her to wait *years* to become betrothed to Daniel?

"Girls, find your seats. The second portion of the evening is starting soon." The dowager sounded like a disapproving governess. But then again, when didn't she? Had she ever been young and lighthearted? What had she been like as a girl, all dewy-eyed and in the throes of a first love?

Juliette giggled at the notion that the pinch-mouthed old woman had ever been in love, and yet surely she had at some time? Perhaps she would ask Charlotte for stories of the dowager's younger days. Or Cilla, who had known the dowager longer and had lived with her after her first husband died and before marrying Hamish Sinclair.

They had not yet reached their seats when Juliette spied Lady Coatsworth standing alone. A flicker of compassion touched Juliette's heart. None of this was fair to her. She had married in good faith, not knowing her betrothed and her father-in-law were being duplicitous. She had not asked for any of this, and she didn't deserve to be shunned.

Juliette caught Diana's eye and inclined her head toward Lady Coatsworth and indicated a bench up the path. Diana nodded and looked over the seated crowd to where Mr. Partridge waited, arms crossed, his eyes never resting in one place long. He nodded and moved to where he could watch over Juliette and the concert, while not standing close enough to overhear anything said by the ladies.

Juliette approached the viscountess. "Lady Coatsworth, won't you take a stroll with me? I've tired of sitting, though the music is nice. We can still hear while we walk."

Stiffly, the lady nodded. "Yes, thank you."

They walked along the path, and Juliette spoke of uncontroversial things. "Don't you love Vivaldi on a soft spring night? I can't remember the last time I felt a mild evening, the weather has been so cold. Perhaps this is the turn we've been waiting for. I've heard that crops are slow to sprout because it's been so chilled. If it warms up, things can grow again. Are you familiar with the composer for the second half of tonight's concert? I confess—I am not."

"I am livid." Lady Coatsworth appeared not to have heard anything Juliette had said. "How dare these people? They have no right to disparage me and my son this way. When our claim is proven true, there will be several people who will receive the cut direct from me, I assure you."

Juliette daren't say, "What if the claims are true?" That Daniel Swann was the heir and Alonzo the baseborn offspring? Daniel wouldn't lie about such a thing, and Marcus Haverly certainly wouldn't either. There must be some provable basis to the claim, or the duke wouldn't have sided with Daniel and be investigating.

"People can be thoughtless and cruel. It isn't for them to be discussing in any case. It's for the Prince Regent to decide when he sees all the facts. I know many do not have faith in Prinny, but I trust Lord Garrow, as attorney general, to present the truth and for our ruler to act according to it. He's been given power, and now he must wield it rightly." Juliette spoke with more confidence than she felt. God had put the Prince of Wales into his powerful position, but that didn't mean he would use his power rightly. The Prince Regent was unreliable at best. One could not predict how he would respond to a given situation. "When one has been placed in a position of authority, he must decide how he will wield that authority. It is our duty to pray for him, that God will lead him in the right path." Juliette had to believe that God, if not the prince, knew what was best and would indeed do so.

"If Alonzo were here, these people wouldn't say such things. He would defend my honor." Again Lady Coatsworth appeared deaf to anything but the fury in her own breast. "Did you know Mrs. Heathford called me . . ." She sputtered to a stop and actually shook, outrage coating her like paint. "She said if the interloper's claims were true, then I was a fallen woman and my son a baseborn commoner. That all the airs and arrogance Alonzo had shown would be rubbed in his face. She only said that because Alonzo wouldn't dance with her whey-faced chit of a daughter at Ashford's bash last Season." The cords of her neck stood out, and her eyes blazed. Was that her teeth grinding as she clenched her jaw?

"Lady Coatsworth, please, you'll do yourself an injury. It will do no good to lower yourself to behaving as these people have. You're above such things." Juliette led her to the bench.

"They're supposed to be above such things as well," she protested.

"You cannot control others, only yourself. They're engaging in gossip and rumor, and they're propagating it. Remember the old proverb, 'A dog who will fetch a bone will carry a bone.'" It was a maxim often repeated by one of Juliette's teachers at finishing school, cautioning against engaging in malicious gossip.

"Dog. That describes Eliza Heathford perfectly." Lady Coatsworth spat the words, but then she let out a sigh and relaxed her spine, sinking against the bench. "You're quite mature, aren't you? A good friend to Agatha, especially in these troubling times. I know you will stand by her, no matter who is slandering Alonzo's good name."

Guilt tightened Juliette's chest. She would stand by Agatha and endeavor to be her friend no matter what, but she feared if and when things broke Daniel's way that Agatha wouldn't want to be friends with her. Grief at the potential loss of her best friend snagged the breath in her throat.

"Loyalty is one of Agatha's best features, and we have been friends for a very long time. This is a difficult circumstance right now, but eventually it will be over, and I hope at the conclusion, Agatha and I are still friends."

"Why wouldn't you be?" Lady Coatsworth looked at her strangely.

Because she didn't know of the relationship Juliette had with Daniel. If she did, they wouldn't be having this conversation right now. *May God work this for the best as well.*

Before she had to answer, movement up the walkway caught her attention. A couple hurried toward them, passing in and out of the gaslight circles on the path. The woman was dressed in black, and she had red hair.

"Agatha." She shouldn't be out and about right now. She was still in full mourning. Who was that with her?

Lady Coatsworth stood and then subsided onto the bench once more. "Alonzo," she breathed.

Mr. Partridge stepped onto the path to intercept the oncoming couple, but Juliette motioned him back. "It is fine. They are friends of mine."

The large man nodded and faded like a wraith into the shadows along the hedge. How could such a burly man move so quietly? He was as silent as Uncle Bertie on a night burglary.

Agatha and Alonzo arrived, panting slightly at their haste. "He's home." Agatha beamed, her hand interlaced with the viscount's.

"How?" Lady Coatsworth asked, rising to embrace her son. "The ship can hardly have had time to reach you, even in the Canary Islands."

"I didn't encounter the ship you sent, Mother." Alonzo removed his hat to speak to her. "I regretted my decision to leave the moment we set sail. When we put in at Casablanca, I disembarked and caught the first ship back to England. I was a fool to leave as I did. I apologize to you, Mother. Agatha has informed me of what transpired in my absence, and bless her, she's forgiven me for running off without leaving word."

Agatha seemed to notice Juliette for the first time, and she beamed. "I told you he would return. Now we can lay to rest these unfounded accusations."

Alonzo puffed up at her certainty, and he raised Agatha's hand to kiss it, a bold gesture. "Yes, and the battle begins tomorrow. Mother, we came to fetch you the moment I arrived at Agatha's. We must begin our strategy. I don't believe you will wish to finish the concert. And Agatha shouldn't be out just now." He indicated her black dress. "I have a carriage waiting at the Water Gate."

Juliette accepted Agatha's jubilant hug. "Word has leaked out. Everyone here knows of the title dispute now," she whispered in Agatha's ear. "Prepare Alonzo. Public opinions are rife."

Agatha stepped back, biting her lip and nodding. "I'll prepare him."

They left, the three of them, backs straight, chins high, as if marching into battle.

Juliette crossed her arms, a chill rippling through her.

A battle. Battles meant casualties.

Would her friendship with Agatha be one of those casualties?

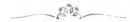

"What do we know?" Daniel asked. He shed his cloak and sat at his desk, surveying the folders, loose papers, and used teacups before him. A cluttered desk was unlike him and accurately represented how he felt about his current case and the distractions that beset him on every side. The inheritance issue sat heavily on his shoulders, and then there was Juliette, and his relationship with his mother.

By far the most pleasant distraction was Juliette. He longed for her, wanted to be with her, to touch her hand, to plan their future together, and yes, to kiss her. Every moment they were apart made him ache. Was that normal? Was this what love did to you? He spent far too much time wondering what she was doing at that very moment, wondering what she was thinking. Of him, perhaps? The need to keep their relationship quiet chafed, though he understood the reasons.

What if, in the delay, she changed her mind? What if she decided the distance between their social standings was too large to span? What if the inheritance claim didn't go his way? Would she realize it was folly to love a mere policeman? Would she determine he was over-reaching himself and withdraw her declaration of love? Haverly had pointed out the gulf that lay between them. How could Daniel ask her to sacrifice all she had and was just to be with him? Perhaps this was God's way of doing the best for Juliette—quietly removing Daniel so she could pursue better.

It wasn't as if they were formally engaged. They hadn't even spoken to her globe-gadding parents yet.

"Swann, are you listening?" Ed asked, and Daniel realized he'd been woolgathering. "You're not ailing, are you? I've never seen you so inattentive."

Ailing? Yes, he was ailing. He was lovesick. What was that Bible verse? *Stay me with flagons, comfort me with apples, for I am sick of love.* Old Solomon had it right on that one.

"My apologies. You were saying?"

"The doctor's examination doesn't tell us much. Haskett was stabbed. There were no scratches or other bruises on the body. Our killer is probably right-handed and of much the same height as our victim, which mostly likely rules out a woman. The wound was delivered with considerable force." Ed read Rosebreen's report, delivered by Owen just that morning. "Then there's the odd mixture found on the clothes. Where is that report from the boy scientist?" Ed searched the papers on his desk and picked up one, lifting it to catch the light from the windows on the far side of the room. He leaned back in his chair and propped his boots on the corner of his desk.

Daniel had tried to describe his trip to Crocombe Abbey, but words couldn't paint a proper picture of the kaleidoscopic impression Rhynwick's home and laboratory had left on him. Crocombe Abbey had to be experienced.

"Grease, horsehair, and pollen are hardly rare substances, even mixed together. I could walk out the door right now and encounter all three within a city block." Ed tossed the report on the piles.

"The only truly unique item so far is the murder weapon." Daniel held Rhynwick's drawing of the vicious knife. "I've never seen anything like this. Did you have any results asking around about it?"

Ed shook his head. "I've inquired at several blacksmiths, gunsmiths, and receiver's shops. No one has seen anything like it before. I even tried down at the docks, asking some of the foreigners if it was native to their country. No results."

Daniel nodded. That had been an excellent idea. The weapon certainly looked exotic. He never would have thought to ask at the docks.

"I think we have to assume it's a bespoke knife, crafted especially for the killer's use," Ed continued. "It could have been made anywhere in the country, or abroad. It would be a miracle if we found the artisan who created it simply by knocking on doors."

"Owen managed to gather the papers from Haskett's office at the Olympian Club." Daniel tapped a crate of documents on the corner of his desk. "Not much to work with. I've taken a cursory glance through it, and apparently Jericho Haskett kept minimal records. Most of what was in his office referred to purchases to keep the club going rather than gambling debts or a membership roster. There are invoices for new drapes, linens for the dining room, a butcher's bill, wages, and the like, but so far I've found nothing of substance. There was a receipt book that recorded daily income. Both the manservant Abel and Alton mentioned Haskett was recording in it the last time they saw him alive. Alton gave me that book, but it has no names, merely the dates and the figures."

"He had to have a way of recording specific debts and memberships, surely?" Ed frowned.

"If he had, we haven't found it yet, and the secretary, Mr. Alton, says he doesn't know where they are."

"Do you believe him?" Ed asked. "This crime does not seem to be random, and most people are killed by someone they know. Is Alton on the suspect list?" Ed smoothed his moustache with his finger and thumb, a gesture Daniel knew well—Ed was thinking hard.

"Everyone is on the list at the moment. I don't know if I believe Alton about the ledgers. He's still in my bad graces. What was he thinking?" Mr. Alton had not waited for Daniel to release the room and had cleaned it thoroughly, going so far as to remove the rug and change the furniture about. Though he'd apologized for overstepping when Daniel reprimanded him, the deed was done and there was no reversing it. Why did the average individual not understand they mustn't alter a crime scene? At least Abel and Alton had possessed the intelligence to close it off at once when they discovered the body. Often by the time officials arrived at a murder scene, the entire neighborhood had traipsed through, and some had even taken souvenirs. The body hadn't been moved in this case, thankfully. But now that the scene had been altered, it would be difficult to gain further clues.

Ed shrugged. "No sense getting into a flap about it now. I asked in Haskett's parish after family or other relations, but it appears he was a bachelor, and no one knew of any other connections. He's been renting a house in Portpool Lane, never a problem with the neighbors or his landlady. According to the watchman on that patch, he was hardly ever home. Had a lady who came in to 'do' for him, laundry and tidying up once a week, but he spent most of his time at the club. He had a regular visitor to his room, but the landlady didn't know his name. Small, well dressed. Came and went every Wednesday evening. She thought they played backgammon or dominoes. She could hear the markers clicking when she passed the door to his rooms."

"She happened to pass the door to his rooms whenever he had a visitor?" Daniel smiled. "We're missing something vital. We haven't kicked the right anthill yet. Everyone has secrets, and everyone is a suspect until they aren't." Truths Daniel had learned from Ed the first week they had been paired as investigators. Daniel had been green, eager, and far too trusting. Ed had reminded him to verify everything he was told, because nearly everyone lied to the police, either by omission or commission.

The door to the investigators' room crashed open, and Daniel jerked. Owen Wilkinson hurried in with Cadogan hot on his heels.

Owen's chest heaved, as if he'd run a long way, and Cadogan yanked his hat off, mangling the brim, his forehead creased.

"There's another one missing. This makes three in the last week. That can't be a coincidence," Owen blurted.

"Three? Three what?" Daniel put his forearms on the edge of his desk. "Stop rushing in here like war's been declared."

"Three boys! I knew you didn't care." Owen glared as he raised his fingers one at a time. "The street sweeper in Blackfriars, the shoeshine boy from around the corner, and now a kitchen boy from the Hart and Hound. All of them gone. And no one knows where."

Cadogan nodded. "I've known all these boys. None of them would have left without saying something. I do fear what has happened to them."

It stood to reason Cadogan might have encountered them since he was all over the metropolis and seemed to know everyone. That the driver was concerned made Daniel's skin prickle. Had he been too cavalier in dismissing Owen's worry? Perhaps there was something to this after all?

"This is the first I'm hearing about the shoeshine boy. Why didn't you mention it?" Daniel asked.

"You weren't interested when I told you Davy disappeared from Fleet Street," Owen shot back. "I figured you wouldn't care about Matthew."

The shaft hit home, and Daniel winced.

"Did you ask at the public house after the most recent boy? Perhaps he was dismissed for some infraction or other."

"Of course we asked. It was the publican Mr. Cobb at the Hart and Hound who came to me, because he'd heard I was looking for other missing boys." Owen scowled. "Cobb said he hired the boy Johnny almost two years ago, and he's been as regular as the changing of the guard. Never missed a shift. The boy said he had a safe place to sleep elsewhere and didn't want to live in the kitchen at the pub, but he was always on time and always polite and respectful."

Cadogan nodded. "I can testify to that. I was the one who got Johnny the job, and I checked in on him regularly."

Daniel paused. Cadogan had unplumbed depths. Though the man had saved Daniel's life, he still didn't know him well. What he did when he wasn't driving his carriage all over London, Daniel had no idea.

It seemed there might truly be an issue with boys not turning up where they were expected. Three had to be more than a coincidence. Four if the rumor from Spitalfields was true.

Still, the Haskett investigation loomed large. Neither he nor Ed could abandon a murder inquiry to chase after missing street children. Perhaps there was another way.

"We cannot investigate at the moment." He held up his hand to stifle Owen's protest. "However, let us consult Sir Michael and ask for an investigation to be opened, with you, Owen, as the principal investigator."

The office-boy-turned-investigator-in-training let his mouth fall open, hope invading his eyes. "Do you think he will approve?"

"We cannot know until we put the question to him. Let us beard him together."

Before Daniel could slide his chair back, the street door slammed out in the hallway, and Sir Michael himself stomped past the investigators' room, pausing in the doorway, face suffused red, to point at Daniel. "Mr. Swann, in my office immediately." He continued down the hall to his sanctum sanctorum, and everyone in the room sat in silence for a moment, jumping when Sir Michael's office door slammed.

"Are you never out of the soup where the guv's concerned?" Ed asked, his tone mild but his eyes worried. "He looks ready to flog you round the fleet."

Forcing down a martyred sigh, Daniel rose. He buttoned his coat, rubbed a scuff off the toe of his boot, and ran his hand over his rather unruly hair. He should make time to see his barber soon. "Perhaps I should tie a rope around my ankle so you can pull me out if he does me in." He pulled a face. "Come, Owen."

"I don't mind waiting until you two have your talk." Owen's face had gone tight. "He really did sound angry."

"The sooner we get his permission, the sooner you can get out there looking for those lost boys. Don't worry about Sir Michael. I'm used to him being angry with me."

In spite of his brave words, Daniel's palms were sweaty and his mouth dry as he entered Sir Michael's office. The director of investigators hadn't taken his seat as he normally did. Instead he paced, his hands in fists at his sides, his back straight.

He tossed a glance at Daniel, noticed Owen, and flicked his hand. "Go away, Wilkinson, and close the door behind you."

"Sir, if I may. Mr. Wilkinson has a case he would like—"

"Did I stutter? Get out." Sir Michael pointed at the office boy.

"Yes, sir." Owen tugged his forelock, bowed slightly, and vanished.

The moment the door closed Sir Michael erupted. "I do not even possess the words. How dare you have the hubris to elect yourself heir to an earldom? Tell me this isn't true! Though I have it from a credible source. You're claiming to be . . . It baffles the mind. I knew you were arrogant, always leering at me in that smug way of yours because I couldn't sack you, but this? Outrageous. I cannot even look at you."

He stared hard, belying his claims, and clearly he had words, because he wasn't finished. "You will drop this nonsense immediately. I had no less than four men question me about the matter at luncheon today, and I looked a right fool knowing nothing about it. I've always known you were trying to grasp and elevate and insert yourself into the aristocracy, but this is ludicrous."

Daniel said nothing, not least because he couldn't have squeezed a word in edgewise in the midst of Sir Michael's spate. Despair and disappointment that word had leaked before the petition could be filed settled into his gut, as well as indignation at Sir Michael's accusations. He had never tried to insert himself into the aristocracy, and no one had been more shocked than he to find out his grandfather was an earl, much less that he, Daniel, was the direct male heir to a title.

"Well? What have you to say for yourself? Don't stand there like a fence post."

Keep your temper. Respect your employer. Do not, under any circumstances, tell him it is none of his affair.

"Sir Michael, the claim is true and will be proven through investigation. The entire matter is in the hands of the Duke of Haverly and my barrister, Sir James Durridge. When they are prepared, the case will go to Sir William Garrow and the Prince Regent. If you have any evidence proving my claim is false, I am certain the duke and Sir James would be delighted to speak with you. Until then, they have cautioned me not to discuss the matter."

Daniel half expected Sir Michael's ears to emit smoke. His choler rose, and a fleck of spittle appeared at the corner of his mouth.

He hissed through clenched teeth, his neck cords rigid. "You arrogant pup. So it is the Duke of Haverly who has been acting on your behalf, forcing me to retain your services." He took a long breath in through his nose, sharp enough to narrow his nostrils. "Fine. The moment the matter is settled—for I know you will be proven a liar—you will cease to be employed in this office. And I will not give you a character to take to your new employer. I don't imagine the Duke of Haverly will want anything to do with you once it is revealed you have hoodwinked him into this charade, and he will not come to your aid regarding your employment here."

Pressing his tongue hard against the backs of his clenched teeth, Daniel counted silently to ten, then fifteen. Deliberately, he relaxed his stomach muscles and lowered his shoulders, drawing a deep, even breath before he spoke.

"Sir Michael, if my claim is proven false, I will resign without a whimper. If my claim is proven true and I am invested the earldom, I am certain we will revisit the issue of my employment. Until then I will follow the direction of my benefactor and my barrister and not speak of this again. In the meantime, the reason I came in here was to tell you that there is a new case pending, and I believe Owen is capable and prepared to investigate. The case involves some missing children, boys all about the same age, who have disappeared without a word. I would like permission to task Owen with the case while Mr. Beck and I continue on the Haskett murder inquiry."

With measured steps, Sir Michael made his way to his chair and dropped into it. It was as if he suddenly realized that if Daniel's claim was proven true, and he was made an earl, then he would vastly outrank Sir Michael and have more power and wealth than Sir Michael would wish to cross. Not to mention having someone as influential as the Duke of Haverly behind him, as well as the Prince Regent himself, for it was the Prince who would make the ultimate decision on the matter.

"You say you have a case for Owen?" His voice sounded strangled. "And you believe he is ready to investigate on his own?"

"I do. Two of the children who have gone missing are street urchins, and the latest is a pub kitchen boy, and there is a possibility of another boy, but that rumor has not yet been confirmed. Those who have been questioned are certain the children would not disappear of their own accord, at least not without leaving word. You may have seen one of the boys before. He shined shoes around the corner on Broad Court and Drury Lane."

Sir Michael nodded and waved dismissively, giving his permission without words. He pressed his palms flat on the blotter, blinked a few times, and took a long breath. "What of your murder inquiry? You've had several days. Where are you on the case? Why is there no arrest yet?" He was back to his waspish self.

"Easter Sunday has put us behind our time. Witnesses were difficult to locate, and the coroner's office and the scientist examining some of the evidence needed time to do their work."

"Do you have a suspect?"

"Not at this time, but I anticipate we will solve the matter soon. We do have some leads." *Thin, thin leads.*

"Very well. Tidy it up soon, since your time here is no doubt short, and I have no desire to sort out your leavings."

Chapter 8

"I don't wish any man dead, but Jericho Haskett was a rum 'un." Cadogan flipped down the metal step and opened the door for Daniel. "How are your inquiries going?"

Daniel paused before climbing in. "Did you know Haskett personally or just know of him?"

The driver shrugged. "I had some dealings with him in the distant past. We lived in the same borough when we were young. I deliver gentlemen to his club now and again but haven't spent time with Jericho in years. He was caught up in some bad dealings before he got that position at the Olympian. Petty theft, smuggling, pocket-dipping. He disappeared for a time, then one day he shows up in a fancy waistcoat and shiny boots, flush with dosh, and sets up that club. I always thought he'd come to no good end, but it's still hard to think he's dead. Murdered."

Daniel tucked this information away as he climbed into the cab. Perhaps it would be another line of inquiry? Haskett's past catching him up? Before the door closed, he asked, "How is Sprite?" The mare seemed thinner than the last time Daniel had seen her, especially compared with the sturdiness of her harness mate, Lola.

"Getting old isn't for the faint of heart, is it?" Cadogan asked. "I've tried her on all sorts of feed, mash, and the like, but she runs off everything I put on her. Still, she likes the work, and I haven't the money for another horse just yet, so we soldier on. I'll have to make a decision about her sooner rather than later, but it breaks my heart to think of it." He shut the door and climbed aboard, the carriage lurching with his movements.

Daniel alighted from Cadogan's carriage sometime later at the curb before the Duke of Haverly's London residence. Light shone from nearly every window of the five-storied structure, and when the footman opened the door, strains of a minuet drifting from upstairs.

"Good evening, sir." The footman took Daniel's cloak and hat. "His Grace is expecting you. This way."

Daniel ran his hand along the glass-smooth banister as they ascended. His feet made no sound on the plush carpet runner. Everything about Haverly's house was quintessentially right. The paint, the wallpaper, the artwork, the brass. A testament to the duchess, no doubt. And money. Daniel had no idea how much it cost to maintain and staff such a residence, but it would far outstrip his wages as an investigator.

They passed the music room at the head of the stairs, and the melody grew louder. Through the half-open door, Daniel spied several ladies and gentlemen seated in orderly rows, listening intently. Was Juliette in there? His heart thudded, heavy and yet light at the thought of her so nearby.

The footman led him up another flight and turned down a carpeted hall to the right. At the end of the hall, the footman, with Daniel's cloak still over his arm, bowed and opened the door.

The room was dark paneled, with heavy drapes and lamps with colored glass shades. Haverly sat at the head of a long table, and also seated were Sir James Durridge, his clerk, Mr. Childers, and . . . Daniel's mother. His stomach flipped and tightened.

They had not parted on the best of terms, and guilt clawed at his innards.

"Good evening, Your Grace, Sir James." He nodded to the other two, not making eye contact, and took a chair. "I apologize for my tardiness. I'm conducting a murder investigation currently, and the task has taken me far afield today."

"Of course." Haverly leaned forward, placing his forearms on the edge of the table.

The room appeared to have no other function than for meetings. There were no gaming tables, no indication as to the purpose beyond the table and chairs and a framed board of cork on one wall. A single bookshelf stood on one wall, and a credenza, but that was all. Daniel supposed someone as influential as Haverly would have many business ventures and partners, and such a room would see much use as a result.

After all, he couldn't use his secret office above Hatchards bookshop for group meetings. That dark, claustrophobia-inducing space was barely larger than a butler's pantry and would never have done for this gathering. In any case, the office at Hatchards was reserved for agents to meet with their leader for orders and debriefings. As he understood it, the secret room had been inherited by Haverly when his own supervisor, Sir Noel St. Clair, retired from service.

With word of the inheritance dispute having leaked and now all over London, there was no need to meet clandestinely at Sir James's either. Daniel gripped his hands beneath the surface of the table and waited.

"I called you all here to go over what I have gathered thus far. And I have to say, it looks promising, though some of the principal parties are no longer with us." Haverly consulted a document on the table before him. "I sent two men, a solicitor and a magistrate, men of impeccable reputation, to Scotland to obtain a record of the marriage of Catherine Swann and William Darby. They have not yet returned, but I have faith that their errand will not be fruitless. The men who perform the marriages in Gretna Green are in such close rivalry, they keep excellent records just to boast against one another who had married the most couples. I understand from Mrs. Dunstan that Joseph Paisley performed the ceremony in the taproom of an inn. My men will find the records, I have no doubt." The duke pinched his chin. "What I *have* been able to verify thus far are the machinations of the Earl of Rotherhide immediately following the marriage."

Daniel's throat tightened as he clamped his teeth. The old man had done everything he could to hide his son's actions and bury his own guilt, but in the end it had proven too much for him.

"Mrs. Dunstan has been most helpful." Haverly nodded to Daniel's mother, who was serene and composed, as if their futures weren't riding on the outcome of the claim. "She gave me the name of the estate to which she was banished, as well as the name of the midwife who attended her. Though Lord Imberlay is now deceased, his estate steward, a Mr. Barron, was able to corroborate the date Mrs. Dunstan, then Miss Swann, arrived at the manor. He signed the statement that said his employer had told him he was taking on the maid as a favor to Rotherhide and that she had gotten herself into a bad way."

Mr. Childers took notes, quiet and efficient, his pen scratching against the paper softly, and Sir James rocked slightly, brows down, considering the information.

Haverly turned another page. "The midwife, a Mrs. Quinton, kept records. She had written in her journal that on March 20, 1791, at daybreak, she arrived at Imberlay Hall and delivered a baby boy to a Miss Swann. The child was healthy and had been carried to full term. In her estimation, the child would have been conceived at the end of June or beginning of July 1790." He set the book down. "That exactly coincides with the date William Darby and Miss Swann fled to Scotland to wed."

"So far, so good. But . . ." Sir James spoke softly, almost as to himself.

"Yes. The marriage and the birth are the easiest to prove. If the solicitor and magistrate return from Scotland with the marriage records, we will be on firm footing there. However, proving the marriage was never annulled is another matter. The earl's valet has delivered the earl's copy of the annulment papers to Sir James's chambers, and I've viewed them. They certainly look authentic. The Archbishop of Canterbury, John Moore's signature is clear. The reason given for the annulment is 'incompetence' because the parties were underage with no parental consent. I've dispatched another solicitor as well as a clergyman friend to Canterbury Cathedral to scour their records. An absence of a record in the church archives, while not conclusive, would strengthen our case."

"Even better if you could find the forger." Mr. Childers spoke for the first time.

Haverly gave the clerk his attention. "How might we go about that? It was all of twenty-six years ago, and William Darby is deceased. He cannot tell us the forger's name."

"Of course, Your Grace. However . . ." The clerk flipped through a leather portfolio beside him and produced a legal document sewn down the side with red tape. "There are not many forgers skilled enough to produce something like this." He laid the annulment papers on the table. "The forgers' community in London is not large, and someone capable of this quality of work would be a legend. I would be willing to check with my contacts to see if anyone knows of a forger of such renown."

Childers had contacts with forgers?

He must have noted the puzzlement on Daniel's face, for he inclined his head. "Sir James works with many clients, and as a result, we have encountered men and women from all walks of life. I find it useful to maintain those contacts, to keep an eye on them, so to speak, to make certain they are not falling back into bad ways. In addition, I wasn't always a legal clerk. Sir James took me in as a young man, but before his benevolence, I was a street urchin. This brought me into contact with a variety of people, both good and bad."

A simple enough explanation, Daniel supposed.

"Though I questioned the wisdom once upon a time, I have found it quite helpful to have a clerk who is familiar with, shall we say, the 'underworld' of London? More than once he's produced a contact with the expertise or knowledge we needed to win a case at just the right moment. He once tracked down a housebreaker who was studying his next target and could testify that a certain member of Parliament was seen leaving an establishment on that street and could not have been two boroughs over, killing a housemaid." Sir James pursed his lips in satisfaction. "That case made my name, and I have Childers to thank for it . . . as does the MP he proved innocent."

"Perhaps he will unearth something crucial to our case." Haverly leaned forward. "Finding the forger would all but guarantee the truth of the claim. He created pristine documents."

Daniel's mother's face tightened as she picked up the papers. "They were certainly intimidating enough to fool me. A messenger from the earl showed them to me two months after I was banished to Lord Imberlay's, though I was not permitted to keep a copy for myself. I never imagined the annulment wasn't authentic. I never thought to question."

"Do not blame yourself, madam." Haverly shook his head. "You were a frightened young girl who had every reason to believe she was being told the truth. You were wronged greatly in this entire matter."

A trickle of pity wove its way through Daniel's chest, but he forced himself to concentrate on Mr. Childers's suggestion instead. "I worked a forgery case previously." Well, he had been on the periphery of the case, since Sir Michael hadn't judged him experienced enough to do more than fetch and carry for Ed at the time. "The man we apprehended was sent to Coldbath Fields. He's probably still there. He might know who could create such a document. His name was Clifford Elliot."

"I'll make inquiries." Haverly penciled a note to himself.

"I could do it for you, since I already have experience of the man," Daniel offered, though when he could find time to ride out to Coldbath Prison he didn't know. Still, he wanted to help. It was his inheritance, after all.

"No. You are to continue to stay away from the investigation. You cannot be seen to interfere at all. Now that the story is common knowledge, it is more important than ever that you remain clear of the proceedings." The duke's tone brooked no discussion.

"Do you know how word got out? My guv confronted me in the office today. He's not best pleased, I can tell you. He said if I lose, I'm dismissed. And if I win, I cannot continue as a Bow Street investigator. It seems I'm out either way." A painful thought, one that Daniel had been trying to avoid since the confrontation in Sir Michael's office earlier that day.

"It did not come from our camp, I assure you." Sir James tapped the table with his index finger. "It had to come from the other side. Speaking of which, Alonzo Darby has returned to England. He's aware of the petition we're preparing, and he is determined to fight it, as we surmised. He's livid enough to have come by my chambers at Gray's Inn to accost me. He was quite adamant that the claim is false, that I'm being led astray by a usurper who has no right, and that I would rue the day, et cetera." He flipped his hand, as if the rest could be filled in by his listeners.

Daniel wasn't in the least surprised, though he was conflicted as to how to feel about Alonzo Darby. He had been arrogant and disdainful from the moment they had met, and it stood to reason he would both accuse and dismiss in the same breath. Yet if everything they had learned was true, Daniel and Alonzo were half brothers. Never having had a sibling, Daniel had no experience on which to fall back. How did one treat a half brother? Or due to the awkward nature of their relationship, did they ignore each other, pretending the other didn't exist?

"Gentlemen." Daniel's mother spoke for the first time. "I am grateful for your work on my son's behalf, but I hope you realize this is painful for all of us. I suffered greatly at the hands of the Darby family—not even realizing the extent of that suffering until recently. My son was denied his rightful place. We were estranged for years while an old man tried to salve his conscience and convince himself he had made everything better by at least providing for and educating Daniel. But the harm done to Lady Coatsworth and her son is no less painful. No matter how this plays out, no matter how the Darbys act, we must remember that they are wounded and scared. I don't believe they are malicious, and I hope you will take care in how you speak of them and to them. I've spent years coming to terms with my life and circumstances, and by the grace of God have been able to forgive the wrong done me. For the sake of my son, I am willing to proceed with this claim, but if I were the only one affected by what we've learned, I would be content to continue as I am and allow Alonzo and his mother to keep what they have always assumed was theirs."

Guilt tightened Daniel's neck muscles, followed by a wave of homesickness. Hearing his mother speak of kindness and forgiveness took him right back to his childhood, sitting beside her in their crumbling cottage or cramped upper-story room. She had done her best to raise him well, with God's wisdom and kindness and love.

Until the day she found a way to be rid of you. Don't forget that.

He tried to cling to the old hurt, but doing so was becoming more difficult. He wasn't a frightened, lonely child any longer, and as a grown man, he could see how the decision to send him away *might* have been a difficult one.

"You are a wise woman, Mrs. Dunstan. We will move ahead with caution. We have no wish to disturb your delicate sensibilities." Sir James patted her arm.

Daniel hid a smile. If the barrister thought his mother a frail flower, he was in for a rude awakening. She had withstood more than her fair share of this life's hardships, and she remained unbroken.

Haverly butted together some papers. "Speaking of proceeding carefully, I have been called to an appointment at Carlton House tomorrow. It seems word of the coming petition has reached our regent's ears, and he is desirous of a consultation."

The duke spoke lightly of an audience with the Prince Regent. Daniel would have been far more nervous were he the one being called to the prince's London residence.

"Why? Do you think it wise to discuss the case with the prince at this time?" Sir James asked.

"I suspect our dear prince is trying to ascertain whether, if he gives the title to Daniel here, will Daniel be inclined to support the prince. Alonzo Darby leans more toward supporting Parliament than the prince, and that factor may have a bearing on the prince's decision on the inheritance matter."

Daniel scowled. "Politics shouldn't come into it. It's a matter of right and wrong, what we're able to prove of our claim. If he's looking for a lackey or a yes-man in return for 'giving' me the title, then I don't want it."

"Should I frame it exactly that way, or do you trust me to be fair and honest with His Highness without giving him reason to despise you?" Haverly's tone was wry, gently reminding Daniel of his position.

Embarrassment pricked his skin. "I trust you to handle the situation, Your Grace. You and Sir James."

"Very well. We will do our best for you both. Meanwhile, continue to avoid speaking outside this circle to anyone about the details of the case. Thankfully, to this point, no one seems to know the identity of your mother, Daniel. I'd like to keep it that way for as long as possible." Haverly rose. "Mrs. Dunstan, my man Mr. Partridge will see you safely back to the Thorndike residence."

Sir James and Mr. Childers gathered papers, and Daniel slid back his chair.

"Daniel, if you will remain for a moment?" Haverly asked. "I would like a word."

Haverly left with the others, and Daniel leaned against the table, thinking of all the ways his life had changed in such a short time. The facts of his case were firming up, making the possibility of him being declared the heir seem more possible. Could he really rise from a base-born tatterdemalion to a peer of the realm?

Would he soon be able to publicly declare his intention to wed Lady Juliette Thorndike, and would society accept the match as a good one for both parties?

Would he have to cease his work at Bow Street, and what would he do instead, should he not be granted the earldom?

If he did inherit the title and the lands and the fortune, what would he do with them? What would God have him use his power and wealth for? He'd barely come to terms, thanks to a frank discussion with Ed, with the idea that God was a benevolent Father. He had little practice wondering what God's will for his life was. Yet if God was his benevolent Father, He had to have a plan. And if that plan included the Rotherhide name and fortune, Daniel was determined to use what he received wisely.

And if he didn't receive the title? Would he still consider God a benevolent Father? Was God truly good all the time, or only when it suited Him?

Following God wasn't easy.

Daniel crossed his arms, wondering what the duke might wish to discuss. The door opened, and his heart shot into his mouth. Not Haverly returning as he had expected, but Juliette.

He couldn't help the broad smile that overtook his features. Her beauty smote him again, the luster of her skin, the curve of her cheek, the brightness in her eyes. She edged round the door and waited, as if unsure.

Until he straightened and moved toward her. She smiled and held her hands out to him. He took them, but it wasn't enough. Pressing her palms against his chest, he put his arms around her. "Ah, my darling."

She looked up at him, as if comparing her memory of his face to the reality. "You are well? You look tired."

She brushed a lock of hair off his forehead, sending a tingle through him. To have someone care so tenderly . . . it had been a long time.

"I've a lot on my mind, but none of it matters now that you're here." He lowered his head slowly, giving her time to refuse if she should wish. But with eagerness enough to thrill any man's heart, she raised herself on tiptoe to receive his kiss.

What he had said was true. Nothing else mattered when they were together. His doubts fled as to the rightness of his feelings for her. As much as he wanted to deepen the kiss, to give her some indication as to the torrent of feelings he had for her, he restrained himself.

When the kiss ended, her eyelids fluttered open. "Marcus told me you would be coming, and he's given us a few moments. I kept waiting for his signal that it was time to slip out of the music room. I've been trapped in the most tedious pianoforte recital."

"So"—he tweaked her adorable nose—"I'm merely a means of escaping societal boredom, am I?" He squeezed her waist and winked.

A laugh escaped her, and his heart soared. How was it possible that so much of his happiness could be tied up in one beautiful woman?

Her face sobered as she stepped back a few inches. "How did the meeting go? I assume you were discussing your case? And are you aware that Alonzo has returned to London?"

"It went as well as could be expected, and yes, I was made aware of his return, though I have not encountered him yet."

"I have. Him and his mother. They are determined, and they are most uncomplimentary to you. Agatha has understandably been drawn into their opinions, and it breaks my heart to think we are on opposite sides of such a crucial issue. I don't want to lose her friendship, but I don't see how it can be avoided. Her loss would be my gain, and vice versa. I never would have envisioned us falling in love with half brothers."

Another jolt went through him at her admission of love, but he also ached, regretting that he was the one to put her in this position. He drew her to him again, resting his chin on her hair as she pressed her cheek into his chest. He didn't want to hurt her or see her hurt. "Would you have me withdraw my petition to the Crown? I will if you ask it." And he would, though it would pain him and deny justice to his mother.

She straightened, her eyes wide. "I would never ask such a thing. Agatha and I will sort things out one way or another, but you must not make such a sacrifice on my behalf. Right must be done regardless of our feelings or what it might cost us. And don't forget—when you are invested with the earldom, there will be no barrier to our announcing our betrothal."

The fire burning in her eyes warmed him, and he couldn't resist kissing her again.

He didn't hear the door opening, and neither must Juliette have done. But both heard the outraged gasp of the dowager.

Chapter 9

THE BLOOD DRAINED FROM JULIETTE'S head, making her dizzy. She gripped Daniel's arms to keep from sagging to her knees.

Of all people to catch them in an embrace, the dowager was the worst.

The woman's expression resembled ice-coated granite. She leaned on her cane, one hand on the doorknob, her lace cap crowding the iron-gray curls around her cheeks.

"Good evening, Your Grace."

Daniel's voice sounded perfectly calm. Perhaps he did not understand their predicament.

"What on earth do you think you are doing, and in my very own house?" The dowager kept her voice low, hissing the words across the room. "Why are you here? You were not invited to this evening's event. Unhand her this moment."

"Your Grace—" Juliette was not given time to speak.

"Have you no thought at all for your reputation, young lady? Or mine? This is scandalous. What would your parents say? If a hint of this gets out, you'll be ruined. And my renown as a proper chaperone will be in bits." Distress and outrage hemmed every word. "I said unhand her."

This time she did not wait for Daniel to comply. She marched across the room, without bothering to use her cane, and took Juliette's arm in a firm grip.

"Come with me, child." She dragged Juliette toward the door, but Daniel hadn't let go either, and soon Juliette was like the bone between two dogs.

She put her hand over the dowager's and removed it. "If you do not mind, I am not a rope to be pulled this way and that, nor am I a child. I am quite capable of both speaking and acting for myself."

The dowager blinked, red suffusing her cheeks. "Impertinence is unbecoming. Especially given that you've been . . . seduced and befuddled by—" She looked Daniel over from top to toe caps, a distasteful curl to her lip. "This . . . person. He's trapped you here to compromise you and force action on your father's part. If Tristan were here, he would challenge this young pup to a duel of honor at the very least. Come with me, Juliette, before your absence causes comment."

Daniel stiffened. "Your Grace, you are misinformed on several counts. First, I *was* invited to this residence. The duke himself issued the summons. Second, I would never stoop to 'trapping' a woman, and if you think—" He broke off, pressing his lips into a tight line, probably before he said something regrettable.

"Madam, why are you not attending your guests?" Marcus's silky voice cut through the awkward silence. "Charlotte, here are Mr. Swann and Juliette, as promised."

His wife glided into the room, skirting the dowager as if she were a garden statue, holding out her hand to Daniel.

Daniel, perforce, had to release his hold of Juliette's elbow to take the duchess's hand. As Daniel bowed, Juliette covered the spot where he had touched her.

"Your Grace. Thank you for having me in your home."

Charlotte Haverly smiled, transforming her face from passably pretty to arrestingly beautiful. "Thank you for remaining here after your consultation with Marcus. I wished to have a word with you." She paused and glanced at her mother-in-law. "We cannot all absent our guests at once, can we? Would you take over my duties until I can return to the music room? I believe refreshments will be served directly."

"Charlotte, do you realize what's been going on here? This upstart has been trying to compromise my charge. I must protect her. She must come with me at this moment." The dowager struck the floor with her cane, emphasizing each word. "I will not have such behavior under my roof."

Juliette's face heated, and her throat constricted. To be chastised by the dowager was one thing, but to be made out to be either a strumpet or ignorant of societal rules in front of Charlotte and Marcus, not to mention Daniel, was going too far.

"Madam, I will remind you that this is *my* roof under which you live. Charlotte and I are quite capable of providing proper chaperonage, and we will speak to them of their actions." Marcus's voice had a subtle sharpness to it, calm on the surface but softly dangerous beneath.

Juliette shivered, praying he never used that tone on her.

"Please return to our other guests, madam."

The dowager's mouth opened, but she must have recognized the warning in her son's tone. She harrumphed, abusing the floor with the tip of her cane once more before turning toward the door. She threw a "we're not finished discussing this, young lady" glare over her shoulder at Juliette.

Dread took up residence in Juliette's stomach, and she pressed her hand to her midriff. The dowager was worse to reckon with than the headmistress of Juliette's finishing school.

When the door closed, Marcus rubbed the back of his neck, leaning against the edge of the table. "This is how my wife's romantic nature gets me into trouble. I informed her of the growing, shall we say *tendresse*, between you two, and she insisted, when she knew Daniel was in the house, that I give you two a few moments privacy before joining you. Against my better judgment, I agreed. I should have known my mother would find you first. The dowager has the scent capabilities of a prize bloodhound when it comes to nosing out any supposed improprieties. I do apologize."

Charlotte squeezed Juliette's hand. "Don't fret. We can handle the dowager. I'm so thrilled about you two, though it will not be easy, your stations being so far apart at the moment. Have you spoken to Juliette's parents, Mr. Swann? Are they amenable?"

"I have not made a formal request, Your Grace." Daniel's eyes looked pensive. "The duke has advised us to make nothing official until the matter of the inheritance is settled."

Charlotte sighed. "Marcus has kept me apprised of the investigation, and I understand his reasoning, but what has reason to do with love? But never you worry. You will prevail. With Marcus on your side, you cannot go wrong. He never fails at anything to which he turns his hand." She threaded her arm through her husband's, looking up at him with such confidence and affection, Juliette's heart ached.

Theirs was truly a love match, something less common in today's society than she had once thought. When she was a girl away at school, she had read the folktales and novels that spoke of finding one's true love and living henceforth only in untainted happiness and thought that the accepted and widespread way of finding your mate.

Now she realized in English society, marriages had more to do with bloodlines, money, and status.

But not for her. She had chosen with her heart and, the dowager notwithstanding, would continue to follow her heart into Daniel's arms forever.

Please, Lord, let his appeal for the earldom be won. It is only right and good. And please, no matter what, let my parents support our union.

"Flattery will get you everything, my dear, but we must not waste Mr. Swann's time. He's engaged in a murder inquiry. You did wish to have a word with him?" Marcus prompted his wife.

"Of course. Mr. Swann, I was hoping you would look into a small matter for me. There is a young girl, Alice, who comes every day to Berkeley Square to sell flowers. She petitions the patrons of Gunter's, across the square. I often buy a few from her in the afternoon because she's so sweet and because she mentioned once that she gets into difficulty if she doesn't sell the entire allotment for the day. For months she's been as regular as the sunrise, stopping by the house after the last of our callers for the day have gone, offering her box of posies."

Juliette looked at Daniel. He had straightened at the duchess's words.

"My concern is," Charlotte continued, "she has not made an appearance for several days. I do not know where she lives, else I would have sent someone around to ask after her. She mentioned once that the flowers came from a farm located on Figge's Marsh in Merton and were brought into town daily by her guv, but that is all I know of her. Marcus feels it is a matter for the police, and I immediately thought of you."

"How old is she?" Daniel reached into his inner pocket for the notebook he always carried. A grim cast settled on his face.

Charlotte shrugged. "It's so difficult to tell with street children because they're often small for their age. Perhaps ten or twelve? Old enough not to have any missing teeth that I could see, but too young for putting her hair up."

Juliette caught Charlotte's eye, aware of what she meant. The child had not yet begun to develop into womanhood, but such a thing would be scandalous for Charlotte to say to a man not her husband.

Marcus caught Daniel's somber expression too, for he asked, "Why does this disturb you so?"

"This is not the first child to be reported missing in the last few days. The first girl that I know of, but they're all of an age and all considered reliable to appear where they are expected." He made notes. "Owen Wilkinson is looking into the disappearances officially through Bow Street. I will give him this information."

"Thank you. I've been so worried but haven't known where to start looking. I didn't want to bother Marcus, as it doesn't really involve national security and didn't seem right to take assets from the agency to attend something like this. Do you think there is a link between the missing children? Is the same thing occurring with each of them, or is this a coincidence?" Charlotte's eyes darkened.

Juliette bit her bottom lip. Uncle Bertie believed true coincidence was rare and should be discounted in an investigation. What could be the motive behind missing street children? She swallowed, gripping her hands together, trying not to think the worst.

"It is certainly not unusual for street children to be unaccounted for, but these are too similar to be happenstance. Something is afoot." Daniel tapped his pencil against his notebook. He cleared his throat. "I do apologize for upsetting the dowager. I hope there will be no repercussions for Lady Juliette."

Her heart warmed that he was concerned for her. He was not solely responsible for them being found together in an embrace, but he seemed prepared to take all the blame.

Marcus put his hand over Charlotte's on his arm, squeezing it and leaning to the side to brush a kiss on her hair. "I shall have a word with Mother about what she thinks she saw here. We're still in a delicate stage of the inheritance petition, and it wouldn't do for her to spread the word about you two. Not that she would, as she would perceive blame might fall her way as your appointed chaperone, Juliette. This will need to be the last time you're seen together for a while. We'll give you a few moments to say your goodbyes. Daniel, if something turns up in the inquiry into the missing girl, and you feel I could be of assistance, don't hesitate to call on me. I didn't realize this might be larger than just one absent street child."

Daniel nodded, sketched a bow to Charlotte, and turned to Juliette as the duke and duchess went into the hall. He took her hands in his, and her eyes prickled.

"I hate that we must stay apart." He raised her hand and kissed it. "I suppose it is too soon to have heard from your parents about when they will return? They will have barely arrived in the Netherlands."

Juliette nodded, unable to speak past the tightness in her throat. It was the Bard himself who said the course of true love never did run smooth. When she had dreamed of falling in love, it had never looked like this. Well, in one respect it did, for she loved a handsome, caring, conscientious man. But in all else, the differences in their social standing—at least for the time being—the fact that they couldn't announce their love to anyone, and that they must remain separate for the foreseeable future . . . she had not planned on any of that.

"Have you made a decision regarding your work for the Crown?" he asked, his thumbs rubbing the backs of her hands.

She blinked. "Things have been at such sixes and sevens, I haven't given it much thought. The Haverly household is full to bursting with family who will attend the duchess's end-of-Season ball. I've been helping Charlotte plan, receiving callers, making calls. All the other social events to which any of them are invited . . . they bring me to everything. Diana—Countess Whitelock—took me dress shopping for the ball, and she has such impeccable taste, picking out exquisite fabric and design with the modiste. I cannot wait to wear it. And then there are the little ones. Diana brings her boys over to play, and Honora Mary, Cilla and Hamish's girl, is here, as well as little Anthony, Marcus's heir. Several of the ladies go up to the nursery every day to play with them. It's been a whirl. I feel as if I've hardly been still a moment."

A twinkle entered his eye. "Too busy to miss me, then, I suppose?"

The ache in her chest swelled. "Never. I miss you every moment."

"It will not be long, though it seems it now." He kissed her hand again. "Once I receive my inheritance, I'll be shouting from the rooftops that you are mine."

Though she yearned for that day, a tinge of worry niggled her heart. What if the petition didn't go Daniel's way? Would he still be prepared to have her for his wife? Would her parents allow the match if he were to remain a commoner?

Would she have to defy them if they wouldn't give their consent?

Juliette squared her shoulders, ready to brave the dowager's silent displeasure as she entered the salon. The concert in the music room had ended, and the guests sat in small groups, partaking of the refreshments. She smiled, though her face felt tight and her heart heavy.

Although she did not feel she had done anything truly wrong, knowing the dowager disapproved caused her unease. She did not like disappointing people, and though her behavior since arriving in London had been somewhat unconventional due to her parents' work for the Crown, she really wasn't rebellious or outlandish by nature. It was circumstances more than anything that caused her to skirt the more rigid societal rules.

If the dowager knew the extent of her activities, the poor woman would have a fit of the vapors. Burgling artwork from aristocrats, apprehending killers in hospital wards in the dead of night, and now . . .

Juliette was at loose ends. Meant to be contemplating her future as an agent, she was avoiding those very considerations. How could she evaluate properly the good and bad of committing fully to becoming an agent when so many other aspects of her life were up in the air? Her parents never stayed home long enough to unpack, it seemed. Even Uncle Bertie had disappeared to the wilds of Dartmoor on an investigation. She had no work to occupy her mind until they should return. For the moment, she was exactly what she had assumed she would be when she disembarked the vessel that had brought her back to England. A debutante wrapped in a whirl of social activities.

How vacuous that seemed to her now. Had she really aspired to nothing more complicated than parties and dresses and suitors? She felt far removed from that young lady, though it was barely four months ago.

Daniel. A tremor swept through her. In her eagerness to declare her love for him, she had tried to squelch reality. The truth was, most everyone she knew would be scandalized when word got out she had fallen in love with a mere policeman. Much like the latest tidbit of gossip had swept through the *ton*—Frederica Fresney had run off with a member of the household staff—Juliette marrying a policeman would appall her peers. No doubt they would calumniate behind her back and give her the cut direct to her face.

The dowager's outrage had stemmed as much from the fact that Daniel was a commoner as her being found in his embrace. If Daniel had been of high rank, the dowager would probably have tutted, but she would have begun planning the nuptials forthwith.

Was Juliette mad to have assumed her parents would consent and celebrate with her at her choice of a mate? Perhaps they would feel as the dowager did, scandalized and forbidding? When it was just the two of them, Daniel and Juliette, she could believe anything possible, but spending so much time with the Haverly guests and family, meticulously following the rules of society and propriety every day, she realized the gulf that lay between their situations. Her parents would be more than aware of the issues their love presented.

Yet what could Juliette do if they did not give their consent? Would she have the courage to defy them and marry Daniel anyway? Would they approve if Daniel was declared a peer, if he won his petition for the earldom?

Of course they would.

He had to win. He just *had* to.

The dowager stared at Juliette from her perch on a settee, her cup stopping halfway to her lips. She gave a prunes-and-prisms pucker, her back straight, one aged hand gripping the top of her cane.

Juliette supposed she would have to make some sort of peace with the woman, or staying in the house would become increasingly unpleasant. She crossed the room, trying to appear contrite.

The dowager sniffed, her eyes like gimlets.

"Your Grace."

"Not now. I am too put out by your behavior. Sit here and don't move from my sight." The dowager sipped her tea.

Juliette stifled a sigh. She would take her punishment and hope whatever Marcus and Charlotte had to say on her behalf would mollify the dowager later. Or at least get her to cease breathing fire.

"I would use Mrs. Stokes's house in King's Place, but it is too small for our needs." Miss Cashel's words caught Juliette's attention. "I envision dormitories, schoolrooms, a hospital ward, and room to teach the ladies various trades. Sewing, baking, laundry, etiquette. Skills that will ensure they can provide for themselves. If I could find a place with some acreage or at least a byre, we could teach some of the ladies to be dairymaids."

"You want a manor house or abbey. Where will you procure money for a property that large, and close to London? Will Haverly fund the lot?" Mr. Burnside, whom Juliette had met earlier, asked.

"He has pledged some, but I refuse to take any more. He and

Charlotte have been most generous, but we cannot put all our eggs in one basket, as it were, nor should they be solely responsible for such a large undertaking. The enterprise needs many donors and supporters." Miss Cashel turned her lovely eyes on him, brows raised. "Gentlemen such as yourself, who are compassionate and not unfeeling toward those less fortunate."

Mr. Burnside tilted his head, as if his cravat was suddenly too tight, color infusing his cheeks. "Of course. I believe my wife is signaling me. Good evening, Miss Cashel."

Poor Philippa. That particular fish seemed to have wriggled off the hook.

"I wish she would not pester the guests. They came for a musical evening, not to be coerced into donating to charity." The dowager tapped her cane on the floor. "Still, Marcus allows her free rein, as free as others under his roof, it appears." A sideways glance at Juliette.

"I understood that you helped Miss Cashel in her work?" Juliette asked, not letting the dowager's tone ruffle her, or at least trying.

"In the country, where our business is private. And limited. Where we can choose carefully the women we allow into the house. Pippa—I mean Philippa—intends to open wide the doors of a London charity to anyone who wants to stride through." The dowager huffed, as if such a thought qualified one for incarceration in Bedlam.

"Didn't Jesus, the Great Physician, say He came not to those who were well but to those who were sick?" Juliette asked.

"You're too young to know what you are talking about. Suffice it to say that I wish Philippa Cashel would keep her fundraising efforts out of my parties."

A footman appeared at Juliette's side. "Milady, there is a visitor to see you. A Miss Montgomery, and if you don't mind me saying, she appears to be in some distress."

Agatha? She shot to her feet, but the dowager clamped her hand about Juliette's wrist.

"Where do you think you're going?"

As gently as she could, but forcefully enough that the dowager would understand she would not be prevented, Juliette removed the grip on her arm. "Your Grace, my friend is in need of me. I pray you will allow me to go to her."

"How do I know this is not a ploy to sneak off again?" she whispered, color riding her cheeks.

"Perhaps you would care to accompany me to see that it is merely Miss Montgomery?" Her face felt tight, and heat pulsed through her. If she wanted to sneak away, she could do it, and the dowager would be none the wiser. She was an agent for the Crown, after all.

Charlotte drifted over. "Juliette? Is there a problem?"

"Agatha has arrived and wishes to see me in private. The dowager refuses to let me attend her."

"Oh, that cannot be the case, surely? Madam would never be so gauche. Go. I will keep the dowager company in your absence." Charlotte winked as she took the place Juliette had vacated.

Juliette nodded, grateful as she followed the footman from the reception room. He led her down to the library, his heels clicking on the parquet floor, the candlelight glinting off the gold braid on his livery.

"I offered her refreshment, but she refused." He held open the door. "Shall I inform His Grace of your visitor?"

"If I need the duke, I shall let you know. Thank you." Juliette hurried past him.

Agatha rose from a chair before the cold fireplace, her face pale, with lines of strain etching her features. "Oh, Juliette, it's too terrible."

Juliette embraced her friend, putting her arm around Agatha's shoulders and squeezing her hard. "What is it? Is it Alonzo?"

Agatha shook her red head. "No, nothing to do with him. There was a murder at my house tonight. And an abduction. Someone has killed one of my footmen, and the murderer has taken a little boy, Peter, who does the boots and shoes and general chores. I was so distraught, I had to get out of my house. It is too soon after my father was killed. I felt the walls closing in about me, and I couldn't breathe." She gasped even now, her hand to her chest. "That poor child."

Juliette's mind reeled. "Sit, please." She guided Agatha back into the chair, noting her icy hands trembled. "Do not stir from this spot."

She went to the door. The footman stood just outside, his back to the wall, awaiting his next instructions. "Would you please have a tea tray brought to the library, and would you inform Their Graces that I need them both? Thank you."

Charlotte had a deep, cushioned chair near Marcus's desk, where she read of an evening while Marcus worked or read, and Juliette went to it, drawing up the shawl that lay across the back. When the footman returned, she would ask him to start a fire in the fireplace.

"Here, wrap up. You're thoroughly chilled." She tucked the paisley print around Agatha's shoulders. "Be sure to cover your hands. They're icy. I've sent for some hot tea, and the duke and duchess will be here soon."

Her head came up. "The duke? Why? I mean, I know it is his house, but does he have to be here? He's so . . . I get flustered around him."

Marcus did have a commanding quality that reassured some and disconcerted others.

"He's a kind man who will help in any way he can. Truly." She answered the skepticism in Agatha's eyes, reaching out to squeeze her hands through the shawl.

"But Alonzo might see it as disloyalty if I converse with the duke. He's the one leading the petition for that policeman to take Alonzo's inheritance. I nearly collided with Daniel Swann at the curb on my way into the house. He was here plotting how to steal the earldom, wasn't he? I told him to send someone else from Bow Street, but I know he will go himself. And now he is on his way to my house, where Alonzo is waiting, and there's a dead man and a missing child . . ." Her voice broke and she let out a ragged sob. "I cannot bear it."

Juliette knelt before her friend, chafing her hands. "Do not distress yourself, Agatha. There is nothing to be gained by worrying about the earldom just now. Let us focus on what happened tonight. Gather yourself, because when the duke and duchess arrive, they will want you to go over everything you know in an orderly and logical manner. Breathe slowly and calm your heart. You were right to come here."

"I could think of nowhere else to go, only that I must get away from Eaton Square." Agatha shuddered and rummaged in her black beaded reticule for a handkerchief. "You're always so sensible, Juliette."

The door opened, and Marcus entered, questions in his eyes. He paused when he spied Agatha. "Miss Montgomery?" He motioned for her to remain seated. "I apologize that my duchess cannot attend. She is seeing our guests off. How may we be of assistance?"

At that moment the footman appeared with the tea tray and set it on a side table. He carried the laden table to Agatha's chairside.

"Would you stoke a fire please?" Juliette asked as she rose and poured the tea.

Agatha's hands still trembled as she took the steaming, fragrant cup. She needed the heat and the comfort of her favorite beverage to settle her nerves.

When the footman had bowed to Marcus and left the room, the duke pulled a chair close and offered it to Juliette. He went to his desk and leaned against the front, crossing both his ankles and his arms.

"Your Grace." Juliette addressed him formally in front of a guest, though she had been given leave to call him Marcus. "There has been a murder at Agatha's house. I understand that Mr. Swann has been dispatched to Eaton Square to look into things."

Marcus's eyes widened at her summation, but he turned his attention to Agatha. "What can you tell me, Miss Montgomery? No detail is too small."

Agatha swallowed, lowering her teacup to her lap. Juliette gently removed it and put it on the tray, and Agatha's fingers knotted. "We were seated at dinner, Viscount Coatsworth and two other guests, Lord and Lady Nettleton." She stopped, guilt striking her face. "Oh dear, I fled the house when I had dinner guests. It was my first small entertainment, just friends of my father's. Lady Coatsworth said it would be appropriate, even given my deep mourning, since they were such intimates of my father's, to host a small dinner party with no games or amusements after."

Juliette patted her clenched hands. "Do not fret about your guests. I am sure Alonzo made your apologies. It was a most extreme time." She wasn't certain Alonzo would make any apologies. She wasn't certain he even knew how.

"As I said, we were seated at dinner, and my butler came in and whispered that he needed a word with me in private." She shook her head. "It was most unusual, for he is extremely proper when it comes to etiquette. I excused myself and indicated Lord Coatsworth should follow, and I am thankful he did. My butler informed us that there had been an incident in the mews. One of my footmen, George, had been stabbed, and the perpetrator had stolen my bootboy, a child named Peter."

Marcus had been concentrating on her words, but at the mention of the child, he uncrossed his ankles and arms and stood upright. "A child was taken?"

"Yes. But who would want my bootboy? He has no family. He certainly has no money beyond his small wages. What profit could there be in stealing him?"

Marcus caught Juliette's eye, and she read the gravity there.

"What happened next?" he asked.

"Alonzo—Lord Coatsworth—took charge." There was a tinge of pride to Agatha's voice, even as she dabbed her lashes. "Alonzo saw my distress and my need to escape and put me in a carriage. I told him I needed to get to Juliette. I knew you were staying here, so I asked the driver to take me to Haverly House. I hope you do not mind?" She slanted a furtive glance at the duke before ducking her chin.

"Of course. Any friend of Juliette's is welcome here." Marcus spoke absently, as if his mind was somewhere else . . . much like Juliette's, centered on the alarming news of a murder.

"Alonzo said he would go into the mews and see to things there. When I arrived here, I met—" Agatha pressed her lips together for a moment. "I met Mr. Swann outside. Though I appreciate you are attempting to help, Your Grace, I do not approve of what Mr. Swann is trying to do to Alonzo. However, when someone is killed, one needs a policeman." Her back straightened, and her jaw firmed. She looked not unlike the dowager, with a disapproving slant to her mouth and the fierceness of loyalty bright in her eyes. "Mr. Swann should confine himself to the area in which he is best suited—dealing with the rabble and detritus of London."

Marcus nodded, his expression neutral. "You will, of course, understand if I have a different opinion. What time did the butler inform you of the killing?"

"It was after ten o'clock. I do not know the precise time."

"Thank you. I will look into the matter. In the meantime, I would like to offer you hospitality for the night. Your house will be the center of the investigation for some time, and you may wish a peaceful place to abide until you can return home. Lady Juliette, if it is not too much of an imposition, seeing as we have many guests residing at the moment, and that Miss Montgomery might wish companionship rather than to be alone tonight, would you share your accommodations?"

"Of course. I was going to suggest that very thing. Come, Agatha. Let's get you upstairs. You can borrow anything you need tonight." Juliette realized she had fallen into familiar lines as she took Agatha's arm and led her to the door. Through their many years at boarding school, Juliette had always been the leader, the one looking after Agatha.

Once they were in nightclothes and Agatha had been tucked into the big feather bed, Juliette found herself restless and unable to sleep. She lit a candle from the banked coals of her fireplace, placed it on a small table, and went to the window seat. She wrapped herself in a blanket and tucked her feet up, parting the drapes to study Berkeley Square below.

"It will kill him, you know." Agatha spoke from the darkness under the bed canopy.

Juliette turned her head.

"It will kill Alonzo to lose the title. Being the heir is all he has ever known. He was mortified when his grandfather claimed he was illegitimate and banished him to the Caribbean. The title is rightfully his. He should not have to fight for it, to be dragged through a dispute. If the petition does not go his way, he will be destroyed. He will have nothing. Mr. Swann had a large settlement from the earl. Why can he not be content with that?"

Juliette hugged herself. What could she say? That Daniel needed the earldom to make him an acceptable match for her? That if the petition proved true, Daniel deserved the title and lands, that what was right was right, no matter who cared passionately about the outcome?

If Daniel won, Juliette would win, but not without cost.

Agatha would be lost to her forever.

Daniel trotted down the stairs of Haverly's massive townhouse, planning to cut beneath the maples dotting Berkeley Square and try to hail a carriage for the trip to the Olympian Club. There had to be more there than he had uncovered thus far, and he intended to bring pressure to bear on Mr. Alton. The records of membership and amounts owed had to be somewhere. Haskett hadn't kept all that information in his head.

Before Daniel could cross the street, a coach bowled up and clattered to a halt at the curb.

"Well met, sir. I was just going to hail a conveyance." Daniel looked up at the jarvey, holding up his truncheon. "Bow Street investigator. I'll get the door." Before the driver could say a word, Daniel opened the carriage door, and Miss Agatha Montgomery, dressed in black, eyes like saucers in her pale face, nearly exploded through the opening.

When she recognized him, she froze, her lips going white. "You."

"Good evening, Miss Montgomery." He kept his tone neutral.

The driver leaned down from his perch. "You're just the man we need, I think. The lady here has had a bit of unpleasantness at her home, and she could use your services, sir."

"Miss?" Daniel asked. "How may I assist you?" He held out his hand.

Her nostrils pinched, and she brushed aside his offer of help. "I have no wish to speak with you, sir. Tell Bow Street to send someone else to my home immediately."

She swept past him up the stairs, and Daniel was left holding the carriage door on the curb.

"I believe you should get in, sir," the driver ordered. "There's been a murder at the Montgomery house. One of her footmen, sir."

Daniel was inside at almost the same moment as the whip cracked and the carriage lurched down the street. A murder? No wonder the lady was so upset.

The trip to Eaton Square was quick at this time of night, and though the horses had presumably just made the same journey, they didn't slacken their pace, pulling up eventually, not in front of the Montgomery townhouse, but in the mews, behind.

Several men, some in livery, stood around a man on the ground, holding lanterns high and creating eerie shadows on the stables. Daniel approached slowly.

He opened his mouth to announce himself in his official capacity, but he needn't have bothered. His eyes locked with the tall man opposite the body and recognition sent a charge through him.

Alonzo Darby, his half brother. Dressed formally, with white linen gleaming at his throat and wrists, the buckles on his shoes casting back the light from the flickering lanterns, Alonzo sneered.

"You."

The same word Miss Montgomery had first uttered upon seeing him tonight.

"Yes, me. What happened?"

"Stand back, men. Let us allow the great Bow Street investigator to work." Alonzo's tone dripped with disdain.

Daniel shrugged. He supposed he would be angry, too, under the circumstances. He took a lantern from a bystander and squatted over the body.

The victim was young. Maybe twenty? And he was dressed in the same livery as two others in the group. "Who is he?"

"George Burghley, footman to Miss Montgomery," one of the men said.

"What happened?"

The man stepped closer. "I was in there." He indicated an open stable door, a black rectangle in the stone walls of the mews, about thirty yards from the body. "Cleaning harness, when I heard someone yell. I came outside, and a chap in a dark cloak and tall hat had George pinned against the wall. And Peter, the bootboy, was laying on the cobbles in a heap." He rubbed his nose with the rag, leaving a smudge behind.

"Then what happened?" Daniel moved the lantern to the dark stain on the dead man's clothing.

"The fellow in the cloak stabbed poor George. I saw his arm thrust forward." The groom demonstrated an underhanded upward strike. "Then he grabbed up little Peter, who was limp as this rag, and run off with him. No way I could catch them up, not with my bum leg, so I went to George, who was still alive, but he was bleeding something terrible. I didn't touch him. Didn't want to cause him more hurt. There's a wee passage here that allows access to the backs of the townhouses, and I scooted all the way up there to raise the alarm. By the time I got back with help, George was dead."

"Do we know what George was doing in the mews? Did his duties bring him here?" Daniel asked.

"It's only the grooms and carriage drivers who work and live in the mews. Peter might be sent round if the lady of the house wants the carriage, but George wouldn't have no business back here."

Alonzo stood with his hands in fists at his side, his mouth as tight as the drawstrings on a miser's purse. "Well, what are you going to do? I don't know why we bother with a so-called police force, when all they can do is bumble about after a killing, scratching their heads and wringing their hands. The purpose of the police is to deter and prevent crime."

Daniel straightened, tiredness weighing on his shoulders. "I need you all to step back and clear the area. You," he pointed to one of the other footmen. "Inform the local magistrate of what has occurred here. And you, go to Bow Street and tell them Daniel Swann is in need of investigative assistance from Mr. Beck and Mr. Wilkinson."

They nodded and left without a word.

"You," He indicated the driver who had brought him to the mews. "Get to Dr. Rosebreen's house and tell him we are in need of his services once again. Tell him to bring a wagon and some sheets." Daniel gave him the address. "Make haste."

The carriage driver had left his team down the mews and stood with the other onlookers. He doffed his hat. "Aye, guv. Be back as soon as we can."

Daniel surveyed those left, an older man with gray side whiskers and an impressive hooked nose, and Alonzo, who looked as if he might burst into flames at any moment.

"Tell me about this boy, Peter. How old is he?"

Alonzo shrugged. "I never met him. I'm not likely to, a bootboy?" He sneered again. "I don't consort with my betrothed's help."

Daniel ground his back teeth before turning to the older man. "And you are?"

"Just call me Beaky." Which immediately drew attention to the nose. "I'm Miss Montgomery's coachman. Live up there." He pointed to the lofted area above the stables.

"What can you tell me about the boy or this man?" Daniel indicated the body.

"Peter's about eight or so? A good lad when he wants to be." Beaky shrugged. "Can't think why anyone would want to carry him off. The boy was limp. Do you think he was dead, too? Do you think that man killed them both?"

"It's too soon to draw any conclusions." Daniel squatted once more and stuck his hand into the victim's trouser pocket. Empty. "Do you know if George here carried a coin purse? Could this have been a robbery?"

Beaky shook his head. "Not likely. We get paid at the first of the month, and we're well past that day. George would have spent it all before now. Had a gambling problem, did our George."

A prickle went across Daniel's skin. Gambling. Which put him in mind of the errand he had set out upon from Haverly's. He had been headed to the Olympian Club to lean on the secretary before he was called here. He'd have to put that off until he had gathered what he could here and seen the body off into Rosebreen's care.

Two stabbings, two men associated with gambling.

Another missing child.

Daniel studied the wound, the tearing of the fabric, the location of the puncture. It all looked oddly familiar. He had examined the fatal injury to Mr. Jericho Haskett, and that wound was decidedly akin to this one. Had the same person committed the crime? Was it the same odd weapon? Rosebreen would be able to tell.

If it was the same weapon, the same killer, how were a footman in Eaton Square and a gambling hall manager linked? And what would the killer want with a child? Were the children somehow linked to the gambling club?

It was much too dark in the mews to determine whether the same strange mixture Rhynwick had identified on Haskett's wrist was present on the victim's clothes. Another task for the medical man.

"Mr. Beaky, why did Miss Montgomery not call upon your services tonight? Why did she hire a carriage to Mayfair instead of her own carriage?"

"I put Miss Montgomery into the carriage," Alonzo said, eyes narrowed, as if daring Daniel to challenge his actions. "I happened to see the driver parked at the end of the street and hailed it, because it would be faster than summoning the coachman and waiting for him to hitch up the team and come around to the house. Miss Montgomery was most distraught that her servant had been killed, and she insisted she had to go to Lady Juliette at once. I wanted her away from this dreadful scene, especially since she is so recently bereaved herself, and thought it wise to use the swiftest means of travel available."

"Most prudent. Thank you." Daniel again strove to keep his tone devoid of emotion. "Is there anyone in the house who can tell me more about the child, or the movements of the footman tonight?"

"The housekeeper will know about the boy. He was in her charge." Beaky scratched his side-whiskers. "You want me to fetch her?"

"No. I'll speak to her once the body has been retrieved by Dr. Rosebreen."

"It's late." Alonzo shifted. "Can you not come back tomorrow to question the staff?"

"Timely investigation increases our chances of finding out who did this."

"That's hardly likely, is it? A stranger came into the neighborhood, abducted a child, when the footman tried to intervene, he was killed for his trouble. How are you going to track one stranger in a city the size of London?"

"Mr. Darby." Daniel refused to call him Earl of Rotherhide or Viscount Coatsworth or anything other than mister until the case was decided. "I will pursue and follow any and all leads that emerge. I will work with other investigators at Bow Street, and I will not stop until the case is laid to rest and someone has paid for this crime. My job would be considerably easier if you were to either go inside the house and wait, or return to your place of lodging until such time as I need to speak to you again."

Alonzo actually shook, his neck muscles tight, and his jaw jutting. "How dare you order me about, insolent pup!" The words hissed through his clenched teeth. "I will not be directed in any way by you or any other mere policeman. I am your better by leagues, and you would do well to remember that. I will have a word with your superiors, and you'll find yourself out on the street where you belong. Not only will I retain the earldom, but I shall bring suit against you for repayment of any settlement my grandfather made you. We'll see how you enjoy being a pauper."

Daniel handed the lantern to Beaky, who was backing away, trying to melt into the shadows of the mews. "Mr. Darby, this crime scene has nothing to do with the dispute between the two of us, and it is also my jurisdiction. If you remain here, hindering me and disregarding my directions, I will have no choice but to arrest you for obstructing my investigation. I have asked you to leave the scene of this crime, and I've asked for the last time."

Alonzo coiled, and for a moment, Daniel thought he might be preparing to throw a punch. Daniel tensed, ready to spring away. He would not engage his half brother in fisticuffs, for he could imagine the headlines in the dailies tomorrow. A fight with Alonzo would be the farthest thing from Haverly's order to avoid drawing attention to himself. Alonzo, after remaining frozen for a long moment, wheeled and disappeared down the narrow opening between the stables.

Beaky breathed out. "Strewth. You're a brave one, taking on a swell like him. He's got his nose so high in the air, it's a wonder he don't trip more often."

Daniel released the tension in his muscles, feeling weak. The last thing he wanted or needed right now was to have a slanging match with Alonzo Darby. Yet, here he was, nearly coming to blows with him at midnight in a mews while standing over a dead body.

He rubbed the back of his neck. Though he had the authority to control any crime scene as he saw fit, Daniel knew he had abused that power just to lash back at Alonzo's supercilious digs.

And he'd enjoyed it, too.

A flaw in his character, no doubt.

Rosebreen sent his assistant Mr. Foster and a wagon rather than coming himself. The footman who had fetched him helped roll the body onto a sheet and load it on the cart.

"The doctor will expect you tomorrow afternoon, or someone can fetch a report," Foster said, prosaic as always. Fetching dead bodies in the middle of the night was nothing new to him, it seemed.

"I need to speak to the employees in the house." Daniel parted with Beaky and followed the footman through the narrow opening between the stables and into a small path behind the walled gardens of the townhouses. They turned up the path until they came to the gate leading into the Montgomery garden. The small patch held a shed, a privy, and a tiny flower patch. Moonlight picked out the white blossoms.

"This way, sir." The footman showed him to the short staircase that led down to the ground floor. "Mrs. Mentieth will be in her sitting room."

The back hall reminded Daniel of the one at the Thorndike's London townhouse, and the sitting room resembled the one his mother presided over.

But not for long, Lord willing. His mother would not be a housekeeper in the future. He would provide for her, set her up in a house of her own, wherever she wished. It was his duty as her son, no matter what she had done to him in the past. Once he was declared the heir to Rotherhide, she would be a countess, and he would see to her care.

Mrs. Mentieth sat in a chair before the fire, a white lace cap on her head, her apron impeccable. She held a handkerchief to the corner of her eye. "Poor Peter. Poor George. It was bad enough the master being killed, but Peter and George? There's a curse on the place, that's what."

Daniel pulled up a wooden stool. "Ma'am, what can you tell me about Peter? How long has he worked here? Has he mentioned anyone following him, or anything suspicious? Do you know his family?"

"He's not been here long. Six months, perhaps? Before Himself was killed at the mill. The last bootboy, Jasper, grew big enough to get another position. He went to a printworks as an apprentice, and a friend of Beaky's said he knew of a lad in search of work. Peter was just seven when he came, and small he was, too. But cheerful and willing. And heavens, could he eat. I could hardly fill him up. And he grew, too. Needed new clothes almost right away. As if now that he had a good place, good food, and honest work, he could get about the business of growing properly." She dabbed her eyes again. "When he first came, he could hardly carry Himself's tall boots down to the scullery to shine them."

"Did he mention anything unusual recently?"

She shook her head, stirring the lace fringe on her cap. "Not to me, he didn't."

The other footman, who had remained in the room, shook his head. "Never said anything like that, sir."

A clatter in the hall caught their attention. Ed and Owen followed the butler into the room.

"Another one. That makes four." Owen spoke as he entered.

"Five," Daniel corrected. "That we know of."

"Five?"

"I'll tell you more later. For now, we need to search the victims' rooms. Ed, if you would look through the footman's? And Owen, you and I will see if there's anything where the boy slept."

The housekeeper showed them to the pallet in the corner of the laundry where Peter had dossed down at night. The footman took Ed up a back staircase, to the servants' rooms. Daniel remembered the layout of the house from his investigation into a stolen painting taken from the gallery upstairs during Juliette's debut ball. The case that had launched their relationship.

"Any notion why the footman would be in the mews at night?" Daniel asked the housekeeper as Owen felt about the pallet and opened the small crate next to it that held the boy's belongings.

She shrugged, spreading her hands. "George went out at odd hours. He was always back for work in the morning, and he never went out on his turn to stay in the front hall overnight, so no one really minded. I heard he liked to frequent a gaming club, but I don't know for certain. Just rumors. I thought perhaps he was meeting a young lady. He had just left the house not long before he was killed. I had no idea Peter was anywhere but in his bed. Perhaps he made a run to the necessary and that's where the killer found him?" Her lips trembled and she blinked hard, dabbing at her eyes. "How could such a thing happen to such a sweet boy?"

"We intend to find out."

Owen straightened. "There's nothing here. A clean shirt and extra pair of stockings. And a prayer book."

"Could Peter read?" Daniel asked.

"He was learning. Mr. Mifflin, Miss Montgomery's secretary, was teaching him after church on Sundays. It was so sweet to see them together. Poor Mr. Mifflin. He's going to be devastated."

"What about Peter's parents? Do you know them?"

She shook her head. "Our Peter was an orphan. A foundling, from what I understood. Before he was with us, he had run away from the Foundling Hospital, and someone had taken him in, along with another lot of children, and taken it upon himself to find positions for them. That's how Beaky brought Peter to us."

Daniel made a few notes, and he covered a smile when he noticed Owen had a notebook identical to his and was penciling in information.

The murder of the footman, in conjunction with the kidnapping, had elevated the missing child case beyond what Owen could manage on his own. If Daniel was right about the same knife causing the fatal blow to the footman, the cases were intertwined and related at more than one point, and Owen would be useful as part of the team.

An hour later, when he left the Montgomery house—through the front door, thank you very much—he found Cadogan waiting at the curb.

"You always turn up when I need you. It's uncanny." Daniel went, not to the door, but to the horses, where Cadogan stood, feeding apple pieces to his team, slicing the fruit into wedges with a sheepsfoot blade that gleamed in the moonlight. "What's this? A new horse?"

"Aye. This is Addie. The timing was right." He sighed, as if the air was pushed out from deep in his emotions.

Daniel didn't want to probe a sore spot, but he was curious. "Where is Sprite now? Did you find a good home?"

"I did. She's going to a place in Sussex, Whitehaven. The estate has become a bit of a place for injured soldiers and military horses to recuperate and get better. A mate of mine at Tattersall's told me about it when I was looking to buy a new horse. He put me in touch with a fellow named Shand, the estate steward, and when I told him Sprite had been an army horse before I got her, he said she could live at Whitehaven the rest of her days. Pasture and a stable, and if she was willing and wanted the work, she could pull a cart for the steward's wife when she went into town."

"That sounds like the perfect situation for her."

"Makes my mind easier, to be sure. And now I have Addie, who is young and learning her business from Lola here, but has lots of stamina and go. I think they'll work well together." He touched the little mare's nose. "They're as mismatched as Sprite and Lola were, but I don't mind."

Addie was a dusky light brown with a black mane, and at least a hand shorter than Lola, though she probably still had some growing to do.

"She looks like a real trimmer. I hope she didn't set you back too much."

"I came into a bit of money recently. Someone finally paid a debt they owed me, so I was able to buy better than I thought." He roused himself, stepping back from the team. "Where can I take you? You're my last fare of the night."

Daniel nodded. "The Olympian Club." They would be open for a few more hours, and he still had to speak with Mr. Alton.

Cadogan pulled a face. "That's a rum place, for all its fancy trappings. Any closer to finding out who killed Jericho Haskett?"

Daniel shook his head as he climbed into the carriage. Not only was he no closer, but he had a sneaking suspicion that after tonight's doings in the Eaton Square mews, he was further from the truth than ever.

Chapter 10

The Olympian Club, while not exactly raucous, was certainly busy for so late at night . . . or rather, early in the morning. Light shone from every window, carriages filled the street out front, and Abel stood at the door, admitting members. He recognized Daniel, lifting his hat and nodding.

"Brisk trade tonight?" Daniel asked. Clearly a murder on the premises hadn't deterred the members.

"Always, sir. If it's Mr. Alton you want, he's in Mr. Haskett's office."

"Thank you. I'll see myself up, but first, are you familiar with a man named George Burghley? Young, light-brown hair, was in service in a house on Eaton Square. He was known to be something of a gambler, and I wondered if he had ever frequented the club."

The man's dark brow furrowed, and he shook his head. "The name is not familiar, and to be honest, sir, the Olympian Club caters to a higher-tone client than someone in service. A household servant would not have the resources to pay the membership fee, much less cover any debts that might arise at the tables."

Daniel nodded. What Abel said made sense. "If you do come across the name, please contact me."

"Is this man in some sort of trouble? Is he likely to cause difficulty here if he does come by?"

"He will not be troubling anyone ever again, I'm afraid. He was murdered, and I am trying to discern if there is any link between his slaying and that of Mr. Haskett."

With a grave expression, Abel nodded. "If I hear anything, I will report it to you."

When Daniel entered the gaming room, the sound of voices, the clack of fish counters, and the flutter of shuffled cards hit him. There must have been at least fifty people at the tables, sitting at the counter, or standing and watching the games.

Olympian Club employees all wore the same royal-blue coats and dull-gold waistcoats and moved amongst the guests with food and drink and small trays of gambling markers, each representing a different denomination. Daniel noted them jotting down names and amounts each time they delivered markers. Were those then taken to Haskett's office to be recorded? They must be.

Cigars and pipes added to the blue cloud of smoke hovering near the ceiling, and the sharp tang of whiskey and the fruitiness of port touched his nostrils.

He wove through the crowd and made for the staircase that would lead him up to the office. The door to Haskett's former sanctum stood open, and Daniel walked in. Mr. Alton sat at the massive desk. Daniel noted the differences since his last visit. The rug had been removed, and the furniture now sat on the painted wood floor. The desk, which formerly had faced the door, had been shifted so that it faced the windows on the left side of the room. It must have taken four men to move the massive piece without scratching the floor. The surface of the desk bore a blotter and an inkwell, and Mr. Alton bent over a ledger.

But by far the most eye-catching additions to the room were the stacks of coins arranged in militaristic rank atop the desk. Alton counted a stack, entered a notation in the ledger, then scooped the coins into a leather sack.

"Is it wise to have all that money out where anyone can see it?" Daniel asked, stepping into the room.

Alton jerked, looking up, a drop of ink splashing his careful columns in the book. A mild oath slipped out as he reached for blotter paper. "Good evening, Mr. Swann. It is less of a risk when one takes precautions." He indicated something behind the door.

When Daniel followed his gaze, a large, menacing visage greeted him.

"This is Vladimir. He was once a bodyguard to Empress Catherine II of Russia. He now works for the club, making sure nothing untoward happens." Alton wiped his fingers on a handkerchief. "What is it I may help you with? Have you found out who killed Mr. Haskett?"

"Not as yet. However, seeing you at your ledgers, I must ask again, where are Mr. Haskett's? We've been through all the paperwork removed from the office, and nowhere is there a list of club members or amounts paid to or owed by those members."

Alton held up the book before him. "This one is new, purchased from a bookbinder just this morning. I was forced to buy one because I could not find Mr. Haskett's, if such a record-keeping system existed. He never showed me a roster of members. Abel knows most of them by sight, which is why I put him on duty at the front door. Each evening he and the card dealers are helping me compile a list from those who have come in."

"Where else can we look for the ledgers? You mentioned the safe in the wall." Daniel indicated the spot, now covered with a painting of a hunting dog with a partridge in its mouth.

"There was nothing inside but money. Which has been removed."

"Removed? Was it stolen?"

Alton shook his head. "No, it was retrieved, as it is each morning."

"Retrieved by whom?" Daniel frowned.

"By men who work for the owner of the club."

"Jericho Haskett didn't own the club?" Why hadn't he been told this?

"No, Mr. Haskett ran the club for someone else, and before you ask, I do not know who. I received a missive the morning after Mr. Haskett was killed, instructing me to keep the club open, to keep good records, and to see that the counted money was available by seven each morning for retrieval. The note was not signed. As I knew this to be the daily practice, I didn't question it and have been following the instructions."

Alton struck Daniel as a man who was good at following instructions. A good second-in-command. How well would he do as the top man in the establishment?

"There must be other records, else how would the owner know if he was turning a profit? Where might they be? Is there anywhere else in the club they could be hidden?"

Alton spread his hands. "You've searched everywhere I can think of. Staff and patrons occupy every nook and cranny of the building. This room is the only one that had stipulations as to who could and should enter." He quickly counted the remaining stacks of coins, noted them, then shook the remaining ink from his quill before putting it into its holder and capping the inkwell. The coins clinked and jingled as he swept them into the sack. He rose and swung the picture on hinges out from the wall and addressed the metal box hidden behind it. A pair of keys were required to open the safe, and Alton had both of them on a ring in his waistcoat pocket.

"Mr. Haskett previously held one key, and I the other, as a safety measure, but I have yet to receive instructions on who should hold the second key now." The metal door opened silently, and he deposited the coins and his new ledger. Daniel could see there were no other books in the safe. Alton closed the door and patted it. "There. That will be secure until morning."

He turned to Daniel. "I apologize, Investigator, but I must go downstairs and make certain things are running smoothly." He indicated that Daniel should precede him into the hall.

"If you don't mind, I will remain here and examine the crime scene once more. Perhaps there is something I missed the other night."

Alton paused. "Very well." He spoke slowly, as if he were not in favor of the notion. "Vladimir will remain in the hall should you need him."

And ensure I don't abscond with the night's earnings, no doubt.

The big Russian said nothing, crossing into the hall, standing where he could still see into the room and grasping one wrist with the other meaty hand at his waist. A wicked knife stuck out from his belt—a long, curved blade like a small scimitar, nothing like the blunt, triangular weapon Daniel sought. Daniel was certain the guard had other weaponry about his person, but it would be a brave man who asked him to surrender them.

Walking about the room, Daniel twitched the drapes, tested the paintings, looked behind a potted plant, unsure why he bothered. The room had been thoroughly gone over the night of the murder and decidedly altered since.

He sagged onto the desk chair. Where would Haskett have hidden his ledgers, for he must have kept some, especially if money was expected to be presented each morning? They were not at his residence, they were not amongst the papers removed to Bow Street, and thus far no one could verify they'd ever seen them.

But they had to be nearby. It was no use keeping them elsewhere. Everything Haskett needed to record occurred here in the club.

And what connection did Jericho Haskett have with a footman from Eaton Square, and what, if anything, did either man have in common with missing street urchins?

This mystery kept growing new branches, tangling into a thicket that was proving impenetrable.

Alton had placed his new ledger in the safe with the coins, and the desktop was clear of paperwork. Daniel slid the belly drawer open, revealing sealing wax, envelopes, and a letter opener. The top drawer on the left held foolscap, an extra quill, and bottles of India ink.

Basic office paraphernalia.

On the right, he pulled open the top drawer, but it stuck halfway. A bottle of cologne, a mirror, and a comb rattled around as Daniel yanked, and with a rush, the entire drawer came free in his hand.

Odd. Why was the drawer so short? It was barely half the depth of the desktop. He set the short drawer on the painted floorboards and opened the drawer on the left once more. It slid out twice the length of the other.

A frisson skipped up his spine.

The desk was old, well-cared for, and expensive. Daniel rose and walked to the front, tapping on the wooden side panels. Knock. Hard. Knock. Solid. Knock. Sturdy . . . *Thunk.* A hollow sound beneath his fingertips.

Somewhere under there, a hidden compartment waited. But how to access it?

He glanced at the hulking Russian who stared at him with the eyes of an adder. Cold, calculating, and ready to strike.

Did he speak English? Did it matter?

Daniel shrugged and knelt beside the desk, pushing and pulling on every ornamented bit of ormolu trim. There had to be a catch or latch somewhere that would release the panel and reveal the hidden compartment. Poke, twist, press. Nothing. He returned to the chair. For practical reasons, the designer must have made access easy for the one occupying the desk.

Removing drawers, pressing on every surface, relocating the blotter, and running his hands over the smooth top. Nothing. Frustrated, he sagged back into the chair.

"I don't suppose you know anything about Louis XIV–era French desks, do you?" he asked the Russian, guessing as to the period in which the desk was created but thinking he must not be far off, as it resembled furnishings in paintings he had studied at university from that age. "Or anything about hidden compartments that might be contained in one?"

"*Da.*" Vladimir unclasped his wrist and stepped into the office. "Many pieces like this at the Imperial Palace."

Daniel blinked. "Any help would be appreciated."

The guard motioned him back, and when Daniel stood, he removed the chair. "Stand there." He pointed to the side of the desk where Daniel had heard the hollowness when he tapped on it.

The massive guard settled his bulk to the floor, sitting with his back to the kneehole, then wriggling and shuffling until his head and shoulders disappeared beneath the desk.

A few muffled thumps and bumps, then a click, and the side panel of the desk tipped out. Daniel managed to catch it before it clattered to the floor, and there they were. Four massive, leather-bound ledgers, each with a gold-stamped year on the spine—1812–1816, the current year.

"Well done, sir." Daniel laughed as the big man writhed out and clambered to his feet. His dark curly hair ran amok, and when he smiled, he was missing an upper front tooth.

Probably knocked out in a brawl.

Daniel laid the panel aside and pulled the books from the space. A tidy little hiding spot. Haskett could probably access the panel while seated at the desk, since he would have known where the latch was without looking.

"You ask *Gospodin Altonov* before you take the books away, *da?*" Vladimir took up station in the doorway once more.

"Of course." Daniel didn't need permission from Mr. Alton, these items being germane to a murder inquiry, because he also had a warrant granting him access to all the paperwork on the premises. "Perhaps you can ask him to return here?"

"I send someone." Clearly he was not willing to leave Daniel alone and risk him absconding with the books. The guard called down the hall to a worker and sent him on the mission.

While waiting, Daniel opened the newest volume. A quick perusal told him that each club member had their own folio. Columns filled the pages with headings such as *dues, rooming fees, refreshments, winnings*. Daniel was most interested in the column titled *losses*.

Every page he studied had some wins, but mostly losses. Sums as small as £5 and as large as £20,000.

Daniel sat back, exhaling sharply. Who could afford to be in debt by £20,000?

He glanced at the name and whistled. That particular gentleman had been sailing perilously close to the wind financially, because just last month, Bow Street inspectors had been sent around with a bailiff to inform the man that he was in arrears on the rent of his palatial townhouse and payment was due within the week, or he would face charges.

The debt had been paid, but whether by the young man or by some of his friends, Daniel didn't know. But the frequency and size of the wagers in this list told him the gentleman had a terrible gambling problem.

There was a separate section at the end of the gaming-club records that showed the daily totals of expenses and profits, along with a notation of the amount of money picked up each morning. Whoever backed this place was making a tidy sum.

About halfway through the book, a velvet ribbon bisected the pages, and another pattern emerged. Pages filled with rows and columns of numbers, but no names, only initials or code words. Surely no one Mr. Haskett had done business with had really been called Squeaky or Boo or Number Six. No titles to indicate what the columns or rows meant either. Haskett must have been able to decipher the pages, but he was dead.

Perhaps Daniel would ask Juliette for help, as she was quite good at cyphers and codebreaking.

He closed that book and opened the oldest one, 1812. Flipping quickly, he noted many of the same names, the same columns, the same sorts of sums. And halfway through, the ledger again switched to the odd code.

Perhaps there was a key in the back of the book? He flipped to the last page.

No easy answers there, just one note, written in the same hand as all the rest.

"Bobby Puck is no more. It's H.C. now. Foot in two worlds. Must ensure he doesn't crush me with those heavy boots of his."

Who was Bobby Puck? Where had Daniel heard that name before? Was it relevant so many years on from when this notation had most likely been written? Did "is no more" mean Bobby Puck had died and someone else had taken over? Was H.C. the mysterious owner of the club, who collected the night's take promptly at seven every morning?

If Haskett didn't own the club but ran it for someone else, had that someone found discrepancies in the bookkeeping? Had the ledgers matched what the backer expected? Had Haskett been skimming for himself? It would be tempting, all that money going out the door each day and only one man in charge of the recordkeeping, to hold some back for personal gain.

Mr. Alton appeared in the doorway, his brow furrowed. "You found something?" His face was pale, and he gripped his hands together.

"I did. I will take these with me for further examination." Daniel began stacking the ledgers into his arms.

"I cannot let you do that. Those are confidential papers that contain the private financial business of several influential and powerful people. I am certain those people would not want their gambling records to be made available to the police."

Daniel noted that Alton did not seem surprised at the existence of the records, only that Daniel had found them. Now he claimed to know what the books contained? Daniel slid the man's name farther down on the "who is trustworthy" list while elevating it on the "who might have killed Haskett?" list.

"Have you been at the club all night?" Daniel still held the ledgers.

"What? Of course I have. I would never leave when we're full of patrons."

Vladimir, hulking behind, nodded. "All night. He never leave."

Daniel nodded, but he would need verification from more than Alton's bodyguard to be sure.

"As to taking these ledgers, the warrant served here the day after the murder covers any and all business paperwork related to the club. I have no desire to expose any of your clients or share their information, but the answer to who killed Mr. Haskett is most likely lurking in here somewhere. The ledgers will be kept in a locked cabinet, and I will have the only key."

"That's not good enough. The owner of this establishment will be most displeased." He trembled. "Please."

"Who is the owner? I will speak to him."

"I am not privy to that information."

Said the man who claimed to have no knowledge of any ledgers in this office.

"Then you best find out." Daniel took his leave, edging past Vladimir, tensed should the man try force. "Or I will find him myself."

The Russian guard stood like a statue, arms crossed.

"Stop him," Alton pleaded.

"I am paid to guard money. Nothing else. You must stop him if you wish."

Daniel had no worry about how he would deal with Alton should the need arise, and Alton knew it.

He went out into the night, the scent of tobacco smoke lingering about him from the still-crowded gaming rooms. He wished Cadogan was there to give him a lift back to Bow Street. A night watchman passed him with his lantern and called out the time. Two o'clock.

When he was an earl, he would keep better hours.

Chapter 11

Twelve hours later, only six of which Daniel had slept, he waited at the coffeehouse for the arrival of Rosebreen and Rhynwick. Both had been busy with the additions to the case in the forenoon and had sent messages requesting a meeting with Daniel in person that day. Rather than traipse all over London, Daniel had sent back missives to meet him at the Grecian Coffee House on Devereaux Square. He'd chosen the meeting place because the coffeehouse off Fleet Street had become a favorite with both the legal and scientific sets in London, and he thought it would be familiar to both of them.

He took a sip of bitter black coffee, chasing it with a bite of cake. He'd been so busy, he hadn't had time for a meal since yesterday. Perhaps he could locate a pie cart after this meeting, because a few tea cakes would not sustain him long.

Owen had turned up at his boardinghouse door early, having already been to Spitalfields to chase down the rumor of a missing chimney sweep's boy. There were too many similarities with the other abductions to ignore. They were looking for someone who operated in a wide area of the city.

Rosebreen arrived first, and Daniel hailed him. The doctor had abandoned his apron, thankfully, but still looked as if he had forgotten to look in a mirror today. His hair was rumpled, as was his coat, and his cravat was askew. If Daniel wasn't mistaken, an instrument or two poked out of his pocket. *Please, let them be clean.*

"It's the same weapon, just as you suspected. It has to be." He flicked out his coattails and plopped into the chair opposite Daniel without preamble.

"And a good day to you as well." Daniel signaled for the waiter. "A coffee and some cakes for my friend, thank you."

Rosebreen pulled a sheaf of papers from his inside pocket. "You'll see I've diagrammed the injury." He passed an outline of a body with the appropriate wounds marked. "This time there were defensive marks on the forearms. A slice and a bruise." He pointed. "Here, and here."

"So unlike Jericho Haskett, the footman fought back." Daniel studied the sketch.

"It would appear so. The other unusual item was a piece of cloth in his hand but pinned beneath the body at the crime scene. Mr. Foster found it when he retrieved the body from the mews. I had my suspicions as to what was on it, but I sent it to Rhynwick for confirmation."

At that moment the young man in question entered the coffeehouse in a bound. Fastidiously dressed as always, he darted through the tables like a homing pigeon headed to his roost.

"Good day, gentlemen." He straddled a chair backward, resting his arms along the top. This behavior drew odd looks from those nearby, but Daniel shrugged. Rhynwick was a law unto himself, and allowances must be made for genius. The contrast between Rosebreen's dishevelment and Rhynwick's dapperness stood out markedly side by side. Yet the intelligence of both emanated in waves.

"It was laudanum. The child was most likely made senseless with laudanum." Rhynwick, too, dispensed with small talk.

"So this was a planned attack." Daniel flipped his notebook open. "No one just happens to have a bottle of laudanum in his trouser pocket."

"Early this morning I visited the place where the murder happened and had a poke around." Rhynwick dug in his pocket. "I found this at the north end of the mews." He held up a blue glass bottle with a cork stopper. "There are a few drams left."

Daniel took the bottle, tipping it to see the liquid. "Could he have forced the boy to take it? Or laced a drink with it?"

"It's possible. The effects would be quickly felt if the child was small."

"He was seven or eight, and slight. I saw one of his extra shirts, and he must be about so high?" Daniel held his hand parallel with the floor, about four feet up.

"Small enough, I would think, to subdue without chemical assistance," Rosebreen observed.

Daniel agreed. "But if silence and lack of struggle were the objective, I could see the use of the drug. It was the kidnapper's, and ultimately the footman's, bad fortune that the snatch was temporarily interrupted. What else did you find?" he asked Rhynwick.

"I was unable to isolate those pollen spores from the Haskett murder, though I've tried several times since you visited the abbey. They're too compromised by the grease. I did manage to identify the horsehair— not the individual horse, you understand, but the color. I believe you're looking for two horses, bay or brown, and chestnut. Beyond that, it's anyone's guess." Rhynwick drummed his fingers on the chair back. "Dr. Rosebreen sent over the footman's clothes, but there was nothing unusual. I did find horsehair on his livery, but that would be expected because he was murdered in a mews where horses go in and out all day. No pollen spores and no grease."

Daniel made notes. Bay and chestnut horses were prevalent in the city. There must be more than three hundred thousand horses in the London area at any given time, from children's ponies in Hyde Park to draft horses pulling brewer's drays. Impossible to pinpoint a particular animal. Even Cadogan had a bay and a chestnut, or he had until he got the new mare.

Rosebreen stroked his chin. "Have you considered the type of person who would carry a knife like the one we're seeking?"

Daniel looked up. "The type of person? You mean a murderer and child kidnapper?"

"Of course you take the crimes into account, but I'm thinking more of the type of person who carries a specialized weapon, almost certainly concealed somewhere on his person. A man of secrets and aggression but not out of his wits. He's not barging about town brandishing this unusual knife, shouting to everyone that he's a killer. Neither is he stabbing in a frenzy. One decidedly accurate thrust." Rosebreen demonstrated. "He must be someone of respectability, at least outwardly, else he would not have gotten into the Olympian Club to murder Mr. Haskett."

Rhynwick leaned back as the waiter brought another pot of coffee and two cups, along with a plate of currant-studded cakes. The young scientist accepted a cup, but he ignored the cakes. While his lean frame might suggest he did not indulge in such confections, Daniel suspected he was slim more because, with his intense focus on his work, he forgot to eat at all.

"Do you think he has an appearance that is not frightening to children? That's how he got close to the boy?" Rhynwick asked. "Perhaps offering a treat?"

Daniel shook his head. "That is one possibility. I should inform you, however, that we're not looking for just one child. We're now looking for at least six."

Rhynwick's head came up, and his eyes sharpened in that peculiar way that said his brain was racing ahead of the rest of the world. "Six? What are the commonalities?"

"Have you ever considered becoming an investigator?" Daniel asked with a smile. "Bow Street could use your skills."

"I *am* an investigator, just in my laboratory. How are the missing children related? If you can find the areas in which they have things in common, perhaps you can find where they are most vulnerable, who would have the opportunity to abscond with them, and why those particular children are targeted."

Daniel scratched his cheek, rueful that Rhynwick had summed up the study of victims so neatly. "They all have employment. They're all close in age. They're all easy prey."

"How do you think our kidnapper is identifying these particular children? And do you think there are more of which we are unaware?"

"In the case of the shoeshine boy and flower-seller girl, the perpetrator could have posed as a customer to get close. The street sweeper would approach someone if offered a coin. The kitchen boy and the bootboy and the chimney sweep would be more difficult, as they were under the supervision of employers, but taking them would not be impossible. These children are accustomed to being helpful, to trying to please adults. In any case, if the kidnapper came up on any of them unaware, it would take little to subdue them. Especially if he is somehow able to get laudanum into them."

Rosebreen put his elbows on the table, holding his coffee cup in both hands. "The real question beyond who is doing this, is why? What does he want with these children? Frankly, the abduction of the girl is the most puzzling."

"Why is that significant?" Daniel asked.

Rosebreen lowered his voice and leaned forward. "There are men who have lascivious natures when it comes to children, but they are usually gender-specific in their taste. If they seek to abuse boys, they don't often have any appetite for girls. The opposite also holds true. If they prefer girls, boys do not interest them."

Daniel's stomach churned. He had given thought to this particular motive for stealing children, and it sickened him. There was no legal punishment too harsh for men with such evil proclivities. But he could not be too narrow-minded when it came to assessing the possibilities just yet, else he might overlook a clue that would unravel the entire case in another direction.

"I've got a clerk and the new office boy at Bow Street searching our criminal records for cases similar to this, and a charge went out to the night watchmen and magistrates around the city inquiring if there are other children missing or if anyone has encountered anything that might tie into our investigation. To my knowledge these efforts have turned up no new information."

"We must return again to the mind behind this crime." Rosebreen tapped the table. "This man is skilled. He is strong and agile enough to kill the footman and make off with the child quickly, but clever enough to surprise attack a grown man in his own office. In the children he identifies victims that fit a particular need of his own. In both cases, he's not frenzied but shrewd. He is willing to kill to carry out his plans, murdering anyone who gets in his way. I assume no one has come forward as a witness to these abductions or murders?"

"Beyond an employee at the Olympian Club reporting a man rounding a dark corner and hopping into a carriage of some sort about the time of the Haskett murder and an old groom from Eaton Square seeing a dark figure kill the footman and carry off the boy, no, we've no witnesses. There was no child abducted from the gaming club. No child worked there. The only thing linking the cases is the strange murder weapon." Daniel rolled his shoulders. "I did find some ledgers of Haskett's late last night, and today's task is to decipher them, as some of the entries are in a private code of Haskett's. Perhaps the motive for his murder lies in his own bookkeeping. The killer may have an entirely different motive for killing Haskett than he has for kidnapping children." He paused. "Have either of you heard of a man named Bobby Puck?"

Rhynwick shook his head, but Rosebreen paused. His eyes went unfocused as he stared through the window into the distance.

"Do you know him?" Daniel asked. "I found the name in the Haskett ledgers, but not as a customer. More like a personal note Haskett wrote himself." He consulted his notebook. "'Bobby Puck is no more. It's H.C. now. Foot in two worlds. Must ensure he doesn't crush me with those heavy boots of his.'"

Finally, Rosebreen stirred. "That is a name I have not heard in a long time. When I was a physician at St. Bart's, a man was brought in badly beaten. His companions carried him inside and threw him on the floor at my feet. The smaller of the two said, 'This is what happens when you try to steal from Bobby Puck.' They left without another word." He blinked, focusing on Daniel's face. "That must have been all of eight years ago. I haven't heard the name since, but it was such an unusual happening, I remembered it. The victim died, by the by."

"Bobby Puck sounds like a charming individual. The note is newer than eight years, as the ledger I found it in was for the year 1812. Did you get the sense that either of the men who brought the victim in was Bobby Puck himself, or that they were merely the messengers?"

Rosebreen shook his head. "I got the feeling they were acting on behalf of someone else."

"I'll have a clerk search the archives at Bow Street. If Bobby Puck was in the business of having men beaten to death, he probably has other crimes to his name." Daniel rose, and Rhynwick bounded to his feet like a schoolboy let out of class.

"If I find anything more, I will contact you. Good day." And he was off like a linnet.

Rosebreen smiled as he rose to his feet. "Brilliant. But eccentric. I heard he was being considered for membership in the Royal Academy of Science. He would be the youngest member if approved, but there are some who are holding out against him for his lack of experience."

"They would be foolish not to admit him and learn from him. I feel the most acute sense of ignorance when he's around. As if he's tolerating the sluglike pace of my mind as his races leagues ahead."

"When it comes to the men of the Royal Academy of Science, it isn't his lack of experience that will keep the members from embracing Rhynwick into their midst. But rather it's that those who consider themselves the most brilliant minds in the land do not wish to appear unlearned next to a dynamic intellect housed in such a youthful person. They hold the power in the situation, and Rhynwick will be hard pressed to be accepted if they are afraid of his intelligence."

"Have you noticed how often people in positions of power abuse that power?" Sir Michael, the Royal Academy, even the Prince Regent, all given intelligence and power by God, but not always using their position to help others. Should God ever grant Daniel any power, he would use it for good instead of taking advantage of others through wielding it.

Of course he had some power, that given him by his office as a Bow Street investigator, and he tried to wield that power equably, though the criminals he arrested might disagree. And for that matter, how would Owen feel Daniel used his position? Daniel grimaced. There was no doubt they'd rubbed each other up the wrong way at times, but he was trying to get on with him, to mentor him. Ed had been correct to remind Daniel of his obligation to do right by the boy.

They stepped out of the coffeehouse, and Rosebreen headed back to his office a few blocks away. Daniel hailed a carriage, noting the horses, a matched pair of bays.

He needed to check in with Ed and Owen at Bow Street. Perhaps they had discovered something that would move this case along.

"I've found no similarities, sir, in these missing children and the others in our files. Either the age is wrong, or the perpetrator was found and had a connection to the missing child." The clerk, Mr. Berry, held a folder behind his crossed arms. A pencil stuck out from behind his ear, and he had dust on his face from combing through the archives. "The truth is, children are easy to lose and difficult to identify. London's streets are full of urchins with no supervision or care, scrambling up to full grown all on their own. The mortality rate amongst these people is staggering. More than a third of all children die before age two. Those who do survive do not have an easy life."

Caleb, the new office boy, stood behind Mr. Berry, holding a stack of files, the wisdom of the ages in his young eyes. He had no doubt experienced this difficult life.

Daniel nodded, sobered by these terrible statistics. "I have a new task for you both. Sift through the archives for the name Bobby or Robert Puck. If you find anything, inform me immediately."

Mr. Berry took the new orders well, but the boy's shoulders sagged, and he scowled, no doubt discouraged by more file searching, but he would have to get used to such chores. The office boy must do as he was told.

"I know it's daunting and does not seem glamorous, but I assure you, Caleb, you're doing important work. More cases are solved by following the paper trail than any other method."

The boy's chin came up, and he nodded. A spark of warmth hit Daniel in the chest at having encouraged the lad.

The clerk sniffed and pushed his glasses up on his nose. "Very well, Mr. Swann. Sir Michael wished me to direct you to his office after I had given my report."

"Thank you." Another confrontation with his superior. Not the best way to get on with his day.

As Mr. Berry and the boy left the investigators' room, Owen entered. "The accountant says he will come this afternoon to look over those ledgers."

"Good."

"What should I do next?"

Daniel took a moment to marvel at the change in Owen. Over the last few weeks, as he had become more involved in cases, his eagerness for work had increased and his surliness toward Daniel had lessened.

"Wait here. You and I are going out after I've seen Sir Michael."

"Good luck." Owen grinned. A flash of sympathy lit his blue eyes, and Daniel appreciated the sentiment.

I may need it.

Daniel tapped on the doorframe and entered the Biddle lair. "You wished to see me, sir?"

"Close the door." Sir Michael's eyes were icy.

When Daniel once again stood on the carpet before the desk, his hands clasped behind him, Sir Michael placed his palms flat on the blotter. "I understand you removed some ledgers from the Olympian Club last night?"

"Yes, sir." How had Sir Michael known? Daniel hadn't told him, and only Owen had been aware of it, for Daniel had sent him to procure the services of the accountant not an hour before.

"You will return them to the club without delay and without examining them."

"Sir? They are evidence in a murder investigation."

"They are not germane to the case and therefore not necessary to keep."

"Sir, how can you say they are unnecessary before we've had them examined?"

"Do not be impertinent. There is sensitive information in those books, powerful men and women who would not care to have a mere policeman meddling in their personal affairs. If they knew those details were in the hands of a common investigator . . ." He shook his head, looking down his long nose. "I will not have private details of the aristocracy leaking out to the broadsheets and newspapers."

Light dawned. Either this was an attempt by Sir Michael to curry favor with the great and powerful who might feel compromised should word get out about their gambling failures, or someone listed in that book was leaning on him to keep the matter hushed.

"Sir, I cannot return the property to the Olympian Club without a magistrate's permission. A magistrate signed the warrant instructing me to remove all records and paperwork from Mr. Haskett's office. Whether or not those records might prove an embarrassment to someone is irrelevant. Whether or not those records might prove someone had a motive to murder Mr. Haskett is extremely relevant."

Red suffused Sir Michael's face. "Am I to take it you are disobeying a direct order?"

"You may take it that I am refusing to disobey a magistrate's orders. If you prefer, we could go upstairs to the courts and locate Lord Creevy, who signed the order, and confer with him as to his wishes."

"Where are those books?"

Daniel said nothing.

"You are walking on a knife-edge, Mr. Swann. Where are those books? I will return them myself."

A hollow feeling opened in the pit of Daniel's stomach, but he stood firm. "Sir Michael, I regret that I cannot accede to your wishes, for to do so would be to obstruct an investigation. Mr. Haskett deserves justice, and I cannot violate the law, no matter who might be embarrassed by where the investigation takes me. My duty is clear."

Daniel hoped Sir Michael would hear the warning in his tone. The supervisor was perilously close to an obstruction charge himself. Perhaps it was time for a bit of oil on the water.

"Sir, I have made certain the ledgers are in safekeeping and will be examined by only myself and an accountant who has worked with this office in the past and has proven himself trustworthy. All information not pertinent to the case will be ignored. If nothing turns up in the records, they will be returned to the Olympian Club in good time. That is the best I can do." He spread his hands. "I have no choice."

"You certainly do have a choice. I cannot allow those names to be read. It would be a disaster." A pleading tone entered his voice, desperation invading his eyes.

Daniel narrowed his eyes. "Is there something I should know? Something pertinent to the case?"

Sir Michael leaned back sharply. "Of course not. Don't be foolish. It's the privacy of certain individuals I am seeking to safeguard from prying eyes."

"I will take the utmost care to keep those records confidential. Only the killer needs worry about what I may find there."

Sir Michael fumed, but there was little he could do if Daniel refused to obey. With the Duke of Haverly's patronage, Daniel could not be fired for this offense. Whoever Sir Michael was seeking to shield, he did not outrank Haverly. Which meant it wasn't a royal duke, because royalty itself was the only possible rank higher than Haverly's.

"If you insist upon keeping the ledgers, then they should be made secure. Bring them to this office, and I will lock them away."

"The ledgers are quite secure where they are." He could not let Sir Michael "safeguard" the evidence. The moment he had possession of the books, they could well disappear. "Unless you would prefer to visit Lord Creevy, the magistrate who signed the warrant?"

Sir Michael's eyes narrowed. Of all the magistrates in the Bow Street courts, Lord Creevy caused the most friction. He was a stickler for following the law, and he called to the carpet any investigator, or supervisor of investigators, who failed to maintain the integrity of evidence or failed to do his utmost to ensure public safety. He and Sir Michael had crossed swords before.

"See that you keep those volumes under lock and key, and return them to the club with all possible speed. Now get out."

Daniel returned to the investigators' room and motioned to Owen.

"You survived." Owen quirked a smile. "You have more lives than a cat."

Daniel said nothing, his gut tight. Fighting with Sir Michael was wearing, but soon that battle of wills would end. Either Daniel would be an earl, or he would be out of work. He and Owen walked out of the building and around the corner toward Drury Lane. A new shoeshine boy sat beside his box and chair on the corner, and when Daniel met his eye, the child hustled forward.

"Thine, thir? Only a penny." He grinned, his middle upper teeth missing and causing the lisp. "I'll make your booths bright."

Daniel nodded, taking a seat in the battered wooden chair and sticking out his boot. "I'll pay two pennies if you'll answer some questions."

Owen dug out his notebook and pencil.

"Yes, thir!" The boy swept up a rag and began wiping the dust from Daniel's boots.

"Your name?"

"Thebastian."

"Sebastian what?"

He shrugged. "Just Thebastian."

"Do you have parents?"

"No." He glanced up, wary. "I take care of mythelf."

"Don't be afraid. I'm not going to haul you off to an orphanage. I'm looking for the boy who worked this patch before you. Did you know him?"

"Yeth. Matthew. No one knows where he went." The boy opened a tin of boot black and dabbed another rag into it, swirling and rubbing it into the uppers and toe of Daniel's boots. "He wath my friend."

"I'm sorry. I'm doing my best to find him. If you have no parents, where do you sleep? Does anyone look after you?"

He brightened, giving his gap-toothed smile. "Oh yeth, I have a place. Dougie looks after uth. We have two rooms, one for boys and one for girls, with lots of beds, and Dougie's wife, Mrs. Dougie, makes thoup. I do get tired of thoup, but thoup can feed lots of people for not much money. And Dougie doesn't have much money. But what he does have, he thpends on us." The boy set to work with a will, expertly popping the rag between buffing. "We all help. We bring our earnings from each day to Mrs. Dougie, and she buys potatoes and carrots, and thometimes, chicken."

He spoke as if chicken were a rare and beautiful thing.

"How many children live with Dougie?"

Sebastian sat back on his heels and screwed up his face. "It changes. Thome kids thtay for a night, and thome, like me, have been there a long time. I came at near Chrithmas, when my old guv died. Dougie found me and my brother and brought us to his house."

"Does Dougie treat you well?" The child looked fed, his clothes were worn but tidy, and he was passably clean.

"I ain't been beat once thince I went to his house. Me and my brother have a bed all to ourselves, with a blanket." Again the wonder of such luxury. "We hafta go to church, and at night, we hafta learn our letters, but ith the best place I ever lived."

The boots were done, and well done at that. Daniel handed over the two coins, which promptly disappeared into a buttoned pocket. Sebastian looked hopefully at Owen, but Owen shook his head. "We have to be moving along."

"One last question. Where is this Dougie's house?"

"Thurston Row, over the Blackfriars Bridge."

"Thank you."

"Where is Thurston Row?" Owen asked as they walked away.

"We'll have to ask someone. I've never heard of it."

Owen shoved his hands into his pockets, matching step with Daniel. "Where to next?"

"I want to question a variety of street children, to see if any of them know or saw anything. First, we'll go to the corner where your little crossing sweeper went missing, then we need to head to Berkeley Square and find flower sellers or other children in the area."

"What about the boy who worked in the pub kitchen?" Owen asked.

"Yes, we'll talk to as many as we can in each of the areas where we know a child was taken."

"Might be faster if we separate."

"No, this is part of your training. The next child we question, you take the lead."

Owen's stride lengthened, and Daniel hid a smile. He well remembered, just a few years ago, his own eagerness as a newly minted investigator and how Ed had taken him under his wing and taught him how to solve crimes.

"Ed has gone to Eaton Square to knock on doors. Perhaps one of the residents or servants in the area saw something of significance regarding the bootboy or the murdered footman."

"Something about all this has been bothering me." Owen stopped on the street corner to wait for a carriage to trundle by.

"What's that?"

"These missing children. Londoners walk past street children day after day, not really seeing them, not even when they interact with them, buying what they're selling, sending them to run errands and the like, but not really paying attention. It's like they're shadows. I know because I was one of them for a long time. Even when my pa was alive, he couldn't find work, so I had to earn money. I've mudlarked, swept streets, delivered messages, cleaned stables, scrubbed chimneys, anything I could. And when I couldn't find work, I stole." He shrugged as they moved to cross the street. "But nobody really knew me. Nobody saw me, the real me. I was one of the lucky ones though. I had a ma at home. She used to be a genteel lady, and she knew how to read and write. She taught me, or I never would have gotten the position at Bow Street. Now I help with my brothers and sisters."

Daniel remembered the cramped room Owen shared with his entire family. A widowed mother and several younger siblings all living in a single room in a row of tenements south of the river. But there was real pride in Owen's voice that he was keeping body and soul together for them all. Every day he walked miles from their place to Bow Street, and never once had he complained.

"Life in this city can be cruel, and life, especially young life, seems cheap. But we won't give up looking for these children," Daniel promised. "It's our job to make sure they don't stay shadows. They matter. Every life counts the same, or else why are we doing this?"

Owen nodded, his chin setting in a determined angle. He showed real promise as an investigator. One had to be determined, and one had to care.

On the other side of the street, a young crossing sweeper leaned on his broom, his hat slouched low.

Owen approached him. "You there. Police. I have some questions."

The boy started to life as if coming out of a sleep, took one look at Owen, and beat a hasty retreat, disappearing around the corner. Owen took two steps after him, but Daniel halted him.

"It's too late. He's gone."

"Little scamp. Why'd he run like that? We meant no harm."

"Think back to your youth. How would you react if someone marched up and said 'Police'? What would have made you stand still for two gentlemen to question you?"

Owen scratched the hair over his ear. "Food or money."

"I doubt much has changed. We need to employ such means to catch our quarry."

"I don't have any food, nor money to buy any."

"I'll take care of the bait. Let's find a costermonger."

Appropriately armed, they found another sweeper. He hurried into the street ahead of them, scuffing aside the horse droppings with his battered broom. "Penny, sir?"

"Would you take a penny and a cake?" Daniel asked.

The boy stopped, suspicious. "What do I hafta do?" His eyes shifted from coin to cake and back again.

"Just answer some questions, but let's get out of the street."

On the sidewalk, the boy said, "The penny first."

"Shrewd businessman. You'll go far." Daniel gave him the coin, thankful for the old earl's bequest, which meant he could fund these fact-finding missions without filling out a reimbursement slip and fighting with Sir Michael over expenses.

The coin disappeared in a familiar move. Daniel nodded to Owen to go ahead.

"Have you heard about the children going missing lately? Children like you?"

The boy's forehead bunched, as if the question caught him unprepared. "You mean like Matthew, from over on Broad Court?"

"Exactly like that. Any notion what happened to him? Or who his parents are?"

The boy shook his head. "He didn't have no parents, not like me. My old dad drives a wagon for a distillery, and my mother looks after us kids. Matthew had a place to stay though. Told me about it once, somewhere south of the river. Stayed with some other kids. I figured he had a guv who gathered kids into his crew. Plenty of those about."

Owen nodded. "Do you know who the guv is?"

"We didn't talk about it much. Too much work to do. This is a good corner, busy all day, so pretty good coin to be made if you hustle. Me and him shared an eel pie once though. Someone flipped him a shilling, and we ate like kings that day." He rubbed his lean belly, smacking his lips at the memory.

Daniel handed him the cake, and the child's eyes brightened. "Did he say the guv's name—was it Dougie, perchance?"

The cake vanished in one bite. "Never said. I best get back to work.

Time's wasting." He put his broom up on his shoulder and went to stand on the curb.

"Sounds like a pocket-dipping gang. With a guv, runners, and distracters, the cannon and the guv take all or part of the haul in exchange for room and board." Owen rocked on his toes. "This Dougie might be running a crew of little thieves."

"Except they're all working jobs. Why pose as workers, and diligent ones at that, if you're stealing? None of the children we're inquiring about has been described as a thief." Daniel checked his pocket for his coin purse just in case. "I suppose they *could* be thieving from people while they work, but that's inherently risky. Especially for someone with a regular position like the kitchen boy or the bootboy. Someone would be bound to remember where they were when they lost their money, and suspicion would fall on the little thief quickly."

"Where to now?"

"Let's try Berkeley Square. Then I have to be back at Bow Street to meet with the accountant to go over those ledgers. While I am thus occupied, you can check with Mr. Berry and Caleb. Perhaps they've found a prior case in the archives that will give us a direction. When we're done at Bow Street, we'll make our way to Thurston Row across the bridge and see if we can find this Dougie fellow."

Chapter 12

"No. I forbid it." The dowager's cane thudded against the Axminster carpet. "I have not spent weeks planning 'The Social Event of the Season' to have you parade in the masses and lower the tone."

Juliette pressed her tongue hard against the backs of her clenched teeth to keep from releasing all the things she wanted to say. It would do little good to vent her feelings to the dowager, for that lady had treated Juliette like a naughty child since catching her with Daniel. Whatever Marcus had said to his mother about the situation had kept the dowager from referencing it or scolding further, but it hadn't thawed her mannerisms toward Juliette in the least.

"The masses?" Cilla raised her delicate brows, looking up from her needlework. "Surely that is an exaggeration? One man is hardly 'the masses.' And he isn't likely to 'lower the tone' of the event. He's handsome, interesting, and quite possibly soon to be a newly minted earl. I would think he is just the type of person one would want on a guest list."

Juliette wanted to hug her.

"I don't know what has gotten into you, Cilla. Ever since you married Hamish, you've grown alarmingly independent. Does he encourage you to be so bold minded?" The dowager sniffed, her lips narrowing. "You used to be such a biddable young woman."

"Hamish encourages me to be myself." She smiled a private smile as she resumed her stitching. Her regard for her husband sounded in her words and glowed in her eyes.

Juliette shuffled a deck of cards, keeping her fingers nimble. It had been over a fortnight since she had last practiced any of her spy craft with Uncle Bertie or her parents, and she did not want to lose ground in her abilities.

She had received a message from Uncle Bertie this morning that he would be returning to London within the week, possibly in time for the Haverlys' Ball, and that he hoped she was behaving herself and not butting into a certain investigator's cases.

If only she could butt in—it would give her something to do and would bring her into contact with Daniel, which she desired to the point of distraction.

Diana Whitelock looked up from her papers and ink. "Your Grace, the invitations went out some time ago. It would be bad form to re-scind one now. And it would mar my seating chart." She held up a neatly columned page. In helping plan the party, Juliette had discovered that Diana loved lists. She had lists for everything. Guests, music, staff, refreshments. She even had a list of lists, which had amused her husband, but, he claimed, did not surprise him. When he had spotted her master list, Juliette had felt a pang of envy at the easy way he had laughed and hugged her, kissing her temple with true affection.

Juliette was surrounded by love matches.

"It would not be bad form on my part, as I was never in favor of inviting him in the first place. What will people think?" The dowager narrowed her eyes at Juliette. "He's a police officer, always surrounded with unsavory people and situations, rubbing shoulders with the criminal element. In addition to his occupation, his character is suspect. Only a grasping, greedy young man would try to obtain a title he's no right to claim. Hardly suitable as a guest or a suitor."

Juliette snapped the cards together and slapped the deck on the gaming table. "I believe I shall get some air. Would someone like to join me for a stroll around the square?" she asked, knowing the dowager would be the last to accept, with her unstable ankle.

Charlotte closed her book and rose. "Some air would do us both good. Let me get a shawl." Though it wasn't bitingly cold, the shawl would hide any signs of her growing child.

Soon, Juliette and Charlotte walked arm in arm beneath the maples.

"One of the many benefits to my marrying Marcus is getting to live in Haverly House with its lovely proximity to Gunter's. Shall we cross the common and indulge in an ice or confection?" Charlotte squeezed Juliette's arm. "Don't fret about the dowager. She worries because she cares, and her worry comes out as scathing comments sometimes. I tell myself that when she's being particularly trying. And do not be concerned that she will be able to change the guest list or dissuade us from inviting Daniel. Marcus honors his mother, but he does not indulge her prejudices."

"Whether she will allow me to have a dance with Daniel is another matter. She is, after all, my chaperone in lieu of my mother, and she is still angry about finding Daniel and me together. When I danced with him once before at Almack's, only having Bertie there to oversee things kept me from being raked over the dowager's coals." Juliette sighed. "It's all so backward."

"What's backward?"

"That others know about Daniel and me before my parents. My fault, I suppose. I should have told them at once, but I held back. I feared what they would say, and I missed my chance. They're gadding about the globe once more, and I'm here, stuck in this odd limbo. In love, not engaged, waiting for the pleasure of the Prince Regent to decide Daniel's fate. I don't know what to feel, only that I seem to be feeling all of it and in no particular rational order. I just wish Daniel and I could be together with no secrets."

"Oh, darling Juliette, I am sorry you've been in such a quandary of emotions. Has Daniel asked you to marry him? Should I be wary of him absconding with you to Gretna Green?" Charlotte spoke lightly, but her eyes were serious.

"He has not formally made an offer for me. He says it wouldn't be proper until he speaks to my father." Juliette gestured in a wide arc. "Why did the Prince Regent have to send my parents to the Continent again so soon? It's so awkward. Daniel and I aren't to even be seen together. We cannot yet let the world know we are in love. This inheritance claim hangs over everything, and I just want my mother." She knew she sounded pitiful, but listing her grievances made each one seem larger. *Pull yourself together, Juliette. This is no way for a grown woman to behave. You sound as overwrought as the dowager.* That thought had a sobering effect upon her.

"You are in need of a hot chocolate and some cake. We cannot solve all your problems today, but we can talk through a few of them."

Charlotte sounded so sensible and kind, Juliette's eyes pricked. "Did you have a sympathetic mother to help guide you through your debut Season?" Juliette asked as they made for the path bisecting the square.

Charlotte laughed. "My mother was sympathetic to a point, but she cannot stand up to my father, who is a tyrant. My debut Season was a disaster by their standards, and it wasn't until I met Marcus in my third, and final, Season that they had any hope for me to marry successfully. They had plans to send me to an awful great-aunt's home in the country if I didn't find a husband with all haste. Aunt Philomena." She shuddered. "At least the dowager doesn't press vegetable tonic on me at every turn like Aunt Philomena."

Gunter's wasn't crowded, but the counter was doing a brisk business. The room smelled of cooked fruit and sugar, and Juliette inhaled deeply. What was it about a baked good that could minimize trouble, at least for a moment?

They found a table in the window where they could watch traffic go by, and soon they had a pot of chocolate and some sweets before them.

"Perhaps I should have a selection of cakes sent over to Eaton Square. Or a nice hamper from Fortnum and Mason's. They might cheer Agatha." Charlotte poured Juliette a cup of chocolate. "Poor girl. I am glad she was able to come to you in her distress. I thought she might stay another night or two. I wouldn't have wanted to be alone in my home after what has transpired. Do you think she will sell the townhouse? So much sadness there lately. Marcus tells me yet another child was taken and that one of her servants was killed."

"I asked her to stay, but we had words last night." Juliette moved her cup in a circle on the tablecloth. "Our loyalties in the inheritance dispute put us at cross-purposes. Not that she knows about Daniel and me. I told her that the decision about the earldom would be correct, whatever it was, as long as justice was done. She didn't like hearing that, as it opened the door to the possibility that Alonzo might be left without the title."

"I see. She believes the title belongs to Alonzo, and you are sure it belongs to Daniel?"

"I am not certain to whom it rightfully belongs, but I believe that an investigation must be done, and the truth, whatever it is, brought to light. Of course I want Daniel to inherit the earldom. It would simplify our relationship, as no one would cavil at me, an earl's daughter, marrying an earl. But I also don't want Agatha to be hurt, and I don't want to lose her friendship. She is very dear to me. For so many years, she was my only friend."

"There seems to be no good solution here, does there? Have you prayed about it? I find when I pray, even though the situation may not be changed, my heart is. I receive peace when I remind myself through prayer that God is both sovereign and good."

Juliette paused. "I've certainly prayed about Daniel and that somehow God would work it all out."

"Work it out to your satisfaction, or His?" Charlotte sipped from her cup and dabbed her lips. "I often find myself wanting to tell God how to do things rather than ask that His will be done and His glory be shown. It does no good dictating to God. That's even less effectual than dictating to the dowager."

Juliette shifted in her seat, staring through the shop glass. Had she been dictating to God? What she wanted, Daniel and her parents' love and attention, weren't bad things, were they? Was it wrong to ask for them?

Had she been asking, or had she been demanding?

She turned to look out the window, blinking rapidly. Her eyes focused. Was she missing Daniel so much that she was seeing him when he wasn't there? She watched through the slightly rippled glass of the shop window as two men crossed Berkeley Square on the diagonal path, and the one on the left walked so much like Daniel, her heart hurt. Then the man stopped and turned, and that same hurting heart leapt with joy. It *was* Daniel.

"What a coincidence. Isn't that your young man now?" Charlotte tracked the gentlemen too. "Perhaps we should chance an encounter?" She signaled the waiter and rose. No need for the vulgar production of coins and receipts, as the shop would send a monthly account to the Haverly secretary to settle the bill. It was the way the aristocracy did business. "I don't suppose you are all that hungry anymore anyway."

They left the shop, walking briskly but not running, as Juliette would like. If she wanted to start tongues wagging, all she had to do was be seen pursuing a man across Berkeley Square. What if he didn't wait? Or was he going to Haverly House? The dowager would be most displeased if he showed up on the doorstep unannounced, but perhaps Marcus had requested to see him again? Had there been a new development in the inheritance petition?

As they neared, she recognized the younger man as Mr. Wilkinson, who worked with Daniel. Their investigation must have brought them to Berkeley Square for him to be along. This was confirmed when the two men stopped before a young girl with a tray of birdseed sacks. The pigeons here were all fat and bold thanks to the governesses who purchased the feed for their small charges to cast about each day.

Juliette and Charlotte paused a few paces away so the men could conduct their business.

"Did you know the flower seller who used to work this patch? Alice?" Daniel asked. He squatted on his heels to put himself on the same level as the girl.

"Yes. Do you want some seed? The birds like my seed." The child held up the paper sack.

"You know, my friend here loves feeding birds also. Perhaps we could have two?" Daniel produced a penny.

A smile split her face and put adorable wrinkles across her nose. She nodded and took the coin, and Daniel handed the two sacks to Mr. Wilkinson.

"When was the last time you saw Alice?"

A furrow formed between the girl's brows. "I don't remember. One day she just wasn't here." She shrugged, the movement raising the box a fraction of an inch.

"Did you ever notice anyone bothering her? Following her?"

A long consideration. "Sometimes a few older boys try to bother us, try to take our money or tip over our boxes. But I tell my guv, and he takes care of the mean boys. My guv doesn't like us to have trouble. Says it keeps us from making him money."

"Who is your guv? What does he do to the mean boys?"

She shrugged. "Mr. Baxter. I don't know what he does to those mean boys, because I never see them again."

"Where do you live? With your parents?"

"No, I live with Mr. and Mrs. Baxter. They sell seeds. Flower seeds, garden seeds, birdseed. There's six of us girls who go out with birdseed to the parks and squares every day. Mr. Baxter makes up the packages at night, and we have to sell them all before we can come home. Sometimes it's hard to sell them all."

Juliette's heart broke for the child, but it warmed to the gentle way Daniel questioned her.

"What street is the Baxter shop in?"

"I don't know the street. It's across from St. Clement's." She bit her lip. "Are you going there? You won't do nothing to get me into trouble, will you?"

"If I visit the Baxters, I will tell them you are an exemplary employee."

The child frowned as he rose. "I'm what?"

"You're very good at your job." He smiled. "Thank you for talking to me."

He rose and turned away. His eyes met Juliette's, and he stopped, his face spreading in a wider smile. He bowed. "Your Grace, Lady Juliette."

She wanted to run into his embrace, or at least take his arm and lean her head on his shoulder as they strolled the square, but neither would be proper nor prudent.

"You remember my colleague, Mr. Wilkinson?"

Owen bowed low, holding the birdseed. "Honored."

"Were you going to call upon the duke?" Charlotte asked. "I'm afraid he's not at home at the moment."

"Not at this time. Our investigation brought us here. We're now looking for other missing children, questioning those who have worked in the vicinity of the ones we know have been taken, hoping one of them will lead us to a viable clue or solution."

"And have they?" Juliette asked.

"We've gathered some information that will require us to follow up, but nothing solid."

"And the poor man who worked for Miss Montgomery?"

His jaw tightened. "We've linked his death to another case, one also involving murder." He grimaced as if he realized this was not a topic considered acceptable for discussing with ladies.

Charlotte must have assumed the same, for she linked her arm through Juliette's. "We will not keep you from your duties, but I am looking forward to seeing you at the ball in a few days' time. We all are, aren't we? In fact, the dowager was just speaking of your invitation today."

Juliette looked at her friend and hostess, biting her lip and raising her brows. Charlotte had a mischievous streak she kept well hidden.

"I can only imagine what the dowager had to say. I look forward to the evening as well, Your Grace. I thank you in advance for your hospitality." He touched his hat brim, elbowed Owen Wilkinson, who did the same, and took their leave.

Charlotte drew Juliette toward the house, though Juliette was sorely tempted to look back over her shoulder and say with her eyes all the things she couldn't say with others present. But she kept with decorum and didn't look back.

Footsteps sounded on the walk behind them, and they stopped. "Lady Juliette."

She turned to face Daniel, only inches away.

He pressed the bags of birdseed into her hands, squeezing her fingers at the same time. "Until the ball."

She nodded.

Please, God, let him be my future.

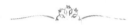

"How could this happen, and here of all places?" Daniel surveyed the wreckage that used to be his desk. "The building is full of investigators and clerks and officers of the courts nearly every hour of the day."

"Why is it only your desk that was broken into?" Ed asked. "What were they looking for?"

"It has to be the ledgers. They're the only thing of value that I had in the building." Daniel picked up the splintered front of the only drawer in his desk that locked. Used to lock, rather. Papers, quills, a letter opener, spare notebooks—every drawer had been emptied onto the floor.

"So we've lost the most important potential evidence in the case?"

Daniel shook his head, his mind racing. Had Sir Michael done this? He had been oddly desperate to get the ledgers returned to the club. Or had an intruder gotten in? But how would an outsider know which desk to ransack? It had to be someone in the building. Sir Michael or someone acting on his orders?

"I didn't feel my desk or the interrogation room we've taken over for the investigation provided enough security. I took them upstairs to Lord Creevy's chambers, and he locked them in his safe for me." Daniel rubbed his palm against the back of his neck. "I was going to fetch them first thing, since the accountant had to cry off coming in yesterday and made an appointment for this morning. He'll be here any moment."

Ed stroked his cheek, his eyes shrouded in worry. "Be careful, lad. This makes me uneasy. I feel as if we're in a struggle with someone very powerful, someone hidden in the shadows but whose reach is growing."

His partner's words echoed what Daniel felt in his gut. "I'll take care, and you as well. I need to go fetch the books. Can you and Owen clean this up before anyone sees it? The accountant will be here at any moment, as will the staff and other investigators. I'd just as soon not advertise the break-in."

"We'll see to it, though hiding that broken drawer front will be difficult."

Daniel clapped Ed on the shoulder as he headed upstairs. The magistrate's courtroom and chambers occupied the upper story of the Bow Street building, and his footsteps echoed in the cavernous court. In an hour or so the room would be filled with those on court business, but for now it remained silent and empty.

He found Lord Creevy's suite of rooms and tapped on the oak door.

"Come," a loud voice barked from the other side.

"Good morning, Lord Creevy. You're here early. I wasn't certain anyone would be about up here just yet."

"Can't uphold justice by lying abed. I suppose you want those books." The magistrate, a spare, angular man with a narrow nose and alarmingly bushy gray eyebrows, motioned him to follow. They passed from his clerk's office into the magistrate's sanctum sanctorum. "They're in the safe." He produced a long brass key from his waistcoat.

"Milord, I wonder if I could share a concern with you," Daniel said.

"Of course." Creevy didn't turn around, bending to unlock the safe behind his desk.

"Someone pillaged my desk last night. I believe they were searching for these ledgers, which tells me there must be information in them vital to the case." He didn't go so far as to cast suspicion on Sir

Michael. He had no evidence, and as far as he could tell, nothing had been stolen from the desk, only scattered about.

"A thief? Here?" Creevy straightened. "Who?"

"I do not know, milord. You may be assured I will attempt to find the miscreant."

"It's good you followed your instincts and brought the books up here. You may use this safe as long as you need." Creevy handed Daniel the stack of ledgers.

"Thank you, milord. I will return them when the accountant has finished with them."

Daniel carried the books downstairs, checking the hallway before he hurried to the interview room he had commandeered for the case.

An anxious hour later, Daniel checked in with the consultant again.

"The ledgers are extremely well maintained. Meticulous record-keeping right up to the evening he was killed." Mr. Drew, who looked as if he could never be anything but an accountant, pushed his spectacles up onto his bald head. "Mr. Haskett had a well-ordered mind." He spoke as if this was the highest praise he could bestow.

"That's fine, but what do the ledgers tell us about the Olympian Club and its patrons?" Daniel kept his voice low as he leaned against the closed interview room door, ensuring only he and Mr. Drew would be privy to the conversation.

"The Olympian Club was doing a healthy business. I've recorded"— he consulted a list—"a clientele of nearly two hundred names from the first half of the ledgers. Now, not all are current patrons. Some have not visited the club for some time. They tend to come and go. New people are added, and some are removed, for a variety of reasons. Some have died, which makes removal simple. Others, it would seem, grew to be so in arrears to the club that their membership was suspended. And they were either reinstated when the debts were paid, or they were struck off the rolls."

"Anything unusual about the records in the first half of the books? We'll talk about the second half in a moment. I want to be sure I am not missing anything there."

Mr. Drew shook his head, sucking his teeth. He wriggled his eyebrows and his glasses dropped down over his nose again. "Everything seems in order in those pages. The only unusual item I found was that Mr. Haskett appeared to keep very little money on hand at the club. Now, for his more well-known clients, members of the aristocracy, that makes perfect sense, as their voucher would guarantee their payment, but for those clients who must deal in gold or banknotes, he seems to have kept remarkably little on the premises. Almost as if . . ."

"As if he was having it removed daily?" Daniel finished for him. "According to the secretary, Mr. Haskett was in the practice of sending the profits of the night before by courier to be banked elsewhere every morning."

Drew nodded. "I see. Do you know where it was being banked? If I could have access to that account, I could compare it with these ledgers and ascertain if the deposits and the amounts taken in matched. Mr. Haskett wouldn't be the first man to have discrepancies between reports and reality."

"I do not know where it was being taken, but I would be surprised if it was in a conventional bank. I suspect the shadow owner of the club is keeping the money in his own safe." Daniel had thus far been unable to penetrate that secret. Alton claimed not to know for whom he worked. Tomorrow, Daniel would attempt to follow the man who picked up the money each morning. "What about the second half of the ledgers?"

"Most peculiar. There are two types of entries on these pages. Some include interest paid, or at least percentages that work out to how I would record interest paid. A moneylending operation, and quite lucrative, as the rates charged are quite high."

"And the other types of entries? You said there were two types?" Moneylending. Had someone who had borrowed money considered killing Haskett a better option than paying?

"I'm not altogether certain, but it reminds me of another case I worked on for Bow Street. That case involved blackmail. These entries are very similar. Clearly not gambling debts, but rather money in at regular intervals? And not broken down into principal and interest as the loans are? If I had to give my opinion, I'd say that's what it was. Records of blackmail."

"How many different blackmail victims are there?" This would certainly take the investigation in a new direction.

"Each account gets its own page, and there are about forty pages that are thus encoded in each book. Some clients carry over from year to year, and some of the code names disappear from one ledger to the next. I would estimate there are about sixty different clients? Fifty or so who have borrowed money and another ten who are paying blackmail?"

"And there is no way of knowing who these individuals are, from these books?"

"I'm sorry, no. Your Mr. Haskett encoded the names of those clients. He was quite up front with the club members accounts, no doubt to be able to show them if any query was raised."

"Did you come across the name Bobby Puck anywhere, other than that one note in the back of the first ledger? And anyone with the initials H.C.?" Daniel had asked him to look especially for that name.

"The name Bobby or Robert Puck does not appear anywhere else in the ledgers. There are three clients with the initials H.C. listed in the first part of the accounts as patrons of the club. And one H.C. in another section." Drew moved the ledgers about, seeking the slips of paper he had used to mark various pages. "The first is one Herbert Croft, now deceased. Account closed two years ago. The second is Henry Cobbler. He has only a handful of entries, and from what I can ascertain, frequents the club in October of each year. Perhaps he lives outside London and his business brings him to the city in the autumn? A farmer or sailor or the like? The last is also a Henry. Henry Canfeld. Silk merchant. He has a home and business near St. James Park. All these men were up to date with their accounts, and none of their gambling is large amounts. The most that was owed at any one time was one hundred pounds by Mr. Canfeld, and he paid the amount due at the end of the month as per usual." Drew dragged the blunt end of his pencil across a ledger page as if drawing a line beneath the account.

"Do any of the clients surprise you? Are there any outliers?" Daniel grasped at anything to help narrow his search.

"There is one little section in last year's records. Here, someone was apparently paying for services rather than financing a loan or paying blackmail. There are half a dozen of them." Again he consulted his papers. "Yes, here. 'Paid for three parcels. Sent via canal boat to Birmingham.' There are others like it. This one says, 'Paid in full for the entire load. Seek new distributor. Current one closing doors.' I do not know if these are part of the expenses of running the club or if he was taking in money for services he provided. It's all unclear. Perhaps if I go through the other papers you've brought, invoices, and the like, I can match up the entries with an expenditure or income."

"Are there names on these accounts?"

"Some." Drew read them out while Daniel wrote them into his notebook. The fourth name on the list made him jerk his head up. "Repeat that name."

"H. Cadogan. And he is in these books from the beginning, and he is the fourth H.C. in the accounts."

Cadogan had business dealings with Haskett? A gambling debt or something else? The jarvey had said he knew Haskett years ago but had given no indication he'd had recent dealings with the man. Just the opposite, in fact. "Was it money owed or money paid to Haskett?" Perhaps it was merely carriage fares, accumulated by club members, and paid through Haskett?

Drew flipped to the beginning of the oldest ledger and ran his finger down a column. "It appears Mr. Cadogan owed Haskett money. At the largest point, Mr. Cadogan owed seventy-five pounds, but it does not appear to be a gambling debt."

"How much is still outstanding?"

"Nothing. The account was closed two weeks ago, paid in full. Mr. Cadogan had been making payments right along in the amount of two pounds per week, which wasn't seeing him get ahead much, as the interest on the loan amounted to fifteen shillings a week."

"That's robbery." How did one dig oneself out of a hole like that?

"I agree. But two weeks ago he put down the sum of fifty pounds and cleared the debt."

Where had a London carriage driver gotten fifty pounds? Cadogan's carriage was old, though well cared for, his horses of ordinary breeding, and his clients not the wealthiest. He worked long hours, hustling to find fares. Add to that he had the overhead of stabling and feeding the mares. He'd also had to buy a new horse to replace the retiring Sprite. He had mentioned coming into funds recently, though he had not specified the origin of the money.

Daniel jotted some notes, plus questions he would have for Cadogan. The man was above reproach and would surely have satisfactory answers. He'd saved Daniel's life, after all. Such a man could not be up to anything nefarious.

"Anything else?"

"Not that I have found. The majority of the clients recorded here also appear in the ledgers of other gaming and gentlemen's clubs I have examined. It is a sort of fraternity. Those who gamble tend to have accounts at several establishments. A few are more in debt than is prudent, but there were no real surprises. The moneylending and possible blackmail—and that is conjecture on my part—I have seen such things before."

"You understand that everything you see here is confidential?" Daniel pointed to the leather tomes, mindful of the promise he had made to Sir Michael to safeguard the information. "Unless or until there is a trial and your testimony is needed, you are to say nothing about what you've found."

Drew nodded, sucking on his teeth again in a mannerism that made Daniel's skin prickle. How did his coworkers stand it?

"I am used to keeping my clients' secrets." He rose, patted his pockets, searched the table, then reached for the glasses perched on his nose. He folded the stems and put them into a cloth case. He'd forgotten the pencil behind his ear. "You know where to find me. What should I do with these?" He pointed to his notes.

"I will keep them with the ledgers under lock and key for now. Thank you for your assistance." Daniel opened the interview room door.

Sir Michael leapt away as if startled, then blinked, swallowing. "All finished? Find anything of note? I was just passing . . . on my way upstairs, you know?"

Daniel stifled a frustrated laugh. Listening at a door? He wouldn't have suspected Sir Michael would stoop to that measure, and then to do such a clumsy job of covering it up?

"Inquiries are ongoing. There are a few things I must follow up on. Mr. Drew has been most helpful."

"Has he? What did you find?"

Mr. Drew donned his hat and picked up his cane. "I shall be going, gentlemen." He edged past Sir Michael, who raised his hand as if to stop the accountant, then let it fall.

"Thank you, Mr. Drew. Send the bill for your time." Daniel went to close the door, but the guv's hand pressed the glass panel, forcing it wide.

"Let me help you." Sir Michael all but leapt into the room.

"No need. I'll just take these upstairs to the magistrate's chamber. He requested that I bring them to him for safekeeping. When I told him you were concerned that certain information would be compromised, he agreed and said he would see to locking the evidence in his personal document safe for the time being." Daniel closed the books quickly, tucking Drew's lists and findings inside and away from Sir Michael's prying eyes.

Sir Michael stiffened and withdrew his hands. "I see. I could take them for you, since I am headed that way."

"Don't trouble yourself." Daniel made his voice as annoyingly cheerful as possible. "I need to speak with the magistrate's clerk in any case." He hefted the books and waited for Sir Michael to move. When he didn't, Daniel went the other way around the table.

"I must know what you've found. I am your employer, and you are required to make regular reports on your progress in your cases."

"Sir, with all due respect, I have no progress to report. Once I have followed up on the leads contained in these books, I will inform you. For now, you can rest assured that Mr. Haskett kept excellent records."

Upstairs, Daniel relinquished the ledgers into the magistrate's keeping, spoke briefly with the clerk, just to be true to his word, then went in search of Owen.

Daniel found him in the investigators' room, sitting at Ed's vacant desk with a stack of folders before him. "Where is Mr. Beck, and did the clerks find anything on Bobby Puck?" He noted that Ed and Owen had made a good fist of rectifying the disaster that had been wrought upon his desk.

"Mr. Beck went to Bethnal Green to speak with the family of the footman George Burghley. He's expected back late." Owen picked up a yellow slip, the paper used for interoffice communications. "The clerks found plenty on Puck, but I don't know that it will do us much good."

"What did they find?"

"He was a known quantity several years ago. Petty theft, which got him a stretch in Newgate, and a few mentions as a possible accomplice here and there, questioned by a magistrate or a constable. But the most recent entry is from 1807."

"He's listed as a possible accomplice? For what? And an accomplice to whom?"

"Horse theft, robbery, malicious damage." Owen thumbed through the folders. "It was suspected that he was part of Black John Killington's gang. But from what I've read here, every crime committed within a hundred miles of London in the eighteen oughts was attributed to Black John."

Daniel hadn't been in London at that time, but the stories were legendary. Black John vied with Dick Turpin as being the worst criminal of the last hundred years.

"So our mysterious Bobby Puck may or may not have been a lackey for John Killington, and he's dropped out of sight almost ten years ago." Daniel sat at his desk and propped his elbow on the blotter, resting his chin on his hand. "Gaol, death, or reformed?"

"I'd place my money on one of the first two. Not many criminals truly reform."

"Anyone in that stack have the initials H.C.? Could Bobby Puck have changed his name to avoid prosecution?"

Owen let his fingers ripple down the tabs on the folders. "Not an H.C. amongst them. Doesn't mean he's not in the archives, just that there's no H.C. that cross-referenced with the name Bobby Puck. But Mr. Berry will be out for your blood if you ask him to comb the archives for all cases where the initials H.C. appear. It would be an impossible undertaking."

With a sigh, Daniel sat back in his chair, drumming his fingers on the arms. "He's done monumental work finding Bobby Puck at all. Are any of those cases involving a man who was beaten and deposited at St. Bart's hospital? Rosebreen mentioned that he'd heard the name Puck in relation to a man who died as a result of a beating. Evidently the man had somehow crossed Puck and gotten trounced for his sins."

Owen frowned and shook his head. "Nothing like that in these files. Was it reported? Who was the man?"

"Another lead for us to follow up. We might be on a hiding to nothing with this angle on the case. The note in the ledger might be nothing at all. It stuck out, unlike anything else written in those books. And Bobby Puck having a criminal past . . . I can't seem to let it go. There's something there, but whether it has anything to do with our case and the murder of Haskett, the footman, and the abduction of street children is anyone's guess."

"Ed says never to ignore a gut feeling. If it bothers you, he says, it's worth following up."

Daniel stood. "Then we should follow up on a few things."

Chapter 13

DANIEL SIDESTEPPED A MAN HURRYING down the path in the Southwark area of the metropolis, his head bent, not appearing to see anyone in his path. Owen wasn't as agile, bumping into the fellow, and if Daniel hadn't been watching for the maneuver, he would have missed it.

"Hold there," Daniel said as he grabbed the man's wrist, twisting it up behind him and pressing the man's chest against the bricks of the building next to them. "Light fingers, haven't you?"

Owen slapped his coat pocket, eyes widening. "Why, you—" He grabbed the man's other hand, wrenching the coin purse from his fingers.

Daniel spun the fellow around, pinning him to the wall with his truncheon pressed to the man's chest. "Just because you have the ability to do something doesn't mean you should. And it's a foolish man who tries to steal from a Bow Street investigator."

The man's eyes widened, white showing starkly against his dirty face. His hat tipped up from the pressure on the back of the brim, revealing a bald pate with a few hairs combed over his dome.

"I never knew, guv. Please. I'm just tryin' to feed me family." A fleck of spittle formed at the corner of his mouth. The acrid scent of gin wafted on his breath.

Daniel reached down and pulled a heavy gold watch from the man's pocket. "You could always take this to a receiver's shop. Unless you stole it?" He flicked open the case. Frankton's on Church Street in Soho. "This has a high tone for a man dressed as you are. Perhaps I should keep this, check it against our stolen goods list, and return it to its rightful owner. If no one claims it in the next fortnight, you may come to the court and retrieve it."

"You're stealing from me." The man wriggled, but Owen stepped close.

"He's not. He's establishing your right to have such an expensive timepiece as this when you've been caught stealing from me. If I press charges, you'll find yourself as a resident of Coldbath Fields."

The man sagged. "I'm caught betwixt the snout and the tail."

Daniel stood him up. "Get out of here. If no one claims the watch, you can come for it, but I wouldn't advise it unless it truly belongs to you." He pushed the man away. "And see that you keep your light fingers to yourself."

Owen tucked the coin purse back into his inside jacket pocket. "You'd think I would know better. I live in a neighborhood just like this. Pocket-divers are thick on the ground south of the river. I got distracted looking for this Thurston Row."

"We crossed the river where the shoeshine boy said. But nobody we've asked knows of Thurston Row or anything like it." Daniel put his hands on his hips, looking up and down Blackfriars Road. "Do you think he was lying to us?"

"He seemed sincere. What should we do now?" Owen checked the sky, where gray clouds gathered. "Feels like rain coming." He flicked up the collar on his coat as a fresh breeze scudded up the street, blowing bits of debris and refuse ahead of it. No street-sweeper boys worked here. No one trimmed the weeds that sprang up in the cracks. No one had the time or money or will. Subsistence living, putting daily bread on the table, was the order of the day. Small shops, tenements, boardinghouses. No parks or wide squares or spacious townhouses to be seen.

If Daniel's mother hadn't been sent to a country estate to get her away from Rotherhide, Daniel would most likely have been raised in such an area, or at the Foundling Hospital or an orphanage. Though some of his lodgings had been humble as a child, at least he had been in the country, with open spaces, fewer people, and land and animals to work. And his current housing was respectable, in a genteel neighborhood.

He glanced up at the street sign fastened to the building above, trying to remember what the child had said. If they couldn't find the street themselves, they would have to go back to the boy tomorrow and pay him to lead them back.

Humbling.

He blinked and laughed. "We're simpletons, Owen." He shook his head.

"What do you mean?" Owen bristled.

"Thurston Row." He pointed to the soot-grimed metal sign. "The boy had no front teeth."

"Sureton Row." Owen smacked his forehead. "Of course. Thurston. Sureton."

"Swann."

He turned. Ed hurried toward them with long strides. "I've had a terrible time tracking you two down." He huffed a little. "I've traipsed all over the city today. Bethnal Green to speak to George Burghley's parents. No joy there, I'm afraid. Then I went back to Eaton Square and broadened my search for witnesses to the footman's death, and then to the Olympian Club to see if anyone had any more information. The guv is going to balk at all the carriage fare I've accrued today."

"What did you learn?" Daniel asked. He would grasp on to anything that would lead them in a specific direction.

"I found a servant at the house on the opposite side of Eaton Square from Miss Montgomery's residence, who had been sent on an errand by his employer and was just coming home at the time the bootboy was abducted. This servant heard a commotion and saw a tall, lean man toss something into a carriage and climb inside and the carriage took off."

"Could he describe the carriage?"

"He said it was fancy, but not like a peerage carriage. No crest on the door, but shiny enough to reflect moonlight. And the horses were mismatched. One was a bay or dark brown. He wasn't sure of the other, but it had a small blaze of white, and it wasn't as dark as the other."

"I'm not certain that helps us much. Carriages of that description are much of a muchness." Daniel tapped his pencil on his notebook.

"Alone it might not, but I also spoke with a midwife in the area of the Olympian Club who was out and about the night Haskett got murdered, and she saw a lean man climb into a carriage that exactly fits the description given by the servant in Eaton Square. Shiny, with mismatched horses, one with a blaze."

Daniel considered this. "It's not enough to identify a suspect, but if we do find one, we can use it to confirm identity. Will either of those witnesses be credible if they're needed to testify in court?"

"The servant will be. Very well spoken, very proper. I don't know about the midwife. She's probably excellent at her vocation, but not eloquent. She's very poor, elderly. I trust her description, but I don't know as she would present herself well in court."

"We'll add both their names and their testimonies to the case report when we get back to Bow Street." Daniel closed his notebook and returned it to his pocket. "We're looking for a Dougie who lives on Sureton Row, who keeps a place where street children can sleep. At least one of the missing children was staying at his place, possibly more."

"I'll join you."

"You and Owen start on that side. I'll take this one. Knock on every door. The street is short, so it shouldn't take much time to find the place."

Daniel entered the tobacconist's shop on the corner. The sweet, sharp tang of the smoking weed hit his nostrils. He didn't mind the smell of unlit tobacco. It reminded him of his past. The head groom at Imberlay Manor had kept a pipe and tobacco pouch in his coat pocket. When he and Daniel had finished the chores for the day, they would go down the lane to the croft allotted to the groom, where they would sit before the fire on a high-backed bench, and the groom would open his tobacco pouch for Daniel to sniff. Then he'd pack the bowl of his clay pipe, take a straw whisp from his shirt pocket, light it from the fire, and puff away until the tobacco glowed red. His wife would give Daniel a hunk of bread and her husband a pint of ale, and they would talk about the horses before Daniel had to scurry back to his mother's quarters for a quick dinner before bedtime.

Of all the jobs Daniel had been given as a child, working in the stables had been his favorite.

He struck gold on his first try. The proprietor of the tobacco shop knew the house Daniel sought. "Three doors down and across. With the blue door. That's the place. Kids everywhere."

Daniel emerged on the street and spotted Owen and Ed coming out of the pub.

"Down the way," Owen called.

Trotting across the cobbles, Daniel joined them. "Think of all the time we would have saved if we had figured out 'Thurston Row' sooner." He grinned and headed toward the blue door. There was one step but no forecourt, the door opening right onto the street. No knocker, so he tapped on the door with his knuckles.

Noises—a chair scraping perhaps, and footsteps—indicated someone was home. The door opened a crack, and a small face peeped out from about doorknob height.

"We're looking for someone called Dougie. Is he at home?" Daniel asked.

The round eyes blinked, and a braid fell over the girl's shoulder as she leaned around the door's edge. "No." She closed the door in his face.

Owen laughed. "Short and sweet."

Daniel knocked again. More scuffling, and the knob turned. A small face peered around the edge, grinning, different from the first. Putting his hand against the blue panel, guarding against another abrupt dismissal, Daniel asked the boy, "May we speak to the lady of the house please? Mrs. Dougie?"

"She wants to know who you are and what you want." The boy pushed his dark forelock out of his eyes. About seven or eight, he had a dirt smudge on his cheek and frayed edges on his collar.

"Tell her we're Bow Street officers, and we want a word with her." Ed held up his truncheon, with the brass plate engraved with his name and occupation.

The child's mouth opened, and he would have shut the door if not for Daniel blocking it. "Go fetch her."

Like a wraith, the boy disappeared, but unlike a wraith, his footsteps thudded and scudded on the plank floor. Daniel recognized the sound of feet in shoes too large for them. He'd worn ill-fitting shoes much of his childhood.

A woman came to the door, wiping her hands on a towel tied about her waist. She had faded yellow hair, tired blue eyes, and red chapped fingers. "Help you, gentlemen?" Her voice held a wary edge.

"We're from Bow Street. My name is Mr. Swann, and these are my fellow officers, Mr. Beck and Mr. Wilkinson. We've come about a boy named Matthew who has gone missing from his place of work."

Her brow furrowed, and she nodded. "Have you found him? Is he in trouble? He didn't come home, and nobody seems to know where he is."

"Is he your son?"

She shook her head. "Hain't got no children of my own. We take in them what has a need."

"May we come in please?"

"O' course. Pardon my manners. We don't get many visitors." She stepped back and held the door. "Not grown ones, at any rate. Little ones I get in plenty."

The narrow hallway had a steep staircase running up on the left and a door opening to the right. Daniel stepped inside and removed his hat. "Is your husband expected home soon?"

"Nay, he'll be out till all hours with his work. Most nights he doesn't get in until half two or even three."

Daniel peeked into the room that opened off the hall. Not a sitting room, or at least no longer a sitting room. Bunks lined each wall, three high, with blankets pulled up over what looked like straw-filled pallets. Neat and tidy. Three boxes sat on the floor below each of the bottom bunks.

"That's the boys' room. The house is a two up, two down," the woman explained. "Boys' room and kitchen down here. Girls' room and me and my husband's upstairs." Two children, maybe three or four years old clung to her skirts, while the boy and girl who had answered the door hovered in the entryway to the kitchen.

"You provide lodging for street children?"

"Aye. Dougie brings them home, or they find their way to us. They come and go. Sometimes it's hard to keep track of who's here."

"Is that why you didn't report Matthew missing?"

"We did report it. At least my husband did. Matthew's been with us more than a year, and we care a great deal for him. We told the night watchman, and my husband says he told you lot at Bow Street."

Daniel looked to Owen. "Did you see a report?" Owen had first told Daniel about it. Had he taken someone's statement? He'd led Daniel to believe he was the one who'd noticed the child missing from his customary place.

"Only after I told you. I had Cadogan make a report so it would be official. I don't know about anyone else's."

The woman nodded, tucking a stray clump of hair back up into her mobcap. "That's right. Dougie reported it. Loves these kids like his own, Cadogan does."

Daniel's chin jerked up. "This is Cadogan's house? The carriage driver, Cadogan?" Cadogan, pronounced Cuh-DUG-ahn. Hence the nickname Dougie.

She nodded. "He's told me about you, sir. About how you nearly drowned at that mill in Hammersmith. I thought you knew it was his house."

Unpleasant pieces began to fit together. A carriage driver with a mismatched team seen at both murders. Street children, of which there were plenty right here, going missing. Even the axle grease, horsehair, and pollen—Cadogan had begun wearing flowers on his lapel and placing them in bud vases inside the cab—found on the murder victim Haskett. Cadogan's name in the Olympian ledgers.

Cadogan who had come into some money recently and paid off his debt.

Too many coincidences.

His gut hurt. Cadogan?

His friend.

The man who had saved his life.

Ed and Owen seemed equally stunned. They had known the carriage driver for as long as Daniel had . . . longer in Ed's case.

Why would Cadogan steal children? And why would he report it? To throw investigators off his trail?

Was he somehow profiting off their disappearances? He didn't live in splendor, but he had purchased a new young horse after pensioning off Sprite. And he had paid a debt to the murder victim Haskett. Where had he gotten that money? From Haskett's desktop when he killed him?

"Can you show me where Matthew's bunk was?" Daniel asked.

"Bottom one, on the right of the door. We've put someone else there now, o' course."

"The boxes contain the children's personal things?" He moved into the room.

"Aye. Their bits and bobs, any extra clothes if they have them. A few trinkets. I moved Matthew's into the kitchen for when he comes back."

"Would you show my colleague?"

"This way."

Ed followed her, his face somber.

Daniel's mind felt as if he'd been punched, and the moment Ed and Mrs. Cadogan were out of earshot, he let out a long breath.

"It isn't true, whatever you're thinking. Cadogan has nothing to do with these children going missing, and certainly nothing to do with murdering two people," Owen whispered fiercely. "He would never do that."

"I don't want to believe it either, but how do you explain the evidence? Two witnesses put someone fitting his description at the scenes—and even more, his carriage and horses' descriptions. He's got several connections to the missing children. Not to mention his name was written in the Olympian Club ledgers."

"Did you ask him about it? It could be something innocent." Every plane and angle of Owen's face was taut.

"I haven't had the opportunity. If he can explain it to my satisfaction, then fine. But we have to talk to him." Daniel prayed these were coincidences and he would not have to arrest his friend.

"You will arrest this man without delay." Sir Michael glared at Daniel. Ed and Owen stood behind Daniel in Sir Michael's office. "Why are you dawdling? You have the evidence."

"But, sir, we know this man, know his character. Why would he kill Haskett and the footman and steal children? He's got a houseful of street urchins." When the trio had returned to Bow Street, Sir Michael had demanded a reckoning of their progress on the case, and they had been forced to divulge their findings.

"You won't know his motives until you arrest him and question him. Perhaps he was seeking to reduce the number of street urchins under his care. He wouldn't be the first." Sir Michael sounded as if he thought Daniel had pillow ticking for brains.

At the moment, Daniel felt as if this might be true.

"You will go upstairs and get a warrant, and I want this man behind bars on a charge of double murder before dark."

"Sir," Ed offered, "perhaps we should go back to the club and fetch the man of all work who says he might have seen the killer. We have some witnesses who saw a man leaving each crime scene. We could fetch one or two of them and have them observe Cadogan covertly. They could look at his carriage and see if it matched what they saw. If they tell us no, then we don't have to arrest him."

"Absurd. Arrest him and then get your so-called witnesses to identify him. The preponderance of evidence is there. If this was any other person, someone not known personally to you all, he'd already be behind bars."

Daniel knew this was true, but he still couldn't reconcile what he knew of Cadogan and the details of the murders.

The missing children bothered him as well. Why would a man nearly overrun with street children in his own house abduct them? What purpose could he possibly have for taking them?

"Well, don't just stand there, or I shall reassign the case to an investigator who does not play favorites with his friends. When the man is in custody, you will return those ledgers to the Olympian Club, and we will hear no more about the matter."

They left Sir Michael's office, and in the hall, Daniel met Ed's and Owen's bleak eyes.

"I suppose we have no choice, but it feels wrong." Owen scuffed his toe on the floorboards.

"I agree. There's something amiss here." Ed shoved his hands into his pockets.

"There's nothing to be done for it. I'll see Lord Creevy and get the warrant. You two put your heads together and think about where Cadogan might be at this time of the evening."

Warrant in hand, they set out. Usually Cadogan was fairly easy to find, as he seemed to know when he was needed and turned up, but this time he wasn't outside the Opera House or the gentlemen's clubs of White's or Boodles. If it had been a Wednesday, Daniel would have expected him to be outside Almack's waiting on a fare.

Finally they came upon another jarvey who had seen him. "He's at the Harp and Hare having a bite to eat. At least he was when I left there not ten minutes ago. Why you want him? I'll give you a ride anywhere you want to go."

"Thank you, good sir, but it's Cadogan we need."

The carriage driver shrugged and climbed aboard his vehicle while Daniel turned up the street. Sure enough, the familiar carriage and team stood at the curb before the public house.

Daniel studied the carriage, standing on tiptoe to see inside. Shiny, and yes, there was a flower in the bud vase. A fresh pot of axle grease dangled from a hook beneath the cab. The mares, Lola and Addie, stood relaxed in their harness, accustomed to waiting.

Lola, dark bay, glossy and sleek. And Addie, the new mare, dun with a white blaze. Sprite had also had a blaze.

When they entered the pub, heads turned and conversations ceased. Cadogan sat at the back of the room, a plate before him. He wore a flower in his lapel.

"Evening, gents. Need a ride? I'm nearly finished." He scooped one more spoonful into his mouth and reached for his hat.

"Cadogan . . ." Daniel's throat hurt. "I'm arresting you on suspicion of murder. Please come with us."

Someone dropped a utensil onto a tin plate, and several gasped.

"Murder?" Cadogan looked befuddled. "Who am I supposed to have killed? Is this some sort of amusement?"

"No one is amused. I'm arresting you for the murders of Jericho Haskett and George Burghley and the abductions of six children." Daniel motioned for Cadogan to rise.

The driver looked from one face to another, still not moving. "I don't know where you got your information, but I've never killed anyone, and I wouldn't steal a street child. I'm the one who reported children missing, remember?"

"We'll talk about all that later. Get up." Daniel felt lower than the gutter, arresting his friend in such a place.

As if in a stupor, Cadogan rose. Ed took one elbow and Daniel the other, and they marched him out of the crowded pub.

At the curb, Cadogan stopped. "My team. My cab."

Owen touched him on the shoulder. "I'll see to them. I know where you stable them, and I'll see they're fed and your missus knows where you are."

Daniel had never felt so oppressed by his job. In most cases, when he arrested a murderer, he was elated and a sense of satisfaction settled into his chest.

Now he felt awful. How could he deny the evidence? And yet something in his heart told him there was more to the story.

"Where are the missing children, Cadogan? If you return them to us, it might go better for you at trial." Daniel knew, though, there was precious little chance that Cadogan would escape the noose if he was convicted. The best that could be hoped for was deportation to the Antipodes.

Cadogan said nothing, setting his jaw, his eyes going so stony, Daniel hardly recognized him.

He wouldn't have time to get more out of the carriage driver tonight. Cadogan would have to spend the night in Newgate, where he would be questioned tomorrow. Ed would find the witnesses he had spoken to earlier and get them to come by the gaol to identify Cadogan.

Daniel had a pressing engagement that he had assumed would be his most difficult task of the day but which now paled in comparison to arresting his friend for murder.

Chapter 14

JULIETTE FELT MUCH THE SAME as she had not so many weeks ago when she stood at the top of the Montgomery staircase for her debut ball. An important night ahead. People to meet, dances, dinner. This time, however, a new layer of excitement and promise filled her.

Daniel was invited.

It would probably be wise if they did not encounter each other, considering what had happened last time, and no doubt the dowager would do her best to ensure they stayed in separate spheres.

But she could meet his eyes across the room, perhaps share a few dance steps if they happened to meet in a foursome on the floor.

She would need to be circumspect, however. If she let her expression reveal her feelings, the entire room would know. It was just such interactions that Uncle Bertie had been schooling her to watch for in others.

The Haverly Party. That was what people were calling it. A prestigious invitation to the gathering of the Season. No expense had been spared—everything had been planned meticulously with the guests' enjoyment in mind.

The house was full of flowers and candlelight. Brass and silver gleamed, and velvet upholstery looked plush enough to sink into. Charlotte had hired extra servants for the evening, who stood ready to assist any guest who even hinted at needing anything.

The foyer could hardly hold another person, and the butler had opened the pocket doors to the receiving rooms to allow the crush to spread out a bit.

The dowager, true to her declared intentions, approached and threaded her arm through Juliette's as if she feared her charge would race away into the night to elope should the dowager let loose of her.

"It will be the talk of the year. Tomorrow's papers will be full of accounts of the party." The dowager smiled, a trifle smug. "I took the liberty of inviting a few newspaper men to look in. Not to intrude, mind you. Just to observe and report."

Does Charlotte know? Or Marcus? Sometimes the dowager's "liberties" overstepped her position.

Juliette kept a close eye on the arrivals, each person or couple presenting the footman with an embossed invitation, their name quietly checked against a list held by Marcus's secretary. Mr. Partridge, Marcus's man-of-all-work, stood on the opposite side of the doorway, arms folded, eyes sharp, looking for trouble before it arose.

Her heart beat quickly, and taking a deep breath seemed futile.

Every nerve in her body buzzed like bees' wings.

"I've arranged for Viscount Coverdale to dance with you first and to take you into supper. He's the son of the Earl of Winslow." The dowager tapped Juliette's arm with her fan. "Perfectly respectable."

She nodded. Henry Winslow had been a guest at her parents' last dinner party. He was pleasant enough.

"Ah, madam, I fear you will have to rescind the offer." Marcus came up behind them, smoothing his lapels. "I accepted a request earlier in the week for Juliette's partnership in the first set as well as permission to lead her in to supper at midnight." He smiled blandly, then quirked his eyebrow at Juliette over his mother's head.

The dowager spluttered. "What? Who? I am this young lady's chaperone. All such requests should go through me."

"Yes, you are her chaperone, but I am her temporary guardian. At least I was. Look who has arrived." He lifted his chin toward the entrance.

"Uncle Bertie." Joy surged through her, and Juliette removed the dowager's hand from her arm, raising her hem to hurry across the foyer to greet him.

"Hello, chicken. You're looking well." He embraced her, pressing his cheek to hers. "And you smell good too. Much better than Dartmoor Prison, I can assure you."

She laughed, relief at having someone of her own with her again making her light-headed. She hadn't realized how much she had missed her uncle's wit and banter. "It's something, at least, to know I smell better than a prison."

"How have the Haverlys been treating you?" He handed his evening cloak and hat to a footman and took her elbow, looking around. "I say, they've done this place up like Vauxhall on a carnival night. And it's just as crowded."

"They've been very kind, though the dowager has been her usual charming self. I'm so glad you're here." She squeezed his upper arm as they threaded their way through the guests.

"Let's go brave the dragon. By the look in her eyes, she's ready to breathe fire. What have you been doing in my absence that has her so stirred up?"

Juliette tugged his arm, stood on tiptoe, and whispered in his ear. "She caught me in an embrace with Daniel Swann. She's been like a prison warden ever since."

Bertie laughed, throwing his head back. "Oh, Juliette, you do like to get into trouble, don't you? I thought I told you to be circumspect. If word gets out, Daniel will have to make an honest woman of you."

"Shhhhh." She jerked his elbow. "Behave yourself."

Marcus came forward, and Uncle Bertie bowed. "Your Grace. Thank you for your kind invitation tonight and for looking after Juliette in my absence. I hope she was not too much of a bother."

"Not at all, Thorndike. We added her to the horde of women who have taken over the place in the last fortnight, and she fit right in. Charlotte has enjoyed her company, as have Countess Whitelock and Mrs. Sinclair. I only wish my sister, Sophie, could be here. I feel she and Lady Juliette have much in common and would be fast friends."

Juliette caught the dowager's eye and realized she had bolted away from the woman without begging her leave. Heat surged into her cheeks, and she was grateful once again for the dark coloring she had inherited from her mother, which didn't show blushes as painfully as those with traditional English-rose complexions.

"I do beg your pardon for rushing away, Your Grace." She spoke to Marcus but included the dowager in her apology. "I was so eager to see my uncle that I momentarily forgot myself."

The dowager sniffed but said nothing.

"I also apologize, Your Grace, for dashing off without hearing to whom you have entrusted me for the first dance." Juliette smiled brightly at Marcus, but her face felt stiff.

The duke tugged his gloves on tighter and smiled. "I suppose, now that your uncle is here, he will need to give his approval, but a certain young man of our acquaintance did ask for the honor. He's just arriving now."

She looked over her shoulder to the front door, her hand gripping Bertie's arm.

"Ouch." He removed her fingers. "Careful there, Jules. That's my damaged wing."

She barely heard him.

Daniel removed his tall hat and handed his invitation to the footman. His eyes roved from one face to the next until they locked with hers, and her heart galloped around her chest.

He looked . . . he was . . . whew. From his carefully tousled hair to the shine on his black shoes, he looked the picture of sartorial elegance. Beau Brummel wouldn't have found fault with him. Pristine cravat, shirtfront, and gloves and inky-black waistcoat and breeches. A strong, invisible cord stretched between them, a thousand things that didn't need to be said echoing through her heart. And Marcus had approved of him partnering her for a set?

"I forbid it." The dowager's cane tip cracked against the floor. "Marcus Haverly, I absolutely forbid it. Not when she is under my care." She ground the words through tight teeth. "Her parents would be appalled, as would the rest of society. For once in your life, stop being a rogue and think of the consequences of your actions."

The lines at the corners of Marcus's mouth deepened, and his eyes narrowed. He turned his head to look at his mother.

The dowager must have sensed his displeasure, for she opened her mouth and then closed it, fumbling for her fan and flicking it open.

"Madam?" A silky, dangerous inquiry full of portent. "Perhaps you should check on some of our other guests."

The fan increased in speed, and the dowager reddened. "I believe I will go see how Charlotte is getting along. Sir Bertrand, I leave Lady Juliette in your care."

Daniel edged around people, keeping his eyes on Juliette, a smile lighting his face. If they were to keep their attachment secret, they should probably stop wearing such telling expressions.

He must have reached the same conclusion, for he paused, collected himself, then approached the duke. "Good evening, Your Grace." He bowed, then looked at the guests, speaking over the many conversations flowing around them. "I believe, though I am no expert, that your party appears to have all the hallmarks of a 'crush.'"

"One can hope. Good evening, Mr. Swann."

Daniel turned. "Sir Bertrand, Lady Juliette. So nice to see you again. I wasn't aware that you had returned to London, Sir Bertrand. I trust you concluded your business satisfactorily?"

"I don't know that there is a satisfactory conclusion to what happened at Dartmoor, but suffice it to say, I have made my report to my superiors. They may make of it what they wish." Bertie, suave as ever, shot his cuffs.

Daniel gave his attention to Juliette, and his sharp gaze sent a thrill through her. She held out her hand, regretting that they both wore gloves. He bent over it, but his eyes never left hers. "Lady Juliette, you look beautiful tonight."

The deep timbre of his voice feathered across her skin, and she wished with all her might that she could walk into his arms and never leave the safety of his embrace. Yet she knew eyes were on her, as they were any debutante when a man was near. Added to that was the news of the inheritance petition that had swept through London society. People were talking, spreading rumors, voicing opinions of the parties involved. She must be careful, not only for her reputation but also for her parents' and her host's. She must do nothing untoward that might jeopardize the case.

"Good evening, Mr. Swann."

"Juliette, this is the man who asked for the honor of the first set. With your uncle's permission, I shall tender you into Mr. Swann's care. And . . ." Marcus looked up the staircase to where Charlotte and the dowager stood on the landing. "My duchess is signaling that it is time to enter the ballroom."

"By all means," Bertie said. "But"—he leaned in and winked—"I'll be watching you two."

Juliette rested her fingertips on Daniel's offered forearm, feeling the warmth through the fabric of his sleeve. Her fan dangled from her wrist, and her white skirts, scattered with silver embroidered stars, swished as he led her up the stairs. They were one pair of dozens, but for all Juliette cared, they could have been alone.

Was this the first of many social functions they would attend together once he was declared the heir? Or . . . She swallowed hard. Was this perhaps the last time? The petition to Attorney General Sir William Garrow would be made soon. A decision could come quickly and change their lives forever.

Daniel and Juliette were near the front of the procession, and when they entered the ballroom, she stopped, gasping. Though she had heard many of the party plans, Charlotte had kept everyone out of the ballroom while preparations were being made. She'd wanted it to be a surprise for all their guests.

And surprise it was. Every chandelier blazed with the light of a hundred candles. Wall sconces with mirrored backs illuminated tall urns of pink and white flowers surrounded by greenery. An orchestra played from the balcony at one end of the room.

But Juliette could not look away from the floor. Where polished parquet had been last week, a pastel mural now graced the space. The Haverly coat of arms had been chalked on the center of the floor, surrounded by floral garland, cherubs, and around the whole, a Greek key design.

Chalking the ballroom floor was reserved for only the most prestigious events. Juliette had heard the Prince Regent had gone to such lengths for one of his parties at Carlton House, but she had never seen it in person.

It seemed a shame to step on it. Others must have had the same thought, for they edged along the perimeter. With each new couple who arrived, there were more oohs and ahhs.

Charlotte's party was a triumph.

"Whew, that must have taken the artists days." Daniel shook his head.

"The duchess has kept everyone out of the ballroom for the entire week. We were forbidden to even peek. I saw the flowers arrive. I wonder how they managed to light all those candles without smudging the floor."

He laughed. "You would think of something so practical." His eyes softened. "The room looks beautiful, but you are breathtaking."

She took a deep breath, treasuring his words, the warmth in his eyes, and the moment.

The room filled, and they were crowded closer together, which she didn't mind, and from the grin on Daniel's face, he wasn't hating the contact either. The orchestra played a flourish, and Marcus entered with Charlotte on his arm. Without hesitation, he led her across the beautifully chalked floor to stand in the center of his family crest. Charlotte wore a turquoise gown with a lovely shawl patterned with peacock feathers. She looked up at her husband, and his return gaze held such pride and love that Juliette's heart ached with joy for them.

The music stopped, and voices subsided.

"Thank you all for coming. Welcome to our home," Marcus said. "We're honored and blessed that you are all here. We hope you will enjoy yourselves tonight. There are refreshments available, a cardroom down the hall, and of course, dancing. If you will take your places for the first set?"

Marcus escorted Charlotte off the floor. In her condition, she wouldn't be dancing, of course, but it saddened Juliette to think that once one married, it was considered bad form to dance with one's spouse. She should cherish every dance she and Daniel could share.

The Whitelocks apparently didn't care about form, for Evan led Diana onto the floor into their places in line. Daniel and Juliette joined them, forming the first foursome for the first dance.

"Sprigs of Laurel, ladies and gentlemen," the conductor called from the balcony.

Juliette almost clapped. She loved this dance. It was the first she could remember learning at finishing school. Daniel pulled his gloves tighter, his gaze intent.

She gave herself over to enjoying the dance, relishing the strength of Daniel's grasp as he turned her, the feel of his body as he passed behind her, the warmth of his smile as they stepped down the line.

As they went down the row, the second couples in the foursomes stepped up, and Daniel and Juliette joined a new foursome, this time with Bertie and Philippa Cashel. Uncle Bertie raised one eyebrow, his expression wry. It wasn't often he could be coerced into dancing. He preferred to spend his time in the gaming room. Unattached males dancing at a ball sent the signal that they were looking for a bride.

Bertie could take care of himself when it came to matchmaking mamas, however, and he was hardly in any danger from Miss Cashel. He'd survived heart-whole to this point, and she was not in the market for a husband.

They performed the foursome movements flawlessly and changed places to form a new one. Daniel paused, causing her to bump into him, and she jerked her attention to where he was looking.

The next couple in line . . . Alonzo Darby resplendent in evening dress . . . but the black scowl on his face boded no good.

"You," he hissed, glaring at Daniel.

"Alonzo, please. This is not the time." Juliette kept her voice low as they pinwheeled. "For the Haverlys' sake, do not cause a scene." She imbued her tone with enough starch to make the dowager duchess proud, and it brought Alonzo up short.

His face turned to stone, and he behaved as if neither Juliette nor Daniel existed. His partner, a pretty blonde young lady in debutante white, shot him a confused look, but the dance steps soon took them farther up the line.

"I am sorry. I didn't realize he would be here." Daniel squeezed her fingers on the turn.

"It was inevitable, I suppose, that you would meet at a social function at some point. I'm sure the viscountess is here somewhere too." Juliette felt as if the lights had dimmed as the tension of the inheritance dispute invaded her thoughts once again.

Pray the song would end soon, preventing them from having to pair with Alonzo and his partner again, at least during this set. *Why does he have to spoil things? This night, this dance, it belongs to Daniel and me.*

Remaining composed on the outside, she smiled, putting a playful look into her eyes. "Never a dull moment when you and I attend the same social function, is there?"

"What do you mean?"

"Let me recount for you. There was the stolen-painting incident at my debut. Then the time you tried to arrest me at a musical recital and reception. Not to mention the wild doings the first time we attended Almack's on the same night. You got involved in a brawl in the cardroom when you arrested Mrs. Fairchild." She gave him an impish grin. "If it is all the same to you, could this evening pass without making a memory of that sort? Surely nothing tonight will have anything to do with your current case."

A shadow passed over his features. "When we have a moment, I have to tell you there has been a development in the murder inquiry." His mouth took a grim set.

Juliette sighed, wishing she could help him bear whatever burden beset him. "Perhaps we can discuss it at supper?" Though they could not dance another set together tonight, she would have his companionship during the midnight break to anticipate.

The music for the first dance ended with a flourish, and she curtsied low as Daniel bowed. After a brief pause, a new song began, and this time they danced mostly in silence. Their paths did not cross with Alonzo or Uncle Bertie, and Juliette gave herself up to enjoying being with him.

When they had danced the requisite two dances in the first set, Daniel led her off the floor. Sadly, the designs were already disappearing from the chalk drawings, smeared and smudged under so many feet. The grit of the chalk did give good purchase to slick-soled dancing shoes, but the ephemeral nature of the artwork reminded Juliette of how quickly things could change.

One must hold on to what one had, because precious things could fade into the shadows when trouble loomed.

It amazed Daniel how quickly things could change. He'd been low, discouraged, and disappointed when he had arrested Cadogan. How could a man he thought of as a friend, a man who had saved his life, be a killer? How could he have abducted children? And why wouldn't he say where they were now?

Cadogan. His friend.

Tomorrow morning Daniel would question him. He'd instructed Ed to have the warden place him in a cell by himself, and he'd slipped Ed a few coins to pay for a blanket and food for Cadogan overnight. Prisoners without friends on the outside suffered greatly in Newgate.

Daniel had hurried through his ablutions, dashed across town to the party, and nearly fainted when he'd spied Juliette across the crowded foyer. A vision in white and silver, her dark hair glossy, her smile radiant. Seeing her was like getting kicked in the chest by a mule.

His mood lifted immediately, his thoughts veering away from his job and the case to the woman he loved so fiercely.

She danced as if borne on clouds, following his lead easily. She fit in this sumptuous environment as if she could flourish nowhere else. Perfect grace, perfect manners, perfect attire, perfectly suited to this world.

Daniel, thanks to his patron of so many years, could dance, dressed well, and had educated diction, but he still felt out of place in such rarified company as a guest at the Haverly Ball.

Which gave him pause. If he did not win his petition, he would lose his place of employment and have to find another means of supporting himself. He had the settlement from the earl, but if he lost his claim on the inheritance because the earl was found mentally unfit to have written his codicil, the courts could take that settlement away. He would be unemployed and destitute.

In which case he would be in no position to support a wife, much less a wife like Lady Juliette Thorndike. He could hardly ask her to leave her parents' palatial London townhouse or rolling country estate and join him in his two-room bachelor quarters.

He *had* to win the petition. There was no other solution.

Daniel sensed someone looking at him, and he glanced to his right.

Alonzo. Seething, eyes hard, jaw taut.

Pausing, Daniel got off step, having to hurry to catch up lest he cause a concertina along the line. Juliette's eyes met his, wide and questioning. Comprehension entered her gaze, and she teased him, no doubt trying to cajole him into a better frame of mind.

He tried, for her sake, but he couldn't stop thinking about what was at stake with the inheritance, all the people involved, and the possible outcomes. A fist of worry closed around his chest at all he would lose if the petition didn't go his way.

Daniel had no doubt that Haverly would keep him on at the agency, but he would most likely change Daniel's assignments. Daniel could find himself searching for anarchists, Luddites, domestic assassins. He would dress and act like a laborer, insinuate himself into the working man's life, attempting to avert trouble before it began.

Noble work, but a far cry from international spies, insider trading, treason in the aristocracy.

And a far cry from Juliette's world. If he couldn't join hers, he would not ask her to leave it all and join his.

He would have to be noble, though it would nearly kill him.

As if that was not enough to deal with, he also had his murder case to consider. He needed to tell the duke what had transpired, but there would be no appropriate time at a party for such deflating news.

When the set ended, Daniel offered Juliette his arm. "I suppose I should return you to your chaperone. Where is the dragon tonight?"

"She will be near the door to the refreshment room. Charlotte had a settee placed there especially for her, as it gives a good view of the doors to the balcony, the gaming room, and the entrance. She can watch all the comings and goings and give her opinions about everything." Juliette leaned close as she whispered, and the scent of roses drifted into his sphere. "Before we reach her, what's happened in your case? Have you found the killer? Have you found the children?"

"We have not located the missing children yet, but I have made an arrest." Daniel took a deep breath. "We've arrested the carriage driver Cadogan."

Juliette stopped. "No. Not that nice man?"

"I didn't want to believe it myself, but there it is." Misery swirled inside.

"Did he tell you why? And where are the children?"

"I'll get to the bottom of his reasons tomorrow when I question him further. He says he is innocent, that he doesn't know where the children are, and that we've got the wrong man. Perhaps a night in Newgate will bring him to the point of confession."

"I cannot believe it. I've ridden in his carriage several times and never once felt in danger."

"I'm hoping to have a moment or two with the duke, to tell him what's transpired and ask his opinion. I value it highly."

They were halfway across the dance floor when Daniel was forced to halt. Alonzo had come to stand in his way. Outrage stiffened every line and muscle of his half brother's frame.

"How dare you appear here? Get out. I won't have you present, pretending you're something you're clearly not." The words were thick and a trifle slurred. Had he been drinking already? "You've no right to show yourself amongst these people. This isn't your world."

Daniel shot an apologetic look to Juliette. People stared and whispered.

"I was invited to attend, the same as you. Now, please step aside." He kept his tone civil. *Do nothing to jeopardize the case. Everyone is looking, including some of the men who will be on the committee, should the case get that far.*

"I'll not step aside for the likes of you, you interloper." Alonzo tightened his hands into fists, his stance braced. "And you, Lady Juliette, are doing your reputation no favors being seen with this lick-spittle. People are talking."

Daniel's muscles tensed, his chest swelling. Gently he guided Juliette behind him, putting himself between her and Alonzo. "It is one thing to insult me, but leave the lady out of it. If you say another word against her, you will regret it." He spoke barely above a whisper.

"And what are you going to do? Plant me a facer? How barbaric." Alonzo sneered. "Something the lower classes would do, start a brawl."

"And I suppose it is high class to cause a scene at someone's party, insult their guests, and call a lady's reputation into question? We're finished talking. Get out of my way, or I will be forced to move you. You do not want to get into a physical confrontation with me, Darby. We would find out which of us had been trained in street fighting and which of us was a soft-as-butter dandy with no stomach for a real battle."

A calculating look entered Alonzo's eyes, and he glanced about them. No one was talking, and everyone was staring, as if waiting for an explosion.

Alonzo straightened, smoothing his lapels and tugging on his gloves. "I would not waste my efforts on you. I'll soon be proven right. You may as well enjoy your evening, because when I prevail, you'll never see the inside of a ballroom again."

He turned on his heel, grinding the chalk beneath his feet, and stalked away, head high, back stiff.

Daniel let out a sigh, relaxing his pose and offered his arm once again to Juliette. "I am sorry."

A shadow of unease crossed her pretty features. "I thought you might be forced to bloody his nose. That would have been terrible, for the duchess to have something so vulgar as drawing claret occur at her party. It would take attention off her fabulous ball."

Juliette was correct, and yet Daniel hadn't sought out the confrontation. It did gratify him that she seemed in no doubt as to who would have prevailed had it come to blows.

They approached the dowager's perch, and Daniel braced himself for her look of disapproval. She never sighted him without pursing her lips and narrowing her nostrils, as if she'd just smelled something unsavory, even when he hadn't nearly come close to knocking out a man's teeth in the middle of a ballroom.

A tall, lean man with a military bearing stood beside the duchess.

The dowager huffed, glared at Daniel, and spoke to Juliette as if he no longer existed.

"Lady Juliette, now that you've fulfilled my son's obligations, you may dance with Viscount Coverdale for the next set."

"Pleased." Coverdale offered his arm with a sharp bow, far too courtly for Daniel's liking.

Juliette curtsied to the dowager. "Thank you, Your Grace. It will be a pleasure to partner you, sir."

She looked at Daniel over her shoulder as the viscount led her back onto the dance floor. Though he wanted to race after her, claim her as his, and shove Coverdale away, he behaved himself. She would come to no harm on the dance floor under the watchful eye of the dowager, and he would give no one further cause to talk about him before the petition was heard. Bad enough with the kerfuffle between himself and Alonzo Darby. He could just imagine the outcry if he began challenging every man who so much as looked at Juliette.

He couldn't deny the jealousy though. Dancing with another partner raised no enthusiasm in him, though he supposed it was his obligation to his hostess. He wanted no one but Juliette. Not to mention, he might find it difficult to find anyone willing to trust their charge to him. He was here at the behest and suffrage of the Haverlys and under no illusions that the rest of the aristocracy was ready to embrace and claim him.

He did spy Anne Victon across the way. He'd partnered her to a dance at Almack's recently, at the command of his patron before he knew that patron was actually his grandfather. The young girl had found it difficult to be accepted into society, as her father wasn't an aristocrat, just immensely wealthy. Her father, Thomas Victon, stood at her side.

Daniel should ask her to dance the next set, but as he wended his way toward them, a young man spoke to Mr. Victon, received a nod, and offered his arm to Anne. She blushed prettily and allowed him to lead her away as the orchestra began the next set.

Perhaps a turn in the cardroom to while away some time until supper when he could be with Juliette again would see his mood improve.

When he reached the cardroom, Alonzo stood in the doorway. If Daniel didn't know better, he would think his half brother was baiting him, trying to get him to swing on him.

Daniel moved to go around him, but Alonzo moved too, blocking his way. Alonzo stepped closer, until their chests were just inches apart.

A hand touched Daniel's arm, and he tensed. Had Alonzo brought reinforcements?

But it was the Duchess of Haverly.

"Good evening, Mr. Swann. I am so glad you could come. I hope you are enjoying yourself?"

He bowed. "Yes, Your Grace. Thank you for your kind invitation."

"Oh, Mr. Darby. It is nice to see you. I hope I'm not interrupting anything important. I was in search of an escort to take a turn out on the balcony with me. I will not be dancing this evening, and it's suddenly quite warm in here. I believe my husband is outside getting a breath of fresh air, and I would like to join him."

Alonzo arranged his features into more pleasant lines and bowed. "I would be honored to escort you."

"Actually, it was Mr. Swann I was after, though your offer is kind. I need to speak to Daniel about a matter I asked him to look into for me. Don't let us keep you from the dance floor. There are plenty of lovely young ladies who would be happy for your attention."

Daniel had to push down feelings of satisfaction at the way she turned Alonzo aside in favor of himself. Those thoughts were unworthy. Gratifying, but unworthy.

Charlotte smiled at him, and Daniel was struck by how pretty she was when she did so. He often thought of her as somber and serious, but when she smiled, she was quite striking. He also didn't miss the intelligent, knowing look in her eye. She had forestalled the confrontation nicely. She took his arm, the ends of her shawl swaying as they walked.

Their path took them back past the dowager, who shot a glare at Daniel and one of long-suffering forbearance toward Charlotte. The duchess squeezed Daniel's forearm. "Don't mind her. She's feeling imperious, put out, misunderstood, and having the time of her life. She'll dine out on the *on dits* from tonight for weeks. It will set her up for the entire summer in Oxfordshire. She's never quite so happy as when she's enjoying a good grumble."

"She and Alonzo Darby are reading from the same sheet music. Both would like to see me pilloried."

Charlotte shook her head as they passed from the brightly lit ballroom onto the wide balcony at the rear of the house. Braziers had been set out at intervals, providing illumination and warmth, with chairs and tables scattered about. A footman stood beside each of the three French doors. A light breeze blew across his face, and Daniel allowed it to cool his irritation.

The duchess patted his arm. "Do not fret. It will all settle out. If Marcus didn't believe in your case, he wouldn't be pursuing it. A day doesn't go by that someone isn't being sent out for information or arriving here to deliver it. Did you see that your barrister is amongst the guests? Sir James is very respectable, and he must see merit to the case. Have you met his clerk, Mr. Childers? He was here much of the day meeting with Marcus and sharing information. I believe they will be ready to present the case very soon."

"Sir James sent his clerk rather than come himself?" Daniel frowned.

"I understand he had to be in court on some matter or other. He sent Mr. Childers, who seems competent and knowledgeable. At least that's what Marcus said. I didn't attend their meeting, of course. Marcus thought he might do a bit of research into Mr. Childers's background, perhaps consider recruiting him as an agent. He's always looking for bright young men like you."

The duke spoke with a pair of gentlemen across the way, each holding a crystal glass, and at something one man said, the duke threw back his head and laughed. His hair was tied at the nape of his neck, longer than current fashion dictated. Such a look would never work with Daniel's wavy hair, but it suited the duke. He stood several inches taller than his companions, and he moved with lithe elegance. He reminded Daniel of the leopard he had seen once at the Royal Menagerie at the Tower.

He could well imagine Haverly creeping into a locked room or fighting his way out of trouble. He was a man's man, a good leader. Daniel could do worse than emulate him.

"We'll wait until he's finished, if you don't mind." Charlotte indicated a pair of chairs beside a small table. "I wanted to have a private word with you in any case."

When they were seated, she said, "I cannot imagine how you must be feeling, with all you've learned recently about your parentage, and now having to encounter Alonzo at social functions. It is not unlike some rather unpleasant family news I received just before I married Marcus. I found out my father had kept a mistress for many years and that I had a half sister. The first time I encountered her in a social situation, with all the *ton* looking on, I wanted to flee. But Marcus encouraged me, and I am so glad he did. Pippa and I are reconciled now, and I help her in her endeavors. She's here tonight, and I am so proud of her."

Daniel knew the story, and he noticed that the duchess did not mention that her half sister had been one of the most sought-after courtesans in the country once upon a time.

She looked out over the railing to the dark yard below. "I am pleased with the way you have comported yourself tonight, especially as I know Alonzo was trying to goad you into a rash action. I was considering your situation this week, and I thought that you and Alonzo are not unlike Jacob and Esau. Brothers on opposite sides of an inheritance dispute."

"Are you sure we're not more like Cain and Abel?" Daniel smiled, mocking himself.

She chuckled. "And which role have you given yourself? Cain or Abel?"

"I've no desire to kill Alonzo. I wish he would leave me alone, if I am truthful."

"What will you do when this is all over? If you are awarded the title, will you ignore him? You will be given power, and you will have to decide what you are going to do with it. How you respond will reveal much about your character."

"Should I not cross that bridge when I come to it? It's pointless to speculate about what I will do, not with the outcome still in question." Though he had considered his options regarding Sir Michael, and even more so Lady Juliette, he had not thought of Alonzo any more than necessary. "It isn't likely that Alonzo will suddenly wish to be friends and behave as brothers if he is successful, and even less so should I prevail."

"No, not likely, perhaps, but it is guaranteed that he will not if you don't make the first overture. He has not hidden his feelings about you, but you have returned that sentiment in word and deed. It is written in your every expression that you do not like him. I am not ignorant of the fact that inviting you both here tonight will cause talk, but both Marcus and I agree that this is your opportunity to be the bigger man. To lay the foundation for a better relationship once the case is finished."

Her words stung. He did not like Alonzo, had not from their

first meeting in the Montgomery drawing room. He didn't like the supercilious tone Alonzo used, and the "I just stepped in something unpleasant" face he made whenever he encountered Daniel. He didn't appreciate Alonzo telling people that the Swanns, mother and son, were grasping, conniving, greedy commoners aiming well above their station. He didn't want to be nice to someone who so ill-used him.

Yet wasn't that exactly what Scripture commanded? To do good to those who hate you and pray for those who spitefully use you?

"I only wish to make you aware that people are watching and ask you to think about your response to Alonzo now and in the future. If you do not want to be thought of as a usurper, perhaps you might contemplate another biblical pair. Do you remember the account of David and Jonathan? Both were on opposing sides of inheriting a kingdom, yet they found a way to be not just friends but brothers of the heart."

Daniel shrugged. "Both parties would have to be amenable to form a friendship such as David and Jonathan's."

"Friendship cannot start until one of you is at least civil. You cannot control Alonzo, but you can control yourself. Neither of you asked for this predicament. You are both victims of the same circumstances. Not to mention the effects your actions have on Juliette and Agatha. There can be no salvaging their relationship if you and Alonzo remain at daggers drawn. I know Juliette is concerned about losing Agatha. They have been very close, and Agatha is dear to her."

"What would you have me do? Drop the petition?"

"No. I believe right must be done and the truth must be discovered. But it would not hurt you to be nice to Alonzo. You can kill him with kindness." She smiled again. "Go heap coals of fire upon his head."

"I shall consider what you have said," he promised. "I have been contemplating what it means to be part of the nobility. What does one do with the power one is given? I see those such as yourself and your husband, who use their power and position for good, and I see others, often in the course of my work, who do the opposite. I want to do right if God should put me in a position of authority. Whether I am awarded the earldom or not, I want to do good in this world. I believe it is one of the reasons I chose to work at Bow Street, for a chance to make the world a better place."

The duchess graced him with another smile, pulling her shawl up higher on her shoulders. "Your desires are noble. I think you are on the right path, no matter what the outcome of the dispute." She paused. "Marcus has finished his discussion with those gentlemen."

The duke crossed the balcony toward them, and Daniel rose. He bowed to his host. "Good evening again, Your Grace."

"Swann. I trust you enjoyed your dances with Lady Juliette?" He rested his hand on his wife's shoulder, and she leaned her head against his forearm. "And you, my lovely? Are you pleased with tonight's events?"

"I am. We've managed to navigate some rather tricky waters, Mr. Swann and I. Alonzo seems to be near the eruption point and has accosted Mr. Swann twice, but Mr. Swann behaved admirably, even when provoked."

"Glad to hear it." Marcus smiled wryly. "I hope you are ready for what is coming, because I believe Sir James will finish his paperwork and be ready to present the case to Garrow in two to three days."

Daniel's insides flinched. Two to three days?

"Did you find all the documentation you needed? And how long do you think it will take before a decision is reached?"

"Some of what I would like to have had cannot be retrieved. No records remain. Mr. Childers, Sir James's clerk? He really surprised me. Not only did he reach out to his contacts, but he found the man who forged the annulment papers. I was astounded. The forger is elderly now and no longer in the trade, as his hands shake too much, but he described the document to my investigators without seeing it, down to the flourishes and even a tiny splash of ink along the edge of the first page. There is no doubt he is the right man."

Daniel's hopes lifted. If they could prove the annulment papers were forged, their case was made.

"As to when the case will be decided, it is anyone's guess. If the King was the one making the decision, it could take months or even years, but with the Prince Regent, he's known for choosing sides of an issue quickly. It is almost as if he wants to get work out of the way to free himself up to play." Marcus shook his head. "I wish he gave more consideration to the matters of the realm placed before him, but there it is. He's . . . given to whimsy, shall we say?"

"How did the meeting go with him at Carlton House?"

"He was, as I suspected, more interested in your political leanings than the rightness and strength of your case. We will have to rely strongly upon Garrow to see to the legalities. But Garrow is a good man, trustworthy, and devoted to the law. He will review all the findings and make his case to the regent."

"I feel helpless, doing nothing to contribute while you all work so hard on my behalf."

"You have not been idle during this time. I understand you've made an arrest?"

Daniel should not be surprised that Haverly already knew. The man had a network of sources that would put Jesuits to shame.

"I wouldn't have thought Cadogan was even in the running. Have you determined a motive?"

"Not thus far. He said he was innocent, but when confronted with the evidence, he became a statue. He's spending the night in Newgate, and I will question him in the morning."

The music ended inside, and light applause rippled out. Juliette passed by on the arm of Viscount Coverdale, and a pang hit Daniel. The set had ended, and another was on the program before the supper break. She would be presented with yet another partner, a bachelor looking for a bride, no doubt.

A footman approached, stopped a few steps away, and waited for Marcus to beckon him closer.

"Your Grace, a messenger has arrived from Bow Street, asking for Mr. Swann."

Marcus nodded, and Daniel bowed to both the duke and duchess. "If it is something urgent and I am called away, I do appreciate your invitation, all the work you've done on my behalf, milord, and to you, Your Grace"—he nodded to Charlotte—"I am especially humbled by your consideration and advice regarding my relationship with Alonzo. I will take your counsel under advisement. If I must absent myself, please give my regrets to Lady Juliette at suppertime." He said the words, trying to ignore the disappointment. If someone from Bow Street was calling for him, the matter had to be significant.

He followed the footman to the entryway, watching lest he find himself in another standoff with his half brother. Alonzo was nowhere to be seen, however, and Ed Beck waited for him on the stoop.

"What's happened?" Daniel asked.

"Owen returned from stabling Cadogan's horses, and on impulse he brought the carriage strongbox back to the station to keep it secure for the night. Sir Michael asked to see it, and he found these tucked inside." Ed opened his handkerchief, and in his broad palm lay a black enamel rose stickpin with a large diamond at its heart and a coin pouch. The letters *J.H.* had been embossed into the leather.

Daniel's heart sank as his last hope that Cadogan was innocent disappeared like a shadow.

Chapter 15

Ed returned to Newgate immediately, while Daniel made a quick trip to his lodging house to change out of evening clothes. Dancing shoes and tails were no attire for the dankness of the prison.

When Daniel arrived at the west entrance of the gaol, Owen waited at the gate, hands in pockets, leaning against the stone wall. He stepped out of the shadows, startling Daniel, who raised his truncheon, ready to defend himself.

"Easy there. It's only me." Owen shoved his hat up, stepping back.

"What are you doing here? It's gone midnight."

"Ed said he was going to fetch you to talk to Cadogan, and I want to hear what he has to say. I won't interfere, but I want to hear it from his own lips that he's guilty."

Owen had been on the case from the outset, searching for the missing children, at one point with Cadogan's aid, and Daniel couldn't blame the young man for wanting answers.

Daniel identified himself to the guard at the gate, wincing as the man held his lantern high, shining it across Daniel's face. "Wait here while I find the warder." The guard's lantern clanked as he walked across the gritty cobbles of the courtyard.

While they waited, Daniel went over what he wanted to ask, the information he needed to make his case against Cadogan.

The guard came back with the turnkey, who carried a baton in one hand and a lantern in the other. "This way. He's in one of the cells in the refractory."

"Is he violent or dangerous?" Daniel asked. The refractory cells were reserved for the most difficult or unruly prisoners.

"Nay, someone put in a request that he have his own cell, and that's the only place where there are single cells. Everybody else is in the wards."

Daniel had made the request, and he was glad it had been honored, though he had not known the only single cells were in the refractory. Hopefully, Cadogan had received the blanket and food for which Daniel had provided coin. Again he felt that odd push-pull. The man could not be guilty, and yet the evidence said he was.

They crossed an open courtyard and entered a long covered hallway. Cells lined the wall to their left, humps of rags on the stone benches at the back . . . humps that were actually prisoners. At the far end, candlelight shone before one cell.

Ed stood close to the bars with a lantern, talking to someone who had to be Cadogan.

"Here he is."

"'Bout time."

"I told you I had to go across town to find him."

Daniel moved to stand in front of the cell. "You ready to talk?"

"I have a few things to say."

"Ed and Owen will listen too, and Owen will take notes."

Cadogan shook his head. "You and nobody else."

"To be official, someone else has to hear it. The court won't take my word alone. If you've exculpatory evidence to give to us, just say it. Prisoners don't get choices." He had to harden himself against wanting to be too lenient. Cadogan was a prisoner and should be treated as such.

Frustration lined the carriage driver's face. "Very well."

The turnkey brought a stool and small table as well as paper and ink. Owen took the seat, and Ed put the lantern on the corner of the table so he could see.

"This first part isn't for you to write down. It's personal to me."

"Just start talking."

Cadogan hitched his blanket higher around his shoulders and leaned against the wall. "I've been driving my carriage all over London for almost ten years now. Before that . . ." He shook his head. "I'm not proud of it, but I was a criminal. This isn't my first stretch in gaol."

Ed's brows went up, and Owen stopped fiddling with the quill.

"Truth is, I did some terrible things in my younger days. I was told I was born in Whitechapel and dropped at the Foundling Hospital the same day. Abandoned children are often left with a token that would identify them to their parents if they should ever come back for them. The token left to me was a wine cork, so you can guess that my mother was probably a drunk. She never came back to claim me, and when I was about eight years old, I ran away. I became a street kid."

Daniel said nothing, but Cadogan's admission made the house on Sureton Row, the refuge for street children, plausible.

"I was canny and totally without morals. I was light fingered, stealing whenever I wanted. I slept wherever I could find a place, and you had to fight for those places. I thrashed other kids, stole a dagger and kept it with me always, and lived by my wits. When I was about ten, an older boy befriended me, and before I knew it, I was part of his street mob. We terrorized people, smashing windows, stealing food, clothes, possessions. We made lots of money stealing gin barrels and selling them at the back doors of public houses. As we became men, the crimes got bigger. Some of the boys started running houses of ill repute, some gambling dens, and some started receiver shops to move stolen goods. If there was a way to make money illegally, we were probably doing it." He wasn't boasting, merely stating facts, almost as if talking about someone else.

"And what was your particular expertise?"

"Running a street gang of kids like I had once been. I was in charge, I had a first-rate cannon, and the rest were learning fast. But I wasn't the top boss. We all answered to one man, someone a few years older than us—the fellow who had recruited all of us to work for him." He shook his head. "Then one of my boys tried to rob the wrong man. He got caught with his hand in the man's pocket, and quick as puffing out a candle flame, the man stabbed him. The boy lived for an hour or so, and my crew carried him home. He died in my arms, and at that moment, I had to ask myself, what was I doing? I had taught that boy to steal. I had been responsible for him, and now he was dead. I had misused my power over that boy, and it cost him his life." Cadogan put his head into his hands. "I knew I had to change my life. I couldn't be responsible for another boy's death."

Daniel waited. How had he never known this of Cadogan? Never even suspected it?

Had never bothered to ask.

"I learned quickly that you can't just leave an organization like that. The leader had a strict code."

"How did you escape?"

"Money. I had to pay. I didn't have nearly enough for the price he set, because I didn't just want to buy my way out. I wanted my whole crew. Six boys. I only knew one way to get the money." He shrugged. "I was a fair thief, but I also had another skill. I hit the gaming tables. Raised like I was, I knew every trick, so I could see it coming. I did well. I earned enough to buy the boys' freedom and to buy the carriage and Sprite and Lola. After that I stayed away from the gambling halls, until recently. One of my kids came to me and said a fancy-dressed man had tried to grab him off the street when he was on his way home. He described the man down to his rose tiepin. I knew it was Jericho Haskett. He was one of the boys I used to run with, and I remember the night he stole that pin."

Daniel felt as if he'd taken a blow to the gut.

"I was at the Olympian Club the night he died." Cadogan straightened and grabbed the bars, letting the blanket fall to the stone floor. "I argued with him. But I didn't kill him. I couldn't. I wouldn't. When I bought my way out of the organization, I started looking for something better to fill my life. I don't know how, but I wound up in a little church in Limehouse. A Methodist church, of all things. But they taught me that there was forgiveness for my sins—even sins as terrible as mine—and a better way to live. Since that day I've tried to live my life the way God says to in His Book. Murder is a sin, and I would never take a life."

Daniel motioned for Owen to begin taking notes.

"You confronted Haskett about trying to take the boy?"

"He said he was recruiting them to fill a new street crew. I told him I wouldn't stand by and let it happen to more children. Ed says you've been to my house. You know I keep rooms for children with no place to go. My wife helps me look after them, and we try to find positions for them and honest ways they can earn their keep. Every little bit helps when there are so many to feed. Haskett had promised one of the boys from my house money, a chance to get rich enough to buy fancy clothes and have a soft bed every night, and everything he could want to eat." Cadogan scuffed the floor with his foot. "I've tried to teach the children that there are mean men out there who might try to hurt them, or lie to them, convince them to do something they shouldn't. Sad bit is, most of them already know it through hard lessons. And this little chap was smart enough to remember what he'd learned. He ran away and told me what had happened. That's when I went to see Haskett. The night he was killed."

"What time was this?"

"After I dropped the last fare for the night. Picked up two gentlemen outside Covent Gardens and took them to a townhouse north of the City proper. It was after midnight, but not by much. I didn't want anyone to see me enter the club, in case there were others from my past still working for Jericho, so I waited until one of the waiters came out the back door and left it ajar. I slipped in and found Haskett's office. He was counting coins like a miser. I closed the door, and we had words. I told him to stick to fleecing gamblers. They're adults who can walk away whenever they choose."

"Was he shocked to see you after such a long time? How did he take your demand?"

"He wasn't shocked, because I had borrowed money from him in the past and had seen him not long before to pay off what I owed. I had come into a bit of money when my uncle died, which is where I got the funds to pay him and to buy the new mare. Haskett thought I had come to borrow more, but I told him I was there because he'd tried to recruit one of my boys. When I told him to leave kids alone, he said he wasn't working for himself. He had an order to fill. And he brought back a name from the past that I thought I had left far behind me. Bobby Puck."

Daniel straightened. "Bobby Puck? You know him?"

"I knew him when I was in that life. He was one of the top boys in the organization. Real close to our boss. Then he disappeared. He was about my age, and I always thought he would take over from the boss. He was intelligent, cunning. All the boys followed him, whether out of loyalty or fear, I don't know. Then he was gone one day. Rumor was the head man suspected he was coming for his position and got rid of him first, or that he'd finally been caught and sent to prison somewhere. Turns out Puck had done a runner like I had, only he didn't get out of the crime business like me. He branched out. Changed his name, found employment, and now lives a double life. Respectable on the outside but an out-and-out criminal on the inside. And he is up to his old tricks, getting his hands on young boys and grooming them to flourish in a life of crime."

"What is the name Puck is using now?"

"Haskett wouldn't tell me. I tried to get it out of him, but he was more afraid of Puck than of me. I heard someone coming up the back stairs, and I knew I had to get away. If Puck knew I was nosing about the edges of his business, he would certainly be capable of snuffing me out." Cadogan shrugged.

"If you didn't kill Haskett, how did his possessions get into your carriage strongbox? The pin and the purse that Owen recovered?" It was the largest accusation in the proceedings. The murdered man's things hidden in Cadogan's carriage.

"I saw the pin on Haskett, but I didn't take it, and I certainly never saw his coin purse. I surmise that whoever killed Haskett must have seen me leaving, known me, and decided to put the blame on me for the murder."

Owen's pen scratched away. Daniel looked at Ed. In his gut he felt Cadogan was telling the truth, though the evidence all pointed to the carriage driver.

"So this mystery killer knows you and is framing you for the murder? Who do you know who would want to kill Haskett and see you take the blame for it?"

"That's just it. I don't know. I've been out of that life for a long time. I paid my way out, so I owe no one from that time. The boys I brought with me when I left, they're grown and living good lives. I found employment for them, saw them trained as apprentices. Some still contact me from time to time. We're all on good terms."

"It has to be someone. Think."

"Haven't I been doing that for hours?" He paced the narrow cell. "I can only assume someone working for Puck got to Haskett, and Haskett told him I was making noise about the children. But why kill Haskett? Why not come after me?"

"We don't have enough information to draw those conclusions. Perhaps Haskett needed dealing with for motives yet unknown, and the killer solved two problems at once by snuffing him and seeing you take the blame."

They were all silent as they considered this.

"Did you grab Haskett's wrist when you confronted him?" Daniel asked.

Cadogan paused. "I might have. He got up from behind his desk, and he dove for the door. I shoved him away. I may have grabbed his wrist. Why?"

"Several substances were found on his right wrist that have been identified as grease, pollen, and horsehair. All items found in your carriage."

"I know it looks bad, but when I left Haskett, he was very much alive. Surely someone saw him afterward? Whoever was coming up the stairs. One of the dealers or waiters or staff?" Cadogan gripped the bars.

"No one has come forward to say so. And the coroner estimates his time of death as being not long after midnight."

"Whoever I heard coming up the stairs must be the killer then."

"We have no witness but yourself who puts anyone on the back stairs at that time. We do have a witness who saw someone leave the building and get into a carriage."

Cadogan snapped his fingers. "Well, there you are then."

Daniel frowned. "Where?"

"It had to be someone else that was seen. I wouldn't get into my own carriage. I would climb up on the seat and drive away."

"He's right." Owen looked up. "He wouldn't get inside his own cab."

The turnkey clanked down the passage. "Are you finished yet? I can't go to bed until you're out of the prison."

Daniel nodded. "Just a few moments more."

He waited to speak to Cadogan until the warder had gone back down the row. "What you've told us tonight is not enough for me to have you released. There is still too much evidence against you. But we will follow up. Ed will check with the servant at the Olympian Club to confirm what he saw. Now that we know Bobby Puck is alive and apparently well, I will begin my search for him."

"What should I do?" Owen asked.

"Go home. Get some sleep. It will be every man to the work at first light," Daniel said. "Cadogan, we'll check what we know against the information you've shared here tonight. The evidence is damning, but if you're innocent, we'll do our best to prove it."

As they passed through the gate onto Old Bailey Street, Daniel felt the weight of responsibility on his shoulders. If there was a chance Cadogan was innocent, he could not let his friend hang for a crime he didn't commit.

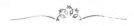

"Are you certain you want to do this?" Bertie asked Juliette. He had come to retrieve Juliette from the Haverlys' house midmorning. Now that he had returned from Dartmoor, she could go back home. But before they went back to Berkeley Square, Juliette prevailed upon him to take her on an errand of mercy.

"Of course. Mr. Cadogan has always been very polite to me, and he saved Daniel's life." She held the basket on her lap, swaying to the rocking of the carriage. Charlotte had helped her pack the parcel, though it was difficult to know what might be appropriate under the circumstances.

"You could have entrusted the delivery to me, you know. You don't have to attend to the errand personally. In fact, I am not altogether certain you'll be allowed in."

"I won't know until I try. If they won't let me inside, I will wait in the carriage while you take care of it." She wanted to see the prisoner for herself and to ask how she might be of assistance to him. Not for one moment did she think he had murdered anyone or stolen helpless children off the street, and she did not believe Daniel truly thought so either.

"Marcus told me, while I was waiting for all your bags to be brought down, that though the case against Mr. Cadogan is strong, it seemed there is more afoot than meets the eye." Bertie covered his mouth as he yawned. "I am too old for these all-night parties. I left at daybreak and only slept an hour or two."

Juliette felt fatigued as well, her limbs heavy and her thoughts wooly. The night had started so promisingly when Daniel had arrived and partnered her, but the moment he'd left on police business, she'd wished she could wander up to her room and be alone. Of course, as a good guest, she hadn't, but she'd wanted to.

The dowager had kept her supplied with partners, and Juliette had danced every set but one. When the last was announced, she pleaded exhaustion, apologized to her prospective dance partner, and taken him to sit with her and Charlotte, who was looking as tired as Juliette felt.

Most of the guests were subdued at the expansive breakfast, and the goodbyes had not taken long. By everyone's comments and compliments, the party had been a raging success and would be talked about for weeks to come.

It was a bit deflating now that it was all over. The planning and anticipation had taken so much time and energy, and now it was a memory. At least Juliette had managed to get a kind word out of the dowager at the end.

"You've behaved fairly well this evening. I was able to keep my eye on you every minute."

Not exactly a glowing report, but better than she'd had in the past from her sometimes chaperone.

Their carriage trundled down the street, turned a corner, and soon they arrived in front of Newgate Prison. Cold stone walls, guarded entrances, and—even here on the sidewalk well away from the inmates—the smell of unwashed humans.

"Stay here." Bertie reached for the door. "I'll make inquiries, and if they will allow you inside, I will fetch you." He muttered under his breath as he got out. "Your father will kill me when he learns I let you talk me into this."

Juliette hid her smile. Bertie liked to pretend he didn't care about things, that he lived life on the surface, a dilettante with nothing serious on his mind, but at heart he was kind, observant, intelligent, and capable. He just didn't want people to know, lest they ask him to do things for them.

He returned quickly. "The guard has said no to your request for an audience with Cadogan. You'll have to entrust the supplies to my humble self." He reached for the basket. "I'll hand it to him once the guard has checked it."

Juliette frowned. "Are you certain I cannot at least see him?"

"Not this time. Wait here. I'll not be long."

She leaned against the squabs and closed her eyes. Her muscles ached a trifle from her exertions last night. It took stamina to dance so many sets, not only physically but mentally. It wouldn't do to forget the steps. It would be difficult to live down if one caused a collision on the dance floor through ignorance. Not to mention carrying on socially proper conversations with a variety of people. Juliette found making small talk, while a necessary skill for a debutante, draining.

When the carriage door opened once more, Uncle Bertie climbed in, followed by another figure. Her heart lurched.

Daniel. Pleasure shot through her.

"Look who I found wandering the prison courtyard." Bertie took his seat. "It seems you two think alike. He was here on an errand of mercy as well."

Daniel smiled as he took the seat across from her. Though she wished he had sat beside her, at least this way she could see his face. "You are looking well, Lady Juliette, especially with such a lack of sleep. Your uncle told me about your generosity to Cadogan, and he's graciously offered me a ride to my next destination."

"Are you returning to Bow Street?"

"No, I am going across the river to Cadogan's house. I promised him I would check on his wife and his horses. I questioned him last night, and I thought of a few more things to ask him this morning."

Bertie leaned back and closed his eyes, pinching the bridge of his nose. "I knew the moment I heard of his errand that you would insist upon going along."

"I do insist. I very much wish to meet Mrs. Cadogan and help her in any way I can. Are you certain of your case against Mr. Cadogan?" she asked Daniel. "I do not mean to question your abilities as an investigator. It just seems so unlikely and out of character on the driver's part to have harmed anyone."

"I thought I had a solid case, but now that I've heard more of the story, I am beginning to believe Mr. Cadogan is being framed. I wish I had not been so precipitate as to arrest him and have him charged, though I really had no choice in the matter. My governor insisted upon it. He's particular about wrapping up cases, especially murder cases, quickly. Our task now is to find a person with motive to murder Haskett, steal children, and be certain Cadogan took the blame. I have a lead, but I have not been able to locate the man I seek."

"What is your lead?" Bertie asked, eyes still closed.

"Bobby Puck. It's a name I found written in Haskett's ledgers, and last night I learned Cadogan knew him years ago when Cadogan was a much different man. Dr. Rosebreen had heard of him before as well, and not in a flattering way. It seems this Puck had requested that Haskett help him find young boys to recruit into his organization, boys who would become pickpockets and worse as they grew up. Boys he could groom to fill places in his criminal organization."

Bertie had straightened at the mention of the man's name, his eyes opening and focusing on Daniel. "Bobby Puck? I haven't heard that name in years. When I first started working for the agency, every crime that went unsolved in London was attributed to Bobby Puck. I thought he was a myth."

"He's real. He went underground for several years, and he's no longer operating under the name Bobby Puck. If the ledger entry is to be believed, his new initials are H.C."

"Have you encountered anyone during the case with those initials?" Juliette asked. "Other places in the ledgers?"

Daniel smiled and nodded, as if he approved of her question, and warmth spread through her. "Astute of you to think of," he said. "None that could be Bobby Puck. We're still looking. Several of the investigators at Bow Street are checking with their contacts to see if anyone has a lead on who he could be. After I visit Mrs. Cadogan, I'm headed back to the Olympian Club to question Mr. Alton, who is now managing the place. Every morning someone arrives to pick up the night's earnings. Ed Beck was going to follow the man in the hopes that he will lead Ed to the man he's working for, who might know who Bobby Puck is now."

Bertie subsided again, but he didn't close his eyes. Two lines formed between his brows, the sure indication his mind was working quickly.

The sound of the carriage wheels changed as they crossed the Blackfriars Bridge.

"You have been to Cadogan's house before? What is it like? What might his wife need?" Juliette asked.

Daniel nodded. "The house is small, and every inch of it is taken up with beds for street children. The Cadogans take them in, feed them, and try to find them employment. They take them to church and help them learn to read and write. Seems they're living a bit hand to mouth. Cadogan's fares pay for bare necessities, and the children contribute their earnings to keep the place going, but it doesn't look like there is much to spare."

"They will need food, supplies." Juliette's mind raced with ways she and her friends could make a difference. "Blankets, sheets, clothing, shoes, stockings. Books, paper, ink, furniture." She would tell Charlotte of the needs. Her friend would be eager to help. And Diana, who would make lists.

Perhaps she would also tell Agatha. They could work together, and perchance the gulf that had widened between them would narrow.

"I admire the way you always wish to help people." The warm look in Daniel's eyes was like a caress. "There are many in your position who either don't know or don't care of the plight of street children. They treat them like little nuisances or shadows that disappear, out of sight and out of mind."

Bertie stretched his legs as far as the carriage would allow. "*Noblesse oblige*. Much like the work we do for the Crown, helping others and using our position to effect positive change is a Thorndike family tradition. We try to follow the teaching of 'For unto whomsoever much is given, of him shall much be required' and 'Love your neighbor as yourself.'"

Juliette pondered this. Her parents did live in such a way, sacrificially. They gave to many in need, did not sort people into those worthy and those unworthy, and they served the greater good through the agency. She fiercely wanted to follow in their footsteps.

She glanced through the window. She had never been in this part of London. The streets were narrow, rutted dirt paths. The buildings were smaller, of wood and grimy brick rather than the limestone and marble of her neighborhood.

Daniel had adequately described the Cadogan home. Small and full of little people. A woman answered the door, three urchins hanging onto her skirts.

Bertie took one look at the grubby little faces and declared, "I shall go up the street to the livery and see about the horses. Mrs. Cadogan will provide ample chaperonage in my absence." He then melted out of the door with a doff of his hat, as if he feared catching a disease from the children.

Mrs. Cadogan stood in the hall with hands on hips, her brows lowered. "What do you want here? Haven't you seen enough? Arresting my husband when you know he would never kill anyone, and he certainly wouldn't kidnap any children. They fill this place to the rafters every day. Why would he need to steal more? And who is this?" She pointed her finger in Juliette's face.

"Mrs. Cadogan." Daniel held up his hands, palms outward. "I'm not here on any sinister errand. I've come with news and to see what it is you may need while we work to free your husband. This is Lady Juliette, who knows Cadogan, has heard of your efforts here, and wishes only to help."

The woman looked Juliette up and down, suspicion in her face. "Help? Her? She probably hasn't worked a day in her life."

Daniel made as if to speak, but Juliette put her hand on his arm. They must make allowances for the poor woman. She was clearly distressed at her husband's arrest and possibly lashing out in fear. "Mrs. Cadogan, I am sorry for the plight in which you find yourself. Your husband has always been kind to me, and I owe him a debt. He once did me a great service." She looked at Daniel. Cadogan had saved her precious Daniel's life, and for that she would be forever grateful. "I have come this very hour from delivering a package to Cadogan in Newgate—a few provisions, a clean shirt, a blanket. Things I thought might make the next few days bearable. I do not believe your husband is guilty of the crimes for which he has been arrested. When my uncle took the parcel inside the prison, for they would not let me in to do it myself, your husband asked if we would visit you. He was worried that without his wages coming in, you and the children would be in need."

Mrs. Cadogan lowered her chin, her arms falling slack. "Pardon my poor manners. I'm that worried about him."

"Daniel, might I have use of your notebook and pencil? Mrs. Cadogan, perhaps we can go into the kitchen and make a list of items that would be most helpful to you." She took the book and pencil with a smile of thanks and followed the lady and the children to her kitchen.

The smell of cooked cabbage and onion permeated the air. The fireplace front was black nearly to the ceiling from years of use, and a small peat fire smoldered on the hob. A few shelves bore cooking utensils, and a little girl of about five summers sat at the table shelling peas.

"I make porridge of a morning and soup for other meals. Soup and porridge can be stretched a fair way and fills up little bellies. We have bread twice a week, and we sometimes have meat on Sunday." Mrs. Cadogan poked a strand of hair back into her cap.

Meat once a week—sometimes. And last night Juliette had sat at a banquet where she had her choice of at least seven types of meat, and that was only one course. Daniel, who stood in the doorway, shuffled his feet, no doubt considering his own comparatively easy existence. Neither of them wondered when, or if, their next meal would appear.

"We shall make a list of items and see what we can get accomplished for you." Juliette took a chair next to the girl at the table and smiled. The child smiled back, showing missing lower front teeth.

At least the place was clean and the children passably so. From what Juliette had observed, keeping children clean took a fair amount of time and effort. "What is most urgent on your list of needs?"

"I wish I could buy a bag of porridge oats at a time. It's less expensive that way, but we never have enough money at once to purchase an entire two bushels. I buy it a pound at a time and thin it with water. And some salt wouldn't go amiss. Dougie loves a dash of salt in his porridge, but we don't often have it to hand."

Juliette wrote, nodding. "What about clothing, blankets, shoes?"

Mrs. Cadogan sank into a chair. "There's always a need, especially for the children going out to work. The oldest ones need new clothes, and theirs are passed down to the little 'uns as they grow."

"I shall make arrangements for a cobbler and a dressmaker to come and measure the children for new things. I understand you are teaching the children lessons in reading and writing? Would it be helpful to have some books and other things sent over?" At this question, the girl with the bowl of peas looked up, her eyes wide.

"Why are you doing this?" Mrs. Cadogan's eyes narrowed.

Juliette searched for an answer that would make sense. She just knew it was the right thing to do. She had plenty, more than plenty, and these children had nothing to call their own. "The Gospel of Luke tells us, 'For unto whomsoever much is given, of him shall be much required.'" The verse Bertie had quoted on their journey over. It felt good to be putting the words into action.

The front door slammed, and Daniel turned to look behind him. "Caleb? Is that you? Why are you here? Did Sir Michael send you?"

Footsteps sounded, running away. Daniel was off quickly in his wake. Who was Caleb, and why had he run off?

Chapter 16

DANIEL CAUGHT THE OFFICE BOY before he could turn onto Blackfriars. His hand closed over the boy's collar, and he eased them both to a stop, not wanting to tumble to the dirt road.

"Easy there, Caleb. It's me." He puffed a bit from the quick exertion. "I did not mean to frighten you." He changed his grip to the boy's arm, because the tightness in Caleb's frame told him he would run the moment he was free. "Did you come from Bow Street?"

He hung his head, squirming. "No."

"Why did you come to Cadogan's?"

Caleb shrugged. "I live there."

Daniel's thoughts stumbled. He was one of Cadogan's street children? "Let's go back there and talk then. There's no need to run like your hair is on fire." Why had the boy fled at the sight of Daniel? The child's eyes darted, as if looking for a way of escape, and red suffused his cheeks. Odd behavior in someone who had seemed happy, confident, and willing to learn at Bow Street.

He behaved now like a boy caught in mischief and afraid to pay the consequences. What had he been up to that had him so ill at ease?

They marched back to the Cadogan house, meeting Bertie and Mrs. Cadogan at the door.

"A friend of yours?" Bertie asked.

"An office boy at Bow Street. It seems this young man may have something to tell us. Perhaps a heavy conscience troubles him." Daniel sent the boy ahead. "Into the bunk room with you, Caleb."

Caleb sank onto a bottom bunk, drew up his knees, and buried his face in them.

Mrs. Cadogan and Juliette entered the room.

"Caleb, child, what is wrong?" Mrs. Cadogan wiped her hands on her apron and sat on the bunk.

"I did a terrible thing." The muffled words choked out on a sob.

"Oh, it cannot be that bad. Whatever it is, we'll help you."

"You don't understand. If the other kids find out, they will hate me." His chin came up, and two tears tracked down his cheeks. He smeared the moisture with a swipe of his sleeve. "You'll hate me." A sob bucked up his throat.

"I'll wait in the hall," Juliette said.

Daniel moved slightly so his hand would brush against hers as she moved past, thrilling at the momentary contact, meeting her eyes for a lingering moment. "Close the door, please."

When she had gone, Caleb asked, "Are you going to arrest me? Am I going to prison?"

"I don't make a practice of arresting children. What is it you've done that you think is so bad?" Daniel leaned against the doorframe.

"I hurt Mr. Cadogan. The only man who was ever nice to me, and I betrayed him."

"How?"

"That pin and that purse." His face crumpled again.

"What about them? They were found in his carriage strongbox."

"I know. I put them there." Caleb sobbed again. "I was sent here to live in this house and to get the job at Bow Street to find out what you knew about the case. And I was given the pin and the coin purse to put in his carriage. When you arrested Dougie, I went to the stables and forced the pin and the purse through the slot on top of the box. And now I'll be killed, because he said if I told anyone, I would be found floating in the Thames." A wail escaped the boy, and he buried his head in his knees again.

Daniel must go delicately, for Caleb was truly in distress. He would not drag the child to Bow Street in irons, though the law gave him such leave. That would be an abuse of his power. No, he would tread lightly, give assurances where he could, and try to help the boy out of the predicament others had slung him into. "You were given the black rose pin and the purse with the coins inside, and you were told to hide them where they would be found by the police?"

"Yes."

"Who gave them to you?"

He shook his head. "If I say, he'll kill me."

Daniel's anger rose, not at Caleb but at anyone who would use threats of murder to coerce a child to break the law. "He cannot kill you if he cannot find you. I will find you a safe place to hide. And if you tell me who the man is, I will arrest him. He can't kill you from gaol."

Caleb nodded. "Yes he can. He can get to anyone anywhere. So many people work for him, do his bidding. They'll find me. He said so."

Daniel pulled his coat aside to reveal the pistol stuck in his waistband. "It is my job to protect people from evil men. You are not the only child with whom he has dealt. There are missing children out there, children this man has stolen off the street. I need to find them."

The boy's eyes betrayed his conflicted feelings. Fear, guilt, and somewhere in there, a glimmer of hope that Daniel must encourage.

"This man, he told you to try to get a job at Bow Street?"

Caleb nodded. "He said they had just promoted one of the office boys to investigator and if I was smart and bright and willing, they would hire me to replace him. I can read and write and cypher, and I know how to get about in London. It was easy to get the job. Harder to get my hands on information. You are in charge of the case, but you're not in the offices much. You don't talk about the case except to Mr. Beck, and you don't leave paper lying around. I tried to get the ledgers, but you locked them away upstairs."

"You were the one who broke into my desk?" They had suspected it was someone who knew quite a bit about the inner workings at Bow Street, but Daniel never would have suspected this child.

Caleb seemed to shrink into himself.

"You are not in trouble. You were acting on orders. Does this man who threatened you carry a knife?"

Caleb shook. Mrs. Cadogan put her arm around the boy, but she looked imploringly at Daniel. "Does this have to continue?"

"If we want to get your husband out of gaol, it does. Caleb." He made his voice strong. "Look at me. What is the man's name? Is it Bobby Puck?"

The boy shot upright, striking his head on the bottom of the bunk above him. He collapsed onto the mattress, groaning. "No, I didn't tell you that. How do you know?"

Daniel knelt beside the boy. "Where I can find him. Tell me and I will protect you. I give you my word." He touched the young man's shoulder, then gripped it, trying to give him strength and bravery.

"He only comes to the place where I meet him late at night. It's a pub off the Ratcliff Highway, The Oarsman. The man"—he didn't seem able to say his name, even now—"has a table near the fireplace. People come and go all night."

"How did he find you and force you to do his bidding? Did he steal you off the street like the others?"

Caleb removed his hand from the crown of his head and wiped his eyes. "I was working at Tattersall's, sweeping the alleys and cleaning the stalls on auction days. One minute I was sweeping up, and the next someone grabbed me and threw me into a carriage. The man forced me onto the floor. He told me to be quiet, or he'd slit my throat."

"Was it Bobby Puck who took you?"

"No. It was someone who worked for him."

"What happened then?"

"He took me to a cellar where there were other kids, and when it was dark, he came and got me. Took me to The Oarsman. I saw the sign as we went inside. That's where I had to meet . . . him."

"What happened?"

"The man who took me said, 'I found this one, will he do?' and shoved me in front of . . . him. He asked me lots of questions, then said I was going to get a job at Bow Street, and I would tell him things I learned there."

"When was this?"

"Maybe three days before I had my first day at Bow Street. I met Sir Michael, and he looked me up and down and said I was hired, and I could start right then by making him some tea."

Which sounded like Sir Michael. "How did you pass along information?"

"The man who stole me told me what to do. The first thing was to find out what I could about the investigation into the murder of Jericho Haskett. Then I was told to come here to this house and ask for a place to sleep, and a few days after that, I was given the pin and purse and told to put it somewhere that made it clear Cadogan had taken them." He hung his head. "I'm sorry, ma'am. I didn't mean for any of this to happen. I was afraid."

She hugged him close. "Don't you mind. Dougie won't be angry. Mr. Swann will put it right."

"Are you going to send me away?"

"Pish-tosh, lad. We turn no one away. Mr. Swann may have a place for you to stay for the next little while, but you'll always be welcome back here."

"I do have a place in mind. Caleb, pack up what you will need to be gone a few days." Daniel slipped into the hall.

Sir Bertrand leaned against the wall, arms crossed, looking warily at the children staring at him from a bench on the opposite wall.

"Where's Lady Juliette?" Daniel asked.

"She went to the kitchen to finish her list of things needed for the house." He never took his eyes off the youngsters, as if he expected them to swarm him at any moment. "Find out anything useful?"

"Most definitely. I'll fetch her. We'll be leaving in a few minutes." Daniel spoke over his shoulder as he walked toward the kitchen.

Juliette sat at the table, the end of the pencil against her lips, deep in thought. Daniel paused for a moment to take in her features, the way the light spilled in from the open back door, shining on her bonnet brim, illuminating her little pointed chin and heart-shaped face. He knew she would smell of roses and that her lips were soft and sweet.

The longing for her to be truly his smote him, and his collar tightened. She was a precious treasure, and he only prayed he would someday be worthy to ask her father for her hand in marriage and that he would be agreeable.

She looked up, her brown eyes serious. "Were you able to help the boy?"

"He had something on his conscience that was too big for him to carry alone. I believe he feels better having unburdened himself. I do have a favor to ask of you. The man for whom he was working has threatened his life. He is in danger, and I would like you and Bertie to escort him to your home, keep him there, and give me time to make an arrest. You could give Caleb some work to do in your home, could you not? As a bootboy or some such? He can read and write, and he's worked in a stable before."

Her brow furrowed. "I do not mind taking him back to Berkeley Square, but Uncle Bertie said he was employed at Bow Street? Did you remove him from that position?"

"Only temporarily. For his own safety. The man who threatened him knows where he works."

She rose, tore a page from his notebook, and handed the book and pencil to him. "I will see he is safe. I will give him into Mr. Pultney and your mother's care. They will know what to do with him."

At the mention of his mother, Daniel flinched. He should go see her. Talk to her. Try to come to some sort of understanding that would alleviate the guilt he felt every time she came to mind.

He stuffed the notebook into his pocket and reached for Juliette's hands. "You are gracious and generous." She was so close, he could enfold her—and he knew she wouldn't protest—but now was neither the time nor the place.

There was a boy to get to safety, and Daniel had a definitive lead in his case.

Daniel went to Ed's home to apprise him of the new developments. He caught his friend just waking from a Sunday afternoon nap and envied him. How long had it been since Daniel slept? A long day yesterday, then the party, then the middle-of-the-night questioning at Newgate, then more investigating today. His eyes felt heavy and gritty.

Ed had a report to make as well. "I went to the Olympian at dawn like we agreed and watched for the money pickup. I followed the courier's carriage east on the Ratcliff Highway, but I lost him in Wapping. I'll try again tomorrow." He yawned, scratching his neck.

"There may be no need. I've got a location in Wapping to try. Caleb gave me the name of the pub where he met this mysterious Bobby Puck."

"I'll get my coat."

"No." Daniel looked at the cozy parlor, the overstuffed chair that sagged a bit, the newspaper on the table. Mrs. Beck and the children had gone to the park, leaving Ed alone to nap. "I need you to go to Bow Street and start work on a warrant for the arrest of Bobby Puck and the searching of a public house called The Oarsman. And the paperwork to release Cadogan from Newgate. If Caleb was telling the truth, we will need to move quickly. I'll reconnoiter at The Oarsman tonight after dark. If I can verify Caleb's statement, we'll need to take the warrant to Lord Creevy's house so we can make the arrest."

"You shouldn't go alone. Let's get Fyfe or Piggott to do the paperwork, and I'll go with you. When was the last time you slept?"

"I'm heading home now to sleep for a few hours, and you need to be the one on the warrant because you know the most about the case. It would take too long to inform anyone else. And at any rate, I'm not making any arrests. I'm just going to reconnoiter."

In the end, Ed agreed, reaching for his coat and hat and following Daniel out of the cozy drawing room and into the street.

Once home, Daniel asked his landlady to knock on his door in three hours, and he fell into bed. Though exhausted, it took him a while to fall asleep, his mind chasing thoughts and turning back on itself.

When he woke, he prepared for the work ahead, reaching into the back of his wardrobe and withdrawing a set of clothes he had last worn on the night of the anarchist rally . . . the night he had first kissed Juliette. Rough shirt, heavy woolen coat, patched trousers, and scuffed boots. His hat had lost its shape through wear and water and had little in common with current fashion. Daniel smiled grimly at his reflection in the mirror.

Perhaps he would add a disreputable cloak to his collection. He could emulate Marcus Haverly in his second personality, Hawk.

He found a cab, but the driver refused to take him all the way to Wapping after dark. That area of town could be jeopardous to one's health, and the driver had no intention of entering it, especially as dusk was falling.

"I'll take you as far as All Hallows, but you will have to walk from there. It's more than my life is worth to drive into that cauldron at night."

Daniel was content with that as his destination, The Oarsman, was only half a mile to the east. Once afoot, he walked briskly, as if certain of himself and his destination, along the Ratcliff Highway. Only a few years previously there had been several murders in this area. Daniel had been still at university, but news of the killings had swept the through the kingdom like the Great Fire of London.

The tavern he sought was midway down a short street that ran south off Ratcliff. He pulled his hat lower, hunching his shoulders, putting his chin down. Though he knew no one in this area of town and had never worked a case here, it would be not to his liking to be recognized, especially by someone he may have arrested in the past.

Perhaps he should have brought Ed with him. No one was more

capable in an altercation, but he was the logical choice to write up the warrant. Daniel would not try to make an arrest tonight. Once he identified this Bobby Puck, he could return with a warrant and apprehend him. They must do everything in strict accordance with the law, for he wanted nothing to interfere with the course of justice.

The taproom smelled of ale and pipe smoke and unwashed men. There were few candles or lamps, and shadows shrouded the corners. There were no card games or dice being thrown. No rowdy singing or storytelling. This was a room of serious drinkers.

Daniel slipped inside, purchased a pint of ale from the publican, and found an empty bench along the wall. He kept his chin low, his hat on, and looked sideways from face to face. Caleb had said the man he knew as Bobby Puck sat at a table near the fireplace.

He felt the curious eyes on him, but in a place like this, the patrons knew better than to ask a stranger his business. After a moment or two, when it became obvious he would keep to himself, they stopped looking and went back to drinking. He leaned forward and placed his elbows on his thighs, holding his tankard in both hands, which gave him a better view down the room. The pub wasn't overly crowded but held enough patrons to appear to be a profitable concern. Most public houses were dark come an evening since publicans did not wish to waste money on candles and lamps, but The Oarsman was inordinately so. More shadows than light, faces hidden. Conversation seemed dimmed too, with voices kept low. Was this customary for the pub, or had they another reason for their subdued behavior?

Daniel spied the table before the fireplace that Caleb had described, set a bit apart from the others, and one of the men sat with his back to the wall, where no one could sneak up on him. Was this the mysterious Bobby Puck? Or was it the other man at his right hand?

Impossible to distinguish features in the darkness, but there was something about them, especially the one on the right, that seemed familiar. He wore a heavy cloak, even that close to the fire, but the way he raised his tankard to his lips, the slope of his shoulders . . . who could that be?

There was no way to casually stroll by the table for a better look. They had positioned themselves well to observe every movement in the room while keeping to the shadows themselves.

The door opened, and a large man entered, the low light from the fire glinting on his watch chain and the golden threads embroidered into his waistcoat. He wove between the tables until he stood before the men in the corner. Perfectly silhouetted against the firelight, he reached into his pocket, removed a pouch, and tossed it onto the table, with the unmistakable clink of coins hitting wood. The newcomer did not remove his hat, nor, from what Daniel could tell, did he say anything.

The seated man who seemed so familiar to Daniel opened a book before him with a slap, dipped a quill into an inkwell, and made a notation, while the other man opened the purse and shook out the coins, arranging them in small stacks. At his nod, the newcomer turned on his heel and left, head down. As he passed, Daniel noted the scowl marring his face.

The publican eased from behind the counter, picked up a poker, and stoked the fire, sending a shower of sparks up the chimney, and as the fire flared, it illuminated the face of the men in the corner.

Daniel stifled a gasp. He knew them both. One was a man he had met before. But even more surprising was the gentleman who sat beside him. A man Daniel knew well.

Or had thought he knew.

One of them must be the fabled Bobby Puck to be sure. Was his companion an accomplice, or had the man tumbled to Puck's identity and was working undercover? Would Daniel barging in to make an arrest upset some long-worked mission of which Daniel had not been made aware?

He must get out of The Oarsman without being seen by either of them, for as surely as he knew them, they knew him.

He must get back to Ed and put names into the arrest warrant Ed was preparing. But getting a magistrate to sign it, even one as fair-minded as Lord Creevy, wouldn't be easy.

Daniel needed to talk to Marcus and then his barrister.

Chapter 17

DANIEL HAD THOUGHT OF NOTHING else all night, and though exhausted, tossed and turned until dawn. Ed had been stunned at the news Daniel had brought, and though he had worded the warrant to reflect the new information, he remained skeptical.

At first light, Daniel traveled to Haverly's house, not wanting to trust his words to a messenger, and arrived promptly at seven.

The duke's valet trotted down the stairs. "May I be of assistance, Mr. Swann?"

"I apologize for the early hour. I need an audience with the master of the house."

"Allow me to confer with His Grace. Please wait here." The valet hurried up the stairs with Daniel's card.

Daniel took out his notebook and checked the notes he had made when he'd returned to his lodgings late last night. Thus far he had no real proof against Bobby Puck. Caleb's statement on who had hired him to plant evidence might not be enough to convince a jury. He would need the duke's help because he could not involve anyone else at Bow Street besides Ed and Owen.

The valet returned. "His Grace invites you to break your fast with him. He will join you shortly."

The breakfast room—still larger than both Daniel's rented rooms combined—had no occupants, but a door on the far side swung open, and the Haverlys' butler entered, carrying a tray with a silver coffeepot and porcelain mugs.

"Good morning, sir. Would you prefer coffee or tea with breakfast?" He seemed completely unruffled at having a guest show up uninvited.

"Coffee, thank you." Daniel moved to a place at the side of the table, assuming Haverly would sit at the head. "Will others be joining us?"

The butler set the tray on the sideboard, poured a cup of coffee, and brought it to Daniel. "Only His Grace this early. Mr. Hamish Sinclair has gone for a ride in the park and will dine with the ladies of the house in about an hour."

"Good morning," Haverly said.

Daniel rose and bowed. "Good morning, Your Grace."

The butler poured coffee without being asked and set it at the head of the table. He also produced a stack of newspapers, placing them beside the cup. "Breakfast is ready, sir."

"Thank you."

A trio of footmen entered, carrying covered dishes, placing them on the sideboard, and removing the cloches. The aroma of the hot food made Daniel's stomach grumble. The past few days had been so busy, he'd missed more meals than he had taken.

They each filled their plates, and Daniel waited until they were alone before he spoke. "I am sorry to come unannounced, but there have been developments in my murder investigation that require some delicate handling." He told the duke what had transpired, both at Cadogan's house and at the pub in Wapping. "So you can see my dilemma. I cannot say which man's identity surprised me the most. But both are problematic for me. I have a witness, a child who swears he was given the stolen goods to plant at Cadogan's, and he can identify the man who gave them to him, but I need more evidence before I can make either arrest. I cannot be seen to be vindictive or serving my own ends. I cannot move too quickly, but each hour that passes means an innocent man is in prison and missing children are in danger."

"You are certain who it was you saw?"

"Yes."

"What is it you would like me to do?" the duke asked. "I do not know that I can interfere in any obvious way, but I can set things in motion covertly." He smiled. "That is where I excel, after all."

"Can you send someone—Partridge perhaps?—to The Oarsman tonight and see who comes and goes and who has contact with Bobby Puck? Partridge is suited to melding into that environment and not being noticed. Have him watch for Puck, but also find any lead on the missing children's whereabouts. They may be being held in a cellar nearby, or they may already have been dispersed throughout Puck's network, with threats of violence if they try to escape or tell anyone what has happened to them."

"Partridge is adept at that particular line of work." The duke crossed his utensils and laid them on his plate.

"And can you find out anything you can on Bobby Puck's past? I can have the ledgers sent to you. Perhaps someone in the agency can decode them. The answers are there, but they'll need unraveling."

"Of course. I will send someone to Bow Street to collect them."

"They're locked in Lord Creevy's safe. You'll need a note from me to retrieve them." Daniel tore a page out of his notebook and wrote the missive.

Marcus's face brightened, and he rose. "Ah, good morning, my love. You're up early, looking as lovely as always."

Daniel stood. The duchess rounded the table and raised her cheek for her husband's kiss, then continued on to Daniel, holding out her hand.

"Hello, Daniel. How nice to see you again. I'm sorry you were called away from the party so abruptly, though I do understand. Are you here on official business? Have you been able to locate our little flower seller, Alice?"

He took her fingers and bowed over them. "Good morning, Your Grace. I have not yet found the missing children, but I believe I am getting closer. I came to see your husband's counsel on how to proceed."

She nodded. "If anyone can help, it's Marcus. He's the most capable man I've ever met."

A pang of envy at their evident regard for one another mixed with a healthy dose of longing for Juliette, making Daniel's chest tight.

"I did not realize we had a visitor." The dowager's imperious, pinched voice accompanied the tapping of her cane. "Oh. It's you."

"Madam. I trust you slept well?" Marcus seated his wife across from Daniel and pulled out the chair beside the duchess for his mother.

She sniffed. "That is my chair." She pointed to where Daniel's plate rested.

"I beg pardon." Daniel reached for his breakfast to move to another chair, but Marcus cleared his throat and looked pointedly at his mother and then at the chair he held.

With bad grace, she lowered herself to the cushion.

"Perhaps I should come back to continue our discussion?" Daniel asked.

"No need. You are our guest. Please finish your breakfast."

Daniel resumed his seat but said nothing more. His very existence seemed to irritate the dowager.

Not unlike the effect he had on his half brother. Daniel had not forgotten the duchess's words of advice, but he had been given little time to consider them, with the murder case turning as it had.

He needed to sort that situation out, but what overture could he make that Alonzo would not rebuff? Forging a relationship with someone who despised him wouldn't be easy. He was having a difficult enough time with understanding people who claimed to love him.

"Thank you for inviting me out. I feel so caged in that townhouse. Alonzo said we should consider renting it out after we marry. I would like to sell it altogether, but he says it would bring in a steady income, as Eaton Square is becoming a desirable address. My father bought it while I was away at school, and I have no sentimental attachment to the place. The house only holds bad memories for me now." Agatha bit her lower lip as they entered Hatchards. She furled her umbrella, shaking droplets off her gloves. "I feel a boat would have been a better conveyance on a day like today."

"Didn't you declare to me, after we finally made it to England from Switzerland, that you would never willingly board a boat again?" Juliette teased. "As to the townhouse, do nothing in haste. There is time to decide what you wish to do with it later. For now, we need books." Juliette mopped her face with her handkerchief. It had been misting slightly when she'd left home, but by the time she had collected Agatha, it was pitching it down with rain. She opened her reticule to consult her list. Though she had originally invited Charlotte on this mission, Charlotte had suggested Agatha instead.

"Perhaps you can do some bridge building. I know you do not like the tension that has arisen between you. However, I insist you take a note from me to the vendors and instruct them to send all bills to Marcus's secretary. I cannot accompany you today, but I do want to have a part in the fun." The duchess had penned a letter, marking it with her own seal. "I know you will find just the right things."

The dowager had looked up from her embroidery. "You're trusting two young girls with that much power? To buy whatever they wish and send you the bill? What will Marcus say?"

"He will say I have done well." Charlotte patted Juliette's hand as she gave her the note with a wink.

Juliette tucked her arm through Agatha's as they perused the shelves at Hatchards, grateful that her friend had accepted the invitation and appeared to hold no ill will for the words they had exchanged a few nights ago. "We need some instruction booklets with letters and numbers, as well as good books for Mrs. Cadogan to read aloud. A history, some morality tales, and fables. I would also like to purchase a few Bibles so that each child may have their own while they do their lessons. Mrs. Cadogan says the Bible is their primary school text."

"We can choose ink, pens, and paper at the stationers too." Agatha's face brightened. "I feel better, doing something for others. I think I have been stuck inside my own head as much as my own house." She toyed with the black ribbon on her bonnet. "The only place I've been for ages is church. Lady Coatsworth and Alonzo are my only callers besides you."

Guilt nudged Juliette. She had been avoiding Agatha for fear of betraying her feelings about Daniel and jeopardizing her relationship with her best friend. Even now she didn't know how to broach the subject. She was grateful that she had been instructed to say nothing until the case was settled, so she had a reason to withhold the truth from Agatha. She would focus on the errand at hand and try to give Agatha a nice afternoon out.

"Do you think this would be appropriate?" Juliette held up *The Elements of Geography and of Natural and Civil History.*

"Perhaps the bookshop clerk could advise us." Agatha paged through *A Young Lady's Guide to Arithmetic,* pulling a face. "I never did like this subject."

Juliette's maid, Miss Brown, who had accompanied them for the day's shopping, ran her finger along the embossed leather spine of a book, her eyes soft.

"Miss Brown."

The maid jumped, pulling her hand away and putting it behind her back. "Yes, milady?"

"Do you enjoy reading?"

"Very much, milady, though opportunities are rare. Most often Mrs. Dunstan reads to us girls in her sitting room in the evening. She teaches anyone who wants to learn how to read. She didn't learn herself until she was older than I am now, and she thinks it a good skill for a young woman to have."

Mrs. Dunstan had unplumbed depths. A housekeeper, an agent for the Crown when necessary, a teacher of illiterate girls, and perhaps a soon-to-be countess. Not to mention Daniel's mother. Did Juliette's parents know of their housekeeper's kindness to her fellow employees? Did Uncle Bertie? They would look favorably on such efforts, and if they knew about them, they would want to help. The housekeeper was a stellar reminder of sharing what had been given to her.

"Please, Miss Brown, choose a few books for yourself and Mrs. Dunstan. I will pay for them myself. Find things you think the other girls will enjoy, but be sure to pick out one especially for yourself to keep."

The maid's eyes lit up. "Oh, thank you, milady."

"You're always doing that," Agatha commented as Miss Brown lost herself in the shelves and possibilities.

"Doing what?" Juliette asked.

"Giving joy to people. It's one of the things I liked best about you at school, and I'm glad returning to England and becoming a debutante hasn't changed that aspect of your character. You're generous and kind, and you like to make people happy."

Heat bloomed in Juliette's cheeks, thankfully hidden by her darker complexion. "You make me sound insufferably perfect. I'm not perfect, as you well know. We've been friends too long for you not to know all my flaws."

Agatha squeezed Juliette's arm. "We know each other quite well, but I stand by my statement. You do have a great capacity for giving joy."

"Good afternoon, ladies. What brings you out and about on such a dreary day?" The Duke of Haverly pulled on his gloves, his hat set at a rakish angle on his long hair. Had he come from the back of the store? Juliette hadn't noticed him, which was odd, since he was such a striking figure.

"We're shopping for schoolbooks. We've undertaken to supply the Cadogan house until Mr. Cadogan's release. They're making do with very limited resources, especially while he cannot drive his carriage, and we've joined with your duchess to fill the need." Juliette felt no fear that Marcus would censure her or his wife for being generous. Quite the opposite, in fact. The duke gave Charlotte free rein to do much as she wished.

"That's very thoughtful of you. Is there any way in which I may assist?"

"You already are. Charlotte has taken it upon herself to fund today's shopping expedition." Juliette responded to Marcus's smile. "She gave us a note asking all bills to be sent to Haverly House."

"I see. That saves me the effort, as I would have made the same offer.

Lady Juliette, I would like a word with you in private if you can spare it. Charlotte's birthday is coming soon, and I would like your opinion on a gift I have in mind for her."

He drew her into the next aisle of books, but from which position they could still be seen by Miss Brown and Agatha. "Actually, I already have Charlotte's gift. I wished to ascertain whether you have considered your future with the agency. Your parents informed me that you would be reflecting upon your decision."

"Your Grace, I have had little time to contemplate, but I feel in my heart I should continue. So much will be determined by the inheritance petition and my parents' feelings of my relationship with Daniel, but I feel my call to the agency and work for the Crown has been given me by God. To discontinue that work would be to disobey what He wills me to do. I've prayed and asked for guidance, and when I think of remaining with the agency, I have nothing but peace. I have been given much in this world, and I feel much is required as a result. If I can help our nation and obey God at the same time, how can I say no?"

Marcus looked grave. "You realize that if Daniel does not prevail in the petition, and you choose to marry him anyway, you must forfeit your position in the agency? You will have drawn so much attention to yourself that it will be impossible to use you in any capacity that includes the aristocracy. I can put Daniel undercover in mills or taverns or the like, but I will not risk putting you in those situations. You will work in the aristocracy, or you will not work for the agency at all."

Her heart tore. "Even if my parents give their blessing on the marriage . . . without Daniel being an earl?"

"Even if. I am sure Daniel would agree with me, though I suspect that without the earldom, Daniel will withdraw his bid for your hand. He is noble, and he will not see you reduced in circumstances."

She knew Daniel's nature and that what Marcus said was most likely true, but it filled her with bleakness. What should she do? What was the right answer? How could God expect her to wait on Him when nothing seemed clear?

"I do not wish to distress you, Lady Juliette, but I wanted you to be prepared. Your parents will return soon, and they will want to know your intentions. Yours and Daniel's. The petition for the earldom will be filed in two days' time." Marcus gave her an understanding look. "Think long and hard about what you want. We will be in touch." He inclined his head and took his leave.

Agatha came to Juliette, watching the duke go out into the rain. "Did you help him with his gift? What does he intend to give his wife for her birthday?"

"What other gift would Charlotte like than books?" She found herself clenching her fists and tried to loosen her muscles.

Hours later, when they reached the Cadogans', Juliette and Agatha laughed at the piles of parcels around them in the carriage. "We might overwhelm the house."

"I hope the mistress of the home won't be offended that we've brought so much." Agatha shifted a box of shoes. "I had no idea one could find so many ready-made items for sale."

Juliette nodded. They had been blessed in a life where everything they wore was bespoke, made to order exactly as they wished. "We've Miss Brown to thank for steering us in the right direction to find what we needed."

Miss Brown, who had not let loose of her book parcel since leaving Hatchards, smiled broadly. "Thank you, milady, for all you are doing. And for allowing me to help."

The Thorndike footman leapt from the carriage and knocked on the house door.

The same little faces peeped out from behind Mrs. Cadogan's skirts. Juliette stepped out of the carriage, holding out her hand to the lady. "We've come to see you again. And we've brought some things. I hope you don't mind."

"Come away in, milady. The place is at sixes and sevens, but you're most welcome." Mrs. Cadogan wiped her hand on her apron before taking Juliette's.

"I've brought my good friend Miss Montgomery with me. Hathaway, would you see to bringing in the parcels?" she asked the footman.

Agatha followed Juliette into the narrow hallway and toward the back of the house, and when Juliette looked over her shoulder, Agatha's eyes were round, looking from floor to ceiling as if she'd never seen such a humble abode before. Perhaps she hadn't.

They passed the boys' bunk room, and Agatha murmured something to herself.

Soup boiled on the hob in the kitchen, and a bit of smoke leaked from the fireplace, giving the room a haze near the ceiling. Children scurried around to stand with Mrs. Cadogan.

The footman and Miss Brown carried in the parcels.

"I wasn't certain of all the sizes, but I think I purchased enough clothing for each of the children on the list. We forgot to trace their feet, but if someone is missed, I will send shoes around as quickly as I can."

"You're generosity itself, milady. How can we ever say thank you enough? What an answer to my prayers." Mrs. Cadogan wiped her eyes with the hem of her apron.

"Oh, and there's foodstuffs, and I made arrangements for the grocer two blocks over to send a standing order weekly until Mr. Cadogan is out of gaol."

"Do you think he will be released?" Mrs. Cadogan asked, all her worry apparent in her features.

"I do. Mr. Swann has never wished to believe in his guilt, and he's working diligently to find out who is trying set the blame on Mr. Cadogan for these crimes."

Agatha opened a package, revealing three dolls as well as some jackstraws, painted pewter soldiers, and a little puppet theater. She took a doll and knelt, holding it out to one of the little girls. "Would you like to play with this?"

The child's eyes rounded, and she looked from the doll to Agatha and then to Mrs. Cadogan. The doll had a porcelain head and arms and a soft body in a bright-blue dress. The girl nodded, but she seemed overcome, unable to reach out for the treasure.

"Oh, go on with you. Take the thing," Mrs. Cadogan said. "And bless you fine ladies for thinking of the children. I've been that worried about how to feed them. I should tell you that it's too much and that we're getting along fine, but that would be a bold-faced lie, so I won't."

"Mr. Hathaway"—Juliette turned to her footman—"there is a livery stable at the end of the street where Mr. Cadogan's horses are kept. Mr. Swann has made provisions for their care, but I would like you to go see how they are. Ask if they have been exercised, and make certain they have plenty of food and clean water."

"Yes, milady."

"Miss Brown, please help us open these parcels. We'll sort them, and the children and Mrs. Cadogan can show us where they should go."

They had barely begun the process when a heavy fist pounded on the door. The young ones scurried to Mrs. Cadogan.

Without waiting to be admitted, the door swung open, hitting the wall. Footsteps thudded down the passage.

"It's the constable!" Mrs. Cadogan gathered the children to her.

"Stop there, madam." The constable, a burly man with rough clothes and hobnailed boots, pointed at the woman. "We've been ordered to take every child in this house into custody."

Two more men crowded behind him.

"Why? They've done nothing." Mrs. Cadogan looked pleadingly at Juliette. "What is this about?"

"You are Mrs. Eliza Cadogan?"

"I am."

"I am placing you under arrest for kidnapping and selling children."

"Sir, there must be some mistake." Juliette stepped between the constable and Mrs. Cadogan. "This woman has no part in abducting children."

"Stand aside, miss. I have a warrant for her arrest and permission to take the children." He looked down on Juliette from his considerable height.

She wrinkled her nose. He smelled of beer and onions. "I will not stand aside. This is ridiculous. This woman is doing her level best to help poor children, and you want to arrest her?" The notion was ludicrous, and she wouldn't stand for it. "Where is the justice in your actions? Whoever wrote that warrant is an imbecile, or he's been fed a pack of lies. Let me see it."

"Miss, if you try to interfere, I will be forced to arrest you as well for obstructing an officer in the course of his duties. The warrant is duly signed. There is a witness who has come forward claiming he was abducted by this woman and her husband."

"Balderdash. Let me see the warrant." Juliette put her hands on her hips.

"Jules," Agatha warned in a low voice. "Now is not the time."

"Now is exactly the time. I am tired of good people going to gaol for things they did not do. Whoever is framing Mr. Cadogan is clearly also framing his good wife." Her ire and frustration boiled over, clashing with what Marcus had told her about her future with the agency, her disappointment at her absent parents, and the entirety of class society who valued only those who could afford to buy their regard. "This great oaf wouldn't know justice if it formed a fist and punched him on the nose."

Moments later Juliette found herself in the custody of the great oaf, pushed into a black Mariah and looking out through the bars. She had been shackled to Mrs. Cadogan, who shook, tears pouring.

Agatha stood at the barred door. "Juliette, what should I do?"

"Get a message to . . ." Who should she say? She wanted Daniel. She needed Marcus, and she should notify Uncle Bertie. "Get a message to the Duke of Haverly. He'll know what to do."

Chapter 18

DANIEL WAITED IN THE HOUSEKEEPER'S sitting room, flexing his fingers, shifting his weight, and telling himself to stop fidgeting. He examined the shelves of serving pieces at the far end of the room, and then the tiled floor, and then the painted crown moldings.

A comfortable, serviceable room and the complete domain of his mother. Hopefully, not for long, however.

Even though he had been waiting for her arrival, he still tensed as the soft jingle of the chatelaine on her belt came from the hallway.

"Daniel." She nodded her greeting. "What is it I may do for you?"

Her tone was guarded, and given the way their last conversation had ended, he did not blame her.

Remembering the happy tunes she had hummed to him while running her fingers through his hair when he was a lad, and the easy way they had been with each other for those many years, made his heart hurt. She had been his whole world until suddenly, she wasn't.

"Thank you for seeing me. There is something I wish to discuss with you."

"Will you sit?" She motioned to the chair opposite the one with the sewing basket.

He perched on the edge of the seat, then shook his head at his ill ease as he slid back and tried to relax.

"There is much I need to tell you, but . . ." He took a deep breath, his face hot and his skin prickly. "I must apologize for my behavior. I have been disrespectful and angry and accused you of doing me wrong, when it is I who have wronged you." The words came out in a rush.

She blinked, and her lips parted. In that instant, her eyes glistened, and she raised her hand to her face.

"I assumed, when you sent me away, that you were glad to be rid of me. That your life would be much easier if I wasn't around. The solicitor who took me away told me you had been so grateful to be rid of me that you had quickly taken the money he'd offered and that you never wanted to see me again. His statement fed into my bewilderment and hurt."

She blanched. "Oh, Daniel, that was a lie. I never took money for you. And I certainly wasn't relieved to have you gone." She shook her head, her hand reaching out for him before dropping it to her lap. "Do you suppose that man lied to you to sever the ties between us more easily? To somehow make the separation less of a wrench?"

"If he was trying to make it less hurtful, he couldn't have done a worse job." Bitterness coated Daniel's voice, as well as a healthy dose of regret. He'd taken out on his mother something that had proven to be a lie.

A tear tracked down her cheek, and she checked her sleeve. With a pang of remembrance, he reached for his handkerchief.

"You never could find yours." The memory was so strong, he felt his own eyes prickle. She had once told him that a man carried two handkerchiefs—one in his trouser pocket for himself and one in his breast pocket for a lady in need. And she had been the lady in need most often in his life.

She gave him a watery smile. "You will never know how I agonized over sending you away. It was the most difficult thing I have ever done. And I had to act quickly. There was no time to prepare you. The solicitor told me I must decide that day, that he would fetch you the following afternoon because the new term at school had already begun. If I chose not to surrender custody, he would have a word with my employer and see we were both turned out. I felt I had no choice but to let you go to what I hoped would be a better life."

"Did you know where they were taking me?"

"The solicitor would not tell me where, only that it was one of the best schools in the kingdom. He assured me you would have a good education, fine clothes, and opportunity to choose your vocation. I received reports every quarter. How you were doing in your classes, your health. I kept every single page." She rose and went to a box on the mantel. "I hungered after every scrap of information. The first quarter, when the report said you were so terribly homesick, I regretted the pain I had caused you. But as the reports improved, I was glad I had been brave enough to send you away. I had to remind myself that it was for you, so you could have an education and a better life."

She handed him the box, and he opened the lid. A stack of papers, yellowing now with age. He pulled one out and held it up.

Daniel has excelled at history, grammar, geography, and athletics. He is disinterested in all forms of mathematics. A tutor has been procured for him for the next term at the university that has been chosen for him, and we expect him to do well. He is in good health and has shown considerable talent in equestrian endeavors.

Odd to read reports about himself. He'd never known what his teachers and professors thought of his academics, had never conferred with any of them as to his future. All that had been decided without him.

"I was miserable in those early days. I built up walls around my heart, shutting you away because it hurt so much. I threw myself into my studies and into cricket and riding so I wouldn't have to remember." He pressed his palms together, pinning his hands between his knees. "I was given all the 'rules' of my guardianship, and the one that hurt the most was not being able to have any contact with you. I let that hurt build up and carried it around with me for a long time. I thought that stipulation had come from you."

"I am so sorry. I was frightened when the solicitor came. He was so forceful, telling me this was the opportunity of a lifetime. That

I couldn't be so selfish as to deny you the chance to become something other than a groom or gardener. The only other time I had been approached by a solicitor, it was to tell me my marriage was dissolved and that I was being shipped to an estate in Norfolk. It felt as if I had no choice in either decision." She shrugged, dabbing her eyes. "It was horrible and unfair to you, and yet God was able to make something good out of it. Look at the man you've become. A university education, a fine job. And if justice is done, you will be the earl. If Rotherhide had not searched for you, had not become your guardian, I don't know if he would have changed his will and confessed their secrets."

Daniel rubbed the back of his neck, remembering how Ed had spoken to him of God working in his life all along, bringing in father figures to mentor him. "Did you love my father?" He blurted out the question. It was a temerity to ask, but he had to know.

She lowered the handkerchief. "I did. I knew he found it difficult to stand up to his irascible father, but he swore his love to me. I didn't mean to fall in love with William. Never dreamed of reaching so high above my station. When I was hired, I was just sixteen, and my first job at Rotherhide was as a scullery maid. I washed pots and helped in the kitchen. Then I was promoted to upstairs maid, dusting and making beds and carrying coal and water. That's when I got to know your father. I 'did' his rooms. And he was kind. I think that's what drew me to him the most. He was kind to the servants, even when his father upbraided him for being soft, telling him that one had to be the 'boss' of his staff or they would take advantage. William was never improper with me. He did not . . ." Her cheeks reddened. "He did not seduce me. His only fault was that he let his father ride roughshod over him."

"I cannot imagine what it must have been like for you. You must have been devastated to realize you were carrying me." He stared at the floor.

"Oh, don't think that for a moment. I was grateful. I loved William so much, and I was happy that I would have a little part of him to keep with me always. I will not lie to you. I was afraid. I did not know how I would care for you or if my new employer would turn me away. When you were born, and you looked so like your father, I cried. You were such a comfort to me. I was no longer alone."

Daniel knelt before her chair and took her hands. "And you will never be alone again, if it is in my power. I am so sorry for the way I have acted since finding you again."

She cupped his face in a caress straight out of his childhood. "I love you, Daniel. I always have. There is nothing to forgive."

His eyes burned, and he relished her touch. Cracks and craters in his heart filled and were made whole again. Peace that had eluded him drove out bitterness and past hurts.

When he had composed himself, he returned to his chair. "I came to apologize and to promise you that I will do all I can to restore your good name."

"I have a good name. Miss Catherine Swann. I adopted the name Mrs. Dunstan because it is always best when a housekeeper has been married. It gives one a certain gravitas with the maids if they assume one is a widow."

"Your name is Mrs. Catherine Darby," he reminded her. "I have the papers to prove it. I want you to have the recognition you deserve."

"The only thing I wanted in life for a very long time, you've given to me today. I wanted to be reconciled with my son. I don't need a title or recognition from anyone. I have everything now." She rose and opened her arms.

He met her in the embrace, inhaling the scent of tea and soap and spices and that indefinable essence that was just her . . . the one he remembered from his boyhood.

"Whatever happens, we know it will be God's will and that He will take care of our future. And Lady Juliette's too." She leaned back, her face grave. "Yes, I know about that. There are many secrets a woman can keep, but being in love is not one of them. She glows at the mere mention of your name. But, Daniel, a word of caution. You and I have been the victims of much hate and hurt because of my attempt to marry above my station. I know the circumstances are different, but there are enough similarities for me to urge caution. If you are not invested the earl, you must not marry Lady Juliette. It would be disastrous for you both."

Daniel wanted to protest, but she was right. If he could not join Juliette's social class, he would not ask her to join his.

"Eventually you might grow to resent one another. Juliette might regret all she forfeited to marry you, and you in turn would carry the guilt of allowing her to have made such a sacrifice. I hope you will pray hard that God's will for you both will be apparent. That if you are not victorious in winning the title, you will take it as a sure sign that God is closing the door on marriage to Juliette."

Juliette met Uncle Bertie's eyes through the bars of her prison cell. She had been shoved into the women's courtyard upon arrival, but when she had given the warder her full name and title, he'd arranged for her to have a private cell.

Beside Bertie, Marcus spoke with the gaoler, signed a paper, and stepped aside for the man to unlock the door.

Juliette gathered what was left of her dignity and kept her chin level with the floor as she walked out. No one spoke until they were standing on the street.

Agatha bolted out of the carriage at the curb, embracing Juliette, her face a twist of anguish. "Oh, Jules, are you well? I went as quickly as I could. I had a terrible time finding the duke but was finally able to run him to earth at Westminster."

Juliette hugged her friend back. The hours she had spent regretting her temper, fuming at the injustice of Mrs. Cadogan's arrest, and wondering when the duke would come had exhausted her. She wanted to go home, send her regrets for whatever social engagement she was expected to attend tonight, and take a thorough bath.

She had barely been released from Agatha's embrace when the one she most longed to see approached.

"Juliette, I came as quickly as I could. What on earth happened?" Daniel looked as if he would embrace her but stopped in time.

"Juliette. What is he doing here?" Agatha tugged on Juliette's arm. "Who do you think you are? Get away from here."

"Agatha, stop. It's fine." Juliette wished she could run into his arms, and knowing she couldn't caused tears to prick her eyes. "He's here to help."

"Perhaps we should take this discussion elsewhere. The steps of Newgate Prison seem a rather unorthodox setting for an assemblage." Bertie's dry wit brought Juliette up sharply.

Agatha's mouth had fallen open, and bewildered hurt glazed her eyes. "But he's . . . he's . . . he's trying to steal Alonzo's inheritance."

"Ladies, Sir Bertrand is correct. This is neither the time nor the place. Get in the carriage now." The duke's tone brooked no argument.

Once inside—with the three gentlemen crowded on one bench and the ladies, including Miss Brown, who still held her wrapped books in her lap, on the other—the duke took control of the conversation. "We are going to the Thorndike residence. There, we will make the appropriate plans for moving forward."

They rode in silence to Belgrave Square, and Agatha held herself as rigidly as if she had been frozen solid. Juliette felt pressure on her shoe and met Daniel's eyes across from her. He winked, and she didn't know whether to sob or laugh. What a farce.

"Your parents are never going to leave you in my care again," Uncle Bertie declared. "Getting yourself arrested. Perhaps the dowager has the correct measure. Perhaps I should lock you in your room until Tristan and Melisande return."

You taught me to pick locks, remember? She didn't say it aloud, because Agatha wasn't to know of her clandestine endeavors, but she skewered Bertie with a look that expressed her feelings.

When they reached the Thorndike townhouse, everyone went inside except Agatha. She sat firmly in the carriage. "I would appreciate you asking your driver to take me to my home. There is no need, nor desire, for me to go in with you. I will dispatch the carriage back here straight away."

"Oh, Agatha, please. Will you not come inside so we may talk?" Juliette asked.

"There is nothing to say. I asked you to sever all ties with this man, yet you persist. You must choose, Juliette, between your friendship with me and continuing to make allowances for Mr. Swann. I cannot and will not side with anyone but Alonzo in this matter, not even you." She reached out and closed the carriage door firmly in Juliette's face.

A stone of regret and sorrow, tinged with anger, grew in Juliette's chest. The severing she had feared had come. Agatha was a loyal friend, but if she sensed disloyalty in someone, she took it to heart.

"Come inside, Juliette." Daniel took her elbow. "We've much to do and discuss." When they reached the Thorndike foyer, he paused, hugging her tight. "I'm sorry. I had no wish to come between you and Miss Montgomery."

She inhaled his scent, her nose pressed into his shirtfront. "It is not your fault. The fault lies in the previous generations who made such disastrous decisions that set us on this course." Her throat felt thick, as if she needed a good cry to release the grief at her severed friendship with Agatha and all the other impossible mountains standing between herself and the desires of her heart.

He tightened his embrace, brushing a kiss atop her head. "The sins of the fathers." He released her, raising her chin so he could stare into her eyes. "There is much we must see to, but hopefully this will all be over soon."

Bertie had taken Marcus into the drawing room, and Juliette and Daniel joined them there.

"Tell us what happened at the Cadogan residence." Marcus wasted no time. He sat in an armchair, legs crossed, hands lax on the chair arms, eyes sharp.

She explained the delivery of the items as she took off her gloves and bonnet. "Then men barged into the house, said Mrs. Cadogan was under arrest for kidnapping children, and I lost my temper. All the children were rounded up to be taken to an orphanage or workhouse, and Mrs. Cadogan, who has already suffered too much injustice, was helpless to stop it."

"So, as it turns out, were you," Bertie observed.

"They said one of the children she was supposed to have taken had escaped and identified her and her husband as his kidnappers."

Daniel, who had leaned against the wall near the door, straightened. "Did you see the warrant? Do you know which magistrate signed it?"

"I was not allowed to examine the document, though I did ask to see it."

Marcus nodded at Daniel, who disappeared into the front hall. "He will dispatch a footman to Bow Street to fetch Mr. Beck and Mr. Wilkinson. Things are moving quickly, and if we do not keep up, the Cadogans may be sentenced before we can forestall it."

Juliette tossed her accessories onto the settee and smoothed her hair. She still felt grimy after being in the prison, but Marcus was correct. They must find a way to stop this injustice before it was too late.

"It will be some time before Mr. Swann's compatriots arrive, and I have other messengers to send out. Lady Juliette, perhaps you would like some time to freshen up? And Bertie, if you could summon your housekeeper and the boy Daniel sent here for protection. I have a few questions for that lad."

Juliette had been well and truly dismissed. Was Marcus angry with her? Bertie she could work around, even if he was a bit put out at the moment, but to have disappointed the duke and perhaps put him even further off the notion of her continuing to work for him cut deeply. She gathered her possessions, bobbed a curtsy in the duke's direction, and went upstairs.

When she returned an hour later, freshly washed and clothed, it was to a larger assembly in the drawing room. If only everyone in the group was privy to the agency, they could have met in the War Room on the top floor of the house. Mr. Beck and Mr. Wilkinson had arrived, as well as Mr. Partridge.

The men rose as she came in. "Please be seated, gentlemen." She went to Uncle Bertie's side, though everything in her wanted to be near Daniel. The greatest difficulty in keeping secrets was remembering who knew and who wasn't supposed to know.

Mrs. Dunstan sat by Daniel in any case, and both seemed quite relaxed in each other's company. Had they reconciled? She prayed it was so. If nothing else came from it, perhaps the petition for the title would open the door to Daniel and his mother to forge a new relationship.

On an ottoman at Mrs. Dunstan's feet sat Caleb, the Bow Street office boy. He'd been given new clothes and a haircut, and he'd been taken in hand by the housekeeper, who was teaching him manners and new skills.

"Young man, you have been most helpful. Thank you for your cooperation. I do not know if you will be allowed to return to your position at Bow Street, but you will not be abandoned. If your former position is unavailable to you, we here in this room will make certain you have a place to live and work." Marcus looked around the room. "You all have your assignments, gentlemen? Let us get to it."

They had held their planning meeting without her? Juliette frowned at Daniel and then at Bertie. "I thought you were waiting for messengers to return before discussing strategy. Why did you not wait for me?"

"Juliette, darling," Bertie whispered, "you are not part of this investigation. Remember how you were supposed to keep a low profile, not draw attention to yourself, and contemplate your future in the agency? Nothing in the charge your parents gave you said to partake in a criminal investigation or get yourself tossed into Newgate."

"But I've helped Daniel on his biggest cases, and this one is important."

"The first one you helped with because you tumbled to our work and got yourself kidnapped, and the second was over my reluctant body, a body that got shot for my troubles, if you will remember? This time you stay well out of it. I'm not even getting involved other than to gather a bit of information for Marcus."

She flattened her lips and crossed her arms. Yet her desire to help confirmed in her mind that she wanted to continue as an agent.

But what about Marcus's challenge that if Daniel did not win his petition for the earldom, and she went ahead and married him, it would put paid to her ambitions as a spy?

"Can you at least maneuver a few moments so that I may speak to Daniel alone?" she whispered. "I have something I must tell him."

"You're certain you are not involving yourself in the case any more than you already have? Getting yourself arrested?" Bertie shook his head, but he smiled indulgently. "I am not the only individual who is counting the days until your parents return. I am not equipped to be a chaperone."

"It's nothing to do with the case, I promise." She held up her palms, innocent as a spring daisy.

"Very well, but keep it to a minimum. For two people who are supposed to not let on that they have feelings for each other, you certainly find ways to be together."

As the men took their leave, Bertie said a few words to Daniel, who nodded. He followed Bertie into the library but sent a glance back over his shoulder at Juliette.

When the hall was empty, she joined them in the cozy room. The panel hiding the wall safe had been repaired and everything returned to normal after the break-in that had occurred a few months ago. The room smelled of leather and wood polish and the indefinable scent of books. She inhaled deeply, drawing comfort from the pleasant aroma.

"I'll give you five minutes, and you'll leave the door cracked open. I may be lenient, but I've not totally lost my mind." Bertie pointed at Juliette.

When he'd gone, Daniel moved toward her, but she put up her hand.

He halted, brows coming down. "Juliette? What's wrong?"

"Nothing is wrong, but there is something I must say to you." Her heartbeat throbbed in her throat. "Marcus told me you might be considering being 'noble' and withdrawing from our relationship if the inheritance petition does not break your way."

His shoulders straightened. "That is correct. I realize it was a complete cheek to even declare myself to you when our positions are so far apart in society. I should have held my peace, but when I saw Duke Heinrich von Lowe kiss you, I lost my self-control. My mother reminded me, however, of the troubles that follow when people attempt to marry across societal classes.

"If I am named the earl, I will ask your father for your hand, but if I am denied the title, I cannot ask you to marry me, to join me in my rooming house, to live on my small salary. Not that I will have that salary once the decision has been reached, for I have been told I will be turned out of my position at Bow Street regardless of the outcome. If Alonzo wins Rotherhide, he has informed me he will sue for the settlement our grandfather bestowed on me, so I will not have even that with which to keep you. I cannot ask you to make that sacrifice."

A wave of shock smote her, and for a moment she couldn't think. It was one thing for the duke to speculate on Daniel's thoughts on the issue, but another altogether to hear it from his own dear lips. "And I have no say in the matter? What if I wanted to be 'noble,' as you call it? Daniel, I have thought of little else in the last few weeks, and I would rather have you and none of this"—she waved to the opulent room around her—"than all of this and not have you."

"You say that now, and I hold it dear to my heart, but I cannot allow you to take such a step. You deserve much better, and I never want you to have regrets. You've been accustomed to nothing but luxury your whole life. You have no idea what it is like to live hand to mouth, hoping the money you earn every day will be enough to feed, house, and clothe you for that day. I'll admit I have not faced those difficulties in a long time, but they are part of my past. I will no longer be a Bow Street runner no matter the outcome of the petition, and I will be forced to make my way in another vocation. I cannot even guarantee that I can support myself, much less a wife and someday perhaps children."

Children. Children with his blue eyes and dark curly hair. Her heart ached.

He continued. "There is every chance that your parents will forbid our marriage anyway."

"I don't care. I would make them understand how precious you are to me. If I would only marry you if you were an earl, how could you ever trust my love, that I married you for the man you are, not the title you hold? I love you, Daniel Swann, and I do not care about money or titles or even being an agent."

His shoulders sagged. "I love you too, Juliette. With everything I am. You are so deeply embedded in my heart, it will nearly kill me to lose you, but if I cannot meet you as an equal, I will not press my suit. I love you too much to marry you unless I can give you the life you deserve." His tone brooked no argument.

"You have all the power to choose, and I have none?" Tears burned her eyes.

He shook his head. "I am powerless when it comes to my love for you. And because I love you, I will make this sacrifice."

"Why is it you can sacrifice, and I cannot? Though I do not consider it a sacrifice to marry you, regardless of your status in society. Please, Daniel." She held out her hand, entreating him to see it from her perspective.

"No, my darling. For your sake, I must say no." He took her hand, opened her palm, and pressed a kiss there. "I am sorry. This is my fault. I should have concealed my feelings for you until everything was settled and I was in a position to offer for you. Unless God does something miraculous and sees fit to make me an earl, I will no longer pursue you. I feel it would be best if we refrained from seeing each other until such time as we are equal in social standing and I can openly court you. If that does not happen, then this is my farewell." He folded her fingers over, concealing the kiss he'd placed against her skin, then walked out of the library.

Chapter 19

"THE WARRANT WAS FORGED, WHICH, considering our quarry, is not a total surprise. Mrs. Cadogan should never have been arrested. He's panicking." Ed held up the copy of the document he'd retrieved from Newgate earlier that day. "How did he manage to remain unknown for so long? I've not heard a whisper of Puck or his organization."

"It's the dual life he leads. The circles in which he currently moves are hardly likely to overlap with the clientele at The Oarsman. I'm certain he takes care that they don't, working through others who do his bidding if there is even a chance of his being recognized. It is only coincidence that I am one of the few people in the city to encounter him in both his personas." Daniel hurried along under the maples that dotted Berkeley Square. His cloak fluttered about him in his haste, but he wished to arrive well before the appointed time at Haverly's. It was nearly full dark already.

The duke had thought it best to meet in his conference room, well away from any of his family but a location that would not arouse suspicion.

Owen had insisted upon coming along, and he trailed behind Daniel and Ed. "I'm glad to have the duke on our side. I don't know how he gets so many things accomplished so quickly, but I wish he was our governor instead of Sir Michael. Criminals would be afraid to put a foot wrong in this city if Haverly was in charge."

If Owen only knew the extent to which Haverly protected the city and the realm.

As they neared Haverly House, Mr. Partridge stepped from the shadows. "Evening, gentlemen." His bass voice rumbled in his barrel chest. "This way. Something to show you."

They diverted down an alley that took them to the back of Haverly's massive residence. Deep shadows surrounded them, and Daniel had to strain his eyes to see Partridge ahead of him. If he didn't trust the man, he would have drawn his pistol and been ready for an ambush.

They turned once more, went through a gate that opened silently—he expected no less from an agent like Haverly than to have well-oiled gates—and down a flight of steps to the basement.

Their footsteps echoed on the tiles of the narrow hall. Partridge turned into the servants' dining room, and Daniel stopped in the doorway.

Seven little faces looked up from their plates. Six boys, one girl. Dirty, with unkept hair but bright eyes.

"This is Matthew, Johnny, Davy, Peter, Lloyd, and little Alice. They've joined young Caleb here for dinner." Partridge tousled one of the boys' heads as he went to the far end of the table.

"You found them." A knot of worry loosened from Daniel's muscles. It was the most concerning aspect of the entire case, the safety and whereabouts of these children.

His mother backed through the swinging door, carrying a tray. The aroma of freshly baked fruit pie filled the room. "Here you are—one for each of you."

"What are you doing here?" Daniel asked.

"Mr. Partridge sent for me, asking me to bring Caleb, and helping to see to the children. The duke's housekeeper is ailing, and he thought I might be of assistance." She set slices before the children and passed a small pitcher of cream. Their eyes grew round, and they didn't wait to be invited to tuck in.

"How did you find them?" Daniel asked.

Partridge motioned for them to step to the side of the room, away from little ears. "Puck didn't show at The Oarsman, but I noticed the publican putting together a box of food and carrying it out the back. He handed it to a skinny man with gold-rimmed spectacles. I followed him, and he wound up at a house a few blocks away. Went right to the cellar door, which was chained shut. When he'd gone down the stairs, I heard young voices."

"Do you think Puck will be tipped off? Might he go to ground if he discovers them missing?" Ed asked.

Partridge shook his head, crossing his arms. "Didn't leave anyone about to tell him, did I?"

A shiver went up Daniel's spine. "You didn't . . ."

The big man shook his head. "Nay, didn't have to. The skinny man dropped the crate and surrendered without a whimper. I set the kids free, and they helped me march him to another pub, one Hawk has an agent in, and I turned him over. Thought I should bring the little 'uns here where they could be looked after proper."

"Well done. Has Haverly given you orders for tonight?"

"Aye." He didn't divulge what those orders were, and Daniel didn't pry.

"Daniel," his mother said, "His Grace is waiting for you upstairs. The meeting will begin soon."

He reached out and squeezed her hand. "Thank you for taking care of the children. Hopefully, by tomorrow they can return to their homes."

"Whatever you must do tonight, take care."

His heart warmed that she was concerned. Her voice sounded so like he remembered it when he was a child, that his eyes prickled.

He drew his mother into the hall for a moment's privacy.

"I spoke with Juliette. I told her there could be nothing more between us unless I received the title." It hurt just saying it.

"Oh, Daniel." She squeezed his arm. "That explains her sadness. She hasn't eaten all day, and only Sir Bertrand's insistence got her out of the house this evening. Poor dear. Still, I think you did the right thing. It is for her sake most of all."

If it was the right thing, why did he feel so terrible about it? It was as if someone had reached into his chest and removed his heart, replacing it with a block of ice. Though, perhaps not a block of ice, for that would feel like nothing. And he felt more than nothing . . . Was anguish too strong a word?

"Thank you, Mother, for your counsel. I must go, else I will be late." He bussed her cheek, marveling that they should have mended so many broken bridges in such a short time.

Pray he had the opportunity to do the same with Juliette one day.

He poked his head back into the dining room. "Ed, you and Owen come with me."

Haverly opened the conference room door at Daniel's knock. "Come in. I have the warrants." He produced the folded papers from his coat pocket and laid them on the table. "It took some doing. I had to enlist the aid of Sir William Garrow. He took it to Sir John Silvester, the Recorder of London. Silvester was reluctant until I provided him with the evidence you've collected. The city will be a tumult when the news breaks."

"I am still amazed at Home Office being able to decipher the ledgers, and so quickly." Daniel had to speak carefully, because Ed and Owen could not know that Marcus was the head of the agency that answered to the Home Office.

"They had some help." Marcus raised one eyebrow. "I sent a couple of men to the Olympian Club, and they persuaded Mr. Alton to help us."

"Persuaded?" Daniel asked.

The duke shrugged, and Daniel caught the gleam of his secret identity, Hawk, in his eyes. "They have their ways. Mr. Alton preferred aiding his government to see that law and order prevailed rather than to be arrested as an accomplice, and he has agreed to testify should he be needed."

"I knew he was holding back information." Daniel scowled. "But I couldn't prove it, and I couldn't get it out of him."

Ed nodded. "How did Garrow crack him?"

Daniel flexed his fingers behind his back, glad that Ed had veered away from the role Haverly had played, assuming the attorney general was the power behind the moves being made.

"Garrow has his ways. To say he was shocked at the information I brought him would be putting it mildly. He was incensed that such behavior could be going on almost under his nose."

"Did Alton give any details about the murder of Haskett or the footman Burghley?" Daniel's heart beat quickly, as it always did at the culmination of an investigation. The pieces were falling into place.

"He did not witness the murder of Haskett, but he has been unwillingly involved in the framing of Mr. Cadogan. We'll discuss it more later. It is nearly time for our guests to arrive. Daniel, you sit at the table with me. Mr. Beck, Mr. Wilkinson, there is a hidden door behind the bookcase. If you two will wait there out of sight, you can listen and come in when you are needed." Haverly pointed across the room.

A hidden door. Of course Haverly would have hidden doors in his house. Ed nodded, and Owen looked as if he was having the time of his life. He hurried over and examined the bookshelf for a latch or lever.

"Pull on the Wollstonecraft book from the top. Tip it toward you."

Owen did so, and the bookcase swung toward him as silently as had the backyard gate. The young man grinned, peering into the space behind.

"Slide the small panel there open an inch or two so you can hear. You will not have a lamp, I'm afraid, as the light may give away your position through the opening."

"Wollstonecraft again?" Daniel asked when his fellow officers were concealed. A copy of a Wollstonecraft book atop one of the bookcases at Hatchards let agents know when it was safe to use the passage up to Haverly's cramped, dark office above the bookstore.

The duke shrugged. "Wollstonecraft has a sharp mind and a sharp tongue, and it takes intellect to read her. She is a favorite author of my wife's." He lowered his head as he moved past Daniel to the head of the table and whispered, "I should tell you that Lady Juliette is in the house. Charlotte invited her to an informal dinner. No other guests, just Juliette. They're currently in my wife's sitting room upstairs."

Juliette was here? Guilt punched him in the gut. This inheritance dispute hung over his head like the sword of Damocles. He wanted to race upstairs and beg her forgiveness, to capitulate and promise to marry her no matter who objected or how poor he was, because he was that selfish . . . but he couldn't. He wouldn't be that weak. It wouldn't be fair or right to sentence her to a future of poverty. He had to be strong enough for both of them.

The pain he had caused had shown out of her brown eyes, and the image haunted him.

The duke slid his pocket watch into his palm. "Nearly time. I trust you are armed?"

"Yes, Your Grace." Daniel took the indicated seat at the table, feeling the pressure of the pistol in his waistband against the back of the chair. He had the gun, his truncheon, and a knife in his boot, should he need it. Ed and Owen were similarly armed, and each had a set of darbies.

A discreet tap on the door was the signal that the guests had arrived in the foyer. Daniel tensed. He breathed in through his nose and out through his mouth, trying to calm his nerves. How could the duke appear so unconcerned, so relaxed?

Moments later, footsteps in the hall. Which one would arrive first?

Sir James Durridge entered, followed by Mr. Childers, who carried his portable writing desk and the familiar leather portfolio. "Your Grace, Mr. Swann." Sir James greeted them. "All is in order with the petition, and I have my audience with Sir William tomorrow. I am not certain what we can accomplish by meeting yet again. Your request that I come at once was most inconvenient for both of us." He pulled out his chair rather sharply. "I had a difficult time locating my clerk on such short notice. We do lead other lives, you understand. I was forced to forgo an excellent concert with friends to be here."

Mr. Childers took his seat down the table. He busied himself organizing his equipment, his expression bland, as if he'd heard his employer's protests at length on the carriage ride over.

"What is it you wish to discuss, Your Grace?" Sir James's tone indicated his barely concealed frustration.

"What time is the meeting tomorrow?" Haverly asked.

"Nine. At Westminster. There is no need for either of you to attend. Childers and I will appear on Swann's behalf."

The small tap at the door sounded again. Their other guest had arrived in the foyer. It was time.

Daniel stood, moving away from the table. "Sir James, you will have to attend the meeting with the attorney general alone. I am arresting your clerk, Mr. Childers, for murder, blackmail, and kidnapping." He drew his gun from his waistband and pointed it at the clerk. "Or rather than Mr. Childers, should I say Bobby Puck? On your feet, Puck."

The clerk sprang to his feet, dragging a pistol from the writing desk, his face a rictus of fury.

Daniel's finger tightened on the trigger, but he didn't wish to kill the man unless he had to.

Puck moved the barrel of his gun from one man to the next, edging toward the door. "You'll never arrest me. How do you know? Doesn't matter. You make one move, and I'll shoot." He appeared to judge the distance between himself and the door and motioned Daniel to move farther toward the opposite side of the room.

The bookcase behind him opened on silent hinges, and before Puck could take another step, Ed pressed his own pistol against his neck. "Drop it, Puck."

Puck froze, eyes widening. He kept the pistol trained on Daniel.

"What is the meaning of this?" Sir James blustered and made as if to rise. "Who are these people, and who is Puck? Childers, put that gun down. What are you even doing with a pistol?"

Puck's hand wavered, and Owen reached over his shoulder and forced his arm down, removing the pistol from his grip after a brief tussle. Ed produced the darbies, and Owen locked them on Puck's wrists behind his back. Owen wore a satisfied grin as he yanked on the connecting chain to make certain the shackles were secure.

"Sit." Ed pushed Puck into his chair while Owen removed the writing desk and the portfolio from the table.

"I demand an explanation." Sir James smacked the table.

"And you shall have one momentarily," Haverly said.

Daniel hadn't seen him move, and yet the duke was on his feet, pistol in hand, cool as a north wind. He looked to the hall door just as it opened, and a footman ushered in the final piece to the puzzle.

Sir Michael Biddle.

Sir Michael took one look at the tableau—Ed, Owen, Daniel, and Puck with shackles on—and turned to flee.

Mr. Partridge effectively blocked his way, turning him around with a meaty hand on his narrow shoulder. "Leaving so soon?" He marched the supervisor of inspectors into the room and closed the door behind him. "I believe these gentlemen would like a word."

Daniel hid a smile. So that was the assignment Haverly had given his most intimidating enforcer.

Sir Michael appeared to regroup, choosing to try to bluster his way out. "What are you doing here, Swann? Beck? Wilkinson? Why are you bothering these fine people? Your Grace, I apologize. Mr. Swann is continually grasping above his station and seeking to ingratiate himself with his betters."

"Perhaps you should have a seat, Sir Michael," the duke said. "Mr. Swann is here in an official capacity."

"He cannot be. I did not dispatch him on any case that would bring him here." Sir Michael eyed Puck, guarded closely by Ed and Owen.

Would he show any sign of recognition?

Sir Michael slowly pulled out a chair, not breaking eye contact with Puck, who fumed and glared but said nothing. Haverly waved to Daniel. "Proceed."

"Sir Michael." He tried to work some saliva into his mouth. "We have arrested this man, known to his employer as Mr. Henry Childers, for murder. His real name is Bobby or Robert Puck, and he is the head of a criminal organization that is guilty of a litany of crimes. Murder, kidnapping, and blackmail are but a few." He paused. "However, you are already aware of his crimes."

"What do you mean?" Sir Michael barked. "I've never met this man and know nothing of his doings, legal or otherwise."

"You were witnessed in his company at a pub known as The Oarsman in Wapping two nights ago. You are well acquainted. He has been blackmailing you for years." Sir Michael Biddle was one of the encoded names in the ledgers, showing regular payments to the Puck organization.

"That is preposterous. I won't stand for these baseless accusations. Swann, you are dismissed from Bow Street. Turn in your truncheon and clean out your desk." More bluster. "Your Grace, you cannot possibly believe these lies? I know you have championed Swann's cause recently, but he has deceived you, just as he has deceived me."

"What proof do you have of these charges?" Sir James asked, his face red as a beetroot. "I've known Childers for years. He's no criminal. He's a law clerk, of all things. And this man is the supervisor of investigators at Bow Street. Neither of them would be involved in anything scurrilous."

Haverly slid the warrants toward Sir James. "Mr. Beck, I believe you should search Mr. Puck for other weapons. Mr. Wilkinson, please shackle Sir Michael and then go through Mr. Puck's belongings in the traveling desk while I search the portfolio. We wouldn't want anyone to do anything foolish. Someone could get hurt." The duke's calm, commanding tone eased Daniel's tension. Haverly would back them.

"Look what we have here." Ed, who had been patting down Mr. Puck, raised a menacing knife. "Stuck in his boot." Thick, heavy, with a triangular blade serrated on one side and with a healthy knuckle guard on the handle. "I believe we might have located our murder weapon."

The weapon closely resembled the sketch Rhynwick had produced. "Rosebreen and Davies will be able to tell us." Daniel nodded his approval as Ed stuck the knife through his belt. He would deliver it to the scientists for examination tomorrow.

"You've no proof I'm involved with this man. So we happened to be in the same pub. That's no crime," Sir Michael said. "Who says we were there together? This is a pack of lies."

"I say you were with him at The Oarsman. I saw you with my own eyes." Daniel replaced his pistol into his waistband once the prisoners were properly restrained. "Puck never thought the Olympian Club ledgers would be found, but once they were, he instructed you to remove them from Bow Street before they could be deciphered. Your attempt to force me to return them failed, and you tried to steal them by ordering an employee to break in to my desk. I foiled those plans by entrusting them to Lord Creevy's safe in his chambers, a place not even you could ransack. When you couldn't find the books, you both decided to throw all suspicion away from the club by framing an innocent man, a man you both knew had a history with Haskett. The carriage driver Cadogan. You forced someone to leave evidence of the crime in a place sure to be found to solidify the case against Cadogan."

"Surely you have the wrong man, gentlemen." Sir James's brows knit across his forehead as the evidence mounted. "I tell you I've known and trusted Henry Childers for years."

"How did you meet him?" Haverly asked.

"It was years ago. At a coaching inn. I'd been traveling, and just as we reached the outskirts of London, there was an accident. The horses bolted, and the carriage crashed. I broke my leg. They carried me to the inn, and there was a young man working there in the stables. Henry Childers. I was laid up for weeks while my leg mended, and I hired Henry to be my . . . my valet, I suppose. He ran errands, copied documents, kept me in touch with my clients in the city. When I was well enough to return to London, Henry accompanied me. He's been my clerk ever since. That was years ago."

Haverly steepled his fingers, resting his elbows on the arms of his chair. "I have verified all of that through my inquiries. What you did not know is that before you met him, he was Bobby Puck, a street child turned aspiring gang boss. He feared arrest as things grew too hot for him in London, and he sought an escape to let things cool down. He thought it to his advantage to change his identity while not leaving his life of crime behind. Slowly he removed or turned every man working for the boss of his old organization until only he and those loyal to him remained. Working for you enhanced his ability to network with other criminals. He has contacts now in every avenue of lawbreaking. You remember how he said he could find London's best forgers and even produced the original forger hired by William Darby to create annulment papers that would fool his father? It's because that original forger was in Puck's employ."

Sir James's eyes turned bleak as he realized the depths of his clerk's deceptions. There was no betrayal as painful as that of a trusted friend.

"Why did you kill Haskett?" Daniel asked Puck. "Was it because he was skimming from your take at the Olympian or because he refused to kidnap more children for you after Cadogan confronted him?"

Puck stared stonily at the wall behind Daniel. He had dropped all pretense of respectability, his face hard and eyes cold. Daniel could imagine him like a spider at the center of his web of thieves and killers. But now the strands of the web encircled and entrapped him.

"I had nothing to do with the murder," Sir Michael protested. "I demand you release me. You've found your killer, and the case is settled. You've only the word of that office boy Caleb that I colluded with Puck to steal those ledgers or plant evidence."

Daniel's gaze sharpened on his employer. "I never said our witness's name was Caleb."

Sir Michael looked as if he'd bitten a wasp, and his face turned ashen.

"Why kidnap children at all?" Ed asked. "You had the gambling club, the protection rackets, the blackmail. What possible use could you have for taking street children?"

Puck refused to answer.

Sir Michael shuddered and his face crumbled. "I'll tell you what I know, but you must speak to the judge on my behalf. Puck was gathering urchins to send north. He had an order for a dozen children to be sent to a mine in Yorkshire as free labor. It was a regular order, every few months. I told him he was acting rashly, that someone would eventually notice the missing children, even if nobody really cares what happens to the brats, but Puck wouldn't listen. No, he always has to do everything his way, even if it lands someone else in the soup."

"Shut your gob, Biddle." Puck tried to rise, but Owen pushed him down, clearly enjoying himself at his first big arrest.

"You have to listen to me. I'm a victim here. He was blackmailing me, forcing me to do his work, to cover his crimes. I had no choice. He threatened my family. He threatened me." Sir Michael pled, nearly sliding out of his chair, writhing in entreaty.

How different he was to the supercilious, petty bureaucrat of only yesterday. Bitter disgust coated Daniel's tongue, and he had to look away from the sniveling, begging husk of a man he had once called his guv.

"Mr. Partridge, the black Mariah should be here by now. I believe it would be prudent for you to accompany Mr. Beck and Mr. Wilkinson in the prisoner transport. Keep the two of these men apart, and do not allow them speak to each other." Haverly stood. "Sir James, my apologies for disrupting your evening. I trust it will not have an effect upon filing the petition on the morrow?"

The barrister shook his head, as if the meeting with the attorney general was the furthest thing from his mind. "I cannot believe this. Childers a criminal."

"Sir Michael, it would be in your best interest to say no more until you have legal counsel at the gaol," Daniel advised him, taking a small measure of pity on the man. "If you wish to make a full confession, I am sure the judge will take that into account when it comes to trial."

Sir Michael sagged, and Ed had to support him to get him to his feet.

Puck needed no such support. He spewed expletives and threats. They would regret trying to take him. He would escape. His men would see them all murdered within a fortnight.

Such a display seemed to put a charge into Sir James. He appeared to now harbor no doubts as to his clerk's capacity for duplicity and murder.

Daniel took Sir Michael's other arm. "This way, sir." He felt sorry for his boss. His life as he knew it was over. He would certainly spend a considerable amount of time in gaol at the very least. Transportation to Botany Bay or death loomed as very real possibilities.

As they walked down the stairs, the drawing room door opened and the duchess and Juliette appeared. Daniel stopped, taking in the sight of her.

Would she ever be his? Would she even want to be, after he had made his ultimatum?

Without a word they escorted the prisoners outside and into the barred carriage for the journey to Newgate.

It was going to be a long few days of taking statements and delivering evidence to the court, but not even that would distract him from the ache in his heart.

Juliette cut out the paper doll she had drawn, handing it to the little girl, Martha, who sat beside her at the Cadogan table. "Which dress would you like for her? Where is she going?"

"To a party. With ice cream and cake and sweets." The little girl's face lit up. "I had a sweet once. It was 'stachio." She smacked her little lips.

Miss Brown smiled at Juliette over the child's head. The maid had been so helpful. All the children had been returned to the Cadogan residence, and Miss Brown had aided Juliette in getting them fed and clothed.

The front door opened, and a shout emitted from the boys' room off the front hall. "Dougie!" Little feet hit the floor, followed by laughter.

Martha shot out of her chair like a lintie, scattering paper dolls in her wake.

Juliette rose, placing her scissors into her basket.

"I'll see to your things," Miss Brown said. "Go greet the Cadogans."

"Thank you." Juliette took one more look around the room, happy the shelves were full of crockery, food, and other supplies. A table by the door held the books and papers Charlotte had purchased through Juliette, and a box of toys sat beneath it, a luxury to which the Cadogans and the children could never have stretched on their own.

She entered the hall to see the Cadogans swarmed with children, each holding one on their knee as they sat on the bench by the stairs. Kids wormed in between and on all sides, and each face held joy.

Mr. Cadogan rose as she approached, snatching off his askew hat. "Milady, thank you for all you did for us. My Missus told me how you defended her, even getting yourself thrown into the gaol."

Juliette took his hand. "It was nothing. I'm only sorry you were both put through this ordeal. I am thankful you were freed and the right men brought to justice. And that all the children were found." She nodded toward Matthew.

"It was Swann we have to thank for all that, him and Beck and Wilkinson. I know now they had no choice but to arrest me, but that didn't stop them from looking for the truth."

Mention of Daniel sent a shaft through Juliette. She held the banister, taking a deep breath. She had declared her love for him and willingness to marry him in spite of her parents, in spite of society's approval, even in spite of risking her future with the agency, and he had quietly refused. He'd said it was for her, because he loved her too much.

How could love hurt this much?

"Are you home forever, Dougie?" Martha asked.

"Aye, lassie, forever, thanks to the sacrifices of so many good people." Miss Brown joined them, the packed basket over her arm.

"We are so very happy with how things turned out." Juliette reached for her bonnet from the row of hooks by the door. "We will take our leave now."

"When you see Swann, give him my thanks. I'm going to check on the horses, and tomorrow I'll be back driving about London. But for today I think I'll stay home and be grateful for all I have, including friends like you." Cadogan shook Juliette's hand.

His wife dabbed tears. "Thank you, milady. I'll never forget your generosity." She bobbed her head.

"I do not believe I will allow you to forget." Juliette pulled on her gloves and slotted her wrist through the strings on her reticule. "I shall most likely make a nuisance of myself, dropping by to play with the children and have a natter over some tea."

"You'll always be welcome. And if I hear Dougie ever charges you for a fare again, he'll have me to reckon with."

Juliette left Sureton Row with a smile, though her heart remained heavy. At least someone had found happiness despite all that had gone on.

Chapter 20

"Darling, I do not know why we've been summoned, but I do know that it is terribly poor manners to be late to a meeting at Carlton House." Mother checked her hat in the hall mirror, meeting Juliette's eyes in her reflection. "Hurry. Marcus will be waiting, and so, I imagine, will the Prince Regent."

The lethargy that had clung to Juliette's limbs for the last week slowed her movements. She could drum up little enthusiasm for anything lately, and even a mysterious invitation to the Prince Regent's London residence brought no excitement.

Her parents had been home five days now, having completed their mission to the Continent. They had made their report to the Home Secretary and fitted back into their societal life as if they had never been away.

Mother had noted Juliette's demeanor and asked several times if she was well. She had even gone so far as to have a physician around to consult. The gray-haired kindly man had prescribed a tonic that Juliette found vile and knew would not cure what ailed her.

Juliette had said nothing about Daniel. Thoughts of him hurt too much. Their only hope rested in a handful of men who, historically, were loath to change the status quo. Formerly unknown petitioners for a title were more often than not rebuffed, dismissed out of hand lest the peccadillos and foibles of the aristocracy in fathering children they wished not to claim became common knowledge.

She had seen nothing of Daniel since that evening a week ago at the Haverlys when he had arrested a murderer and his own boss. The newspapers had been full of nothing else since, and Juliette had sat through a long dinner in which Uncle Bertie had brought her parents up on the story, including Juliette's small part, which had landed her in gaol for several hours.

They had been sympathetic but also cautioned her against rash behavior that would draw attention to her in ways that might undermine their work as agents.

Bertie had also apprised them of the inheritance petition for the Rotherhide title, the principal parties, and the basic known facts, along with several rumors. Though her mother had looked at her long and hard during the telling, Juliette had kept her face expressionless.

Neither parent had questioned her about her decision to continue working as an agent or not. Perhaps they felt she had not had long enough to consider? She did not broach the subject either, since she could not really decide until the petition was heard.

They now climbed into the Thorndike carriage—Mother, Father, and Juliette—and set off for Carlton House.

"Darling, I'm worried about you. I hope the upcoming trip to the seaside will cure whatever ails you." Father patted Juliette's knee. They were scheduled to leave for Brighton soon. Father had a holiday residence in Hove on the south coast, and the Prince Regent had requested they accompany him on his annual trip to Brighton.

The knot in Juliette's stomach tightened. Anxiety stalked her at night and sadness during the day. It would be the same in Brighton or London or at the family estate at Heild House in Worcestershire until the petition decision was rendered and she knew for sure.

The longer the wait, the more certain she became that things would not go well for Daniel.

Several carriages stood at the curb in front of Carlton House. She spotted the Haverly crest on one.

And the Rotherhide crest on another.

A lump formed behind her breastbone and rose to her throat. Alonzo was here? He had been using the coach, living in the townhouse, assuming he was the rightful heir.

Was this a meeting to deliver the Prince Regent's decision? If so, why had they been invited? Was this Daniel's doing, or Haverly's?

She couldn't breathe. If it was indeed the decisional meeting, she had never imagined she would be present for it. She had hoped that Daniel himself would arrive at her parents' house with the good news.

They were shown in and taken through the massive house to a magnificent room with deep carpets and heavy velvet drapes of crimson. A long table covered in green satin was flanked by gilded chairs upholstered in the same crimson velvet as the drapes. Every surface on walls, floor, and ceiling was ornamented in gilding, carving, plasterwork, or paint. Cherubs chased one another in a massive medallion on the ceiling, and a chandelier that must be all of fifteen feet in length hung over the center of the table. At the far end, a throne sat beneath a red velvet pelmet, flanked by gilded candelabra. Her feet sank into the carpet, and she realized her mouth hung open. The opulence in this single room would have fed the Cadogan household for a score of years.

As she had assumed, Marcus Haverly was there, his hair pulled back smoothly, his lapels embroidered with gold threads. Every inch the capable gentleman, he did not look a whit out of place in such a splendid room.

Alonzo Darby and his mother sat stiffly across from him. Agatha had the chair on Alonzo's other side, but she did not turn to look at Juliette. Her head was down, her face pale. A pang of loss swept over Juliette. Today would decide many things, her friendship with Agatha amongst them.

Sir James Durridge was there, sans his clerk, who now cooled his heels in Newgate, awaiting trial. Alonzo's legal representative sat opposite him, beside his client.

Mrs. Dunstan was placed beside Sir James, demure and calm. How could she be so serene at a time like this?

And lastly, Juliette allowed herself to look at Daniel. He gave the barest of nods as he rose. His features were tight, showing the strain he must be under. All the gentlemen stood as the ladies approached.

"Tristan, Melisande, welcome back." Marcus rounded the table, pretending this was his first meeting with them since their return. He had debriefed them the night after their ship docked, but that wasn't for everyone in the room to know. He kissed Mother's offered cheek. "Do sit down. His Highness will be with us shortly, I am sure."

Juliette took the chair the duke pulled out for her, down the way from Daniel and opposite the Darbys. The table formed a line of demarcation between the sides.

Haverly took the seat at the foot of the table, at Juliette's left hand. There were two chairs at the far end still empty. The most ornate of these must be for the Prince Regent, and the other for Sir William Garrow.

The silence suffocated her. Why was she here in a room with no air? Where was the prince? Did he not know that his delay was torture?

Mrs. Dunstan leaned forward and caught Juliette's eye, giving her an encouraging smile. Daniel's mother had said her calm trust came from the Lord.

If you've any extra calm, could you pass it down, please? God is in control. God already knows what the Prince Regent will decide. His heart is in the hand of the Lord. Like a river of water, God turns ruler's hearts the way He wills. Please, Lord.

Juliette knew the truth of this, and yet trusting it, leaning into it, being reassured by it was still a struggle. Charlotte had asked the hard question of whether Juliette had prayed that God's will would be done, or if she was praying that God's will and hers would align. At this point Juliette didn't know what to pray. *Please, Lord* was all she could muster.

A door at the end of the room opened, and a large, florid-faced man with a paunch and a waistcoat that strained to conceal it entered.

The Prince Regent himself.

Everyone pushed their chairs back and rose, and as he drew near, the men bowed and the ladies curtsied. Juliette did the same, sinking low and keeping her eyes down.

Another man followed him in, gray of hair and sober of demeanor. Sir William Garrow.

Juliette took her seat after the prince was seated, and she gripped her hands in her lap. Her gold and garnet ring bit into her finger, and she twisted it round and round.

"A most serious subject, the succession of a title." The prince had a fruity, deep voice, and he spoke with no introduction or welcome, almost as if continuing a conversation he'd been having. He licked his lips frequently, and the resulting glimmer of moisture made Juliette's stomach flip. She studied the far wall, where a portrait of an Elizabethan courtier stared back at her, then turned her face back to the prince, lest she be exhibiting bad manners by not giving him her attention.

"I have given the matter much thought and have conferred with both Garrow here and Haverly on the matter. Having examined the proofs provided by both sides . . ." He droned on for some time.

Why wouldn't he get to the point?

"I am reluctant to go against tradition and expectations, and for that reason I have decided that Rotherhide will be inherited by Viscount Coatsworth, Alonzo Darby."

Juliette closed her eyes as Lady Coatsworth gave a sob. Rushing water sounds filled her ears, and her breath caught in her throat.

It was over. In spite of the evidence, in spite of all the work everyone had put in, in spite of what was right and just and all her prayers . . .

She opened her eyes to see Alonzo put his arm around his mother and hold his hand out to Agatha. Agatha blinked, and two tears raced down her cheeks.

"Thank you, Your Highness," Alonzo said.

Juliette wanted to be happy for her friend, and maybe someday she would be. But not now. Now she could barely avoid being crushed by her disappointment.

She was glad she could not see Daniel's face in that moment, down the way. She could not look at Marcus. He had done everything humanly possible to prove that Daniel was the rightful heir.

This was a miscarriage of justice, but they were powerless to change any of it.

Poor Daniel.

"However, I am convinced that though for form's sake I must side with Darby as to Rotherhide, Mr. Swann has a rightful claim. This dilemma has caused me not inconsiderable effort, and I believe I have come up with a solution. A rather Solomonic solution, if I do say so myself." The prince patted his stomach with satisfaction, licking his full lips again. "Mr. Swann, you and your mother were unfairly treated by Rotherhide, and you deserve compensation. You are the legal first-born heir, and though I cannot give you Rotherhide, I have decided it is only right to confer on you a title of your own."

Everyone on Daniel's side of the table straightened.

"Your Highness?" Daniel asked.

The prince smiled broadly, as if pleased to have stunned everyone. "That is correct. There is a title lying fallow at the moment. Aylswood. I am conferring on you the title Earl of Aylswood and shall create the title Viscount Swann as well. There is property north of Banbury, a house and estate that come with the title. They have been maintained by the Crown up until now, but you will take over their upkeep and ownership. I believe the previous Earl of Rotherhide left you a considerable sum as his ward before his death. You shall keep that bequest. Also, there will be no aspersions cast upon your lady mother. Though it is unconventional, this is an unusual circumstance. By rights she would be a countess now, and while I cannot confer that title upon her, she will be known as Lady Catherine, Viscountess Swann."

No one had lit a candle or opened a curtain, but the room seemed brighter. Juliette still struggled to breathe, but for a different reason.

Two titles? The solution had never occurred to her, and she was surprised it had occurred to the prince.

God really did move in mysterious ways.

"That is a very sensible plan, Your Highness. Most clever of you to have thought of it." Marcus spoke smoothly, complimenting the ruler without being obsequious. "Aylswood is a beautiful estate. Some of the best stables in the land, I understand."

"Sir William will see to the paperwork and meet with the necessary people in transferring the title from the Crown to you." The prince waved his hand, as if it were a trifling task. "Haverly here has informed me of your service in keeping the King's peace. Bow Street will be sorry to lose you, but as a new peer, your time will otherwise be occupied. I'm certain Haverly will assist you in learning your way. He did the same for another new earl, Whitelock, not all that long ago." The prince pushed his chair back and rose, shoving his bulk upright.

Chairs slid back on the carpet as they all scrambled to their feet.

"It's time for morning tea." He patted his stomach again. "I'm peckish. Someone will show you all out."

There was barely time to bow and curtsy before he was gone.

Had it all really happened? Was Daniel now an earl? Aylswood, not Rotherhide? Did she dare hope?

Alonzo puffed out his chest. His every line showed his satisfaction. In his mind, he no doubt thought he had been vindicated. His mother dabbed her eyes with her handkerchief, her hand shaking. For all those on the outside, her marriage was declared legal and true, her son the rightful heir.

Agatha rounded the table, hugging Juliette. "Isn't it the most wonderful thing? You are happy for me, are you not? Though I'm not certain why you are here? Had your parents something to do with the Prince's decision?"

Juliette was spared having to answer.

"I asked the Thorndikes to come," Marcus said. "They are here to support Mrs. Dunstan as her employers. Though no longer Mrs. Dunstan, but Lady Catherine." He inclined his head to the new viscountess.

"Your Grace, it will take some time to become accustomed to what has happened. Did you know the prince had these plans?" she asked.

"He consulted with me yesterday."

The way the duke said it had Juliette wondering if the solution had originated with Marcus and that he had somehow convinced the prince that it was an idea of his own making.

Marcus winked at Juliette, and she suppressed a laugh. He *had* influenced the prince. She was sure of it.

"We will be taking our leave," Alonzo said, his lips stiff.

Daniel crossed to him. "Rotherhide, we've had our differences, but going forward, I would like to put the daggers away. We are, whether we like it or not, half brothers. I believe we are both big enough men to behave, if not warmly, then at least civilly to one another." He held out his hand.

Juliette held her breath.

For a moment it appeared that Alonzo would refuse, but in the end he jabbed his hand forward, gave Daniel's a brisk shake, and turned away.

It was a beginning.

Agatha joined the Darbys, taking Alonzo's offered arm, looking back with joyful eyes to Juliette. Her beloved had gotten what he wanted and thought he deserved. She was content, her future assured. And she appeared more than ready to resume her friendship with Juliette and totally unconcerned that Daniel had been given a title. What happened beyond Alonzo mattered little to her at the moment.

Sir James and the other barrister gathered themselves, shook hands all around, and departed, leaving the Swanns, Thorndikes, and Marcus.

"We're most pleased for you, Mrs. Dunstan. Or should I say Lady Catherine. I suppose this means we will have to find another house-keeper." Father bowed over her hand.

"I confess, while I am happy to have been here for you, Lady Catherine," Mother said, "I'm still mystified as to why you thought we should be present, Marcus."

"Ah, that. Well, I believe that will become apparent soon. Daniel, would you like us to absent ourselves?"

"Not just yet, Your Grace, if you don't mind. There is something I would like to say to Lord Thorndike." Though he was not speaking to her, his eyes never left Juliette's.

"Yes?" Father asked.

Daniel turned to face him. "Sir, I love your daughter. I had no business revealing those feelings to her when I did, a month and more ago, but I was delighted to know she returned them. I should have come to you immediately, but I was called away on a case, and then you and your countess left the country. In my previous station as a Bow Street investigator, I could not possibly have hoped you would look on my suit favorably, and though Juliette had declared she would marry me no matter my station in life, I could not in good conscience ask her to reduce her circumstances to that degree. I held on to hope that the Prince Regent would see the rightness of my claim to Rotherhide and that as an earl, I would be an acceptable match for Lady Juliette."

Father's brows rose, and he looked at Mother. "I see. It must have been a crushing blow to you when the prince awarded the title to Darby."

"It was the worst moment of my life, sir. Worse even than when I was taken away from my mother and banished to boarding school as a child." His eyes met Juliette's again, intense and eloquent. "But when His Highness said there was still an earldom for me, it was like sunshine bursting through the clouds. All the shadows fled. Sir, I would like to marry your daughter, and I would like your blessing."

Father pursed his lips, narrowing his eyes. "Juliette, is this true? Do you love this man?"

"I do, Father." Her voice came out squeaky, she was so overcome with hope.

"And you were prepared to marry him even if he had not received a title?"

"I was." She nodded for emphasis. "No matter what it cost me, though it would have pained me greatly if I did not have your approval."

He stroked his chin. "Haverly, you've had him investigated thoroughly, have you not?"

"I know more about him, Thorndike, than he knows about himself.

I've spent the last six weeks looking into every aspect of his origins, and before that, you know I had him checked out as a potential operative for the agency."

"Hmm. Melisande, what do you think?"

"I think you should stop tormenting them and give your blessing. It's clear now what has been ailing Juliette since we arrived home. She's been pining." Mother hugged Juliette to her side.

Father laughed. "I can never fool you, Melisande."

"Father, please," Juliette said.

He inhaled sharply. "I give my blessing, Swann, not because you are an earl but because you are a good man. You have integrity, honesty, and kindness, all of which qualities will serve you well in the future. I give my blessing to you both, but I will ask one thing."

Daniel's relieved smile had Juliette biting her bottom lip. "What is it you require?"

"I would ask you to wait to marry until autumn. You have not known each other for long, and in mostly extreme circumstances. It would be wise to spend more time in each other's company, preparing for marriage. And I would like Juliette to be married from Heild House, at St. James the Great Church in Pensax."

"September?" Juliette asked. That was only four months from now.

"I was thinking November, but perhaps we can compromise on October?" Father faced her and leaned down, placing a kiss on her forehead. "I believe we will make our way toward the carriage. Daniel, I trust you will say what you have to say and bring Juliette to the front door in a few minutes?"

"Yes, sir."

Juliette clasped her hands before her, hardly able to believe what had transpired in the last few minutes. The moment the door closed, Daniel embraced her, holding her close, kissing her temple, her hair, her forehead. At last he cupped her face between his palms.

"I've been waiting all my life for you, Juliette. You have helped me heal from hurts I didn't know I carried. Every day you inspire me to be a better man. I love you. Please, will you marry me?" His voice was thick, as if damming up more emotion than he knew what to do with.

"I will, on one condition." She stared hard into his eyes, wrapping her fingers around his lapels.

"Name it."

"Never again will you consider doing something 'for my own good' without allowing me a say. I understand your reasons, but I never want to live through anything like the last week again. My love is unconditional. I loved you before you were given a title. I loved you before you knew you were entitled to one. I love *you*, Daniel Swann, not your prospects, your social standing, or your wealth, potential or perceived."

His face softened, and he lowered his face until their foreheads touched. He moved his head so that his nose brushed hers. "I promise, and I love you all the more."

She raised her face to his, wanting to show him as well as tell him how much he meant to her. His arms came around her, folding her close, his lips firm on hers, giving and receiving, promising and anticipating.

Every shadow dissipated in the light of his love and their future together.

Suddenly, five months seemed a long time to wait.

Epilogue

"I hope the prince doesn't mind too much our being late to Brighton." Juliette took the chair Daniel pulled out for her at the Thorndike's dinner table. Guests laughed and found their place cards. "He left last week."

He took the seat beside her, letting his hand linger on her shoulder, inhaling her rose-scented perfume. "I wish we didn't have to go at all, but as long as we can be together, it won't be so bad."

"There's so much to do here, and you've yet to see your new property. Have you been to the Banbury area before?"

"I have not. It's still hard to believe I have a manor house and lands. The last couple of weeks have been a whirlwind. Haverly has made quite a point of introducing me around, sponsoring me for membership at White's, procuring invitations, establishing me in society. Your father has been helpful too. And your uncle."

Everyone had found their places, and Daniel studied the guests. Across the table, the Dowager Duchess of Haverly examined the silverware and crystal, Haverly bent his head to listen to Countess Thorndike, and Miss Cashel adjusted her skirts, a regal expression on her flawless face. The new Earl of Rotherhide and his betrothed looked quite pleased with each other, though she wore half-black mourning attire.

"I'm happy for them," Juliette said, following his gaze. "Agatha was certainly surprised when I told her of our betrothal, but as long as you didn't take Alonzo's title from him, she's happy for us both."

Daniel's mother, beautiful in a burgundy dress with ostrich feathers pinned in her hair, caught his eye and winked. She was still unaccustomed to the finery, as well as being a guest in a house she had overseen as housekeeper less than three weeks ago. He had rented a townhouse for them both, not a mile from Berkeley Square, and she had been seeing to hiring staff.

He must guard his resources, for he did not yet know what sort of income his new estate would provide, and the bequest from his grandfather would not last forever. How did one stay afloat financially when one was supposed to be the idle rich? Something on which to consult Haverly, and soon.

Footmen popped corks and filled glasses with champagne. At the head of the table, Tristan Thorndike rose, holding his glass. "Ladies and Gentlemen," he said, his voice raised.

Conversation ceased and heads turned.

"Tonight is in way of a celebration. My only child, my beloved daughter, Lady Juliette Thorndike, is formally betrothed to the Earl of Aylswood, Daniel Swann. Please join me in a toast to their happiness. I wish you as successful and blissful a marriage as your mother and I."

Everyone raised their glasses and drank. Daniel caught the eye of the dowager and only just refrained from tossing her a saucy wink. He didn't want to make the old girl choke on her wine.

Down the way, Sir Bertrand took a long gulp from his glass, his eyes unfocused, his movements wobbly. Once again he was playing his role as a sot. Who was he spying on now?

Daniel reached for Juliette's hand under the edge of the table and gave it a squeeze. She was by far the most beautiful woman in the room, surpassing even Miss Cashel. Juliette outshone them all. In any room. Anywhere. He raised his glass to her and let his eyes twinkle at her, drawing a laugh.

Dinner lasted far into the night, something else to which Daniel was trying to become accustomed. He covered a yawn as they rose. So many courses. He would have to pace himself better if they were going to eat like this often. It was all a long way from the hastily gulped eel pie or pasty from a costermonger's cart that he was used to.

When most of the guests had gone and he knew he should be taking his leave as well, Tristan asked him and Juliette into the library. "A few things to discuss before you go."

The Duke and Duchess of Haverly were already there, as well as Sir Bertrand, miraculously sober now, and Lady Thorndike.

"Well celebrated. Congratulations, Daniel, on your betrothal, and I wish you every happiness, Juliette." Marcus kissed her cheek, then shook Daniel's hand.

"Thank you." Daniel was glad Juliette kept her arm threaded through his. He liked her touch and that everyone could now know that she was his intended bride.

"I brought you all here in a sort of official capacity, as I have some news, and I have a question. First, the question." Marcus slid back his coat and put his hand in his pocket. "Lady Juliette, before your parents went to the Netherlands on their mission, they gave you a task. They asked you to consider for certain whether you wished to continue in the service of the agency as an operative for the Crown. I know you have had a few other trifling matters on your mind." He smiled. "But I hope you have given it some thought."

"I have. And I have discussed it with Daniel. It is my wish to continue both my training and to be useful in any way I can to the agency. If you are able to keep your word and not send my parents on any more missions for a while"—she inclined her head at him—"they will have a part in my training, guiding me, along with Uncle Bertie."

"Excellent. I hoped that would be your decision. Now, to my news. Daniel, as a member of the peerage, you are hardly able to continue in your current job at Bow Street. You still have your burgeoning role as an agent, but there is another position that is open, and I have it on good authority that it can be yours if you wish."

Daniel lowered his brows. "A position?"

"It seems the office of supervisor of investigators is vacant. If you were to fill that situation, think how useful you would be to the agency. And to London. You will be a valuable intelligence and information source, as well as being able to continue your police work, if in a changed capacity. As you will have to spend some time at your new estate each year, I would advise bringing Mr. Beck on as an assistant supervisor. What do you say?"

Take over Sir Michael's office? Direct investigations rather than carry them out. He would still have his hand in police work. And he would still have Ed as his partner. Daniel looked at Juliette, brows raised.

She nodded, squeezing his arm. "It's a perfect opportunity."

"If I take the position, there are some changes I would like to make, starting with petitioning Parliament for more funds to hire and pay more investigators. Having only six for a city the size of London is ridiculous." His mind raced at the possibilities.

"I can see we have the right man." Marcus clapped him on the shoulder as he passed. "I'll put the process into motion on the morrow. I'm now going to take my lovely wife home. Congratulations again, Daniel and Juliette. I am glad to retain both your services."

The Thorndikes followed him out into the hall, and his mother said, "I'll get my shawl and wait for you."

"Thank you, Mother. I won't be long."

When they were alone, Daniel kissed Juliette. "Ah, I've been wanting to do that all evening."

She laughed, sending warm trickles through his veins.

"Oh, I have one more surprise for you. I forgot until just now." He took her hands.

"What now? I hardly become accustomed to one change before something else happens."

"I think you will like this one. I told you my mother was hiring staff for the townhouse? She made a brilliant new hire today."

"Who?"

"It seems an earl is in need of a carriage and driver, and she hired Cadogan for the job. He and his wife and all the children will be moving into the living quarters above the stables behind the house I'm renting. He will keep his carriage and horses, and I will rent them from him. He will drive me, and eventually us, anywhere we wish to go."

Juliette's smile would outdo the sun on a cloudless day. "Oh, that's perfect. You've thought of everything."

"It wasn't me. It was my lady mother."

"I'm so glad you two have reconciled. And that the Cadogans and the children will be close by enough that we can help them with the things they need."

He folded her close. "And hopefully someday maybe our children can play with their children, and they will all be the better for it." The thought thrilled and satisfied him.

"And you will have your job at Bow Street, and I will have mine with the agency, and together we can do some good in the world. Use our blessings to bless others."

"That's enough to be going on with, I think. For now, let's think about a wedding." He kissed her again. How far they had come since that first meeting only a few short months ago when she was a debutante and he a detective.

And how far might they now go as an earl and his countess?

Acknowledgments

THIS BOOK WAS A CHALLENGE to write, and there are some people I need to thank for their help along the way.

My daughter, Heather Drexler, who helped me flesh out the plot, filled out Post-it Notes, wrote on whiteboards, pulled on plot threads until they unraveled, and listened to me tell her the story several times as I worked it out in my head, certainly deserves thanks.

Thank you to my patient husband, Peter, who never complains at the long hours, the research books that just show up at the house, or all the times I am preoccupied, living in the story world in my head.

All the people at Kregel who help get this book from a wisp of an idea into readers' hands. Thank you. Janyre, you champion my projects and help me fix the big-picture items. Dori, you sort out grammar and consistency and my prodigious use of commas. Katherine, Kayliani, Sarah, Catherine, Lindsay, Rachel, and so many more people behind the scenes, you are appreciated.

Thank you to the Jane Austen Society of North America–Minnesota Chapter for hosting a workshop on English Country Dancing. I learned the steps to Sprigs of Laurel at that workshop and thoroughly enjoyed myself!

To the Facebook group Inspirational Regency Readers. You are amazing! That group is my favorite place to hang out online, and it's because you all make it so fun.

And to you, dear reader. I am grateful for you. Thank you for

Acknowledgments

coming along on my writing journey, for caring about these characters, and for keeping their stories alive in your minds and hearts.

To my agent, Cynthia Ruchti, of Books & Such Literary Agency, who guides, guards, and occasionally goads me.

To writer friends Julie, Michelle, Gabe, and Mary—thank you.

Recommended Reading

REGENCY FICTION TAKES QUITE A bit of research, and I thought I'd share a few of the books I used while writing this story. This is by no means an exhaustive list, but if you enjoy Regency history, you might find these of interest.

Louise Allen, *Regency Slang Revealed: Grose's Dictionary of the Vulgar Tongue* (CreateSpace, 2016).

Teresa DesJardien, *Jane Austen Shopped Here* (Teresa DesJardien, 2020).

Susana Ellis, compiler, *Ackermann's Repository Fashion Prints 1815–1818* (Susana Ellis, 2018).

Horace M. Hayes, *Stable Management and Exercise: A Book for Horse-Owners and Students* (Arco Publishing Company, 1974).

James Hobson, *Passengers: Life in Britain During the Stagecoach Era* (Fonthill Media, 2021).

Richard Horwood, *The A to Z of Regency London* (Harry Margary, 1985).

Titles and Forms of Address: A Guide to Their Correct Use, 12th edition (Adam & Charles Black, 1964).

Carlton House: The Past Glories of George IV's Palace (The Queen's Gallery, Buckingham Palace, 1991).

Make your debut in the online salon!

Join like-minded fans in the Inspirational Regency Readers Facebook group.

From new book announcements from Regency authors you love like Erica Vetsch, Michelle Griep, and Julie Klassen, to contests and giveaways, to exuberant discussions about favorite Regency reads, new and old, you'll find hours of entertainment with this growing community.

No letters of introduction needed to take part! Just jump right in by searching for "Inspirational Regency Readers" on Facebook or visit https://www.facebook.com/groups/2568745689914759.

THORNDIKE & SWANN

REGENCY MYSTERIES

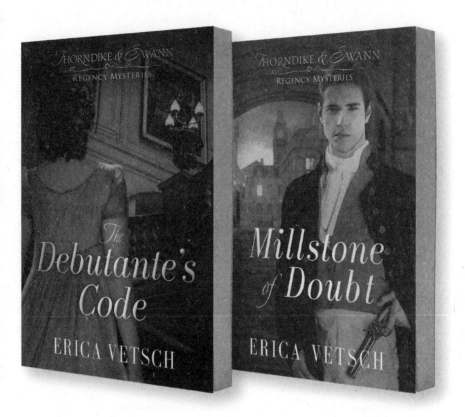

"A propulsive tale about a family of spies. . . . [Juliette and Daniel's] slow-burning romance comes together naturally. . . . Fans of Jen Turano will delight in this pleasing mystery."

—*Publishers Weekly*

"Carefully crafted Regency mystery. . . . An inherently fascinating series that combines mystery and suspense with elements of Regency-era elegance, decadence, adventure, and romance."

—*Midwest Book Review*

KREGEL PUBLICATIONS

Return to Regency England with Erica Vetsch and the Serendipity & Secrets series

"Vetsch's impeccable research and compelling Regency voice have made Serendipity & Secrets one of the strongest offerings in inspirational historical romance in years."

—Rachel McMillan, author of *Th e London Restoration* and *The Mozart Code*

"I love the way Erica Vetsch creates characters I care about. Get them deep into trouble, and in the end, loyalty, bravery, love, and faith save the day."

—Mary Connealy, author of *Braced for Love*

"Vetsch's rich writing and carefully crafte d stories sweep the reader into Regency England with all the delights of this fascinating genre."

—Jan Drexler, award-winning author of *Softly Blows the Bugle*

KREGEL
PUBLICATIONS